CASHBOX
· · · · · · · · · · · · · · · · · ·

Richard S. Wheeler

A TOM DOHERTY ASSOCIATES BOOK
NEW YORK

CASHBOX

Copyright © 1994 by Richard S. Wheeler

Cover art by George Bush

A Forge Book
Published by Tom Doherty Associates, Inc.
175 Fifth Avenue
New York, NY 10010

Forge® is a registered trademark of Tom Doherty Associates, Inc.

ISBN: 0-812-52143-9
Library of Congress Catalog Number: 94-2343

First edition: June 1994
First mass market edition: April 1995

Printed in the United States of America

0 9 8 7 6 5 4 3 2 1

To the memory of my delightful parents,
S. Lawrence Wheeler and Elizabeth S. Wheeler

Eastward I go only by force;
but westward I go free. . . .
I should not lay so much stress on this fact,
if I did not believe that something like this
is the prevailing tendency of my countrymen.
I must walk toward Oregon,
and not toward Europe.

HENRY DAVID THOREAU

PART I

1888

CHAPTER 1
················

It was said of Cornelius Daley that no sparrow could fall but that he knew of it. The silver king considered it a modest exaggeration. But he did have the amazing capacity to see what others missed. On the road to Cashbox he studied a high-banked ford that would be treacherous after a deluge. From the coach window he plotted the likely railroad grade to connect the silver town with the Northern Pacific. They passed a Livingston-bound stage and he counted its passengers and noticed their attire. Two men dressed like whiskey drummers were leaving Cashbox.

The coach lurched into a ford, throwing his thickening person into the salesman beside him, and then labored up a sinuous grade. He remarked the exact condition of the nine-passenger green coach operated by the Cashbox Forwarding Company as it rocked over the rutted road along Allebaugh Creek. His coach carried eight passengers: six jammed into its opposing seats; two more on the roof. The population of Cashbox would blossom this day, as it had for a year.

The young woman who sat across from him, her high-topped black shoes between his, attracted his careful scrutiny. She wore a costly gray suit, a puffy white blouse with a high collar, and an ivory cameo suspended on a black velvet choker. Everything about her was respectable except her sulky eyes and faintly amused mouth, both of which were utterly disreputable. She wore a thick gold ring on the wrong finger.

Next to her sat two men of the sort he called dealers, though their profession was not cards. This type flooded into new mining camps looking for quick killings, and rarely stayed more than a month or two. They exploited the unsettled conditions, often selling a property before they owned it. One sported a Van Dyke, while the other had scraped his face, but both had the telltale look of calculation in their eyes. And both had surveyed the woman, at first furtively, then boldly.

None of the six said much, other than to exchange pleasantries about the fine April day. But the silence vanished when the coach turned onto the Allebaugh Creek road, six miles below Cashbox. The dealers brightened. The drummers beside Daley smiled.

"I can smell the money," the bearded dealer said. "Everything in the world is for sale if you have the price."

"Why, that's a maxim, Ben," said the other. "Throw a dog a bone and you've bought him. Throw a man a bone and you have his property. Throw a woman a bone and you can pleasure her."

The dealers eyed the woman to see how she might react. Her lips compressed slightly, but that was the only sign that she had even heard them.

"I take it your bone is thirty pieces of silver," Daley said softly.

"Thirty pieces—" said the bearded one. "Oh, that's rich." He eyed Daley speculatively, noting Daley's attire. "What's your line, friend?"

"I'm a poet."

"A poet? Now how can you make a competence at that? Do you give readings?"

"Never. A poet examines souls. Yours wants attention."

The woman smiled suddenly, and Daley detected a flash of gratitude in her wry expression.

The coach toiled up long grades cut into the flanks of grassy foothills. They had been climbing ever since stopping at that pestilent station on the Shields River. The team had been changed only once during the seventy-odd miles from the Northern Pacific station at Livingston, and Daley could feel the horses straining in their harness.

"Everyone out," the driver bawled. "These here critters are done in."

Daley opened the veneer door, stepped down and lent a

hand to the woman. She took it, negotiated the tiny iron steps, and leapt to the rutted road far below, staggering as she landed. The rest followed her while the two on the roof clambered down from the driver's perch.

Even in the nippy air the nondescript horses had worked up a sweat which had frothed under their breeching and stained their withers black. The Jehu snapped four sets of lines. The coach creaked forward and disappeared around a bend.

Daley patted dust from his black suit and smoothed his waistcoat while she watched. Morning sun shot coy warmth into his travel-stubbled jowls. The passengers fragmented into groups. The two drummers, sporting green brocaded waistcoats and red brocaded noses, walked ahead. The roustabouts who had traveled on the roof began the hike up the grade. The dealers stuck together.

The lady fell in beside Daley, her long legs whipping the woolen skirt to its limits.

"I know who you are," she said matter-of-factly. "Con Daley."

She faintly surprised him. Most people knew him by his other name. "You have the advantage of me, madam," he said.

"I have the advantage of most people," she replied, with husky amusement. She let him puzzle that for a while. "I am Sylvie Duvalier."

She said no more, and he didn't ask. Walking beside her was as cheerful as a double shot of Crab Orchard over chipped lake ice. They rounded the bend and spotted the coach stopped a half mile above.

"I just knew you would come to Cashbox," she said. "It'll change everything."

"How will it change anything?"

She chuckled huskily, without replying.

"You still have the advantage of me, Mrs. Duvalier," he said. Her matrimonial status remained an enigma.

"You want to know my intentions," she said. "Why does anyone come to a mining camp? A place like—this?

I'm chasing rainbows." She waved a slender hand at solemn pine-clad slopes and distant peaks.

"You've come to the right spot."

"It's all will-o'-the-wisp, but a lady has to try."

"I hope you succeed—whatever you want."

"I want to see where the rainbow ends. But they had to
build some hotels there first. I waited, like you."

She was probing him but he didn't mind. "They all
want to get in on the ground floor. And I always let them.
It's easier to let things sort out for a year or two."

"I'm a second-story lady myself."

He eyed her and she smiled faintly. She would be used
to the ogling of men, he thought. Her tall, lithe figure drew
attention. She had displayed it with a tight-fitting suitcoat
that pinched her slender waist. Her curly chestnut hair fell
in an unruly mass that would defy a battery of barrettes. It
framed an angular pale face that betrayed only determination.

She took the upslope easily, but he felt his heart begin
to labor. A rail spur to Cashbox would come none too
soon to suit him. Business was so easy from the stuffed
chair of a private palace car. "The town wants a railroad,"
he said.

"And you'll build it."

"We'll see."

He helped her into the creaking coach and settled himself opposite her. The interior smelled of sweat and leather
and tobacco, and the breath of the hardware drummer next
to him betrayed a fresh infusion of ardent spirits. She
veiled herself in silence once again. He heard a thumping
on the coach roof and then the mutter of the Jehu, threatening pain to sulking horses. They had four miles to go by
Con's reckoning.

They passed ox-drawn freight wagons carrying rolls of
flat braided steel cable, the kind used in the hoists. The
contents of the wagons did not escape his alert gaze. On
one roll he spotted a waybill that read Giltedge Mine. Another freighter carried a walking beam for a mine pump.

Two miles from Cashbox they met several freighters heading toward the railroad with bedloads of dull black bricks of ore concentrate, each weighing a hundred pounds. These, he knew, were destined for a smelter, where they would be reduced to pure silver and a lot of lead. The treasure was not guarded; there wasn't much that bandits could do with it. One thing that did not issue from Cashbox was shining silver bullion, ready to be minted into Liberty dollars or a Tiffany teapot.

They topped a rise guarded by twin cottonwoods that looked useful for hangings, and he beheld the town, or at least the part he could see by leaning out of the coach window. He had become perfectly familiar with it from attentive study of a plat map, copies of claims, and a topographic map. He had, among the papers in his portmanteau, the name of every owner of a town lot, the owner of every mining claim in the Cashbox district, and more. In coded form he carried the confidential results of every assay done in the district in the last year.

Cashbox lay upon a sloping plateau at the foot of the Cashbox mountains. Two years ago it hadn't existed. Prospectors had thrown up log huts and tents in the narrow gulch north of town where the axe of God had cleaved the mountain apart. Daley had been tempted to buy the town lot company that had platted Cashbox in 1887 but he had passed it by as something too trivial. It had subsequently sold ten thousand dollars' worth of twenty-five-dollar lots. Now, in April of 1888, Cashbox was showing signs of permanence, with a rude scatter of log buildings and even a few of native stone along Main Street, the road they were traveling.

He had never seen the point of rushing to a new camp before it could provide a few comforts, unless you were a saloonman. They always arrived at the beginning, with a barrel of rotgut and a couple of tin cups. They would dispense their wares at awesome prices and then retire five thousand dollars richer. But that wasn't worth his time.

They passed a hand-lettered sign perched on a post.

Cashbox, it said. *Where no till is empty.* Suspended beneath it by its arms was an ancient red union suit with its trapdoor hanging open. He smiled faintly. There would be few tills in Cashbox. There'd be little cash in Cashbox because there was no bank. Most business would be done on credit. That suited him fine. He had upon his bosom a sheaf of Treasury notes in high denominations.

At the mouth of the gulch several rude stores huddled, looking as if the next hiccough of nature would turn them to rubble. He gazed at the familiar names: Baker's Mercantile, Aller's Hotel, a snaking log thing that stretched to the creek; the Carbonate Miners Saloon, Fogel's Bakery, a log real estate office promoting townlots, and a barbershop. A knot of ne'er-do-wells and sharpers clustered before the rock-fronted log post office and express office, waiting for the stage, which creaked to a stop.

"Haryar," the Jehu cried, leaping to earth. He spat. A horse yawned.

Con Daley opened the little door and squirmed out into the poised and shining metropolis, knowing exactly what would happen in the next moment because it had happened a dozen times before. He was not disappointed.

"It's the Silver Fox!" cried some jackanape. "The Silver Fox!" Half a dozen gangly males of assorted vintages raced toward the mines up the gulch.

"I told you so," said Sylvie.

He sighed, feeling the ache in his posterior where the stage had pounded it, knowing he was the cynosure of all eyes.

CHAPTER 2
. . . .

Sylvie Duvalier eyed the rooming house dubiously. It was Regina Maltz's place. They had told her down on Main Street that a proper woman might find shelter there.

The two-story house looked as rawboned and temporary as everything else in Cashbox, its real glass windows interrupting the unpainted shiplap sides like the spots on grimy dice.

It would beat sleeping on a saloon floor on a heap of beery sawdust, she thought. She had tried the hotels but the clerks had mocked her. One of them had silently led her to the dormitory which was the hotel's sole accommodation. There she beheld perhaps fifty straw-filled pallets lining the walls of an odorous room. Half the pallets were occupied by men with their clothes on and boots off.

The oily clerk had an amused leer on his face. "Four bits a night, and you provide your own towel," he'd said. "Slop pail out back, beside the necessaries."

"There's no place for a married woman?"

"Lady, there's no place for men. They're sleeping in tents and huts. Saloons fill every night. Ten cents a flop. Costs an extry two-bits to sleep on the billiard table. There ain't room; not with fifty pilgrims showing up every week. This here's luxury compared to some. We got the biggest, fattest bedbugs you ever ate. Tell you what. You got some cash, maybe you can try Regina Maltz's place up the slope. But she don't take any woman. Of course, if you ain't particular. . . ."

He had winked at her and pointed to the far slope, across Cashbox Creek, where a snaky log building nestled into the grassy slope, dug into earth at one end and on stilts at the other. It looked innocuous by day. A red-painted sign hanging askew on the front said "Minnie's Sporting House."

But Sylvie was particular.

She collected her breath and pushed open the door of the boardinghouse, which opened on a two-story foyer and stairs. Here were real rooms with real doors, and a stairway with a bannister. Even a cornice at the ceiling.

"I'm not in there, I'm in here," came a woman's voice. Sylvie peered through a corridor that led to a kitchen.

She discovered a hefty woman peeling potatoes. Sunlight caught her blond hair and haloed her face, but a palpable sadness lay upon Regina Maltz, permeating her heavy features. The landlady studied Sylvie uncertainly, looking for the subtle signs of pedigree—and virtue. It was obvious to Sylvie that the inspection had resulted in no conclusions.

"I'm filled up," the woman said, while a long potato peel curled away from her paring knife. "Got all the rooms double-rented. When one's on shift the other sleeps. Shift bosses, clerks, men like that. Miners can't afford this. They're in tents and flophouses."

"I need a room."

"Well, maybe you should just get on the next stage out."

"I'm waiting for—my husband's at Marienbad, in Bohemia—you know the place. Taking the waters. So curative, you know. He's not well. The silly goose drinks too much. I'm, ah, going to wait. And start a business."

All of that was true, sort of. Beauregard Pitt was indeed at Marienbad trying to cure his gout. She was married in a sense, at least not divorced. But she was entirely on her own.

"There's no rooms. I'm desperate."

Regina Maltz stopped her paring and rose, shaking potato eyes from her apron. She smiled, something luminous in her heavy face. "Never be desperate," she said. "The Good Lord didn't put us on earth to be desperate. Trials, yes—by fire and ice. We can't escape trials. But there's no need to wring your hands."

Sylvie didn't want lectures, and she turned to leave.

"Now where are you going, young woman?"

"To find a billiard table."

"No you're not. I don't know your business. I don't know why you've come to my door. But I know thirty, forty men that'd build you a palace overnight if you said the word. Have you means?" She looked apologetic. "It's none of my business—but I need to know."

"Some. I'm going to start a club."

"Well, it's none of my business what it might be."

"A club for gentlemen."

Regina Maltz stared at Sylvie, registering that.

"A quiet place. Where men can gather. Fine French food. A glass of port and a cigar . . . a place with, you know, amenities, a few big rooms—much nicer than a hotel. Men like a place to do business with each other."

"I've never heard the like. You'd want to be cautious."

Sylvie sighed. "I'd best be looking," she said.

"If you don't mind a straw-filled tick, you can stay in my own room. Maybe you can help me. I don't think one of those hotels would be—suitable."

"I've always managed, Mrs. Maltz."

"It's Miss."

Sylvie realized suddenly that she was beholding a weary old maid, a woman who had no doubt struggled alone for more years than she could remember. A woman too big-boned and lantern-jawed to light fires in men. Sylvie wondered how this creature had persuaded the carpenters and masons to build her boardinghouse before almost everything else. Something in Regina Maltz's eyes spoke of sympathy, as if she'd been put on earth to nurse the feeble and foolish.

"For a little while, Miss Maltz," Sylvie said. "But not for charity's sake."

"My pay is the keeping of your reputation, Mrs.—why, bless you, I don't know your name."

"Sylvie Duvalier."

"What a pretty name. I've never enjoyed either of mine, but I make do. Have them bring your trunk."

"We haven't discussed the rent."

Regina Maltz beamed. "Yes we have. I'm amply paid."

"You mean—you're not charging? I couldn't permit that—"

"Welcome to Cashbox. Is this your first camp?"

"I've never been to a mining camp. It seems chaotic."

"This is my third. I've always had boardinghouses. When the mines fail we all move, you know. The devil takes the hindmost."

"Why don't you find a town that—"

"Then I couldn't be helpful. Besides—I am what I am." She eyed Sylvie. "These are rough places. You'll want to be careful. If you're not sure, why, ask me." She smiled a smile that said she knew everything there was to know about mining camps.

"How do you know when the mines will fail? I'd want to know that. If I start a business."

"People look after me. Now fetch your things. We eat at six."

Sylvie paused outside the front door, which was a raw hole in the building unadorned by even a small veranda, and reached by two stumps serving as stairs. Before her, shimmering in the spring afternoon, the town's muted frenzy drifted to her, lifting her pulse. The boardinghouse stood upslope from everything. She could peer down into the business district, crowded with wagons and buckboards and saddle horses. Elsewhere, carpenters swarmed like ants over half-built houses and shops made of planks and studs so green that sap oozed from them.

The staccato of a hundred hammers ruined the peace. A whirl of sage-scented air reached her nostrils. There were no lawns; only silvery sagebrush, with buildings poking out of it. Some rough men were erecting their own log dwellings with bare earth floors and sod roofs.

The rawness and madness of it smacked her senses and made her wonder about herself. This wasn't a town—this wasn't even civilization. This was a hive of feverish action, fueled by dreams. She could feel it. The animal sweat of men floated in the breeze, along with their hopes and need to build empires.

She'd been lucky. Here she was, with shelter, food and privacy handed to her by a strange woman whose reward was to preserve something Sylvie didn't really want. Sylvie couldn't bear cloistered Philadelphia—not its academies and institutes, not its stuffy society and blue laws. Nor Wilmington, either, where she and her sister, Tennessee, had grown up.

The thought of her childhood dredged up old frustrations. She'd been born in quicksand and had spent all her life trying to reach a shore. She'd been raised by a mother, stepmother, governess, and an aunt. She'd had a father, stepfather, and two "uncles" she had later discovered were her stepmother's lovers. She'd been inculcated with Episcopalian virtues, hedonism, atheism, Unitarianism, and homeopathy. One aunt was a monarchist who worshipped the Hapsburgs, another a syndico-anarchist follower of Mikhail Bakunin, while the governess had subscribed to Orson and Lorenzo Fowler's *Phrenological Almanac* and smoked a pipe. Her stepfather was a vegetarian and prohibitionist except for wine, which he imbibed with every meal. All she had ever wanted in life was solid ground—which was the impulse that had brought her to Cashbox.

She didn't regret coming here in spite of the harsh reality before her eyes. Here she could do anything she wanted and it'd turn out fine. That had been the only article of faith she ever possessed. Something delightful would happen in this wild place. She would just go hunting for the rainbow's end until she found it.

CHAPTER 3

Con Daley peered genially at the six gawkers, looking for some slight sign of intelligence and finding none. "Take your bags, sir? You staying somewhere?" Con beheld a gawky adolescent in knickers, skinny as a cigarillo.

"Why, lad, you can take those two black valises into the express office."

"You're not staying nowhere?"

"Oh, I'll get around to it."

That news stirred the gawkers. The Silver Fox would stay a spell. He watched the boy heft the heavy bags into the stone building, hand them to the clerk, and return, wondering whether to stick his palm out for his reward. The boy opted to stuff his hands into his knickers.

"You want a guide or something?"

"What's your name, son?"

"Casper Penrose. I can fetch and take."

"I admire your enterprise. A feisty lad'll go somewhere. Why, I remember shining Commodore Vanderbilt's shoes. I remember saving for a bicycle so I could run messages. We all start somewhere, right at the poor-boy bottom, and then we succeed or fail. Now, Mister Penrose, you've shown me a fine spirit—a young entrepreneur."

"Well, I want to earn something."

"You will. I'm going to hire you right now. Take me to the cemetery."

"The cemetery?"

"Yes. People do die here, don't they?"

"You want me to take you *there*?"

"I believe that's what I said."

"How much? I mean, what's it worth?"

"Casper, I'll pay what you're worth. You're too sharp. All business is built upon mutual trust."

Casper Penrose looked confused. "I want to be sharp. Like John D. Rockefeller," he muttered. He motioned for Daley to follow, and set off down Main Street.

Daley followed, and so did the gawkers.

Daley stopped. "Gentlemen, you surely have something better to do. Let a man pay his respects to the dead."

He watched the lot of them drift back to the express office. Then he fell in beside the boy.

"You got someone buried there?" the boy asked. "I don't know of nobody that's your kin."

"My kin are all the fallen men and women and children of every silver mining camp there is, son."

"Yeah? Who says?"

"Casper, you must respect sentiment. Your heart needs softening."

The boy led him three blocks down Main, and then across a rude plank bridge that spanned the trickle of

Cashbox Creek, and into open fields that sloped toward a nearby ridge. This quarter of Cashbox seemed less desirable than the more level areas.

"See that over there?" The boy pointed at a low log structure notched into the slope. "That's a cathouse. And that there—" he waved further upslope "—that's another one. We got seven. This here one, nearest the flat, it's the fanciest. They got real witchy girls. They won't let me in yet. I know the name of the madam. She's Charlotte Keiserling. I guess she's some old dolly."

"I think we should be paying our respects to the dead, Casper."

"I want money so I can visit one. I need to earn two dollars. Ain't it funny that the whores and the dead are all mixed together? Maybe they do business." Casper emitted a nasal adolescent giggle.

Con Daley sighed. The boy's juices were flowing.

The cemetery burst into view after they pushed through hip-high timothy grass. Cashbox neglected its dead. Not a grave had an iron or picket fence around it. He saw no headstones, only rude crosses or headboards with a name burned into them. Plainly, the new metropolis had devoured its living.

"See that one over there?" Casper said, pointing to a distant clay mound. "That's the Chinee. Up there's the whores. They all gotta be buried in white wedding gowns—you know, to make up in the next world. Soil's shallow up there so that's where they go. We're standing in the Catholics. We had one we didn't know, maybe greaser or Injun, so we just dragged him over the ridge. The rest are white people. We got one murder—him there, we don't know his name, he was shot by One-Eyed Jack Wool two weeks ago. Wool, he's a snively gambler—but don't you tell him I said it. Say, what are you looking for?"

"Facts."

"I never knew there was facts around here."

Daley studied the headboards, missing nothing. Each told its pathetic story of life wrestled and lost.

"Casper, what happened in September, last year?"

"Oh, that. The cholera come and took away a whole bunch. Eleven grown-ups and a few children too. My friend Timmy, he was okay one day and croaked the next."

Timothy Patrick Costigan
Born July 5, 1875 A.D.
Died September 17, 1887 A.D.
R I P

"They'll get better water soon. It's from springs up Allebaugh Creek. The town lot company's doing it."

Quietly, Daley surveyed the tattered rows until he found a cluster of Cousin Jacks. Some Trewarthas and Polweals, a Fenno, Trenoweth, Polglase. If you knew the old mining camp ditty, you could point to the Cornish as easily as you could point to the Irish: "By Tre, Pol, Pen, and O, The Cornishman you come to know."

Daley studied these headboards closely. Like so many miners, these had lived a short and brutish life, dying in their twenties and thirties. Dying wholesale on a certain day.

"Casper, what happened on November seventeenth of last year?"

"Oh, the big cave-in. It trapped a bunch."

"What mine?"

"The Giltedge. That rock's so rotten it don't stay up. Hugh Trego, he's a-fightin' old Webb for more timber, but old Webb, he says the mine hasn't made a dime."

"There's a Penrose here."

"Yeah, him that was a cousin of my pa, from Padstow."

"What happened, Casper?"

The boy shrugged. "Rotten bloody rock. It come thundering down and trapped five right at the end of the shift, and it took a week to get 'em loose, and they come up the shaft blue, with the women weepin'."

"There wasn't enough timbering?"

"Old Webb, he's got the timber sets on five-foot centers, like it was hardrock. Me pap, he's afeard to walk through that crosscut."

Daley nodded, and continued his rounds, pausing at each grave. He was looking for a name and didn't find it. A lot of children. A handful of wives and daughters. Not very many miners, and those were the veteran Cornishmen who had carried their trade with them when the tin mines went bad.

Dull, eroded clay covered them now, rimmed by sagebrush and short grass. Some of the markers had fallen, and no one had come to put them up again. He lifted the fallen markers looking for the name, feeling glad not to find it.

"Come see the whores!" Casper cried. The boy stood in the middle of an isolated quarter, segregated by an invisible wall. Daley clambered upslope. The bawds had all been buried at a slant. That was a novelty after a horizontal life. Here, at least, the varnished headboards were fancy. An incredible eleven women lay here. Daley found only one with a Christian name on it: Katharine Glory O'Meara. She had lived twenty-seven years. That one bore the image of the cross, and a tired brown bouquet lay propped against it. But the rest had chosen their noms de guerre: Irish Queen, Little Gold Dollar, Molly B'Dam, Straight Edge, Pegleg Annie, Contrary Mary, Coal Oil Georgie. Two were labeled A Woman. One was labeled Few Clothes, 1862–1887.

"I wisht I knew Few Clothes," Casper said.

"You are very young, Casper."

Daley was through. He hadn't found the name. Five had died in a mine collapse. Another dozen had probably died in single accidents. Some perhaps from pneumonia. The Giltedge stood three-quarters of a mile from town, a long wintery walk for a man coming out of the sweaty hole at the end of his shift. All the other mines were still higher up the gulch.

"You going to get a place to stay now? You go over

there to that place, they've got red velvet wallpaper and fourposter beds and a stove in every room. I seen it through the windows lots of times. It's a fancy place there, and the women are fancy too."

"No, I'm going to the Carbonate Miners Saloon," Daley said, starting back.

"You gonna buy the billiard table to sleep on?"

"Oh, no, I never lack for a place."

"I can't go in there. I can sometimes, but mostly I can't. I had a beer there once and no boyo said nothing."

"What do your parents think of that?"

"Him's in the mine all night; her is sleeping, and me twitty sisters don't know. I guess I'm pretty much grown up."

They paused at the grimy door of the saloon. The boy waited eagerly. Daley found some change and dropped a dime into the boy's palm.

"A dime! That ain't much for you."

"Spend it wisely."

"You need anything, you jist fetch me. I live in that place up there." He pointed to a square frame house. "I'm going to run errands and get my start just like you did with them financiers."

Daley smiled. "We all start humbly. But we all start."

"Yeah, well, I'll be seeing ya, boyo."

Con Daley entered the dark saloon, which was lit by a single coal oil lamp over the bar. The mine shift would end soon. He would have time for a sandwich before the Cousin Jacks arrived.

CHAPTER 4
• • • • • • • • • • • • • • •

Thaddeus Webb stood at the grimy window of his superintendent's office admiring the mine he had built. He did that often. It suffused him with pride to see this crea-

tion of his. He had finished the mill only a few days ago,
and now he could hear it thunder, and feel its vibration
through his soles.

He loved the gritty tableau afforded by his window,
finding beauty in it where other men might find only a
hellish blot upon nature. The Giltedge Mine lay like a
crouched monster partly up the side of the gulch, beneath
the denuded slope of Cashbox Mountain. Its headframe
rose like a giant guillotine, naked to the sky.

Next to it stood a great board and batten shed which
housed the twin boilers and steam engines that drove the
hoist and operated the giant Cornish pump that sucked water from the bottom of the main shaft. The shed also
housed a smithy where a blacksmith put new cutting edges
on the worn-out star bits of the drill steels, and repaired
the machinery. Next to it was the timber foreman's shop
where thick logs were hewn into the timbering needed to
keep the drifts safe.

One tramway led from the headframe to a trestle where
slack was dumped from ore cars. A modest pile of worthless rock lay at the end of the elevated rails. Another tramway took ore cars to the mill. There, two Blake jaw
crushers, each capable of pulverizing a hundred tons a day,
reduced the ore to pellets. Three California five-stamp batteries thundered day and night to reduce ore to the consis-
tency of flour so that the precious and base metals could
be amalgamated or roasted into concentrate and shipped to
a smelter. The roar of the mill never ceased, and its thunder shivered the panes of glass in his office, and set his
pencils to humming on his raw plank desk.

It might be a monster, but it was a marvelous one, employing all the technology he had mastered at the Columbia School of Mines and since. For two years he had
poured his engineering genius into this. For almost as
long, his men had been boring into hard rock to get at the
most incredible body of silver ore he'd ever worked. But
only this week, on completion of the mill, had he started
to ship concentrate by ox-drawn wagon to the smelter at

Wickes ninety miles to the west. Only now would the mine begin to return something to its patient owners, John and Henry Hammon.

He returned to his creaking wooden swivel chair, unable to put off any more the task he loathed more than anything else. He had to write his semiannual report. If the tableau outside his window was ugly, his office was even worse. The bare plank floor and pale green walls and plank benches for his visitors had only utilitarian purpose. No lithograph or painting graced its walls. Only a calendar. Nothing in his office was kind to the eye, but Thaddeus never noticed. An office had never been anything more than a place to get work done. In fact he got a lot more work done simply because it was so grim and uncomfortable that guests never tarried.

"I'm going to start the report, Baghote," he yelled to his clerk, who toiled under a green eyeshade in a reception area that was even less inviting than Webb's lair. "Bring me the production data."

"You don't need it; it's all in your head anyway," Baghote grumbled.

"Yes, but I have to make sure my memory doesn't trick me," Webb replied. Above all, Baghote hated those lawless moments when papers weren't in their proper pigeonholes and ledgers.

Webb was not a man of words. He'd sooner study the mine's black silver-lead galena in its gangue of jasper and quartz than write words. He'd sooner be in the blacksmith shop seeing why the drilling steels were dulling too fast than trying to explain things to owners who didn't know a Bickford fuse from a Cornish pump. He'd sooner get into a shouting match about the timbering with Hugh Trego.

By noon his office would be littered with crumpled balls of paper, and his fingers would be black with ink. He would offend Portia again by not showing up for lunch, and he would have to soothe her with some little confection. He glared at the frosted glass door, imported clear from Valparaiso, Indiana, daring someone to come in. But no one did. His icy reception of unwanted intruders maintained his privacy.

The Giltedge Mining and Development Company was a financial rathole, even though the values of its ores were good—27.4 ounces of silver to the ton, in galena ore that was 60.7 percent lead. That, in fact, was the assay value of the first ore shipped from the mine that very month. What's more, the dimensions of the vein had yet to be plumbed, but were plainly of the bonanza variety. They had sunk a shaft to the hundred-foot level, and run drifts through ore in both directions, a distance of almost two hundred feet, without coming to the limit of the vein.

Better still, the assay values were improving with depth. Ore at the surface had assayed at fourteen ounces of silver to the ton. How, then, could he tell John and Henry Hammon that they would have to invest another hundred thousand dollars before the mine would turn a profit?

Webb jabbed his nib into the ink bottle and began scratching thick, dark, stiff words. It was in him to begin with the bad news and not try to soften it first with anything hopeful. He had never been very politic; over three decades his bluntness had won him the superintendencies of several mines. And also gotten him in trouble.

Never had he loved and hated a mine as much as this one. Never had a mine imposed such difficulties, or driven him to such inventiveness. This one was his angel and devil. He had fought it and wooed it and gradually subdued it.

Dear Sirs:

The sixty-degree angle of the ore body, he wrote, made its extraction difficult. He had first tried to drive the shaft straight down the lode, but the slant had been awkward and the ore stretched in every direction from the shaft. Then he had driven a vertical shaft through the sedimentary rock, mostly limestone, that bordered the ore body. At the hundred-foot level he had run a crosscut to the ore and then two drifts. All at terrible cost.

He grunted his displeasure. Until the great carbonate

strike at Leadville, Colorado, no one had ever imagined that ore could be found in what once had been sedimentary rock, metamorphosed by solutions of mineral salts from nearby igneous formations. He knew only that such rock was treacherous, the strata at that angle ever threatening to collapse and murder his men. No amount of shoring seemed to be enough. The volcanic disturbance had crumbled the limestone into lethal pieces that now hung malevolently above his miners.

As if that weren't bad enough, the silver vein had grown so large that the ore would have to be gouged from huge galleries which would require special timbering, level upon level, like a several-story building inside the womb of rock. What a paradox: a mine so rich it was breaking the owners.

He arose and pounced through the frosted glass door.

"Barkley, get me Mueller's assay reports—seventy-nine, eighty, and eighty-one."

Barkley Baghote scowled. "You have the figures in your head," he said.

"I need them now. And the projected costs of the smelter."

"I will delay as long as possible because of your tone."

"Baghote, let's not. Not today."

"Have you ever considered what would happen if I altered every statistic in the files?"

"No, I haven't considered it."

"I might, you know. You don't pay me enough to ensure my loyalties. My mind is elsewhere."

"I don't doubt it," Webb growled, and settled back to his writing.

In due course, Baghote laid the assay reports on the desk, but Webb scarcely noticed. The clerk waited, refusing to leave until Webb had studied the figures in the printed forms and handed back the files.

"That's fine, Barkley."

"You should give me a bone. Sit, Bowser, sit. I don't know why I stay on."

The Hammon brothers faced some hard choices. It simply was not economic to ship concentrate by ox-team. They could sell out; they could shut the mine and wait for a railroad to make the mine profitable; they could form a stock company and sell shares; they could mine and stockpile ore until the time when it could be hauled cheaply—at a dead loss until the payoff. Or they could build a smelter, which was Webb's choice.

Not that a smelter would be ideal. The ores were self-fluxing but it would cost thirteen dollars a ton just to ship charcoal from the railroad. The Giltedge Mine—and all the rest in the district—wouldn't show much profit until a railroad connected Cashbox with the Northern Pacific. But at least the smelter could profitably reduce the ores of neighboring mines, and might be the best proposition.

Webb wrote furiously. He recommended a public corporation and floating some stock. He surprised himself by not throwing pages away, as the pile of paper grew. Each page bristled with dizzying statistics: assay values, shipping costs, the price of labor, the losses from highgrading by miners—which he estimated at twenty percent of the assay values of the ore—and most ominously, the declining price of silver, currently $1.20 an ounce, and of lead, currently 4.5 cents a pound.

The rattle of his office door interrupted his reverie. He discovered Baghote standing there in his gartered shirtsleeves, his green eyeshade as askew as his lips.

"Mister Webb, this is an occasion. It's infernal news. Like the Ottoman Turks seizing Boston."

"What? What do you want, Barkley?"

The horror playing over the man's broken features announced catastrophe. He had a ten-trapped-men look in his wild eye.

"It's marvelously bad news, sir. I've never heard the like in twenty years. Wrack and ruin. Blood and guts. He's come, he's come here."

"I'm afraid you'll have to explain this better, Barkley."

"The Silver Fox! The Silver Fox!"

Cornelius Daley. A coldness spread through Thaddeus Webb as if the fire in the stove had gone out.

"He got off the noon stage. So I'm told. Like a Byzantine prince."

"Thank you, Barkley."

The clerk squinted, as if to squeeze an ounce of gossip from this occasion, and backed out the door.

Thaddeus Webb sighed, read through his five-page letter once again, and then tore it into tiny bits, not stopping until he had turned it into confetti.

Chapter 5
. . . .

Hugh Trego stepped off the hoist into blinding sunlight, feeling as sour as a sore-toothed bear. He blinked, orienting himself to the surface once again. Around him the lads shuffled away, their day's toil done, some to the company boardinghouse a few rods away, and others like himself to Cashbox, down the gulch. Today he would have a mug or two at the Carbonate Miners Saloon. It would have to be on credit; he wouldn't have a dime until tally and exchange day.

"Damme, old son, I'm ready for the kiddley broth," said old Trenoweth.

Trego grunted. "She was a bad shift," he muttered.

Before they had gone down the hole, Thaddeus Webb had told the men he was building a clothes-changing room. He had talked about their health as if he cared. Now he had said, the men wouldn't fetch pneumonia walking to town through bitter cold in their sweat-soaked clothes.

But oh, that mouthpiece of the bloated capitalists. All that pious talk about the men's health wasn't at the core of it. The changing room was nothing more than robbery, just another way to oppress brave men who risked death every day for a miserable three dollars and a half, barely enough to keep a family together. No, that miserable bleddy Webb was going to rob the boys of an ancient right—unspoken but always a part of working in the holes—of taking a dab of ore as a little bonus. Some had a false crown in their oil-hardened felt hats and stowed a bit of ore up there. Some had put false pockets into their britches—but the changing room would stop that.

Those fat capitalists called it highgrading but it was nothing more than a bit of the wage. For weeks now, the shift boss, Timmons, had shaken each man's lunchpail as he came off the hoist. If it rattled, he had opened it—and usually he didn't find food. The maddening thing about this mine was that it was too bleddy rich: they were driving drifts through solid galena ore now—above, below, in front, and on all sides. There wasn't any slack. Every ore car was run straight to the mill. The men couldn't slip a little ore into the cars heading for the slackpile and then recover it later from the heap of slack. That had been the time-honored way, almost a right belonging to any good miner who braved the pit.

No, there wasn't a chance, and the men were the poorer and meaner for it. Oh, that ugly, slave-driving, mean-hearted Webb. Someday, when the fat capitalists were raking in their loot from the Giltedge, Trego would start a bleddy union. But not now. Not until the mine started paying. Otherwise she'd just be shut down, and they'd take fifty jobs away.

That hadn't been all of the bleddy hell this day. There was a hangfire at one of the faces, and they waited it out for half an hour after the shift started before any man had the courage to go back in there for a look. One of the Hercules lifter charges didn't detonate. They spliced the Bickford fuse, blew the charge, and then mucked out ore in air thick with the lung-murdering fumes of giant powder. And just to make the day pure bleddy hell, a ton of rotten rock fell into the crosscut not far from the shaft, and had to be mucked out by men afraid for their lives because there wasn't enough timbering. That damned Webb had promised more, but no one had seen a stick of it.

Trego lumbered down the gulch, oblivious of the sweet spring afternoon, needing a beer to make the world right again. Anna could wait. She'd waited many times before. She had started waiting supper in Cornwall when he first braved the tin stannaries. The scowling slopes of the gulch hemmed in his spirits, but in a few moments he'd sip a mug and feel better. By the end of each shift he'd had enough of tight places.

His mouth anticipated the dark draft beer that would be drawn for him the moment he walked into the Carbonate. That was his kind of saloon, plain, rockwalled and long as a snake. For over a year it had been the club of those who braved the Giltedge hole, though plenty of men from the other mines came there too. It had been festooned with workingmen's things. From its rock walls hung miner's picks, old drilling steels, coal oil lamps, and an out-of-place elkhead with a great rack. Two Brunswick billiard tables with lamps over them filled the rear. A twenty-foot rosewood bar brought by ox-train from the railroad stood on the right, with a mirrored backbar behind it. Nearer the double door, the only decoration was an Anheuser-Busch lithograph of Custer's Last Stand. The sawdust on the floor always stank of beer and pine pitch, but it was the bed of dozens of homeless men each night, waiting for Cashbox to put a roof over their heads.

As he plunged through the battered double doors he sensed at once that things weren't the same. A knot of lads clustered at the bar, gathered like a Methodist choir around some bleddy preacher in black. Only it wasn't some preacher. It was the blood-sucking pirate Cornelius Daley, who stood there, mug in hand, elbow on the cherrywood, shiny shoe on the brass rail, like he had a right to be there.

Hugh Trego didn't like that a bit. Would this blood-sucker never leave a workingman alone?

Joe Wales handed him a foaming mug. "It's on Daley," he said, answering Trego's stare with a shrug. Hugh downed it in great chugs, feeling the cool brew bubble away the thirst that always built in him after every shift. The mine sweated a man dry. Wales filled it again, and this time Trego sipped quietly, letting the draft beer soak his pores.

"You're the ones that make it work," Daley was saying to Anselm McGuire and the rest. "The supers up top don't know what's what. They don't know how much water's running. They don't even know the ore. All they've got to go on is an assay now and then. But you chaps know. You know where the trouble is, you know where the highgrade is."

It was all horse apples. The bleddy man was sucking up to the miners. Everyone knew how Con Daley liked to live. Give a silver camp a fancy saloon or a pretty lady or a good chophouse, and Daley would be there, smoking fat Havanas, wearing headlight diamonds on his cravat and six fingers, ordering caviar and brie cheese for some blonde who wouldn't look twice at a Cousin Jack.

"I've hardly been down in the holes myself, but I know what being poor is. I was an express boy, running messages for a dime tip." Daley smiled and sipped at his mug.

"If you ever knew poor times, you've forgotten it," Trego muttered, but no one was listening. He could tell a man who'd been poor—and Daley didn't have the marks.

"Now Webb's a good man," Daley said. "He'll make that mine pay if anyone can. But I suppose he forgets sometimes just who mucks all that ore out of there."

"Damme, Webb's a bloodsucker," answered Peter O'Grady. "We naught get a spare set of timber when the roof's fallin' on our ears."

"It's a poor mine that can't buy wood," Daley said gently. "The Hammons are out of development cash."

"Is that so. They won't put a spare stick in the cross-cuts, and we get rock on our heads."

Hugh Trego *knew* what Con Daley was doing. He was collecting information so he could steal the Giltedge. Sympathizing with the men and sucking up news like it was silver bullion.

Trego pushed himself toward the center, elbowing past friends and rivals until he loomed squarely over the silver king. "You're not a shift man, Daley, and this isn't your place. Drink up and leave now, and quit mining the lads so you can do your bleddy deals."

Daley eyed him quietly, without antagonism. "You have the advantage of me, sir. You know me, but I don't know you."

"Hugh Trego it is, and I'm saying she's our club here, and you can find something more to your taste up a block or two. You'd not come in here but to use us like cannon fodder."

"A Cornishman. I'm always in awe of the Cousin Jacks, Mister Trego. We couldn't dig a shaft without you."

"Damn, me heart bleeds," muttered Sam Polweal. "This from an Irishman, too."

"I'm not a man to be flattered," Hugh said. "I know what you're about. You come to town to make a killin', only it's us in the holes likely to be killed."

"You're a man to be admired, Hugh Trego. You're a man to stand up for your lads. I wish I had you as a shift boss in some of my holdings. You'd see to the safety of the men."

"You can't soft-talk me, Daley. I bleddy well know what you're doing, and so does every jack in here. They're just eyeing a man that gets his name in the papers a lot—and a man that signs a lot of vouchers. Now this Carbonate's a place for us and our kind, and I'm saying it plain. Get out."

"He's bought us rounds, Hugh," said someone.

Daley smiled. "Mister Trego, I'm looking for information—but not the kind you think. I'm looking for a man named Ambrose Gill. I want to buy his claim." The financier peered around him amiably. No one responded.

"Have none of you ever heard of him? Is he here? Alive? Dead?"

"He wouldn't come in here," said Peter. "He'd not be a wage man. The prospectors and glory hunters have their own place. Most of 'em wouldn't rub shoulders with a man that goes into the hole."

"You don't think he's here—in Cashbox?"

"Damme, I know him," said Anselm. "He had a claim above the Giltedge, but she don't amount to spit. He wanted me to dig on shares, but I wouldn't. He said he was getting some values over to one edge, but it wasn't worth mining. Yeah, he's around somewheres. Buy him a drink and he'll probably deed the whole outfit to you. He's a taste for corn spirits."

Daley surveyed McGuire quietly. "You've been helpful to me and I won't forget it, friend. Anything you ever want or need . . . come to me." He turned to the rest. "Any time you need something . . . come to me. I've a spot in my chest for any man that works and starves and dreams of better days. I've been lucky and I like to share what I have."

"Damme, ain't she sweet," muttered someone.

"Luck be damned," Trego said. "Luck had nothing to do with it, Daley."

Con Daley set his mug down on the wet rosewood and stepped free of the bar. "Trego, my friend, you're a chap to get ahead in the world. If ever you're down on your luck—come see me. Any time, any place. I'll be here. Maybe a long time. I'm looking for investment properties."

"I'd sooner do business with Webb," Trego growled.

Daley extracted a gold eagle from his pocket and handed it to Joe Wales. "Set 'em up, my friend. It's on Con Daley tonight."

CHAPTER 6
. . . .

An amazing gale whipped wind through May Goode's thin dress when she stepped off the immigrant coach. She drew her black knit shawl about her shoulders and hunched toward the elegant brick station. The coach, with its yowling infants, frightened families, and hardwood seats, had been an ordeal. Every jar on the wheels had pounded through the shaped wooden benches into her weary body. She hadn't slept since leaving Minneapolis. The only comfort had been the coal stove, which had spread its suffocating heat through the jolting coach. After three years of never being warm, she welcomed the heat.

It had cost her $17.40 to come to Livingston. She had ten dollars left, the amount she would need for the coach ticket to Cashbox. She had an apple she had bought from the candy butcher with her last dime. She had no luggage, only her little reticule, which contained a few rags and a gaptoothed comb she had found. Within the station, where everything echoed beneath its vaulted ceiling, she paused, studying Livingston. The town lay in a corner of the pine-clad mountains, and was prettier than anything she had ever seen before.

She braved the wind to cross Park Street, and let herself into the ticket office of the Cashbox Forwarding Company. A pale man with hair parted in the middle awaited her pleasure behind a grilled wicket.

"Cashbox," she said, extracting her ten-dollar bill.

He grunted and pulled out a ticket. "Eleven dollars," he said, pushing it to her. "It leaves in an hour."

The price stabbed her. "I—I was told it was ten," she said. "I mean, back—"

"Eleven."

"I don't have it." She turned away bleakly. Maybe she

would have to settle for Livingston. But no, not Livingston. Not with two passenger trains a day disgorging people from back there. Someone might recognize her. Someone might know. "I have to get there," she said. "Is there any—discount . . . or something?"

"Nope, eleven it is, ma'am. Sorry."

She fingered the thin gold band that still encompassed her ring finger. Frank's two-dollar prison. "I have this. Ten dollars and this." She dropped it on the counter.

He eyed it, and something softened in his gaze. "No, you don't want to give me that, ma'am. Not that." He eyed her closely, his knowing gaze taking in her skeletal face, cheap dress, so shabbily made that the shoulder seams were already pulling apart. She endured his scrutiny, suddenly afraid. They all seemed to know everything about her. She could see it in their faces. The contempt. The horror. "You got any luggage?" he asked.

It startled her. She shook her head. "Just this."

"That saves me forty pounds. Ticket's good for one passage and forty pounds. We can take a little freight to make it up. I'll let you on for ten."

He shoved the pasteboard ticket across to her and her worn bill vanished beneath the gray marble. "Good luck," he said. "Midnight eating stop; you can get a box lunch at the NP station there, four bits. Arrives in Cashbox noon tomorrow."

She nodded. She had the apple.

She settled on a bench fashioned from curved oaken slats. Cashbox tomorrow. All she knew of it was what she had read in the *Tribune*: "Cashbox, out in the farthest reaches of Montana Territory, bids fair to become the queen silver camp of that wild land. Ever since its fabled deposits of galena silver were located two years ago, it has bloomed like a rose in the wilderness in spite of being eighty miles from anything called civilization."

That was all. It was what she needed. Eighty miles from anything and a thousand miles from those who knew her. She would find something respectable to do there. They always needed women in those camps. She might cook or sew or keep house. But oh, God, she would never escape the past. It lay upon her so heavily it crushed her soul. She could flee to the farthest ends of the earth and her past would be there. She would never be released from the memories she couldn't bear.

She boarded the stagecoach nervously and found herself wedged between a whiskey drummer and a preacher, hell and salvation. She knew too much about salvation. Half the books in the prison library were tracts placed there by the uplift societies of the Baptists, Methodists, and Lutherans. They all had the same scripture on the frontispiece: The wages of sin is death.

She was the lone woman on the coach. They stared furtively at her and she was sure they knew her secret, her name, her criminal act, her whole miserable life.

But they didn't. They gazed out the windows as the Shields River Valley crawled by, and the spinning sun stitched the faces of the mountains. When darkness settled, they all stared out the windows anyway, as if they could see the land parade by. She welcomed the darkness because no one stared at her. Somehow the drivers of the lurching coach knew where to go, but to her it all seemed like a trip down a tunnel. She smelled bad breath, the fumes of whiskey, the odor of armpits, and the interiors of shoes. But the coach was warmer than the stone-walled prison.

Manslaughter.

But that wasn't the proper word. Child slaughter. She couldn't remember it happening, though she remembered what followed, and most of what went on just before. Frank had abandoned her—vanished one day—leaving her on a hardscrabble few acres with their little boy, Robby, four years old. After that she had survived, but only barely, toiling in her huge vegetable garden; preserving foods so they might eat; washing neighbors' clothes; cutting and selling firewood; mending neighbors' nightshirts, suits, stockings and shirts; ironing until sweat ran off her;

baking bread for the bachelor farmer down the road. Pennies here, dimes there; keeping going somehow. And always the boy, who looked so much like Frank, always in her way. She had loved Robby even so.

She had taken him to New Ulm to buy shoes; he had whined the whole while, maddening her. She had been weary, sick with flu and despair, and her head hurt. Then something happened she couldn't remember. But three witnesses at the preliminary hearing said she had screamed at the little boy and struck him again and again, her slaps cracking his head back, until he had fallen to the paving stones inert.

She remembered none of that. But the next part she remembered so painfully she could hardly bear to think of it. Robby took a long time dying on the cobbles of New Ulm. He shuddered and spasmed while May sobbed and held him and silent men and women watched. Some time later Robby sighed and lay still, his small life gone, and the doctor and constable took her away. She was in the newspapers—oh, yes. There she was in print, for all her neighbors to see. There she was, a killer.

She hadn't a cent for her defense, and they all said she had done it, so she told the magistrate to do what he would. How do you plead? he asked. She said she didn't know. He entered a plea of *nolo contendre.* "You didn't intend to kill the child," he said. "There was no malice aforethought. But neither did you control yourself, as any adult must. This is manslaughter." With that, he sent her away for three years. They sent Robby's little body to her parents in New Ulm, but they would not let the killer go to her son's burial.

She sat in the darkness now, feeling the stage lurch under her, throwing her into the preacher and then the whiskey drummer while the bleak night eddied by. At some grim lantern-lit place they stopped and changed teams. In the cold dark she devoured her apple, core and all, so she might have strength the next day. It was the only food she'd had since leaving Minnesota and it wasn't enough to drive back the dizziness. She walked in the frosty air to make her limbs work and then climbed in again.

"Madam, I have a little tad for you," the whiskey drummer said. "I didn't want it." He handed her half a loaf of coarse bread. So he'd noticed she didn't go inside with the rest. Maybe he was seducing her. But the bread felt so soft and sweet in her hands that even her fingers hungered.

"I don't need it," she muttered.

"Take it, or I'll feed it to the fish at the next creek."

"Thank you," she said, and took it. She hoped it was too dark for the others to see her tears.

She had discovered that prisons were dark and cold. The quarried walls permitted no heat to enter in summer, and kept none inside during winter. They gave her no candles. She had missed Robin and wept for him, raged at the demon within her that had killed her darling boy. But it had been no good to weep, for the burden of her sorrow never lifted.

She had found few books in the women's wing and begged the matrons for some. Finally they had brought some in from somewhere. In her term she had read over four hundred books. They didn't let her have novels that might inflame her criminal mind but she read botany, astronomy, essays by Emerson, medicine, and several thousand judicial decisions. Toward the end they let her read poetry, romances, and female hygiene.

She was not yet twenty-seven when they let her out on a raw February day, after giving her two dollars and the thin gray wool dress she wore. She had nowhere to go—certainly not New Ulm—but the two dollars took her to Minneapolis. She worked a few weeks as a saloon girl, serving drinks and fending off propositions, saving, saving to escape.

She beheld Cashbox a little after noon, and the sight filled her with dread. Someone here would know who she was and that her last name wasn't Goode. She stepped down from the coach into an ungainly town, and peered at a scatter of log buildings huddled beneath timbered slopes. Bewilderment overtook her. What could a penniless woman do? Her fellow passengers scattered. The Jehu unloaded the stage and drove it off. A few nondescript men stared at her, flooding her with fear.

"Miss!"

A woman beckoned to her from the brightest gig May had ever seen, enameled canary yellow, with green spoked wheels. The woman herself wore yellow silk with mink sleeves and collar, as gaily dressed as her chaise. A black cape clasped at the throat kept the woman warm. Reluctantly, May edged toward her.

"Are you waiting for someone, dearie?" the woman asked.

"Yes! Yes!" May cried.

"Men can be bums—keeping a lady waiting," the woman said. May thought she was gorgeous in a flashy way, with huge brown eyes beneath a nest of wild hair. The woman used paint.

"He'll come," May said.

"Of course. But if he doesn't come, dear, I can help you. I'll just wait a while. I'm in no hurry. Isn't Cashbox a delight? I'm Charlotte Keiserling—in case you ever need me."

May nodded, and strolled up and down the rutted street, jumping over muck and soaking her cheap shoes. She didn't know what to do; she didn't want to go with the woman. She felt dizzy with hunger again, and it would be icy tonight.

A while later May saw the gig approaching, the sleek mare stepping delicately through the slop in the street.

"Men are bums," said Charlotte Keiserling. "Come along dearie, and you can wait for him in comfort. It'll be cold soon."

Numbly, May Goode climbed in beside the woman in yellow.

CHAPTER 7

. . . .

There was a side of Willard Croker that he didn't like
much. He could be the politest, smiliest, kindest fellow
the world had ever seen. He could be the affable chum of
men, women, boys, and dogs, although he drew the line at
cats. He could charm old maids and ministers. But he
didn't consider any of that his true self. It was the mischief
of his ambitious mother, who had never ceased forming
and correcting her son. Long after he had fled home and
become a printer's devil in Carbondale, Illinois, he was
still getting letters from her about gentlemanly habits. In
his mind's eye, his true self was rough as hog bristles.

In time, he had become the proprietor of a small weekly
paper, perhaps because it permitted him to be affable to ladies and rough as hog bristles at the same time. He had no
competition in Cashbox, which allowed him to say what
he pleased and report stories from any angle that might put
coin in his empty pockets.

He tightened the form containing the first page of *The
Plain Truth* and slid it from the stone onto the steel bed of
the press. With a hand-roller he applied sticky proofing ink
to the type, and then gently laid a sheet of newsprint over
the type. He cranked the manually operated flatbed press,
which rolled a drum over the paper, imprinting it with the
ink.

He lifted the page, wary not to get any more of the
smeary ink onto his stained fingers, and set it on the typesetting table under the coal oil lamp. Then he perched his
half-spectacles on his bulbous nose, and began proofing.
He hoped to put this week's edition to bed before he addressed Portia Webb's Cashbox Women's Club about the
civic pride of Cashbox, Montana Territory. He would have
to be careful about what he said: most of those dears

formed themselves on every other Thursday into the Woman's Christian Temperance Union.

He turned to the most important, and most recently composed, article, the last to go into this issue:

"Arriving on the Cashbox Transfer stage this 12th instant was none other than Cornelius Daley, the renowned Silver Magnate of Helena. The purpose of Daley's visit is unknown, but it bodes well for this fair metropolis of the Northern Rockies. Daley never visits a mining camp until it is established and has a strong and lively future.

"His arrival has been known to transform a raw camp into a fair city. We fully expect Daley's interests here to turn Cashbox into the next Denver or Tombstone of the west, a place that may grow into a thriving Gotham of 50,000, living upon the inexhaustible wealth of Great Mines, while supplying commercial and banking services to the surrounding District.

"No doubt the canny entrepreneur, vulgarly called the Silver Fox for his legendary skill at acquiring an interest in the richest Silver Mines in the West, has been closely watching the fortunes of Cashbox, and is well aware that this Fair City is the fabled Golconda of the Territory, the Ophir of the Western Hemisphere.

"We have learned that Daley has taken rooms in the unfinished Palace Hotel from Messrs. Whitmore and Lake, who expect to open Cashbox's first two-story hostelry, eatery and saloon by May 1 at the latest. Daley's presence brings a cachet to this fine spa that will serve it forever.

"The proprietors are planning gourmet cuisine that will excel the finest culinary arts of Paris and Terre Haute, along with a rococo lobby and Gilded Saloon that will be the envy of San Francisco, Leadville, and St. Paul.

"Leave it to a man of Daley's genius to arrange for rooms in such an establishment even ahead of its Official Opening. We trust that the inconveniences will be slight these first days, and that those astute hostelers Whitmore and Lake will take good care of their special boarder.

"We eagerly await the moment when our newest citizen

divulges his purposes in fair Cashbox, but all our doughty
citizens can take heart. When Cornelius Daley sets foot in
a silver camp, everyone prospers. Town lots become precious; mining claims rise in value; stores flourish; trans-
portation companies boom; true and honest wealth
blossoms, as if by an Ethereal Hand, from the generous
rock, and blesses us with schools and churches, civic
pride, enterprise, and above all, an increasing population
of law-abiding and industrious citizens.

"Even now Cashbox boasts eight hundred fortunate
souls, and it is said fifty more a week arrive upon our Alpine Shores. This very week, thirteen splendid frame
buildings have been completed along with twelve new log
structures; and within the month Cashbox will possess
over forty more, if enough nails are shipped in, along with
ready-made glass windows. In two or three years Cashbox
will be the Shining Light upon the Hill, offering the hand
of opportunity to all."

Not bad, he thought, considering how little he knew. He
could not even say whether Daley intended to stay. But it
was just the kind of story he loved: it would raise the
value of every property in the district, including those
he was acquiring just as fast as he could snatch them. In
the next issue he would rewrite the same story. In fact,
he'd rewrite this one half a dozen times and probably double property values in a few weeks.

He still had to proof the rest of page one, and turned to
the story about the lawsuit. One Homer Ingstadt had alleged that Bass Boehm had jumped his valuable silver
claim just south of Robinson, and was suing to remove
Boehm from the premises and recover damages. The slan-
derous suit, Willard Croker had written, had no merit, and
libeled Boehm, an outstanding citizen with a reputation for
probity in his land dealings.

The article urged Justice of the Peace Anselm to dismiss
the suit forthwith, along with two other suits against
Boehm. In a sidebar Croker had written that the plague of
town lot jumping had reached such proportions that sev-

eral good citizens were being dislodged each month by ruffians who simply took over lots and waved deeds somehow gotten from the Cashbox Town Lot Company.

The Plain Truth pronounced this to be a scandal and urged the election of a constable who could deal with the ruffians. In particular, it recommended Rodwell Boehm, younger brother of the aggrieved Bass. Rodwell Boehm, the paper concluded, would be the ideal citizen to deal sternly with these nefarious ruffians.

Croker discovered half a dozen typos in these two lead stories, but none of them required fixing because they didn't cloud the meaning and he was in a hurry anyway. Hastily he proofed the rest of the page: An Odd Fellows ball, two miners' dances, business openings, the first concert of the Cashbox Cornet Band, arrivals, new buildings, silver and lead ore shipped, a birth, three deaths. He found more errors but let them slide.

He hated the tedium of typesetting a paper, the loathsome business of plucking each letter of type from its casebox and sliding it into a device that held the line of type. It was dull, mean labor, fit only for printer's devils. Willard Croker knew he was made for better things. The paper was useful, of course; in fact, necessary. But he dreamed of the moment when he could turn it over to the gypsy printers and brainless boys.

At the last, he discovered an error in a headline, and turned to the bins of Caslon 18-point display type to replace a *V* with a *W*. That meant loosening the wingnuts on the form and extracting the line of type. Errors in text were one thing; errors in the headlines weren't so piddly. Swiftly he replaced the offending letter and tightened the form again. He eyed the seven-day clock shelved on the log wall and realized he could not print 230 copies and still be at Portia's on time.

He didn't mind. Each of the little talks he'd given to Portia's circle had won him the trust of the best people in town. He knew himself to be something of a ladies' man though he'd never taken one to wife. His rhetoric had been polished until it glowed like agate. Once he divested his six-and-a-half-foot body of the grimy inkstained apron and entered the world as a gentleman of great wisdom, he was always taken for one of Cashbox's leading lights. Which he occasionally was.

He carefully scrubbed black ink from under his fingernails, and soaped his hands until they were as clean as a cherub's even if the rest of him wasn't. Then he locked the door of his little log building on Cashbox Street with a skeleton key, and headed for the Silver Saloon for a sandwich, a snort, and a dill pickle to hide the aroma from the dear ladies.

After that he would toil up the grade to the calcimined frame house with the gingerbread trim on McDonald, where the door would open even before he rapped on it and Portia would gush him in to a perfumed parlor. He'd have a glowing report to drop into their little pink ears. It would be all about Cornelius Daley, give or take a few inventions—nothing off-color of course—to spice his account of the silver magnate. He would tell them that Cashbox was born again.

Then they'd beam, offer him all the finger food and tea he could swallow—which was as much as was on the platter—and invite him to come again. This evening he would do what he usually did on Tuesday nights after putting *The Plain Truth* to bed; he would put Charlotte Keiserling to bed after giving her a free five-cent copy, with the ink not quite dry.

CHAPTER 8

• • • • • • • • • • • • • • •

May Goode felt bewildered. Why was she letting this happen? Had she no will? Had her years in prison turned her numb? She sat beside the woman in costly yel-

low silk, Charlotte Keiserling, as she steered her gay yellow rig across a plank bridge and up a relentless slope.

May had no illusions about the woman. She knew why
Charlotte Keiserling often met the stage. May's years in
prison had introduced her to a netherworld of a sort she
knew nothing of in her protected life at New Ulm.

She searched herself. Was it starvation that had goaded
her? The promise of warmth and a roof? Or was it simply
her helplessness when she stepped off the stage into a
strange town, without a cent?

The madam steered the gig toward a chinked log building with small windows, and halted under a rude porch.
The sporting house bore no marks of infamy, and for a
desperate moment May thought it might be just a boarding
hotel. A man limping on a pegleg rounded a corner and
took the lines from Charlotte, grinning wickedly at her
from behind a huge brown beard.

"Thanks, Amos," the lady said, and turned to May.
"Come in, dearie, and have some tea. You look tired."

"I think—"

"Oh, bother! You come in now, and we'll get to know
each other."

She sounded as if she'd said this very thing to a lot of
women over the years. "Just some tea," May said. Tea
would be a treat and would help her recover her courage.
And also—she confessed to herself—she was intensely curious.

"Most everyone'll be asleep," Charlotte said, opening
the door and ushering May into a parlor that lay shadowed
except for a brilliant rectangle of sun blazing across the
floor. Someone had civilized the room. The logs had been
whitewashed; crimson settees and chairs filled the spaces,
along with an upright piano with sheet music on its rack.
Above, a cut-glass chandelier held six unlit coal-oil lamps.
A worn Brussels carpet covered the raw plank floors. A
painting of a fat nude, with diaphanous gauze entwining
her thighs, hung in a gilded frame. May had never seen a
painting like that, and it stirred some unnamable emotion.

"Our private quarters are in the back, dearie. There'll be some hot water on the stove," Charlotte said, herding May down a long corridor wreathed in night and metered by closed doors at regular intervals, each lacquered a Chinese red. But in a moment they reached light again, pushing through velvet drapes into a kitchen no less cheerful than the parlor.

So this was the secret life of such women, May thought, the house of which no proper woman spoke, as if its name, *brothel*, when whispered aloud would invite sulphurous fumes rising from hell. Here, made gaudy and papered over with minor luxuries, was the lair of harlots.

No one else was in the sun-streaked kitchen.

The madam poured hot water from a marbled blue pot into a China teapot, added a charged tea strainer and soon poured the brew into teacups. Then she produced a tray of sweets.

"Have a tart," she said, and laughed heartily. "We have our little jokes here. We take a tray into the parlor each night and ask 'em if they'd like a tart."

May wolfed down three before she thought to hide her appetite from her hostess.

"You've had some tough luck, dearie," the woman began. "You want to tell me about it?"

May shook her head. She would not tell anyone, ever.

Charlotte Keiserling shrugged. "Suit yourself. I just thought I'd lend you a shoulder to cry on. Me, I don't have a hard-luck story, but some girls do. I love the life. I'm a natural. I got into trouble when I was fifteen—oh, no, dearie, not the way you think. I was just too fast. I'd discovered boys. I liked to fool around with them. I never had such fun. They'd never met a girl like me. I did things with them, and we'd laugh until we were silly.

"But I got caught. I didn't care. I've never stopped foolin' around and having fun. I'd rather be entertaining men than anything in the world. So I figured I might as well get paid for it, long as I was ruined. Oh, it's easy. You've never met a woman so ruined. Why, there's a party here every night, and everyone has such a good time. We sing, someone plays the piano. We tell lots of—ah, jokes. We serve the gentlemen a little bourbon or rye if they wish, and they have fun too. Why, life's just a party."

May nodded. Her years in prison had thrown her into contact with such as these, and she hadn't found any joy in them. "Thank you for the tea. I'd better go now."

"Oh, what's the rush, dearie? You stay on as long as you want, treat's on me. Stay an evening. See the life. No one's pushing you. Stay here in the kitchen if you want. The girls'd love to meet you. See that alcove with the curtain? Stay there tonight all by your little self."

"Why did you come to a place like Cashbox?" May asked.

The woman shrugged. "I move every once in a while. When a town gets dull. Or when a camp starts to die. I can't stand that. I left some like that; got out. Isn't this a cozy town? Last town, the bluenoses chased me out. Oh, was that something. Same ones that climbed atop my curved body and kissed my ruby lips started makin' laws. Well—it's a good life. Warm in the winter, and happy— why, you don't even know what the word means, I bet. I'm safe. You'd be safe, too."

"I can't. Don't you see I can't?" May blurted.

The madam patted May's arm. "Dearie, you can't feature yourself in the life. You have a sort of, well, notion of vice. It's like a corset. Oh, the happiest day in my life was when I unlaced the corset." She bawled happily, and May couldn't help but like this cheerful lady. "Are you married, dearie?"

"I was—yes. I can't do this."

"Left a man and some wee ones behind, I bet."

Tears bloomed in May's eyes. "No, no," she whispered through a choked throat.

"I'm sorry, dearie. None of my business."

"No, it's none of your business."

"Have you a name? Is it secret? Most of my girls don't use their real one, but they all answer to something—like

Texas Rose, or Little Bucking Mare." She laughed uproariously. "She's well named, Little Bucking Mare. I don't even know what her name is."

"I'm not—I'm not . . . interested. I have to go now."

"You poor starved little thing; you just sit right there and eat. I won't let a hungry thing like you walk out. You trust Charlotte. I'm like a mother, lovin' all my sweets. Why, the girls, they're just getting up and scrubbin' and puttin' on their warpaint. You just settle there and you'll meet some just like yourself, only you're sweeter."

"I'm not sweet," May whispered. "You don't know me."

"You listened to some preacher too much, dearie. It's their way of tellin' women what to do. You ever studied the Testament? Have they ever got a mess of rules. Hey, you're not in Persia; this is the United States. A woman—she can do what she pleases. You're going to be queen of Cashbox. Oh, a queen—after you fiddle around with your pretty hair and learn to please the gents. I'll teach you that. You're gonna have gentlemen bringin' you flowers and silver dollars. They'll be lickin' their chops for the taste of you."

"I don't want that, I just . . ." May felt tears welling up. She hadn't come all the way to Cashbox to violate herself, like she was ripping some fabric she was made of. Why, if she'd do this—this!—then she was just as bad as everyone said; she was just a . . . killer.

"Hon, have some more tarts. I never did see such a half-starved little thing." Charlotte shoved the tray closer. May wanted them. She could taste the pastries, thick with jam in the middle. She ached to wolf down the whole silver tray of them. But she shook her head, at first slowly, then with some fiery need as if her whole future depended on it; not one more tart; not one more sip of honeyed tea, hot and cheerful as it slid down her throat. One more sip, one more tart, one more minute in this warm kitchen and she'd—

She bolted upright and rubbed away the tears.

"Whoa, up, missy. You sit down. It still frosts up at night. You don't have to go anywhere; I'm not pushing you into anything. Why, I'll get Amos. He'll set you right down and talk to you sensible about Cashbox. He's a good man, dearie; he's gentle and can, ah, make this pleasant—"

But May Goode drew her black shawl tight, clutched her reticule, and fled through the long black hallway with its dollared doors. Some were open. She glimpsed young women in dishabille—and a bald man in his gray drawers sitting on a bed and laughing. She burst into the parlor, fled past the piano, scattering waltzes and mazurkas. She pried open the heavy door to the music of announcing bells.

"You come back, dearie. When you get cold, you come back."

She felt the cold afternoon air brace her. She ran as fast as her long skirts would let her, fearful that the peglegged man might catch her. She tumbled down the slope, her breath rasping, her throat so constricted it ached.

She crossed the plank bridge over the tiny creek, and slowed. Still near tears, she clambered up a steep grade to Main Street, a different, colder, meaner part of town. She didn't know where to go or what to do; she had only an hour or two before stores closed.

She paused, letting her pulse slow, looking about. She hadn't even had time to examine Cashbox before the lady with the yellow rig had chased her to the ground like a fox hunter and his hounds.

She felt better. She could never know happiness because of the secret in her; the mark of Cain, preachers would say. She was Eve, cast out of the Garden of Eden. The thing that had nauseated her in the sporting house slowly died. She was not one of them. She had faced down temptation.

Cashbox lay in a glorious wild, huddled together because of the vastness of the mountains. Far to the south, the snowy peaks of the Crazy Mountains bloomed in the late sun. Closer at hand, dark piney slopes vaulted to high

ridges. She studied Cashbox, which lay pastel and sweet in
the brisk air, perfumed with eddying wood smoke and
sagebrush. She saw no picket fence to keep her in or out.
She saw no walls, and this place without walls touched a
need in her.

She was free. She didn't have a penny. She didn't have
food. She didn't have enough clothes to resist the onrush-
ing night. But she was free. No one knew her name or her
past. No one would shut a door because of what had happened. She could walk in any direction. She could go anywhere, be anything. But this shocking freedom was more
terrifying than the prison.

"Oh, God," she whispered: "What will I do?"

CHAPTER 9
· · · · · · · · · · · · · ·

Cornelius Daley eyed the dray horse, a beast of dubious
ancestry, as the hostler wiped dust from the seat of the
buggy. "You'll need the whip. He can be a slacker. Pop
him good and he'll go good."

"What are the blinders for?"

"Oh, them? He takes notions he's in a race sometimes
. . . when some other horse draws up beside him. He's got
brakes, though. Most of the time he's jist an old bobcat."

"I trust you have insurance," Daley said blandly. He settled himself in the quilted leather seat and steered the mis-
begotten blue roan toward the gulch, handling the lines
with practiced ease. The weather seemed uncertain, with
an overcast hooding the peaks and sawing off summits.
But he had never permitted weather to govern affairs of
the purse.

In a few minutes he had his first glimpse of the Giltedge
Mine. It stood on the left, just above the soggy road and
the rivulet that passed for a creek, crowding the vaulting
and naked slope behind it to make room. The works were

wholly familiar to him, not only from sketches he had seen, but also from his encyclopedic knowledge of silver mining. The headframe stood naked to the weather. Beside it, the engine house roared, its stacks erupting black smoke that hung under the overcast, choking the gulch. He eyed the grimy office building, knowing he would enter it later. He examined the thundering mill, belching its own smoke and vibrating like something berserk. A tramway connected the mine to the mill, and another carried slack out on a trestle where it was dumped. The pile of slack was not large.

He steered the buggy off the rutted road to make way for the constant freight traffic, and let the beast nip the new grass. He wanted to watch. He extracted his Hamilton pocket watch from his vest and noted the hour. Almost 10:30. This shift would be well along, which is how he had timed this trip.

He felt mist on his face but no rain; his black greatcoat would turn it, and he had no need to hasten. He settled back to observe, knowing it would take an hour to find out what he needed to know. Down at the faces, or stopes, muckers would be shoveling rock blown loose by the previous shift's blast, the worthless slack going into some cars, the ore into other cars. At the headframe—"on the grass," they called it—a tophander and cagers, the ones who rode the cages along with the ore cars, pulled the cars off the hoists onto an iron turning sheet, and then onto the tramways leading either to the slackpile or the mill. That was the operation that Daley wished to observe.

As the minutes ticked by, he saw one after another mule-drawn ore car roll down the tramway to the mill, and the empties parade back. But he saw not a car headed for the slackpile. Could it be? He was not a man easily awed, but what he was witnessing was beyond the wildest imagination: they were mining a body of ore so thick and wide and rich that it yielded no slack. They were working in the bowels of a huge vein.

He knew what the assay values were. Johann Mueller,

the assayer in Livingston, had kindly supplied them for an absurd recompense, the amount being exactly the $1.50 he charged the Giltedge Mine. Mueller, a graduate of the Freiburg School of Mines in Saxony, had been taught the world's finest assaying techniques, and was better at it than his American colleagues.

An assayer was, at bottom, the operator of a tiny, lab-sized mill and smelter, operated on the same principles as the giant ones that handled nonferric ores. Mueller amused Con Daley. If a man was going to be dishonest, he ought to be crooked on a worthwhile scale. Daley would gladly have paid fifty times more for the confidential information that Mueller penned on his printed assay forms and then copied for him.

Daley waited patiently through another hour, ignoring the mist. In the whole period he never saw a car headed for the slackpile, which taxed his credulity. Satisfied at last, he cracked his whip over the rump of the surly horse, and headed for his next destination a few hundred feet distant. The Giltedge had been erected on two original claims while its milling and future smelting operations were located on worthless limestone nearby. But what interested Con Daley was the claim immediately above the Giltedge, owned by one Ambrose Gill, a man who seemed to have vanished after doing his initial assessment work.

Daley could find no place on the cramped road to pull off, so he continued ahead until he found a wide spot that would permit the heavy traffic of ore wagons, freight wagons, mule trains and carriages to squeak past. That suited him fine; he didn't want it known just where his interests lay. He pulled out a carriage weight and clipped it to the bridle—not that this wreck of a dray horse was going a step farther than it had to. Then he walked back to Gill's claim, muddying his glossy hightop shoes. He studied the shoulder of the road, looking for stakes or cairns, and found none at first. But at last he located a steel pipe over on the Giltedge side. The next six hundred feet belonged to Gill, and there would be one bore in it, not far from the Giltedge line. Beyond Gill's claim was the Ophir Mine.

Daley had quietly bought half of the Ophir, not because it was succeeding—but because he expected it to fail in a year or two. Sometimes a failing mine could be more profitable than a good one, especially if it were organized as a certain kind of public stock company. The thought cheered him.

Gill's bore, several rods from the Giltedge line, had been driven straight into jasper. Mueller's assay report indicated almost an ounce of silver to the ton, traces of gold, and some lead, none of it in values worth pursuing. Unless you were Con Daley.

He found the shaft behind brush. It pierced horizontally into the steep hillside from just above creek level, following the jasper as it angled toward the Giltedge line. Ashes on its wet floor suggested it had been used as shelter, but most of the year it would be too wet even for a homeless man. Daley walked in a few feet, uneasily eyeing the dripping timber sets that held up the fragmented rock. He wanted to know whether the shaft had been driven ten feet or more. A small detail like that could be important. Ten feet was considered the minimum distance needed to patent a federal mining claim. It was the equivalent of the hundred dollars of assessment work required by the government. This shaft obviously pierced much farther. Daley eased back out, relieved that the world hadn't fallen on him.

Gill's claim, filed with the mining district registrar, read much the same as a thousand others Daley had read: "I, the undersigned, claim one claim of six hundred feet by one thousand five hundred feet on this silver-bearing surface lead, extending west and east from this notice, with all its dips, spurs, and angles, variations and sinuosities." One copy had been posted in the exact middle of the claim; the other copy had been filed.

For Daley's purposes, the language was ideal; it laid claim to all ore in the vein wherever it went. The Federal

Mining Act of 1872 allowed a locator to mine a vein that apexed, or surfaced, on his property even if it laterally entered adjacent claims. Gill's claim was perfect: the assessment work had been done and the claim was patented; and the presence of some values in an assay by the renowned Johann Mueller anchored it all down. All he had to do was locate Gill, sober him up enough to sign a deed, and pay him fifty dollars for it. With that in hand, he would soon own the Giltedge.

What court would deny that the incredible Giltedge lode had apexed right where he stood? But an apex lawsuit would be the last resort. The devious master of federal mine law and apex legislation, J. Ernest Potter-Pride, Esquire, would eat the silver and leave Daley the lead.

There had to be a cheaper way. But financing the Hammons would probably not be it. He had lunched twice with those affable merchants at the Montana Club to explore that. The pair had built a giant retail business specializing in the mining camps, now the largest mercantile firm in the territory. They sold more petticoats, bloomers, corsets, bust enlargers and drawers than Con Daley had seen in a Montgomery Ward catalogue, but they knew nothing about mining. They knew only that they had an incredibly rich lode and it was all theirs.

Daley smiled. His reputation had preceded him. The Hammons had feared the Silver Fox, and had shaped the company with a jaundiced eye toward speculators. The Giltedge had been organized as a private partnership with a lot of boilerplate intended to keep outsiders at bay if either brother died.

Still, the mine had taxed them to the limits, and that smelled like opportunity. Daley had contacts among bankers and brokers, people he lunched with regularly who often had a tidbit for him. He, in turn, tipped them off about excellent mining prospects. From them he had learned that the Hammons could lose their shirts unless they came up with more capital. What a pleasant prospect for the Silver Fox.

He clambered into the buggy, feeling the mist that had beaded on its seat chill his buttocks. He drove a mile up the gulch before he found a place wide enough to turn around, but he didn't mind. It gave him a view of the Ophir, the Midas, the Silvertop, the Queen of Sheba, the Exchequer, and the Delirium Tremens, named for the shaky operation it was. He might toy with them someday. But not now.

He steered the buggy down the gulch, dodging mule teams and ore wagons, and turned into the muddy flat in front of Webb's offices. It was time to catch the crusty superintendent in his lair.

CHAPTER 10

. . . .

Thaddeus Webb eyed his famous visitor warily. The man's overindulgence had begun to take its toll. A web of red capillaries bloomed on his nose; the man's raptor face had softened, and his body had thickened with the years.

They had met before. Con Daley managed to meet most everyone connected with silver mining. He had an affable way about him, and was as much at home with Cornish miners as he was with superintendents. Webb wished that he could deal with others as easily. But he'd always been a driven, curt, energetic man goaded by visions of excellence. He could not suffer small talk. Neither could he change himself.

"Well, Con, what brings you to Cashbox?" Webb asked, trumping the small talk and ersatz geniality.

"Ah, my old friend, I'm just looking over mining properties as usual. Promising, promising. This one, for a fact."

"The Hammons aren't selling."

"How right you are. I lunched with them twice in Helena, and made several generous offers."

That was news to Webb. The owners hadn't bothered to tell him, which irked him a little. If the Silver Fox was sniffing around, he ought to know it immediately. "It's a privately held company," Webb said.

"That'll change, my friend. This mine needs capital, and lots of it. The Hammons are sitting on . . . shall we say a bonanza? But they could easily go belly-up."

"You seem well informed—as usual," said Webb dryly.

Con Daley chuckled. "I like facts," he said. "I collect them. Let me tell you a few things about the Giltedge. Right now, you're boring through an incredible lode. You don't even know its dimensions or how deep it runs."

"You have good informants."

"No, my friend. It's simpler than that. I've just spent a while watching from the road. Twenty-three ore cars went to the mill; not one car went to the slack pile. I can read ore cars, even if some can't." Daley chuckled so infectiously that Webb laughed too. "I'll tell you more. The Giltedge is incredible. Maybe the richest silver ore body in the world. But she's a devil, too."

"How do you know that?" Webb asked. He did not lack respect for the pirate.

"Oh, lots of ways. You're going to sink a new shaft. The hoist cable came in a few days ago." His eyes twinkled. "I saw it from my coach. That suggests that the ore lies on a tricky incline. You've had trouble getting to it from the old shaft. And you're skimping on timbering. It's not a safe mine, Thaddeus. You really ought to do something about it."

"Daley, I've done what I can. This mine hasn't earned a nickel yet—the first concentrates left for Helena a few days ago. I don't have—" He stopped. Daley was squeezing a song out of him as if he were an accordion. "How do you know it's not safe?"

"I visited the cemetery."

Webb sighed, his mind filled with bad memories. "It happened before we reached ore. We didn't know how bad the rock was. It haunts me every waking moment."

"Now you know what kind of rock. You're still not giving your men the timber sets. That's what I'm here about, Thaddeus. I want to talk to you about capitalizing this mine properly."

Webb sat back, his mind swarming with thoughts he couldn't organize. "If the Hammons aren't interested, don't come to me. I'm not the owner and I'll not sneak about."

"Thaddeus, you know as well as I do you can influence them. The mine wants capital immediately, or the Hammons'll lose it and take the worst bath of their life. They don't know mining. They hired you because they needed a man like you. They told each other you'd make it pay. You above all. But even you, Thaddeus, need working funds. They're extended—everyone in Helena knows that. You need another hundred thousand or it'll all collapse on their heads—and yours—and your miners'."

"Daley, I'll listen to an offer but not behind their backs. Everything you tell me I'll faithfully repeat to the Hammons. They're coming here soon."

"Ah, Thaddeus, my friend, that's what I want to hear. Now these fine brothers—they know they've got something good. What are the values, eh? Twenty-seven ounces to the ton, and getting better, eh?"

Daley's accurate information didn't surprise the superintendent. He didn't respond.

"I've seen people like the Hammons—sheep, really—take the plunge. They don't really understand it. They know they've got a fortune in the rock and it makes them suspicious of people like the old Silver Fox. They're like a man that falls overboard clutching a bag of gold. He won't let go of it even to save his life. He has to let go and swim to the surface, but he can't." Daley shook his head. "That's how they are. They'd rather go under than open the mine to the development that'd save it."

Webb smiled. Daley was having a good time.

Daley settled back into the wooden chair, oblivious to its discomfort. "The Giltedge needs a smelter and a railroad to the NP to be more than just marginal. It needs working capital for timbering and development. You sit there by the hour, worrying that another collapse of rotten rock'll murder your men. Ah, yes, murder. That's what the widows would call it, and then the press."

Webb recoiled from the words he couldn't bear.

"You want those timbers in there as badly as the Cousin Jacks. But where's the cash? There's not even enough for payroll. Can you fill up those envelopes next tally day—next Saturday? Ah, I can see it in your face, my friend. Don't say a word. You live in a private hell, and the Hammons aren't helping you a bit. Now you've summoned them. The crisis is at hand."

Webb smiled thinly. "And you'll supply some cash out of the goodness of your heart."

They laughed.

"I'd want fifty-one percent of a closed partnership. I'd ante a hundred thousand immediately—that would buy a smelter, timbering, and a few months of operating costs—and I'd raise more if there's reason down in that mine to build a railroad." He cocked an eyebrow. "And I'll wager there's ample reason."

"Control," Webb said. "You may as well be talking to a rock. They might borrow at interest from you. But your reputation precedes you."

Daley smiled. "I need control. The Hammons know that. Without it—" He shrugged, amusement rising in his face.

"Without you around, Mister Daley, I could run it as it should be run, for long-term profit. For the benefit of all the owners. The Hammons want an investment that'll yield good income for many years; something for their widows someday. Something for their children and grandchildren. Something that'll still benefit Cashbox fifty years from now." Webb said it lightly, wondering whether Daley got his meaning.

But Daley only chuckled, somehow communicating more with the amused convulsions of his big frame than he ever could with words. "I'd make them rich," he said. "But I don't suppose they want that."

"They already are."

A clamor of bells penetrated through the window. Webb listened alertly.

The pattern he dreaded came clear. Seven bells. Seven bells! Insistent, urgent. The emergency signal. Seven bells told the hoist man in any mine to lower the cage at once, no matter what, and bring it up upon further signal. Seven bells was the tolling of the dead.

"Sorry, Daley," he muttered, springing from his chair and out the door. He raced toward the headframe, where the cage would arrive and disgorge its burden. Somewhere behind him Daley was following.

Within the engine room, the hoist engineer carefully watched the giant needle that indicated the exact position of the cage as it slowly twisted toward zero, and then he braked as the open-sided cage burst from the earth.

It bore an injured man, and several others, including that firebrand Hugh Trego. The man's head oozed blood from lacerations, and something looked wrong about it. Webb didn't recognize the man.

The miners tenderly lifted the injured youth—he seemed barely beyond his teens—off the cage and onto the clay, and covered him. They stared helplessly at Webb. No doctor had as yet arrived in Cashbox.

"Who is he?" Webb asked.

"Kermit Reilly, sir."

"What happened?"

This time Trego replied, enraged. "A rock fell on 'im, rotten rock out of the bad place where no timber spares a man. He lives alone in a cabin; he's got not a soul to nurse him back—if he ever comes back. And this bleddy mine's not got an infirmary where he can lie. By God, Webb, this be it. Ye'll get timber sets up or not a man of us'll enter the bleddy pit again."

Trego balled his terrible fists, as if wanting to pulverize Webb.

"Take him to the office, please. I'll get some women to clean him up and—"

"We'll not let your pampered women work their charity upon Kermit Reilly. We'll have none of that. We'll have a safe pit or none; we'll have a doctor; we'll have an infirmary; we'll have a hole that won't keep our wives worrying themselves sick every time we walk from our houses—worrying whether they'll see us alive again—"

Tenderly they lifted the red-haired youth into a makeshift stretcher and carried him toward the company boardinghouse across Cashbox Creek. No man among them paid the slightest attention to Webb, or the black-suited man beside Webb.

"It's hard to live with, Thaddeus," said Daley, after the sorry procession had vanished. "How can you bear it?"

"I can't bear it," Webb said, fighting back a wetness in his eyes.

"A man's hurt and it's on your conscience."

Webb whirled on Daley.

"It's not a time to talk business," said Daley, leaving Webb standing in the mine yard.

But Webb had the feeling that Daley had never stopped talking business.

CHAPTER 11

Regina Maltz patiently spooned chicken broth into Kermit Reilly, who swallowed it slowly, an act requiring all his will. It pleasured Regina to nurse the young miner; it filled her with a sense of giving and nurturing—things that had been absent from her humdrum life. She wiped a small dribble from his chin and spooned in more.

She had seen to his comfort twenty times a day, peering in on him while he slept, adjusting his blanket, worrying about the bloody bandaging that wrapped his lacerated head and the other bandaging that had soaked up the blood of his mauled shoulder and immobilized his right clavicle. Kermit could not use his right arm and no one knew whether he would ever be able to again.

The rock had plunged without warning from the top of the crosscut, glancing off his head and smacking into his shoulder, knocking him into the muck. It had been a miracle that it hadn't killed him.

"Have you had enough?" she asked.

He nodded. The pain had glazed his eyes with a haunted, desperate, half-mad stare. He needed laudanum, but none was to be had in a camp without a doctor—except perhaps from those unfortunate women across the creek.

The miners had come to her after the accident and asked whether she might nurse him. Reilly lived alone, they told her.

"Miss Maltz," Hugh Trego had said, "you're known in every camp where miners gather; you're known as the one haven a miner can go to for help. Would you be so kind as to nurse this fine lad back to the living?"

"Of course," she'd said. Always of course.

Never in her many years in the camps had she turned away anyone. This camp had no hospital. The greedy mine supervisors squeezed blood from their men—and never gave them a place to heal. Silently she condemned Thaddeus Webb and all of his ilk for their neglect.

Regina wondered why she had been elected to care for every broken-winged bird. Perhaps it was because she didn't know how to say no. She had always nodded, and soon the sick or wounded were carried to her doorstep. She had cared for them; spent her meager earnings on them; sent a few east with a ticket she had purchased for them—and had rarely been repaid, except with gratitude. But that was a gift in itself that stilled the ravening of her own starved soul.

She had coaxed two of her tenants, Herbert Trenoweth and Anton Bosnick, into abandoning their first-floor room for a while. Like all her roomers, they double-rented, each possessing the room for twelve hours. Others in the boardinghouse took them in for the duration. After that she had hovered over Reilly, held his icy hand through the worst of his splitting headaches, calmed him when he convulsed, and wiped his body clean when he had sweated out his fevers. She welcomed these chores like a mother tending her children.

She had gotten no help from Sylvie Duvalier and wanted none. Sylvie couldn't mother a stray cat, much less a wounded man. Sylvie had been out each day tracking down masons and carpenters who might build her clubhouse, but with no success. No carpenter would spend a minute on such a thing while the town's newcomers slept on saloon sawdust for the want of boardinghouses, hotels, restaurants and homes.

She set aside the bowl and held Reilly's clammy hand. He lay with his eyes closed, and she could see pain throb with each weak pulse, a feral migraine crouched within him.

She wondered about him. Who was he? She knew his name, an approximate age—twenty-five, she guessed—and a few facts. He mined for the Giltedge and he lived alone in a log hut. He had an Irish surname but she didn't know whether Kermit Reilly had immigrated or was a native son. She knew he was a wounded mortal with some sort of dreams, large or small, locked within him. Had he grand designs—would he claw his way up the ladder and be rich? Or did he only want enough in the tally and pay envelope to buy a little ale, throw darts in the pub, and laugh with his friends?

He had friends. The Cornishmen had brought the Irish youth to her with a ferocity in their eye, as if daring death to snatch away their brother who shared the danger of the pit.

She had to shop. Feeding her boarders required a trip to Baker's market every day. Uneasily, dreading to leave the youth to cough and die alone, she donned her old cloth coat and ventured into the April sun, discovering a mean wind that sliced through the fabric.

At the mercantile she handed Stearn Blevins the list. This would be a heavy load—last fall's potatoes, a fifty-pound sack of wheat flour, a crock of lard, twenty pounds of onions, any fruits that could be had, a case of cabbages if available, a crock of butter, and a jug of milk.

"Stop at the butcher's too, Stearn. He'll have some beef to send me."

"Sure, Miss Maltz. You want your letter?"

"A letter?"

He surprised her. She rarely received mail. He hastened to the wicket in the corner that served as the Cashbox post office, and returned with the envelope. A copperplate script read *Regina Maltz, City*.

"Thank you, Stearn. Please be quick about it, or I'll be feeding my men late."

She lumbered up the slope to her boardinghouse, wondering why she had chosen to live in a place so raw. Cashbox had no tree-lined streets or green lawns or sidewalks or pleasant houses in a row where settled people raised families. It just was in her to pick these places, she supposed, some unanswerable restlessness, some vague revulsion toward weary cities that seemed to snuff hope out of people. In these raw places hope bloomed and second chances swelled on the smoke. Cashbox was the bedground of a thousand intoxicating dreams, including her own, the ones she barely acknowledged when they flitted darkly through her unguarded mind.

Even before removing her coat, she peeked in on Kermit. His chest rose and fell rhythmically. He slept. Satisfied, she slipped into her own quarters and sat down to read her mysterious mail, hoping that someone, just one of all she had helped in her many pasts, had remembered her tenderly.

She pried open her letter and withdrew a printed form with certain blanks filled in by hand.

Dear Miss Maltz,

*As attorney for Mr. Bass Boehm I am writing to in-
form you that you are being evicted from a certain
Cashbox Town Lot Company lot, Number 22, which
he possesses by valid deed. He is requiring parties
who are trespassing on his deeded lots to vacate said
lots within seven days of receipt of this letter, along
with all goods and chattels and tenants.*

*As you no doubt remember, the original Cashbox
town patent application filed with the Federal Land
Office in March of 1887 by the Company was rejected
on technical grounds because of a faulty survey. The
Company rectified the error and refiled in June of
1887 and was subsequently granted a federal land
patent covering eighty acres.*

*Since all the deeds conveyed to buyers by the Com-
pany between March and June of 1887 were invalid,
the Company offered to supply new and properly
dated deeds to those who held the invalid ones. To
this effect the Company posted two public notices
during the month of November, 1887, one located in
the offices of the Cashbox Town Lot Company on
Main Street, and one on the east side of Cashbox
Creek on the front wall of Minnie's Sporting House.
An additional notification was posted in the legal notices section of The Plain Truth, in two subsequent issues.*

*Those who, through their own negligence, did not
apply for the new deeds lost their ownership of the
lots. My client, Mister Boehm, purchased a number of
these in January of this year, including lot 22, and is
now its rightful owner. I enclose a certified copy of
Mr. Boehm's recorded deed, supplied by the county
clerk at White Sulphur Springs.*

*While eviction is regrettable, Mr. Boehm has an in-
alienable right to his own property, which I will pros-
ecute vigorously as befits these circumstances. Your*

*best recourse is to cooperate fully and peaceably and
be out of the premises by April 29.*
   Sincerely,
   J. Ernest Potter-Pride
   Attorney-at-law.

Regina read the letter numbly, again and again. No one
had notified her of anything. She wondered how such a
notice had escaped her eye or ear. She wondered darkly
whether such a notice had been posted at all, and why she
had not been informed by letter. She wondered if this were
not more of the town lot jumping that had plagued almost
every mining camp, including Tombstone and Leadville.

That crook! Bass Boehm and his hard-eyed cutthroats.
That sleazy shyster Ernest Potter-Pride. Good heavens,
they would take her boardinghouse from her. She would
still owe the White Sulphur State Bank for the two-
thousand-dollar mortgage she had only begun to pay off.

She wondered what to do. A lone woman in a mining
camp could be easy prey. She couldn't afford a lawsuit,
and if all this was true, a lawyer couldn't do much anyway. Her boarding fees paid her mortgage and bought the
food, and what little profit she made on it seemed to slip
from her fingers because of her foolish habit of helping
the Kermits of this world.

Regina Maltz sighed. All her years as a woman alone in
the camps had girded her soul with a strange sort of steel.
She would not despair. Her first step, she decided, would
be a trip to the gilded office of that skunk.

CHAPTER 12

• • • • • • • • • • • • • • • • •

Sylvie Duvalier eyed the Palace Hotel speculatively. It
was going to be splendid. She eyed the parqueted floor,
the wainscoting, and the black walnut registration desk

with approval; these were the marks of a classy joint. A naked brass-railed bar and mirrored backbar stood in the darkened saloon off the lobby.

She spotted no one but she could hear the hum of saws and hammers, and the thuds of heavy objects being moved. It would be perfect if she could afford it. She had to find something: that very morning, Regina Maltz, tight-lipped and upset, had hinted that she was about to lose her rooming house to lot-jumpers. It had frightened Sylvie into instant action, and she had headed here. If Con Daley could rent in advance, then so could she.

The thought pleased her. She had business to transact with him. She poked around the unlit lobby until a dark-haired man in shirtsleeves descended the grand stairway.

"We're not open, ma'am," he proclaimed.

"Of course you're not. But you rent to Con Daley. I thought you might rent to me, too."

He studied her until she felt like hanging beef. "I don't know that we can," he said. "You're unescorted."

She thrust her left hand at him. "This ring escorts me."

"I'm not sure our guests would approve—"

"If they don't approve of me, they shouldn't be guests."

He laughed, a new appreciation blossoming in him. "I'm Loren Whitmore, from Ann Arbor, out here civilizing Cashbox."

"I'm Sylvie Duvalier. I'm here on business."

Whitmore sucked his mustache. "Most unusual," he said.

"That's why I'm here. I'm unusual. Now what'll you charge for a good room? A room occupied by me every day is worth more than one with no guest."

"We'll be charging three dollars a night. But . . . we really aren't prepared—"

"Prepared! You want me to sleep on the street? Where else can a lady get a room?"

He shrugged, apology in the gesture. "Things are a bit—raw, still. We'll have no running water for two months—have to wait for the Cashbox Water Company to bring its line from the springs up Allebaugh Creek. That means—primitive facilities."

"It won't bother me a bit. Now how about seventy-five a month in advance?" She plucked some notes from her reticule.

The sight of that lettuce wilted him. "There's one at the rear of the second floor," he said, gesturing. She followed him up the grand stairs and down an uncarpeted hall, past rooms filled with painters and drapers. He steered her into Number 12, a spacious and sunny room without a stick of furniture in it. She liked it at once. It had a stove in the corner and a window with a view.

"I'll take it," she said, smacking bills into his hand before he could change his mind. "Have it furnished by evening."

"Ah—I was going to show you the rest." He steered her into the hallway toward the lavatories. "I shan't go in with you, but you can see we'll have ... comforts when the water comes. For now, there's a pump out back—and the rest."

She plunged into a tiled room that contained two water closets, each with a Modern Sanitation Company oak commode; some washbasins with gold-plated faucets; and a four-claw bathtub of noble proportions. The Palace was trying to live up to its name.

"I'll move right in," she said. "Which is Mister Daley's room?"

He eyed her suspiciously. "We ensure the privacy of our guests," he said.

"He's a friend. I was just curious."

His gaze settled over her like a fishnet. "I'm sure you'll bump into him," he murmured. "Come back late in the afternoon and we will be ready for you. I presume you have a trunk?"

"At Miss Maltz's."

He nodded. "I'll tell my partner, Walsh Lake. I hope you'll be comfortable. Ah, what did you say your business is?"

"I didn't. My business is getting rich."

He beamed. "Mining, perhaps?"

"My sex was mining yours before we got put out of Eden."

He smiled. "I, ah, trust you're on the proper side of town."

She jammed her wedding ring into his face, and he danced backward. "Never insult a semi-lady," she said. "I am one-half refined and one-half dangerous."

That was it. By evening she had settled herself in her new room, which still smelled of varnish. She was the mistress of a fine brass bed with goose-down pillows, a rocking chair, a blue-striped settee, an oak armoire, a small escritoire with a ladderbacked chair, a cut-glass double-chimney lamp, and a dry sink with porcelain pitcher and basin.

At dusk she heard a small commotion in the hall and a door closing toward the front of the building. She slid into the corridor and studied the closed doors until she found one with a streak of light yellowing the wooden floor under it. She knocked.

Con Daley opened, surprise on his face.

"How would you like to take a lady to dinner?" she asked.

"Ah, Sylvie. You have the advantage of me. I've never yet refused a beautiful woman."

"Have you eaten?"

"Oh, no, I've been out poking around mines—it's a business you know. . . . I have assorted appetites. Silver, money, food, spirits . . . beautiful ladies. Just now, a good bourbon poured over some lake ice would suit me."

"I'm a bourbon lady myself."

"Why, Sylvie, I'm amazed."

"Where will you take me?" she asked. "They haven't opened up downstairs. Where can you take a whiskey-sipping lady?"

"Why, let me think. I suppose I could have the Silverado Cafe send us a meal for two—unless you prefer

to go somewhere. . . . And some ice? I have the spirits."
He nodded toward a corked bottle beside the glowing lamp
on his table.

The amused lift of his brow engaged her. She nodded.
"Bring the ice. I have a proposition for you after a few
drinks have softened you up. I'm going to make you my
silent partner."

"Ah, you're going to take advantage of me. I might enjoy that. But maybe I'll take advantage of you. Who
knows what a little Crab Orchard will do to a lady." He
peered at her amiably. "Well, in that case, private dining is
the thing. Far from funneling ears. But I should warn you,
I'm already softened up. Attractive ladies do that to me. I
don't know anything about anything, except silver."

"Neither do I," she retorted. "I guess we'll just have to
fumble along over filet mignons and asparagus. And then
I'll make you a proposition."

He laughed pleasantly. "Forgive me—I'll have to run
over there and order. Make yourself at home."

"I live here now," she said. The words arrested him. She
smiled and pointed at the corridor. "Number 12."

He nodded and vanished down the broad stairs.

She waited quietly on a settee identical to the one in her
room. He hadn't made his bed. Impulsively she made it
for him. She discovered three black suits hanging in his armoire, and a row of shiny black shoes, and several cravats.
He had gone through most of his spare shirt collars. Perhaps he hadn't found a laundress yet. She spotted a black
pigskin Gladstone, and supposed it was his office. It
seemed to radiate secrets and power and she wished she
might riffle through it. She guessed she'd find a silver
flask in it filled with ardent spirits. On his dry sink was a
Nero razor strop and a silver-handled straight-edged razor.
And a box of Hilt's Best cigars.

He fascinated her. On the stagecoach coming to Cashbox his penetrating gaze seemed to pluck everything there
was to know about her, and behind those eyes lay a lively

intelligence that made sense and order out of what he observed.

Then she had discovered an amazing thing about Cornelius Daley. He was utterly unassuming, even though he was a rich and powerful man. His quiet courtesy was the hallmark of his character. She couldn't even imagine him strutting about like some vainglorious Napoleon, or insulting servants, or feeding his own vanity by reciting the failures of others.

And lately she had discerned the most important thing of all: he was a serious man. His every act had serious intent. There was no frivolity in him. She knew it was his seriousness that gave him intelligence. His serious nature had made him rich. She admired that quality in him, especially after all those years of Beau Pitt's frivolity. She had known all too many dandies and dreamers back east.

There was something formidable about Con Daley; something that drew her to him in ways she couldn't fathom. Suddenly she felt a rush of gratitude. This older man would be her comfort here; maybe more than a comfort.

She heard him coming and settled herself on the settee.

"Ah, you've tidied me up."

"It goes against principle," she retorted. "I have no domestic instincts."

"What instincts do you have?"

"I'm a hunter, I guess. Always looking for something."

"Do you ever find it?"

"No. Whenever I capture something I want, it crumbles in my hands. Rotten luck. That's why I came here. I'm looking for something that'll last."

"You'll never find it."

"I know, but a lady has to look."

He laid a block of lake ice wrapped in *The Plain Truth* on the dry sink and began chipping at it with a pick. In a moment he handed her a tumbler of ice and bourbon.

"Well, what shall we toast?"

"Us," she said.

CHAPTER 13

· · · · · · · · · · · · · · · · ·

May Goode stood in the middle of Main Street, examining the businesses the way whist players studied their cards. She knew only that this afternoon was dying and she had perhaps an hour to find succor—or face a brutal night. She scolded herself for wasting time with that woman. But anger did no good; she had been angry for three straight years, and it only kept her from making the best of things. She set those feelings aside, and faced a block of hulking buildings that radiated their indifference.

She tried the mercantile first, pushing into a cramped cavern with a grocery counter on the right, manned by a young man as pimpled as a potato; dry goods and clothes on the left; and hardware at the rear. Dirty front windows cheated the sunlight.

"I'm looking for a job. I can do anything. I can cipher, wash, sell—"

"I'm not the owner—"

"Well, I need to eat. Those windows—look how grimy they are. I'll wash them. I'll clean the counter. Mop this gritty floor. Make it sparkle. All I want is some food. Tins of peaches or candy or anything. . . ."

"I can't. Mister Baker, he's gone home. I keep the store until six. Maybe tomorrow . . ."

"I need something to eat!"

"I ain't allowed—" The man shrugged.

"Can you tell me where I can find a job?"

"How should I know? Ask the newspaper." He turned his back to her as a dismissal.

She fled into the rutted street, defeated but undeterred. She tried the Cashbox Town Lot Company next door, but it was dark and locked. She passed Ike Cobb's Tonsorial Parlor. Through its small window she could see the barber

clipping a man's hair, and others waiting. That would be
male territory. Next was a saloon, The Carbonate Miners
Saloon, it said. The grimy window revealed a few rough-
looking men with their feet on the brass rail staring at a
taxidermist's antelope as if they wanted to kill it. She spotted a glass jar of pickled eggs on the bar that brought
juices to her mouth. But it was a man's place.

She came to a busy intersection. Cashbox Street. The
name had been daubed on a board. To the right the street
bridged the little creek, and in the gulch beyond stood a
two-story stone-walled saloon. Its gilded sign heralded The
Oriental. She turned that way reluctantly, not wanting to
leave the safe side of town. But she had been a serving girl
for a while and she could do it again for a day or two—
anything for food and shelter. Almost anything. She hesitated. This had no front window. It would be dark inside.

She opened a surly door and found herself in gloom. At
the rear, lamps glowed over green baize tables. A skinny
man with a black eyepatch perched there shuffling a deck
idly. On each wall hung one of those plump nudes she'd
seen in the brothel.

Nearer, at a gaudy bar, a woman server in amazingly
short skirts watched her.

"You looking for work, sweetie?"

"Uh—what kind of work?"

"You want to hustle drinks and anything else? You get
to keep the tips—and whatever you pick up on the side.
We could use you."

"On the side?"

The serving girl laughed. "On the backside, hon." She
gestured toward a stairway that May had missed at first
glance.

"No . . . no. I—I'll try somewhere else." She backed
away, and then saw snacks arrayed for the evening
crowd—three slabs of cheese, pickled eggs, a bowl of
rolls. She hesitated.

"Could I have a roll?"

"Work or get out," said the skinny man with the eyepatch. "Damned bloodsuckers."

She fled across the plank bridge, never stopping until she had reached Main Street again.

To the west slouched the Silver Dollar Hotel and Eatery, a log affair that dared the unwary to enter. She plunged into a gloomy foyer where unnameable odors compounded from sweat, tobacco, and fried foods smacked her. The place boasted no lobby; only a tiny cage manned by a balding bleary-eyed drunk who looked like a narrow-necked bottle.

"We don't have no rooms for wimmin," he announced in a whiskey-graveled voice. "We got jist one room upstairs, sleeps forty men and five thousand bedbugs."

"I'm looking for work. I can do anything. I can cipher, keep books, clean, scrub sheets—"

"We don't have sheets."

"I can clean. I need work right now."

"We're clean as we need to be, and not a bit cleaner. I prefer honest dirt m'self. Wimmin always want to scrub something to death. Once you do that, you git spoilt."

"What about the cafe? I can cook. I can do dishes. I can serve. I can cashier."

"He don't want nobody. He's a loner that needs leaving alone."

"I'll go ask."

She plunged through a doorway into a log room with trestle tables and benches in front and a Majestic cook-stove and kitchen worktables at the rear. There were no customers. The smells, rank and intoxicating, tortured her. A graying man with delirium tremens stirred a pot on the stove, refusing to acknowledge her presence.

"I'm looking for a job," she said to his thin back. The back, as stiff as celery, ignored her and the trembling arm kept assaulting the kettle.

"Excuse me, I'm hungry; I'll do any work you want. I'll wash dishes."

The man refused to turn around. His kitchen seemed a

shambles, greasy and begrimed. The smell of rot slithered through the air.

"I'll clean everything. Just for a supper. I'll scrub every inch. Your customers'll be happier."

"Beat it," he said. "Vamoose! I don't need nobody. Use tin plates and cups, and just drop dem into a soapy bucket and hang dem up to dry." Never did he turn to face her.

She addressed the celery-back again. "Would you feed me? I'll pay you tomorrow."

"How many times I hear dat?"

"I'm going to clean your place anyway," she said desperately. "Whether you like it or not. I'll serve people and wash those tin plates. Maybe I'll get some tips." Maybe, too, she could gulp down the customers' leavings.

He didn't reply. With his free hand he lifted a green bottle and swilled its contents down. She had yet to see his face.

She set her battered reticule next to a grimy log and hunted for a washrag. Some scummy water stood in a zinc sink. She drained it and added some Gold Dust Washing Powder from a box on the floor. She approached his stove to draw hot water from its reservoir. He turned sharply away.

"I don't want no one in here," he said.

She ignored him and began scrubbing the trestle tables, scouring off layers of slime. Her stomach hurt; food smells had driven her body to a frenzy. She ignored that. Somehow she would earn a meal here.

She worked furiously, and all the while he kept her back to her as if she were the South Pole. She found no mop but put a rotted straw broom to good use after splashing soapy water on the sticky floor. Then she tackled the kitchen area of the open room, puzzled about the man's conduct.

"I'm May," she said. "I'm just doing this for a meal—if you'll give me on."

He mumbled something.

"Would you mind turning around so we can meet? I'm

just a regular person, like you're a regular person. I'd like to be welcome."

"You get out now."

She detected pain, maybe anger, in his outburst. "Well, what's on the menu? What do I offer tonight?"

"Same, same. Dey don't get no choice. Dey just get a scoop of slop. For two-bits how much more should dey get, eh?"

Even his slop looked delicious to her. She'd seen potatoes, chunks of gray meat, flour, chopped cabbage, and some salt tumble into the blackened kettle.

She began working on the tin plates and cups and spoons. This establishment had no knives and forks. She scrubbed hard, peeling away accumulated gum.

The first evening customers, a pair of bearded men in work-tattered clothing, settled themselves at one end of the far trestle table.

"No wimmen—you get out!" yelled the cook.

"I'm going to help."

He threw up his spindly arms and muttered something. Then he ladled his concoction onto the metal plates and carried them to the customers.

Now she saw it: the puckered white and red ruin, the half-face devoid of an eye. She recoiled as if bitten by a snake.

"Now you go!" he said.

"I—I think you have courage. Whoever you are. I—admire you. . . . How did it happen?" she asked timidly.

He stopped suddenly, and she saw something in his good eye that looked like acceptance. "Giant Powder. I was in dem mines once."

"Well I like you and I'll help you."

"Do what you want!" he yelled. He grabbed the green bottle and gulped its contents until he stopped to gasp.

May served herself a large helping, wolfed down the tasteless muck gratefully, and waited for the evening rush.

CHAPTER 14

· · · · · · · · · · · · · · · · ·

J. Ernest Potter-Pride downed some milk of magnesia to quiet a stomach rendered dyspeptic by his business associate, Bass Boehm. They had quarreled over tactics. Mister Boehm preferred the blunt approach, while Attorney Pride counseled discretion in the matter of the town lots.

But that was the way of Bass Boehm, he thought. The man was fashioned upon the model of a blackjack. Where a cranium should be there was only double-ought buckshot encased in thick leather.

The chalky stuff sifted into Attorney Pride's slim belly and began at once to soothe the turmoil there, putting him into a philosophic mood.

Once, long ago, he would never have let Bass Boehm into his office, much less associate with him in business. He had had scruples. For a fleeting moment he let himself think of happier times, when he could walk down a Menlo Park street and greet his neighbors. When he was an esteemed counsellor at law whose honor was unquestioned, and whose future glowed as bright as his former neighbor Mr. Edison's incandescent bulb. But that was before the disciplinary hearings. That was a closed door, and now he guzzled milk of magnesia, hobnobbed with men like Boehm and wished his life could be clean and honorable again.

Yes, Boehm was a hellish man, Pride thought. Boehm had wanted to evict every businessman on Main Street from his building, erected on land he thought he possessed but didn't. The lots were owned by Bass Boehm and Attorney Pride in equal numbers.

Pride was the attorney of record for the Cashbox Town Lot Company, which he had seen as a rare opportunity to fatten his purse. It had all been so simple: a small fee to the surveyor had rendered the land patent application invalid, and in due course the federal land office had returned it for amendment, mooting every deed the company had issued, unbeknownst to its perfectly honorable owners in Butte.

After that it had been a mere matter of seeming to inform the deedholders that the company would issue a new and valid deed upon application. He had posted proper notices in dark corners, and had persuaded Willard Croker to publish the notice in the legal columns of *The Plain Truth*—or at least seven copies of two editions, six of which went into Pride's files. After running seven, Croker had inserted a subscription advertisement in the hole where the notice had been. That was enough to prove to any slack judge that the remedy had been widely trumpeted, and if the deedholders were too negligent to do anything about it, that was their loss. Willard Croker's payment had been six lots. He could have demanded twenty and gotten it.

Attorney Pride and Bass Boehm, between them, owned most of Cashbox. But Attorney Pride knew prudence, while Boehm knew only blunt instruments. It would not do to leave town wearing unsightly tar and feathers, especially when he prided himself on his sartorial elegance.

The jangle of the outer door announced the presence of a client, and J. Ernest Potter-Pride smoothed silvery hair which gathered into a bun at the nape of his neck. It haloed his clean-jawed, youthfully masculine face. He adjusted his silk cravat while rounding his polished desk. Then he admitted to his inner sanctum the well-known and much-admired Miss Regina Maltz.

"Ah, my dear Miss Maltz, how delightful to see you," he said, hiding his distaste of the woman with the speckled plum pudding complexion and a form like a pie safe.

"I have your letter," she said without preamble. "I think we can come to an agreement. I'll buy my lot at its current market value from Mister Boehm—if he really is its owner. I wasn't informed. Not a word. He's a lot-jumper. I've seen it in three camps. I paid twenty-five, and now it's worth a hundred. I haven't that much, but I'll come up with it and that'll settle it. I haven't an attorney, and couldn't afford one. Now, tomorrow I'll come for the deed, and—"

"Ah, ah, Miss Maltz. Mister Boehm is quite adamant about possessing that lot. He was here this very hour, angry about your trespassing. He won't sell that lot under any circumstances. He intends to house his business colleagues there."

"He wants the boardinghouse. I suppose he'll steal it. I have a mortgage on it from the White Sulphur—"

"It's a pity, Miss Maltz. Yes, I feel for you. But after all, the notices were posted on two sides of town and published in two successive editions, and you neglectfully—"

"Oh, rubbish. You're lot-jumpers, the bunch of you."

"Ah, my dear, your language is a bit harsh. You're distressed—"

"Oh, rubbish."

Attorney Pride sighed dolefully. "It's his choice. You'll be out in a week; you, your tenants, and your chattels, or he'll keep whatever he finds there."

"He'll have to carry me out. He'll have to carry poor Kermit Reilly out. He's too ill to be moved. I won't budge. I think the people of Cashbox'll take my part."

"Now, now, you're being irrational. You call a drayage company and have them load you up. You tell your tenants—"

"I'll tell them to stay put, that it's lot-jumpers we're dealing with. I've had enough. Possession is nine-tenths of the law. You can tell that to *Mister* Boehm. Tell him I won't move; there'll be blood on the floors. Let him wave his revolvers. If he wishes to shoot me, let him shoot. Tell him he's a crook and I'm fed up with mining camp crooks—including you."

Attorney Pride cleared his throat in the hanging silence.

"I'm sure you didn't mean to impugn my integrity, Miss Maltz."

"What integrity?"

"Tut tut, Miss Maltz."

"You tell the lot-jumpers I'm not moving, no matter how much they threaten. They'll have to bury me first."

"Now, Miss Maltz, it's a matter for the courts. If you won't move, a writ from the court and some action by the deputy will do it for us."

"No it won't. I won't budge. If you try, you'll be dealing with a few hundred miners and teamsters."

That was a real possibility, he thought. The angel of Cashbox would call her markers. "Ah, the angel of the mining camps! Now, you and I know it isn't altruism that inspires you—is it?"

"I don't know that word."

"Selfless concern for others."

A wounded look shot through her as swiftly as lightning. "Do you mean, do I care about the ones I help? The broken and hurt and down-and-out? Yes. Do you mean that I get my reward? Why yes, it's my reward that the humble men of the camps cherish me. If that's a black beetle crawling in my soul, then I'll agree. I didn't know that I should have no reward, even if it's only the kind given to a . . . sister or a stranger. I know what hurt is; I don't think you do. That's the difference between us: You dish out hurts. I heal them."

She turned to go. "I'll shoot the man that tries to put me out of my house. I suppose that doesn't fit your definition of a mining camp angel."

Astonished, he watched her leave, and glimpsed her as she walked toward Baker's Mercantile.

The encounter depressed him. She had pierced through his veneer and exposed him for what he was, as bluntly as that New Jersey judge years before. He sighed, wondering how he had slid into this desolate life. He had never been desperate, had never lacked means. It had arisen out of a perverse pleasure in skinning people. Why, he'd practi-

cally made a career of skinning other boys out of their
marbles, especially the big aggies they cherished. After
that it became habit. He had no cure for it. Occasionally
someone with a sharp eye—he would credit Miss Maltz
with the sharpest eye of all—could see right through him.

But it was no use thinking about what he might have
been.

He spent the next minutes applying his fertile mind to
the situation. Boehm should back off. He was asking for it,
going after a legendary saint of the mining camps. But Attorney Potter knew he could no more stop Boehm than he
could stop a tusked boar. That meant he would have to resort to other means—such as a little publicity.

He plucked his black derby from the antler coatrack and
settled it over his silvery hair, making sure that his locks
weren't hidden from admiring view. The next edition of
The Plain Truth would appear tomorrow, and there might
still be time to plant a little front-page oompah-pah.
Willard would go along; he always went along, even when
he grumped about it. Big, toothy, affable Willard Croker
would run the story just as it was dictated to him. Who
knows? Maybe Attorney Potter-Pride would emerge as the
new angel of Cashbox.

CHAPTER 15

* * * * * * * * * * * * * * * *

Hugh Trego had organized the walkout at the Carbonate
Miners Saloon the night before: not a man would go
into the Giltedge hole until it was safe. A few had resisted
him, saying they couldn't afford to lose pay. But the rest
had overruled: they couldn't afford to lose their lives or
face terrible injuries, like poor Kermit Reilly.

Now, a half hour before shift, he wondered if the discipline would hold, or whether he'd see hard-pressed men
with wives and children and debts step into the cage and

let themselves be lowered into that hole once again. He couldn't stop them, not without a union and its discipline. And he couldn't turn against them either, not his brothers in daily toil and danger.

Trego stalked toward the superintendent's building to have it out with Webb. Maybe the bleddy supervisor would fire the lot of them. That would be better than being trapped in the hole, dying by slow degrees as the air gave out. He'd as soon pull up and leave Cashbox as not.

He stalked past Baghote straight into Webb's spare office. At least the bleddy super didn't squander company money on flocked wallpaper, carpets, shiny desks, stuffed chairs, and the rest. Webb's office was as functional as a monk's cell.

"Trego!" exclaimed Webb. "I was just going out to find you."

"Well, I've found you, and I'm here to tell you that not a bleddy man'll go into the hole until we get more timber in it. It's our lives you're toyin' with."

Webb nodded. "Not a man, eh? I'd expected it after Reilly was hurt. How's the young man doing?"

"That's a hand-washing question, Webb."

Webb stared, hard as granite. "I'll ask it again. How is Reilly? I want to know."

"He's poorly. We've got him at Miss Maltz's boardinghouse. She'll do her best. He's hurtin' worse than any mortal should ever hurt. If we had a doctor and an infirmary or even a bleddy nurse—"

"I know."

Odd how that phrase dignified Webb. Trego hated Webb for it. He itched for Webb to be something he wasn't: an uncaring boss. Instead, Trego had confronted a man who was making the best of bad situations; a man who respected his employees, even though Hugh Trego had a bad time admitting it.

"Anyway," Trego muttered, "not a man goes down the hole. If you plan to fire us, be about it." His truculent tone hung in the air.

"I was going to tell you that we won't be mining today," Webb said, startling Trego. "I've talked to the timber foreman. We've enough wood for about thirty sets. I was going to use it to wall the new shaft. But I'm closing that whole operation down for now. I'm putting half of you in the timber shop cutting sets and wedges; the rest of you—if you will—in the crosscut doing some timbering . . . wherever you and the shift foreman see fit."

"Thirty sets won't do it, Webb."

"They'll cover the worst places in the crosscut. You can put them on two-and-a-half-foot centers where the rock's rotten."

"It's not enough."

"It's all the wood on the premises."

"Order more."

"I've spent our first three months of production income even before seeing a dime of it. The other mines are bidding up the price of the logs; it's wood or wages. And that's just the tip of my troubles."

"Don't give me that; ye're backed by bleddy rich capitalists with pockets that haven't got a bottom. Don't tell me ye can't buy wood."

"The Hammons are coming in a few days. I've summoned them. Now, will you put up the sets or not?"

Trego pondered it. Thirty sets would cover the worst spots but it wouldn't make the Giltedge safe. The sets, consisting of two upright posts and a notched beam, were normally spaced on five-foot centers in good rock. Each set was erected and pinned into place with wooden wedges as the tunneling progressed, and soon the terrible pressures and the plastic nature of the rock pinioned them tightly into place. But timber was forever rotting in the wet mines, and rotted posts and beams had to be replaced regularly. Trego applied a simple calculus to such questions: would he work in the hole with the new sets in place? He would—for a limited time.

"I'll talk them into it—for now. But it's not safe. You

don't care enough about the lives and limbs and eyes and bodies of the ones that muck your bleddy ore."

"You're kinder to me than Con Daley was yesterday, Trego. He said I was courting murder."

"Well, the bloated capitalist is right."

"Sit down, Trego. It's time to talk about the Giltedge. I'll be telling you things in confidence."

"Nothing's in confidence. You're not buying me, Webb. Every word that gets spoken here is a word I'll share with my men."

"All right. Those are fair terms."

Trego sat in the hard-bottomed chair opposite Webb, feeling ready to storm away if Webb tried to separate him from his brothers who mucked rock under the earth.

"It's not just the mine; the mill's losing money. We have to run a hundred tons of ore through it a day to make it profitable. With only two stopes being worked in the Giltedge, we're not even close. The custom milling we do for other mines helps. But we need to open two more stopes fast. That's why I've been pushing the new shaft down.

"We need a railroad. It's a long haul to the smelter. The concentrate goes out of here by ox-team, and that costs so much that not even this rich mine can earn a profit. If we had a smelter we could ship silver and save the lead until later, when we get a railroad. You know that."

"So shut her down, Webb."

"That's why I've asked the Hammons to come. We need more capital fast, or we'll have to. And something else, Trego: if they don't give me cash to buy timber, I'm resigning. I've got my resignation letter written—that's it right there—and I'll hand it to the Hammons if I must. No matter what you think, I care about your safety. That accident in the development phase—it was more than I could bear. You can believe me or not."

Trego believed him, and hated himself for it.

"What about Daley's offer?"

"I can't discuss that with you."

"What about the Hammons—will they come up with it?"

"I shouldn't talk about that either, but I will. They're overextended. And they don't know mining. They know they're sitting on a huge lode of the best silver ore in the world, and they want it all. They're obsessed—ah, they're unduly eager to keep speculators like Daley out. I don't think they appreciate the conditions here but I plan to tell them. I intend to take them into the mine—if they'll go. I'm not going to mince words about safety. And their own reluctance will serve as the lesson."

"They want us in coffins, is what."

"You don't believe that."

That was Webb. He didn't give an inch. Hugh Trego could hardly bear to admit what was whispering within him: Webb was an honorable and good man. "I'm not through with you, Webb. The air's bad in the hole, and it's burning out our lungs. We want air or we won't go down."

Webb didn't flinch. "I'd planned to run some winzes when we got the new shaft down, to give you some circulation. I've nothing to offer you now. In fact, the farther you go with the drifts, the worse it'll get. I don't have piping to pump it in."

"It's up to the Hammons, then, isn't it."

"You've got to remember, Trego, they're pinched. They can't get a loan until we have some notion of our reserves. We don't even know the size of our ore body."

Trego nodded, wanting more to complain about. But he felt the old helplessness, the sense of not being in control that afflicted the humble of the world. "I'd best tell the boys we'll be timbering today," he muttered. "Maybe they'll go down the hole to muck rock tomorrow, maybe they won't."

"Thanks for stopping by, Mister Trego."

Hugh plunged into the quiet predawn gray, and found his lads milling about the headframe. The shift foreman had already told them what was in store but they were waiting for Hugh.

"I've talked to himself. I told him we'd put up the sets—and see. He's got enough wood in the timber shop for maybe thirty sets and some lagging on top of them. It's a little, for the worst spots. After the new wood's in, we'll stand down there and see how she feels. Then we'll decide about this bleddy hole. I've things to tell you after the shift, things himself is saying. But that'll wait."

They trusted him. The doubts in their eyes vanished, and they shuffled off to the timber shop to begin. But misgivings clawed at the gut of Hugh Trego.

CHAPTER 16

• • • • • • • • • • • • • • • •

J. Ernest Potter-Pride knew all his skills would be put to the test. Across from him sat Bass Boehm, who was as unpredictable as nitroglycerine. Jar him once and nothing would happen. Jar him again and you'd be a crater.

His client had recently read the latest edition of *The Plain Truth*, or affected to, since his rendering abruptly stopped whenever his forefinger encountered an unknown word.

"What is this? What is this?" Boehm growled.

"It's an article I planted in the paper to keep you out of trouble."

"Whatcha talking about? Pride, I'm gonna wring your neck."

"Well a neck's what we're talking about—only it's yours. I think you overreached, putting the bite on Regina Maltz."

"What's she got to do wid it? I'm moving in and that's the end of the tale."

"She happens to be the Florence Nightingale of Cashbox."

"The what?"

"Never mind. The miners and teamsters love her. Putting her out was not delicate."

"I'll boot out anyone that gets in my way, including you, Ernie the Attorney."

Pride sighed. "It's Ernest, as I've told you before. That form of address is repugnant to me." It had been offensive ever since the yellow newspapers of New Jersey called him that during the proceedings. "My purpose, Bass, was to keep your thick neck out of a hemp noose that might interfere with your breathing. Which is what you'll face if three hundred angry miners decide you need a lynching."

"They don't scare me. Point a scattergun at them and they fly like quail."

Attorney Pride cleared his throat. "I'm going to read the column, and you're going to tell me what you object to. I don't think you understand it."

J. Ernest Potter-Pride considered Croker's front-page article in *The Plain Truth* adequate, but no more than that. The man suffered genetic limitations. Even so, since the paper's publication the day before, no less than a dozen good citizens of Cashbox had hastened to shake his hand and congratulate him on his civic virtue. It had filled him with rosy cheer. Odd, how the acclaim had diverted him from his usual business, which was to get rich.

The article had appeared under the headline, "Cashbox Lawyer Donates Town Lot," and was placed at the top of the news column of page one next to the Baker's Mercantile ad.

"On Friday instant," Attorney Pride read, "Cashbox attorney J. Ernest Potter-Pride conveyed a town lot deed to Miss Regina Maltz, owner of the boardinghouse on McDonald Street. The deed, for Lot 36, was one of several owned by the attorney, and has a market value of approximately one hundred dollars.

"Attorney Pride's charity was occasioned by the sad dilemma of Miss Maltz, who is to be evicted from her present premises on Saturday by the owner of the lot upon which her building stands, Mister Bass Boehm.

"Unfortunately Miss Maltz neglected to apply for a new deed from the town lot company when it was brought to public attention that certain deeds were invalid because of clerical errors. In January Mister Boehm bought the lot.

" 'I represent Mister Boehm,' the attorney said, 'and it became my sad duty to inform her of her eviction. She stands to lose a great deal, having erected the boarding-house on a lot she didn't own. Of course I sympathize, but she was negligent about obtaining valid title. I've endeavored to persuade my client to delay the eviction until Miss Maltz can relocate, but I am informed that Mister Boehm has urgent need of the lot for business purposes.'

" 'Miss Maltz visited me, understandably distressed. I can only do what is necessary for my client, but it occurred to me that this worthy woman, known as the Angel of the Mining Camps, ought to receive the benefactions of the Community she has helped so much and so often.'

" 'Just to start matters in the right direction, I have donated Lot 36, which had been in my possession. I trust the rest of Cashbox will follow suit and see Miss Maltz and her boarders properly moved into a New Building. It is the least we lesser citizens can do for a Grand Lady who even now nurses a young man injured in the mines.'

" 'I invite others to join me in this charitable endeavor,' he concluded.

"*The Plain Truth* commends Attorney Pride for his civic generosity in this Age of Greed. We are blessed in this rising young Community with men of outstanding Moral Courage, willing to surrender their own hard-won Wealth for the comfort of others less fortunate."

Pride set down the paper. Boehm glowered.

"That," said Pride, "is known as trumping trouble. I'm charging your account for the lot and fees, one hundred fifty in all. Consider it a minor cost of doing business."

"I ain't paying."

"Of course you will. Now I want you to give her a one-month extension. I think Cashbox'll build her another house. Give her a month and you'll be deemed an upstanding citizen."

Boehm laughed uproariously. If there had been other knees to slap, he would have slapped them. But then he reverted to his usual explosive self. "No. Out she goes. And I move in. That's a five-thousand-dollar joint I copped."

"It won't look good."

"Won't look good." He sparkled like a lit fuse again. "That's rich."

"Uh, Bass, I don't think you quite understand the nature of your faux pas. Miss Maltz is a saint. Saints have a little fence around them. You're treading on majestic toes."

Boehm exploded into a guffaw.

"Bass," Pride chided, "she has no intention of being pushed out. She's going to resist. Her fanny'll be glued to the floor. This is a tricky business. Get that through your skull."

"So? I toss her out Saturday."

"Sunday. She has until midnight Saturday to vacate."

"No, Saturday. Why wait?"

"Bass, I can't help you when you violate the terms of your own eviction notice."

Boehm shrugged. "I'll say Boo! She'll scream her way clear to Main Street. I get the furniture, too."

"She's nursing a badly injured miner, Boehm. It won't look good if your boys haul him out on a litter and leave him in the street. He might die."

Boehm didn't reply. The plight of Kermit Reilly obviously didn't interest him.

"I don't think you're listening."

Boehm eyed Attorney Pride innocently. "There's always ways," he said. "It's gonna be a circus."

"I've kept you and your plug-uglies out of trouble so far, Bass. But that won't help you after Saturday."

Boehm erupted from his chair like Mount Etna, startling Attorney Pride, but Boehm was only making his way to the door.

"Sunday," shouted Pride.

"Saturday," Boehm retorted.

From his window, Potter-Pride watched Boehm sputter down the street like a lit fuse.

The attorney sagged into his swivel chair. He wondered how he had slid into this sort of life. The ten-minute interview had drained him. Noon had come and gone, and he thought to remedy the emptiness of his belly, and calm his nerves with a quickie or two at The Palace. Suddenly he'd become the hero of Cashbox. It lit rosy lights in him. They thought he was a noble fellow. Maybe he could run for office. They'd all support him.

Happily, he plunged into the April sun, pausing only to settle his brushed black homburg on his wavy hair. At lunch he'd eat more than food; he'd devour the compliments of all the splendid merchants in town, and hint that maybe he'd do even more for the unfortunate Regina Maltz.

CHAPTER 17
. . . .

When Con Daley finally got wind of Ambrose Gill, it was too late. That very evening, said his informant, there'd be a wake for Gill at the Shamrock Saloon, on Cashbox Street, where a Celtic soul could mop some ale.

The informant, Peter O'Rourke, looked as if he wanted a tip, so Daley obliged him with four-bits. A *wake*. Con Daley felt as if his long and intimate romance with Lady Luck had come to an end. Fate had been cuckolded long enough. The bad news threw him into a funk.

Daley had spent days in his livery buggy wandering patiently from mine to mine asking about Gill. Maybe the man had wandered off, but the more Daley probed, the less likely it seemed. Plenty of people knew him and said he was around. Gill, it turned out, was a canny prospector who could track down sulphuret or carbonate ores like a

ferret. He vanished for long periods with his mule and
prospecting gear, only to return now and then for a blow-
out in Cashbox.

Daley decided to go to the wake. He nourished the forlorn hope that he might still purchase Gill's claim, perhaps
from a relative or partner. It didn't look good, though. His
plan to pry open the Giltedge had probably died with Ambrose Gill. If the forthcoming meeting with the Hammons
didn't yield any fruit, Con Daley's business in Cashbox
would come to an end.

At four that afternoon, as the mine whistles blew, Con
Daley knotted his cravat before his mirror in the Palace
Hotel and marched resolutely toward the Shamrock Saloon. He knew his presence would dampen the wake but
he couldn't help it. All those squinty Irish miners and
teamsters would study the financier, turn quietly to their
mugs, slide into a sulky silence, and wait for him to depart.

Con Daley had never been to a wake, but he feared it
was in his blood to sing songs or share some maudlin hi-
larity beside the coffin of the late departed. He supposed
that all Irishmen were burdened with such unruly emotions. His patrician New York parents had considered them
vulgar. He'd been schooled at Phillips Academy with Protestant boys, and had thus been veneered with the codfishy
feelings of the Boston upper crust as well as their muted
tastes. He hardly knew whether he was Irish anymore, or
what he really was. It often bewildered him, being an
Irishman with the manners of a Congregational deacon. But
that was only the exterior. Down inside, when it came to
having a good time, he knew he was no bloody heretic.

He entered hesitantly, and found the saloon much the
way he had imagined it, noisy as a horse track and packed
with gents in their only suits, all of them getting a head-
start on grief. By midnight they'd all be weepy and sentimental. To the rear, on a table, rested a handsome coffin of
polished oak, its lid open. A pair of lamps above it illu-
mined the burden within, while banks of columbine and

cinquefoil surrounded the departed, along with a black funeral wreath.

It seemed odd to see all those weathered faces and sunburnt hands embalmed in stiff white shirts and suits that had probably been folded into cedar chests since the last wedding or christening or funeral. But there they all were, two score Irishmen, knotted together in ritual circles with tonsil varnish in hand. He spotted not a tear or mournful countenance among them, and it seemed a bit callous. Had none of them the nerve to pay their respects to Ambrose Gill? They noted him, as all men in the camps noted Con Daley, but his presence didn't slow the revelry a bit, or even give pause to this Celtic ritual.

He fished in his pocket for a frogskin and bellied up to the bar to equip himself for his ordeal. "What'll it be, captain?" asked the keep. "Order what ye will; it's all on our sainted Gill."

"He arranged it; he willed it?"

"Ah, God, what a blessed man he was, sir. There's no ill to speak of Ambrose Gill, for the saints have preserved his generous spirit. He's throwin' a party fit for a lord."

The mixologist, wearing a chalk-striped suit beneath his white apron, eyed him from behind a scarred rosewood bar with the usual towels hanging from it to permit a man to wipe foam from his mustache. "You'll be Cornelius Daley. Our old friend Ambrose, he'd be honored by your presence. I'm called Sourmash Charlie behind me back," he added. "Also Tomato Nose. Facewise I'm Brendan Toole. Now, I'll start you on some Jameson Irish upon January ice, a fittin' gift from old Ambrose. We also have Valley Tan, Medora Busthead, and Old Gideon."

Daley sipped the cold Irish whiskey, found it bracing, and nerved himself to drift to the rear and see the man whose death had thwarted his designs. He edged through mourners entirely too cheerful for his taste, past brass cuspidors and calcimined plank walls decorated with lithographs of bay and black thoroughbred horses with arched tails and roached manes.

The diamond-shaped oak coffin smelled of cash; the departed was not leaving the world in a pine box. That vaguely disturbed him too. Bargains might be gotten from the desperate, but rarely from the affluent. Somehow, Ambrose Gill had minted money.

Daley fortified himself with a generous slug of Irish whiskey, felt it scour his tonsils, and edged up for a gander at the man who held the fulcrum of fate in his dead hand. For one so dead, Gill seemed uncommonly rosy of cheek.

An eye opened, black and insidious, and closed again. Con Daley spilled some of his whiskey.

"It's you," said the corpse. "Heard you was looking for me."

"You're dead right," said Daley, rising to the occasion.

"Well here I am. Enjoying my wake?"

"I hope to before the evening entirely unravels."

"I thought you might come. You're the honored guest." The deceased opened both eyes long enough to survey his visitor, and then closed them. "We can talk a bit," he said. "But not for long. It'd ruin it. What'd you want to see me about, old boy?"

"It can wait," Daley said. "Are you ill—expecting to depart from us soon?"

"Oh, no, lad. Not a bit, unless me luck turns wicked. I thought to meself, Ambrose, you nary have a wife or child, and if my brothers and sisters, or me dear mother, still live in Waterford, I don't know it. A man that's got only a few friends ought to enjoy his own wake. It's wicked that a wake is wasted on the dead, I says. I'd like to hear what all the lads have to say to me; whither they weep and whither they be as kind to an ould fart that lies croaked and cold, as they was when they was speaking to his face. So I decided to find out. So far, they've been too kind, and I don't believe the lot of them. All wicked blarney if you ask me. But let the ale loosen their tongues a bit, and then we'll see. The wicked bastids is so kind I hate the whole devil-hearted lot of 'em. Now I've got to shut my mouth and lie quiet."

"When are you going to return to life? I'd like to do a little business."

"Oh, not for a while. I thought later on I'd git up and join me friends—if these damned devils're still friends—and cap the night with a few mugs. Ah, God, Daley, never hold your own wake—it's the devil's own temptation. Miserable curs. Biggest mistake of me worthless life. Look at 'em!"

"This isn't a good time. Where can I find you tomorrow?"

"Nursing a wicked hurt to me soul and carcass. Who says we can't do business now? State it and I'll say yes or go to the devil."

"I want to buy your claim—the one between the Giltedge and the Ophir. I'd give you a good price."

"Now what do ye want to buy that worthless thing for? Eh?" The deceased glared at Daley from two malevolent eyes.

"Any claim lying between two good mines is worth buying."

"Ha! It's all slope, good for nothing. No, I won't sell a foot."

Con Daley felt off-center, dealing with a man lying in a coffin. "I'll met you tomorrow, Gill."

"Naw ye won't. Tomorrow I'll load Mother Dear with some grub and go out again. I got me a sulphuret ledge—not worth patenting because it's only a few feet deep, but it buys a man a wake when he needs one. I want to close me eyes agin and listen to all these wicked buggers sham their grief."

"I'd give you fifty dollars for it."

"No."

"I'll give you a hundred."

"No. It's not for sale."

"I'd—consider your price."

"Ah, God, a dead man in a coffin can't be selling his

worldly goods, mind you now. He'd never get to heaven. He'd be booted out like a pore wicked thing. I'd niver get to see me pa. Maybe I'll give 'er away some time."

"Give it away? Give it? How about right now?"

"Ye wicked mick, shame on you, doin' business with a man fresh in his coffin."

"How about after the wake?"

"Not now," Gill roared. "Maybe when I feel like it." The deceased sat up in his oak box. "Yer spoilin' me wake," he grumbled.

"Where can I meet you tomorrow, man?"

"Maybe I will and maybe I won't. I won't make up me mind now. You go enjoy my party, and I'll be listenin' and I'll make up my mind tomorrow. Shame on ye for doin' business with a man newly laid in his coffin."

With that, Ambrose Gill resumed his moribund state. The party roared. Con Daley joined in, hailing every old friend in the saloon, hoisting more tongue oil to his lips than he'd ever swallowed at one time. Tonight he felt the blackness. That's what he called the gloom that lurked just beyond his mind and pounced on him whenever he reached one of his goals.

CHAPTER 18

• • • • • • • • • • • • • • • • •

The pine floor near the stove bit at May Goode all night, but she didn't mind. It was paradise compared to the night outside. Not that the man approved. He had tried to push her out when he closed, but she begged him to let her stay, and finally ignored his angry muttering. She toiled all that evening. When she wasn't serving customers she continued to scour the grubby eatery. In the darkness, after he stormed out, she used the last of the hot water in the stove reservoir to wash herself and her hair, a luxury so grand that she sang lullabies in the dark.

She awakened to a clamor in the lobby and wondered at it. The door from the hotel burst open and two men entered, dimly visible in the predawn gray. Hastily she tugged her skirts down about her ankles, and sat up.

"Der she is. Get her out of here."

She recognized the voice of the angry owner.

"Get a light," said the other.

A match flared, blinding her. She stood, shaking dirt from her skirts as an oil lamp threw yellow light.

The other man wore a star.

She panicked. They'd come for her. They'd take her back to prison. She waited bleakly while the burly man in a mackinaw looked her over.

"You're trespassing, ma'am," he said. "You won't leave even though you've been asked repeatedly. Is that right?"

She nodded.

"I toll her git out, I toll her she's no right to be here. I toll her I don't want her around, but she just wouldn't git."

"Clement, you just relax, now. I'll take care of it. What's your name, ma'am?"

"May . . . Goode."

"Well, you're trespassing. Where're you from?"

Her pulse lifted. "Wisconsin." She hated the lie but she would never say Minnesota.

"Why, that's where I'm from, ma'am."

She dreaded the next question, the *where*, but he didn't ask it. "How come you to Cashbox? You have a husband?"

She shook her head miserably. "I was—" she just couldn't say anything. Finally she held up her hand so he might see Frank's miserably thin band on her ring finger.

"Troubles. You're obviously running. Well, I've got to get you outta here. Clement, he's about ready to swing his butcher knife at you."

"Could I have breakfast first?" she cried. "I worked—I worked all last night. Look! Look at what I've done."

"Get her outta here," said Clement.

"Looks purty nice in here, Clement. The lady's a scrubbin' dervish," said the lawman.

"I didn't hire her. Get her out."

The lawman shrugged uneasily. "Better come along," he said. "He's not going to feed you no matter what you done for him." He gestured, and she followed docilely.

They stepped into cold mountain air laced with the perfume of woodsmoke. Cashbox lay still and sleepy.

"I don't suppose you've a cent," he said.

"I ran out of money. I'm looking for a job."

"Well, ah . . . a proper job?"

"Anything! Washing. Ironing. Sewing. Cooking. Cleaning. I can cipher. I can read. I can write the Spencerian hand."

"How'd you get into this little fix?"

"I—" He had caught her off guard again. "I have domestic problems. I want to start over. That's what people come out here for—to start over."

Something relaxed in him and he smiled. "I'm Slug Svensrud, constable here. I can't help you much but I've got a hot stove and hot coffee on in my jail."

"No! No!" she cried. "I don't—"

He seemed puzzled. "You're plumb safe there, ma'am. Wait for the stores to open."

She peered at him doubtfully, but she saw nothing in him that menaced her. "All right," she said. "Thank you."

She followed him meekly to a log building on Main guarding the gulch like a prison door, and then into a rude office with plank benches. He busied himself at the potbellied stove.

"Here. It's only a week old," he said, handing her a mug.

She took it gratefully. The constable smiled.

"Here's to luck," he said, eyeing her in a way that invited her to talk about herself.

"Do you know where I could find work? And a place to sleep?"

"A job? Most anywhere. Not many women in camp.

Try *The Plain Truth*. Croker's always grouching about setting type. He's wanted a printer's devil for months."

"But those are boys."

Svensrud smiled, revealing even white teeth. "It don't matter out here. Try the lawyer, Potter-Pride. I don't know if he needs someone or not, snaky devil that he is. Try any boardinghouse—like Miss Maltz. She does a heap of cooking."

"I tried Baker's Mercantile yesterday."

"Nah, they wouldn't need you. You want to go into business? There's hardly a laundress in town. Not even a Chinee."

"I—don't have anything. . . ."

"The barber—Ike Cobb—he might let you wash clothes in the back—between baths."

"He rents baths?"

"Yeah. He's almost the only place a man can get a soak."

She eyed the constable dubiously, and he grinned. "Not for you, eh? But the Palace Hotel, on Cashbox, it's opening soon. Lots of jobs for a woman, I bet."

"I can't wait that long."

"Yeah, I forgot. You runnin' from something? A man?"

His intense gaze frightened her. He peered at her from penetrating blue eyes that never seemed to blink. "I'm divorced," she mumbled, shrinking from his attention. "How'd you get your name—I mean, Slug."

"I was a mean kid. Regular bully. I beat up dogs and stabbed frogs and pulled girls' ponytails. They called me Slug and it stuck."

"Uh, are you still?"

He chuckled. "I get paid to be mean."

"You're a sham," she said, and didn't know why she said it.

An hour later she knew a lot more about him than he knew about her. When his wall clock chimed eight, she felt relieved. Now she could start looking.

"Thank you for the coffee. It wasn't as bad—"

"It was worse." He seemed amused "Look, you're in a tight corner. If you can't find anything, I mean a place tonight, try here." He nodded toward a pen that filled the rear of the little building, divided from the office by log partition and a strap iron door. "I'm not supposed to, but if I don't have some drunk in there—"

"No!" she cried. "No!"

He seemed puzzled. "You'll be safe," he said gently. "Door'll be open; you can put wood in the stove. Benches in there're pretty hard, but no harder than a restaurant floor."

"No!"

"I don't live here," he added. "I got a cabin."

"No, I'll find something, thank you."

She fled, feeling his curious gaze upon her back until she hurried around a corner. Never, never would she sleep in the jail. She paused to gaze at the mountains, glowing incandescently in the early sun. Their vaulting majesty reassured her. She had come to a place with no walls. That's what this wild West meant to her.

The law office wasn't open. She rattled the door and then walked toward the newspaper, situated in a low log building off Cashbox Street.

She turned into the building and found a big beefeater of a man in an ink-blackened apron breaking up type, deftly tossing each metal letter into little bins. It awed her that every letter of every word had to be assembled by hand for each edition, and then returned to its little home.

"You want an ad or a subscription?" the man asked, never pausing.

"I'm looking for work."

He paused, examining her carefully, his cheerful gaze raking her face and form. "I don't have any," he said.

"The constable thought you would. I can cipher and read proof and keep accounts and—"

"Proof that page," he said, pointing to a sheet lying on a counter. "Do you know proof marks?"

"No."

"Well, circle the typos—the errors. What's your name, little lady?"

"May Goode."

"Well, we'll see."

She found a stubby pencil and set to work, discovering that the page was covered with sticky ink that smeared at the slightest excuse. The page had already been proofed. At least he had made some odd marks on several errors. She knew he was watching her back and there was something in his alert smile that seemed almost indecent, but she didn't mind. Maybe she could earn a little here. She began reading, and found it hard to concentrate on the spelling and not get lost in his stories. He wrote vividly, she thought; all about booming Cashbox and its bright future, and how some Irishman, a big financier, had come to town to invest.

Maybe he wasn't such a good proofer after all. She found a dozen errors he had missed. When she had finished, she turned to him with a shy, tentative smile. He stopped breaking down type and examined her work.

"You're good, but I can't pay you. I don't have the advertising. Maybe you could sell papers on the streets on Tuesday nights and sell ads in between—on commission."

"I have to have a job right now. I guess I'll—"

"No, hold up. You want to be a devil? Learn printing and everything? Set the type, write stories, run the press, sell ads, shake the change from the pockets of nasty subscribers that think their views are better'n yours?"

She nodded. "If you can give me something to get by on," she added anxiously.

"That's my quarters back there. You can stay there."

"Will Mrs. Croker approve?"

He laughed in a very worldly way. "You want a job, you can have bed and board," he said.

"I want a dollar a day and I'll find my own keep."

"You drive a hard bargain."

"And I want some now, too. So I can eat."

"Six bits. And you can stay here."

"I won't stay here but the rest is all right."

He shrugged. "There's a printer's apron. Put it on unless you want that dress to turn black. It'll get mussed up anyway. Now, you can start breaking down this page. Every letter into its box. The font is Caslon. And watch out for the italic."

"I need a dollar first, and I'll be back in twenty minutes."

"I'm a sucker for a pretty woman," he said, and gave her some two-bit shinplasters.

They looked like hundred-dollar bills to her. She held back her tears until she was out the door, and running to an eatery.

CHAPTER 19

· · · · · · · · · · · · · · · · ·

The mine felt better to Hugh Trego as he and his friends walked down the crosscut and into the right-hand drift where they'd be working. The new sets had done it. A man could trudge along the tunnels without dreading that the world would fall on his head. They even joked now, instead of falling into a grim silence as they made their way into the blackness.

They pushed an ore car along the rails, empty except for their steels, eight-pound hammers, picks, round-nosed shovels and lunchboxes. Their glassed candle lanterns lit the way. Each of them had a lantern, a wrought-iron candleholder, and three candles, enough to burn a half hour longer than their ten-hour shift.

The acrid smell of exploded dynamite lingered in the dead air, the residue of the previous shift's final act, which was to fire the round it had loaded into native rock. If they had done their job well, the head would be advanced three feet, and there would be about thirty-two tons of blackish galena ore to muck out. The ore would be lying on a turn-

ing sheet, a plate of boiler steel pushed against the face
that made it easier to shovel ore and turn ore cars around.

They reached the head and paused silently, each studying the rocky face, looking for a hangfire, a smouldering
watersoaked fuse that hadn't detonated the fulminate of
mercury cap that would blow the charge. They looked also
for a charge that hadn't blown. Both could be murderous.
It was the powder man's responsibility to count the blasts
at the end of the shift from the safety of the shaft vestibule, and if he didn't hear all seven or feel their puffs, to
leave word of trouble for the next shift. That would be
George Polweal, and he hadn't left word.

"Looks all right, my beautays," Trego said. He'd been
in good spirits ever since the new timbering had gone in;
almost as if he could claim this cold, wet hole as a snug
home.

"Still pure ore," said Sam Fenno. "I've never seen the
like. A seam like this and no slack. Will she ever end?"

"She's a handsome lode, old son," agreed Tim
Trenoweth. "And not a bit's going into our pockets."

They jabbed the pick ends of their candleholders into
the nearest timbering and lit the naked candles in them,
saving the lantern candles for their travel through the tunnels.

The fourth among them, Jarvis Jones, a silent Yank,
crawled over the rubble to the face and studied it. He
rarely spoke to the Cousin Jacks and seemed an alien
among them. But he toiled harder than the rest, as if
driven by some dark anger. Trego suspected that he
highgraded more ore than anyone working the Giltedge,
slipping it into tubes sewn into his jumper, or stuffing it
into a false crown for his felt hat.

Jones and Fenno, the most junior in this crew, would
muck the ore while Trego and Trenoweth would begin the
doublejacking as soon as they had cleared space to work
next to the head. But until then they all would fill the ore
cars.

They lifted the heavier chunks by hand and dropped

them into the car with a deafening clatter. They swiftly raised rock dust that triggered fits of coughing. Even before the first car was filled, more cars were arriving on the tramway, pushed along by lads whose task was to move the laden cars to the turning sheet at the mine shaft, where the cage man would wheel them into the lift and take them up to grass.

Hugh felt his muscles quicken and then hurt as he staggered to the ore car with one large chunk after another. Sometimes the larger pieces had to be shattered with hammers before a man could handle them, but he scorned that. He loved the fine feel of weight in his arms. They all worked silently; there'd be time enough for talk at the break.

He wondered how he'd come to mine, to spin away his days in a score of black holes, as if he hated the sun and wanted to spend his hours in the darkness that comforted the wicked. The tunnel felt cold, but he worked up a heat and stripped off his shirt and unbuttoned his union suit and let it hang from his waist. A mine was a hellish place, and yet he'd found a life in it. He enjoyed the cooperation of his fellows, the occasional grin, the unspoken conversation, the fierce, reckless bonding that held true above and below the grass. And so he mined, ruining his ears and his lungs while darkness abraded his soul and hid his iniquities.

"Well, Timmy, it's time we started her," he said.

Tim Trenoweth gathered the hammers and the steels for the doublejacking, selecting the Black Diamond bull steel, a foot long and an inch and a quarter in diameter. They would first drill three holes in the middle of the new face, making a triangle of them. Hugh flexed his arms and began, slamming his eight-pound hammer against the bull steel being held by Trenoweth, a steady fifty strokes a minute. Between each stroke Trenoweth rotated the steel.

When the steel had dulled, after penetrating about six inches, Trenoweth pulled it and slid in the second, and then they changed positions so swiftly that they scarcely missed a beat. The second steel's diameter was a thirty-second of an inch smaller than the bull steel, and it was six inches longer. It, too, would dull after six inches, to be followed by another a fraction narrower and still longer.

When each steel dulled, they exchanged jobs. One would rest by rotating and cleaning steels while his partner hammered at a target scarcely larger than a quarter, their rhythm punctuating the roar as the muckers shoveled ore into the cars. They each entrusted their hands and arms to the skill of the other; a missed blow could cripple them for life. It was a task that the experienced Cousin Jacks kept to themselves.

The tool nipper happened by, and Trego yelled at him for more steels. It took a set to drill each of the seven holes.

"And clean the candlebox, ye lazy devil," he added.

The red candleboxes, set next to the hoist shaft and filled with dirt, provided the only sanitation in the mine. Their stink could pervade the whole works, and worse, conceal the smell of smoke. Fire was the enemy in the holes; fire shot suffocating smoke through the tunnels, murdering every living thing in them. A man wanted to be able to smell smoke instantly. The nipper was supposed to keep the boxes fresh, and also pick up dead rats and quicklime the area where they lay, for the same reason.

They broke mid-shift and lunched on pasties, the seasoned beef, potatoes, and vegetables cooked in their thick elongated pastry shells, a filling meal easily eaten with the fingers. Letters from 'ome, the Cornishmen called them. They heated water in cans set on pedestals fashioned of nails, using their candles, and soon they all had hot tea to wash down the pasties.

Ah, the breaks were good times. A quiet cheer replaced the harsh rattle of ore cars and tumbling rock, and the clang of hammer on steel.

"Jones, my beautay, how long're you going to muck rock?" he asked the silent stranger.

Jones shrugged and smiled. He alone had no pasty, but

bread and cheese. "I'll never git rich down here," Jones said, after the Cousin Jacks had all supposed he wouldn't reply.

Hugh wondered about that.

"She's callin' us back," he said after they'd had a rest.

They toiled through two candles and part of their third. Trego and Trenoweth completed the first three holes and set to work on the remaining four, drilled into the corners of the face. Drilling the lifter holes meant holding and hammering steels above their heads, but even that was easier than drilling the edger holes close to the bottom. But at last they completed their seven holes. The muckers shoveled away the last of the ore, and pried the turning sheet into the face of the drift to receive the next six cubic yards of ore.

Then Trego, the powder man, set to work on the charges. From a box of Du Pont explosives brought by the tool nipper, Trego extracted a red-wrapped stick of Hercules-brand dynamite, or Giant Powder, and gently, oh so gently, pushed it into the first of the holes, using a wooden rod to drive it to the back of the hole. Then he cut a four-foot length of Bickford fuse and slid it into a copper fulminate cap, and crimped the end to anchor the fuse. Bickford burned at a steady thirty seconds a foot; this charge would detonate two minutes after he ignited it.

The Bickford had always been a marvel to Hugh. It alone had made large-scale mining possible. It consisted of a core of powder wrapped by strands of jute, and then wound with string and two layers of tape, the outer one waterproofed with tar. If it failed, it failed safely by sputtering out. It never leapt ahead toward a premature and murderous detonation. He loved it, loved its coarse tarry feel in his hands. His intent was to detonate the charges in a certain order, the center three first, to blow rock into the drift so that the lifters and edgers could blow their rock into the vacated space.

He sliced open the paper wrapping of a stick of Hercules and inserted the cap into the gelatinous explosive. Then he bound his fused stick together and even more gently pushed it home. The fulminate would explode on concussion as easily as from a spark. It raised a sweat of sheer terror in him, but he loved doing it almost as much as he loved the suspended moments when he lit those fuses. The primer, or cap, was always attached to the second stick, so that some of the fuse would burn inside the hole, undisturbed by the detonations of the surrounding charges.

After that he pushed home the remaining sticks of dynamite and plugged the hole with mud to contain the explosion as much as possible, which added greatly to its effect. The fuse dangled down the face like a long rat tail. He was alone; the nipper had collected the equipment. The powder man worked alone while the rest did tunnel work, laying tram rails or deepening the waterbearing trenches to either side, or doing some timbering.

Tenderly, sweat beading on his forehead, he loaded the rest of the charges, cutting the fuses to the length that would fire the round in proper sequence: the center charges first; the lifters second; and the edgers last. One hole had given him trouble, and he'd cleaned it with a tiny scoop on a wire until the obstructions fell out. But at last he had his charges in the face, each sealed by muck; seven rattails dangled before him. He had an inch of candle left; the shift was almost done.

Trego peered about, checking for forgotten tools, stray sticks of dynamite, caps, valuables, clothing. He saw nothing. The nipper had collected it all, save for the roll of fuse and his lantern. He cut a length of Bickford fuse that was shorter than the shortest fuse on the charges, measuring carefully. This was the spitter, the piece of fuse he would use to ignite the rest. Its shortness was his insurance. If it burned to his fingers he had to get out no matter what; he would have thirty seconds before the first detonation.

"Fire in the hole!" he cried, the traditional warning to all mortals. He felt his pulse elevate as it always did in this mesmerizing moment. He lit the spitter and held it to each rattail, the longest ones first, waiting for each to spit into life. This was always the moment of his testing; the moment when he had to will himself not to bolt. It seemed like a new struggle each time, as if God and the Devil were wrestling for his soul all over again. He lit the third, watching it spit orange sparks, and the fourth and fifth and sixth. And then the seventh. He plucked up his lantern and the roll of fuse and raced out of the drift and into the crosscut, his unruly heart wild in his chest.

CHAPTER 20

H ugh Trego hastened out of the drift and through the crosscut until he had almost reached the vestibule where the rest of the men waited for the hoist.

He paused out of earshot of their voices, and waited. The detonations shivered the rock, the booms almost on top of each other. He felt the pulses of disturbed air as the Hercules charges tore rock from the bones of the earth. Seven, he thought. But something was odd. These sounded throaty and deep, rumbling like thunder. It lit his curiosity. He waited, his canny ear trying to decipher what had been different. He shrugged. Nothing he could describe.

The cage reached the vestibule, and some of the men entered, to be lifted to the grass above by the hoist engineer. Amid the clamor of bells the hoist rose while the exhausted miners balanced themselves carefully. The cages had no sides, and woe to the man who teetered into the moving rock wall of the shaft.

"Hurry up, Hugh; she's coming down again," said Fenno.

"Tell them to wait for me; I'm listening a wee bit."

He closed his eyes and strained to understand what he had heard; he didn't want to leave word for the next shift that all was well if it wasn't.

The cage clanked to a halt, and the rest of the men clambered into it.

"Hurry, lad," cried someone.

"Tell Timmons I'll be up in five minutes—I'll have me a look. She's done something."

"Don't be crazy, Hugh," yelled Trenoweth. "She's all right."

"Tell 'em to wait a wee bit."

"You're a stubborn man, Hugh. It's no good arguing with you."

With that, the cage rattled upward again. The shift foreman and the hoist engineer would be angry at him; their shift was ending too, and his delay would tie them at their posts.

He eyed his candle; an inch left. He was going to do something crazy; walk into air thick enough to burn out his lungs; walk into something wrong. He trudged through the crosscut bored through limestone and into the drift, his lamplight reflecting whirling dust. The toxic fumes of detonated dynamite seared his throat and lungs.

He pulled his jumper over his nose, knowing it wouldn't help much, and groped through murk, gasping for air. He reached the face, and found the usual tumble of blown rock before him on the turning sheet, barely visible. It was still settling, and each thump and rattle of rock jarred his nerves. He wondered what he had come for; his lungs ached and his throat burned. He'd thrown away the safety of waiting.

But that strange sound had driven him. He lifted his lantern and then saw it through the murk: a blackness at the face. Coughing hoarsely, he clambered over the rubble, scrambling toward the darkness. The ore settled under him, careening him forward almost into the darkness. He slammed into the right side of the face. Next to him was an abyss.

He held his lantern up, trying with weeping eyes to make out what lay there, and faintly discerned a cavern, its black walls winking at him in the moil of the settling dust.

He felt his heart race. He could not see its bottom. He kicked rock into the abyss and heard it smack rock not far below. Above he caught the black lustre of ore. The bleddy hole looked as big as a large house.

A vug. He'd never seen one in all his years in the pits. He pulled a fist-sized chunk of lustrous black rock from the opening. It felt heavy and cold in his hand. A vug was like a giant geode in the bowels of the earth, a cavity lined with incredibly rich ores deposited by solutions over the eons.

A bleddy vug!

He coughed and backed away, scrambling over rock, and wheezed his way back to the lift, his lungs aching and his eyes leaking. His candle had blued down for want of air but now it flared again. He fingered a piece of rock that was mostly silver and lead. The cage was waiting for him, and so would be the shifter up on the grass, who would roundly cuss him out. He belled the engineer and felt the cage race him upward while he coughed and gulped air.

He burst into the blinding light above, and into the anger of Coke Timmons.

"Have ya no sense? Give me your lunch bucket, Trego," yelled the shift boss, snatching it and shaking it, the ritual shift-ending gesture of mistrust. He thrust it back to Trego, who stood coughing. "What's that in your hand? Why it's ore. Highgrading, are you? Keeping Watkins and me hanging around while you help yer old self. Give it to me."

"I will not," Trego growled. "I'll not be giving you this to stick into your own britches. She's too rich. You see what she is, and next thing all you'd be robbing the mine—and blaming the boys for her when Webb finds out."

Trego coughed again, and sucked in the clean alpine air. He knew he had hurt his body.

"I said give it to me, Trego."

"And I'm saying I won't. You and me, we're a-marchin' up to Webb and we're putting this bleddy rock in his hands. The lads and me, we'll not be takin' any blame. It's a vug I blew into down there, and it's a vug I'm tellin' himself about."

"Hand it over, Trego—or out you go."

Trego balled his fists, one of which had the ore in it, but the shift boss darted backward.

"All right, have it your way. But I'm telling Webb you've broken rules—and out you'll go."

"And I'll tell him the whole of it; you wanted to pocket this juicy little plum for yerself and all the shift bosses and supers. Get rich and blame the Cousin Jacks. I'll tell himself, thankee, and he'll hear me out."

"Look, Trego, he's in a meeting. The Hammons are here. We can't go busting in there."

"I can and I will, and you'll not stop me. Not with a vug down there."

They marched to the offices, Trego's breath still searing his throat.

"I'm comin' to see Webb, and right now," he growled at old Baghote.

"But you can't—he's meeting with the Hammons."

"You'll fetch him or I'll go in meself."

"Better get him," muttered Timmons unhappily. "Trego's acting like a mad dog."

Uneasily, Baghote edged toward the closed door, knocked and entered. A moment later Webb appeared, looking testy.

"What is this, Trego?"

"Here's what it is. I blew open a vug, that's what she is. Look at her." He deposited the black metal into Webb's hand.

Astonishment lit Webb's face. He hefted the ore, studied it, pursed his lips, unbelieving.

"A vug," he muttered. *"A vug!"*

"Big as a bleddy house."

"You went back? After firing the round?"

"I did."

Webb shook his head. "And wrecked your lungs and risked your neck. That wasn't smart."

"Maybe it wasn't. I'm a stubborn beautay. But you needed to know before the supers and shifters did." He let it hang there.

"Trego kept us waiting and broke half the rules," Timmons growled.

"And I'll break every bleddy one if I have to."

Webb studied the rock as if it were something alive and malign, tossing it in his hand as if to fathom its contents by playing with it. Then he turned to Coke Timmons: "I'm going down there in a bit. Put the next shift in the other drift—or on the grass. Tell the blacksmith I want a strap-iron door and an iron barrier in this drift immediately. And a good six-lever padlock. Fast. It'll be worth a bonus for him and his men."

The foreman glared at Trego like a man who'd been betrayed.

"Am I fired?" Trego asked, truculently.

Webb sighed. "No, you did the right thing."

"You could thank a man."

Webb smiled. "I've a bonus in mind for you too, Hugh Trego. Keep this quiet. Maybe you've saved the Giltedge for the Hammons."

"Quiet? I'll not keep it from the men. I won't have your thirty pieces of silver if it separates me from them."

It took Webb aback. "You're loyal to them—I like that, Trego. All right. I'll ask this: would you keep it quiet long enough for us to block that drift?"

"I don't know why, but I will."

Webb smiled suddenly, like winter sun in an overcast sky. "I'll have this assayed. I've never seen ore like it. This piece in my hand could have several ounces of silver in it—*several ounces* of silver in about three pounds."

"And the men won't be seeing a dime of it," Trego muttered.

CHAPTER 21

· · · · · · · · · · · · · · · · ·

Christmas had arrived in May. Thaddeus Webb hefted Christmas in his hand, feeling its metallic weight. It would take an assay to determine the values, but he knew he was holding many dollars' worth of silver.

He set the mysterious dark ore on his desk, where it radiated a spell, like some alchemist's magic. The Hammon brothers eyed it idly, not knowing the sorcery before their eyes.

Closeted with the Hammons, Webb had been bounced all day between two conflicting wills. John, the elder brother, was an ascetic fussbudget, skinny as a stack of dimes, brimming with worries about pouring money down rat-holes, while Henry was quite the opposite, a chubby optimist who wanted to spend enough to make the mine work.

If they agreed on anything, it was that the Giltedge should be kept in the family, and that speculators like Daley should be kept out. But such was their desperation that they had seriously weighed the offer Daley had conveyed to Webb. It seemed better than a public stock company.

Webb hefted the ore. "This is probably your salvation. That was the powder man on that stope. He's hit a vug of this. If it's what I think, there'll be a fortune there for the plucking."

"What's a vug?" asked Henry.

"I'll show you. I'm going in there as soon as the hoist engineer's on shift—ten minutes."

"You're going down there? But you've been telling us the mine's not shored—it's dangerous!" exclaimed John.

"Risk. That's what mining is about, John. Are you coming? I'm about to look at the most important thing that has ever happened to me—or to you."

"Not I! Not with all that rock over my head."

Webb smiled. He had bent their ears for half an hour about inadequate shoring.

"I'll go," Henry said. "This sounds like a dream."

"Good. I want you to see this. I'll get a jumper you can put on over that suit. But leave your suitcoat here."

Minutes later, armed with a canvas collecting bag, a pick hammer, and a coal-oil lantern, Webb took Henry Hammon into the bowels of the earth and led him into the drift. The acrid fumes of the dynamite still lingered but the dust had settled.

"I can hardly breathe!" exclaimed Henry.

"Now you know something about the miners' lives," Webb retorted.

"Are you sure this is safe?"

Webb eyed the timbering. "No, it can all land on your head. But you're a brave man."

"My itch is to turn tail and run to that shaft."

Webb laughed shortly.

"Everything's so—strange. Suffocating. Echoing."

"You can bless the Cornishmen who brave this every working day, Henry."

The reflector lamp shot light here and there, glancing off ore-black walls. They came to the stope, and the mountain of rubble in front of it. Webb lifted the beam to the new face, and discovered a yawning hole perhaps six feet in diameter. His pulse lifted. He felt like Heinrich Schliemann unearthing Troy; like an archeologist piercing into Pharaoh's tomb.

"We'll have to crawl over this—careful now."

He helped Henry clamber over treacherous rock and then they stood before the gaping hole while Webb played his light over the lustrous walls of a huge gallery. Trego's round had blown into a corner of it; almost all of it lay to the right and below their viewpoint.

Henry Hammon gasped.

"That's a vug. First I've seen," Webb said. "That's the best ore you'll see in a lifetime, deposited by accretion, mineral salts in water. I don't know what this is worth, but we may be looking at a hundred thousand dollars of ore."

"My goodness. That much? In sight?"

"Visible ore."

"You're just guessing."

"Call it an educated estimate."

"I'm speechless! Are we done? Let's get out of here."

"Be patient, Henry."

Webb could not get to the floor of the vug without a ladder, so he confined himself to chipping off samples around the edge of the jagged hole, while Henry wheezed and coughed.

"I've got to get back to better air," Henry said.

"All right. I'll be there in a minute."

Webb's eyes were leaking tears and his esophagus burned. It was still too soon after the blast for the air to have cleared. He collected half a dozen more pieces of ore—all he could carry—and crabbed backward over the rubble and out of the drift with nothing worse than a skinned knuckle and a twisted ankle for his effort.

"Are we rich?" asked Henry at the shaft vestibule.

Webb smiled. "We'll see what Mueller reports."

"We can take it to him in Livingston and wait for the report," Henry said.

"I'm having the drift sealed," Webb said.

"Sealed? You mean they'll steal it?"

"The miners think it's a prerogative."

"But it's theft! Blast them all!"

Webb sighed. This world wasn't like the Hammons' world with all of its moral certitudes. Most of the men in the pits considered the enrichment of their daily wage an ancient right.

"This'll be sealed. Which means that only the shift foremen and the men on the grass, who'll take it to the mill, and the mill men will snatch it!"

"But it's mine!"

Webb shrugged and steered Henry into the cage, which lurched upward, tugging at their stomachs.

They divested themselves of their jumpers in the new changing room, and returned to Webb's office to face the dour John.

"We're rich, John. I saw something beyond belief," Henry cried.

"Maybe we shouldn't be rich. Maybe Divine Providence has decreed that we should stick to our stores. We should be starting one in Cashbox, Henry. These good people need a Hammon Brothers Mercantile. The women need yard goods and ready-mades. The men need hardware. I tell you, we're letting Baker steal it away. Our true business awaits us, Henry." He sighed dolefully. "Our greed has led us astray."

"John, for heaven's sake, listen to Thaddeus."

Webb settled himself into his wooden swivel chair, wondering what to say. The School of Mines didn't offer classes about handling mine owners.

"Well, John, I've just shown Henry a fortune in almost pure ore, all of it visible in a cavity—a gallery—that we blew into. It's the size of a house. I've got enough ore—" he waved at the canvas sack on his desk "—for a few assays. I'd say we're looking at a hundred thousand dollars of easily refined ore. At the very least. That's bankable, John. It's a proven reserve. Once we have some assays and some measurements—why, you should be able to soften the heart of the flintiest banker in Helena. Listen to what I'm saying: this gives you the development cash we need to survive."

"But anything could happen. The tunnel could cave in before you get to it. Nothing's a sure thing. No, it's just an excuse to pour more wealth down the rat-hole."

"Let Thaddeus show it to you, John," said Henry. "Then you'll see."

"Now, confound it, I don't doubt either of you. But I'll not put my good and honorable name to a loan contract obligating me and my heirs to such a debt."

Henry seemed helpless in the face of such adamant resistance.

Webb stared at them and thought he might resign after all. He hadn't brought that up, but the letter was on the desk, face down. He decided to try one more time.

"John," he said. "With that vug you could sell this mine for half a million in an hour. I could send for Cornelius Daley right now and you'd have more than twice the two hundred thousand you've invested in development. If that's what you want, I'll get him and you'll have a handsome profit. On the other hand, if we develop this mine you stand to make a lot—maybe a million."

"Million?"

Webb nodded. "Quite apart from the vug, that's the largest body of ore I've ever heard of—we don't have any idea what its dimensions are, but it's huge. I've been conservative. I'd guess that vug alone'll provide enough quick cash to pay most of your development costs—including the loan. We can mine that vug in two or three weeks and you'll have your cash out and the loan paid as fast as that's smelted."

"Two or three weeks? Enough to pay a loan that large?"

"Yes—if it assays the way I think it will."

"Two or three weeks?" John acted as if he could scarcely believe it.

That settled it. Something in John gave way. The Hammon brothers instructed Webb to turn down Daley; they did not want his money. They agreed to take the ore samples to Johann Mueller and wait for the assays. Then Henry would deliver the reports to Webb while John talked to bankers. Above all, they intended to keep a mine worth a million dollars to themselves.

CHAPTER 22

• • • • • • • • • • • • • • • • • •

Saturday afternoon J. Ernest Potter-Pride was awakened from an erotic siesta by a clamor at his office door. He hastened shoeless to the front of his house and admitted Constable Svensrud.

"You're Bass Boehm's attorney, aren't you?" Svensrud asked.

Attorney Pride nodded.

"Well, he's fixing to commit murder and fetch himself a noose. Maybe you'd better talk him out of it. No one else can."

Pride skewered his hightop shoes, laced them, and hastened into silvery sunlight. He had no idea where the constable was leading him until he beheld the largest crowd of men he'd ever seen in Cashbox. Not just men, but wagons and teams in numbers too great to count—all of them surrounding Regina Maltz's boardinghouse.

Midnight would be her eviction hour.

It took Ernest Potter-Pride only a moment to see what was afoot. They were going to move her boardinghouse to the new lot. Miners, teamsters, storekeepers, and roustabouts had all gathered for the event, which they'd obviously kept secret from him. Over on Lot 36, the one he'd donated to her, crews were laying up a dry masonry foundation of limestone from the slackpiles of the mines. Elsewhere, crews were skidding log rollers into place, cutting sagebrush, trimming away bumps and filling hollows with their shovels. He spotted Thaddeus Webb, who was dragging logs into a sort of tramway.

But the great majority of townsmen—Potter-Pride estimated two or three hundred—stood silently around the boardinghouse, crowbars in hand, waiting for something. They were being held at bay by Bass Boehm and half a dozen hard cases, bristling with bandoliers, cartridges, revolvers, rifles, and double-barreled shotguns.

"You better yak at him before someone gets killed," Svensrud said. "He's jumping a house he don't own—not until midnight."

Pride needed no more encouragement. He wove through the silent and angry crowd into the no-man's land between the movers and Boehm's cutthroats.

"Pride—you tell that devil he don't own that house and he's never gonna own that boardin' house and he's fixing to own himself a noose," yelled Svensrud.

Regina Maltz approached, dry-eyed but agitated. "Please help me, Mister Pride. You're the only one that can. They dragged me out of my own house."

"There, there," he said, smiling dutifully. "You'd best step out of the way."

"I will not. I'm going into my house. They'll have to shoot me to get me out."

Pride patted her hand and proceeded to Boehm, who grinned at him. "Yellow, ain't they?" he said, waving toward the hundreds of silent men. "I tell 'em this here's my house; they come a foot farther and they'll be pulling buckshot out of their bellies. That done it."

"Bass, this isn't yours—not yet."

He shrugged. "I already took it. Now you scram—or you'll take some buckshot too."

"Look, Bass. You can't go back on your own terms."

Bass Boehm grinned. "Well, I'm doing it. This here joint's worth five grand and I'm nipping it. Some chicken lawyer you are. I hired youse to keep me outta trouble, not get me into it. Tell 'em to scram."

"Bass—it's your thick neck I'm talking about. That's Svensrud over there, ready to act."

"Well, he'll be the first to get a load of double-ought, Pride." He chortled. "Look at 'em, six shotguns holding off three hundred. What vaudeville. Now you tell the old sweetheart to scram. We got her place and that's how she's wrote. Like you keep sayin', possession's nine-tenths of the law."

Attorney Pride walked beyond Bass toward his cocksure troops, who seemed to be enjoying the moment. One of them was Bass's younger brother, Rodwell.

"It's your lives," he said. "You murder anyone and you'll hang from that cottonwood over there in about two minutes, without a trial. That's a lynch party out there. I count eleven nooses they're swinging. Bass doesn't own this, and every man out there knows it."

They eyed him uncertainly, and he decided to force the issue.

"Bass. I'm telling those men to come on in and move this house right now; you won't shoot," he said. "You fire one shot and you won't see another sunrise."

"Hey, Pride. You forgot her. They come a step closer and I grab her."

Pride ignored him. He found himself loathing Boehm more than ever. He sensed that the man's bravado was merely veneering his fear. Miners were waving the nooses.

"Miss Maltz," he said, "follow me."

"I won't budge one inch."

He sighed. She was on her own. He walked out to the waiting townsmen. "You can go in now and move the house. None of them'll pull a trigger."

But no one dared to move.

He signaled Thaddeus Webb. "Come along with me, Webb." Unhesitatingly, Webb followed, carrying a pry bar.

They walked through a ticking silence toward the boardinghouse, in a quiet so deep that the caw of a crow seemed as loud as the Giltedge Mine whistle. But none of Boehm's gang swung a shotgun toward them. Then Boehm motioned his men away.

"You're fired, Pride," he yelled, when he reached his saddler.

As fast as the toughs retreated, cheering miners and teamsters swarmed over the lot to begin their charity. The

Angel of Cashbox would be moved before the witching hour.

Pride watched one crew enter the house to anchor down the furniture while another crew began levering up one side of the building and sliding jacks under the frame. Others readied long rollers. Still others worked teams of draft horses into place. It amused him, this sentiment in the midst of a greedy mining camp.

Regina Maltz watched quietly at his side, sometimes muttering fierce things he couldn't catch.

With so many on hand, and matters so well organized, it took amazingly little time. When the house rested on rollers, the teams were hooked up and scores of men grabbed ropes attached to the rear, ready to brake the motion if needed. Then the teamsters cussed and whipped, while the ox teams and horses strained in their collars. Slowly the boardinghouse creaked along on its rollers. People cheered. The building sailed down the gentle slope like a galleon, well under the control of the hundreds of men whose sturdy hands and powerful animals guided it. An hour later it stood upon its new foundation, looking like it belonged there.

Regina Maltz wept, dumfounded by the spectacle.

But these gents weren't done. Much to Pride's astonishment a crew of carpenters erected an outhouse at the rear, while others built a fine stairway and porch at the front door. The miners laid a flagstone walk to McDonald Street and another to the outhouse. Well before dusk Regina Maltz's establishment was complete. Bass Boehm wouldn't drive *this* woman into the streets.

"It has a better view," she said, over and over. But that was plainly because she couldn't think of anything else to say. As men began collecting pry bars and jacks and saws and ropes, she wandered among them, wet-cheeked and smiling, clasping their hands between hers, whispering things they couldn't hear but knew to be her love and gratitude. She never stopped until she had clasped every hand of every man, even as they drifted away into an uncommonly cheery evening.

Ernest Potter-Pride had watched it all transfixed: reminded of the mighty power of tenderness, something he had forgotten though his life had once been filled with it. He understood what he had just witnessed, but it upset his plans, his future, his schemes—his life.

He knew what he'd do: he'd have Willard Croker write another inventive piece about him. He would be the hero of Cashbox, and he'd prosper more than ever.

"Glad you could settle it, Pride," said Constable Svensrud, who had hovered nearby the whole time. "You done a fine thing."

"Well, ah, my client needed counsel." Compliments troubled him these days.

He plucked a fragrant cigar from his breast pocket, only to be interrupted by Regina Maltz. For a long moment in that quiet dusk her eyes searched him, asking silent questions. Her cheeks glistened. And then she clasped him, her thick arms clamping him to her ample bosom, and he felt her melt into him, felt her wet face bury itself in his shoulder.

"There, there," he said, patting her, wanting to light the Eventual five-cent cigar in his right hand. He patted her thick left shoulder and springy hair even as her clinging sent some emotion long forgotten through him.

"You've given me my life back, Mister Pride," she whispered from some nook in his shoulder. "I don't know about you. Sometimes I think . . . you're someone else. I won't ever forget. You'll see. Not ever."

"There, there, Miss Maltz. I was simply advising my client," he objected, as crisply as a lawyer addressing a judge. Silly woman, oozing sentiment.

He wanted to light his cigar, but she was a long time letting go and he didn't know how to pry her loose.

Chapter 23

. . . .

The arrival of John and Henry Hammon at the newly opened Palace Hotel did not escape Cornelius Daley. From his upstairs front window he spotted an elegant black Victoria parked below, while its driver lounged patiently. Sure enough, moments later the Hammons climbed into its lacquered body and the Victoria wended its way toward the Giltedge Mine.

He found Loren Whitmore at the registration desk.

"Ah, Whitmore. When the Hammons return, please make sure they get this." He handed Whitmore an envelope that contained an invitation to dinner in the hotel's new Silver Queen chophouse. There, he supposed, the three men could come to mutually profitable terms. "It's a dinner invitation. Is your kitchen ready? Have you gotten all your spirits in?"

"Oh, they're still coming in, but we can treat you to a fine meal. Only a few things are short."

"Very well, plan on seven o'clock—if they accept, which I imagine they will."

"I'll tell the chef, Mister Daley."

"They may prefer tomorrow night."

"No, they're staying only this night, sir."

Daley nodded. After the icy shower of Webb's news, they'd be ready for some Château Lafitte, some fine filets, and some fine credit from the Silver Fox.

He pierced into a chill spring afternoon and hurried to the Shamrock Saloon on Cashbox Street, which probably would be opening up. He entered a beery darkness, but he made out Sourmash Charlie laying fresh sawdust on the newly swept planks. The oak coffin had vanished, along with the bouquets and the black wreaths, and only the Brunswick billiard table occupied the rear.

"Ah, Mister Daley. A little snort you'll be wanting," said the professor of mixology as he set down his pail of sawdust.

"No, I'm looking for Ambrose Gill. He said he might be here."

Sourmash sighed unhappily. "Mister Daley, sor, it came to a sad ending about midnight. Poor Ambrose had a fit. He rose up out of his box like a spectre from a grave. 'You don't care about me,' he sez. 'You're havin' ale at my expense and not a tear do you shed for poor old Ambrose, your old friend from Connemarra,' he sez. 'Here I hold a wake so's to know how it'll be when I depart bye and bye, and you never pay your respects at my box. You ignore a man and drink his ale and forget that Ambrose Gill ever was among you,' he sez. And with that, Mister Daley, he slaps two double eagles on the bar and walks into the night, and that was the last a body's seen of him."

Daley sighed. "I don't suppose he left a message for me."

"Nary a thing, sor."

"Did he say when he'd be back?"

"He swore upon his mother's grave he'd never come back; we were all put out of his mind forever more."

"Do you know where he went?"

"To his ledge, sor. He's got a silver blende ledge he works himself."

"Where's that?"

"He doesn't tell a soul, sor. Not even me."

"Will he get over his—unhappiness?"

"Oh, no, sor. You know how it is. He'll nurse it and water it and let it flower in his noggin, and things'll never be the same."

"Can anyone get word to him?"

Sourmash Charlie shrugged, as if the question weren't worth answering.

"Well I'm looking for him. If he comes in, let me know immediately."

"I'll do that, sor. You sure you don't want a nip?"

"What I want and what I do are two different things, Sourmash."

He retreated to the Palace, determined to find Sylvie. She would be good company. In fact, he would include her at dinner. Henry Hammon would enjoy her; John would tolerate her and privately wonder what their relationship was. It amused him.

Her idea for a gentlemen's club appealed to him. In Helena, the Montana Club had been his lair, an ideal place to negotiate a contract or just enjoy a few whiskeys with other gentlemen. Its rose damask tapestries, cut-glass chandeliers, parqueted floors, along with a staff that saw to a man's comforts, had won it a choice clientele of gold and silver men, cattlemen, timber men and copper kings from Butte. There he could put whole enterprises together without even leaving his leather wingchair.

And so it might be in Cashbox, if the town grew the way Helena had. It just might, he thought. But it would all depend on a railroad. Sylvie didn't realize that. She didn't know about boom towns. She would have no clientele for her club unless someone built a spur down to the Northern Pacific.

The memory of that first evening filled him with benign pleasure. He'd thought he was going to be seduced, but he had been wrong. Sylvie Duvalier might some day end up his lover, but it would take more than a dinner. She was available, but not at the drop of a double eagle. They had finished their dinner; he lit a Cub, and she invited him to become a partner in her business. She lacked the cash. He politely deferred his answer. He might invest in her club, but only after he knew more about the future of Cashbox. After that, she gossiped about people he didn't know, including her sometime husband, always with a wry wit. And then, with a twisted smile, she bade him good night. He found himself staring at the door, wishing she hadn't vanished through it.

But Sylvie wasn't in the hotel this afternoon.

Late that day he watched the Victoria pull up again. The

Hammons emerged from it and returned a little later with their luggage. Then the driver steered the lacquered carriage south. Astonished, he hastened down to Whitmore.

"Uh, they left, Mister Daley; didn't even stay the night. I gave them your letter. They seemed in an awful hurry. Mister Henry Hammon opened it and said, 'Just tell Daley we regret, and we'll see him in Helena some time.' That was it, sir. As fast as that. I'm sorry we couldn't accommodate them."

Gone. In a rush.

Daley hastened up the gulch, wanting to catch Webb in his offices. The man worked nonstop, twelve or fourteen hours a day, driven by something. Webb would have the answers.

Daley pushed into the Giltedge Mine office at the moment that old Baghote was lighting a lamp so he could see the ledger before him. The clerk settled the glass chimney over the lamp and nodded. "I'll tell him you're here, sir."

A moment later Daley entered Webb's office, just as Webb was sliding a desk drawer shut. Daley had the feeling that whatever lay in that drawer wasn't for his eyes.

"Con?" asked the superintendent.

"The Hammons were here, Thaddeus. Did you convey my offer?"

"I did. They aren't interested."

"Not at all?"

"Not a bit. They've other plans, I'm afraid."

"I don't suppose you'd elaborate."

Webb smiled. "No," he said.

"Are they going to build a smelter? A railroad?"

Webb looked amused.

"Sell the company? If they are, I'd like to bid."

"No, not sell it, Cornelius."

"I can supply what they need."

"They don't need a thing."

"Thaddeus, a few days ago this mine was on the brink of collapse. No payroll, no timbering, work stopped in the new shaft. Now they don't need a thing."

"It's been a pleasant visit, Cornelius."

Daley grinned. "And so it has, Thaddeus."

Con Daley closed the door behind him and eyed Baghote, who was furtively watching him from under his green eyeshade.

"Ah, what a hard day, my friend," said Daley.

Baghote shook his head.

"The Hammons here and all. I guess you've been busy."

"No, not a bit," Baghote said.

"How about a nip, man? Have you tried the Palace saloon yet? My treat."

Baghote raised his head slightly and glared. "I may not earn as much as these silver kings, but I have my integrity."

"Oh, I just thought we'd have a nip. You're a man to have a nip with."

"You're looking for information from me, Mister Daley. I'd give it away before I'd let myself be bought. My price is not two-bits."

"Of course not. You're a loyal man."

"Yes I am, considering what I'm paid."

"Well, I'll not offer you a nip, then. You're too fine a man. I just saw John and Henry Hammon at the Palace. Everything changed in a hurry, didn't it. I've never seen them happier."

"Why, they've every right to be, Mister Daley. It doesn't happen every day, you know. They burst in here— the powder man and the foreman—right in the middle of the talks. Why, in they came, carrying a lump of ore that looked like the roof of Hades, sir, but it was pure metal, right out of the vug."

"Vug? Oh yes, the vug. I've never seen the Hammons so pleased."

"A giant, sir. Bigger than a locomotive factory, and lined with pure silver. No one's heard of the like since the Comstock."

Daley laughed. "You tell Webb that I congratulate him, Baghote. I never dreamed he had a vug up his sleeve."

The man nodded and disappeared under his green eye-shade.

Con Daley sighed. This one was harder than he'd ever imagined it would be.

CHAPTER 24

• • • • • • • • • • • • • • • • • •

Sylvie Duvalier jammed another barrette into her unruly hair but it didn't do any good. Her hair had a perverse will of its own. The best she could do was keep it out of her face. She brushed it faithfully every morning but it always looked as if she'd just gotten out of bed, a condition that did not escape the attention of gentlemen.

Something about the Wild West was demolishing the last of her respectability. She had tried to be a proper belle in Wilmington, but propriety had eluded her. Her sister, Tennessee, had been married off to a prominent Du Pont executive. But hapless Sylvie had scared eligible bachelors off until her irritated guardians began to trumpet the dowry. That attracted Beau Pitt, who had married her and promptly spent it.

The problem, she assumed, was that she had always preferred the company of men, especially the company of captains of industry. She yearned to do what they did. And she loved their worldly ways. Back in Wilmington, the amount of time she spent in the company of men raised a lot of eyebrows. And when people realized she favored the company of older men, and rich ones at that, the eyebrows shot even higher.

She anchored a green-ribboned straw boater to her mop of hair with oystershell hatpins and examined the cock-eyed result dubiously. Everything about her was always dubious, she thought wryly. She had arrived at a comic mood. They possessed her once in a while, and usually got her into trouble.

This rare day in May she would buy the lots for her club. She knew the very ones she wanted: number 80, on the west side of Cashbox Street, and 81 too, if she could afford it. They would be the perfect site, just off Main Street with its hotels and mercantiles. Both of them belonged to Willard Croker, the owner of *The Plain Truth*. She had found that out at the town lot company office.

The Plain Truth issued once a week from a grubby log building that lurked behind the mercantiles. She found it by prowling alleys, and entered upon a gloomy workplace lit only by one lamp. Under it a woman bent over a form filled with type. It surprised Sylvie to see a woman. This one glanced at her furtively and seemed about to speak. But then Croker emerged from behind a curtained partition, beaming like a lighthouse.

"You're Mister Croker," she said.

He surveyed her with lusty good cheer. "That's me. What can I do for a lovely lady like you?"

"You can sell me a lot or two."

It surprised him. "Well now. I didn't catch your name."

"I didn't offer it. Sylvie Duvalier. That's Mrs. I'm interested in Lots 80 and 81. They told me you own them."

"You've seen them?"

"Up the street. I'll give you seventy-five apiece."

"Seventy-five?" He seemed taken aback. "Why, they're worth two hundred each," he said, his gaze upon the expensive cut of her velvet suit.

"I've been advised, Mister Croker, that lots here run from a hundred down to thirty or forty—the higher prices along Main Street. This isn't Main. Seventy-five's a fair price."

Croker hemmed for a moment. "I'll have to think about it," he said. "I was expecting more."

"It's three times what you paid."

"Things appreciate. I think—"

"And I'll want a warranty deed. Poor Miss Maltz. What a scandal that was."

"Oh, that was a scandal. I've editorialized against lot-jumping, but it doesn't do much good. A warranty deed? Now what's that?"

"You're going to warrant that my title is unclouded; that I can enjoy my property without being subject to a claim upon the land from someone else."

The beam in Croker's face lessened slightly. "You've been talking to an attorney . . . Potter-Pride?"

"No, Con Daley. He explained it to me, and he'll look over the deed before I pay a nickel." That dinner, she thought, had benefitted her more than Con would ever know.

"Con Daley! Now, are you some . . . friend of his?"

"Exactly."

"What, ah, are you going to build on these lots?"

"A gentlemen's club, with suites upstairs, dining room, kitchen, saloon and club rooms downstairs. And my quarters to the rear."

"Pretty fancy for Cashbox."

"I'm assured from reading *The Plain Truth* that Cashbox has a glowing future; soon there'll be thousands of happy citizens, rich mines, rich ranches, an electric power company, streetcars, waterworks, and a railroad."

"A gentlemen's club. A dignified gentlemen's club," he said.

"Where substantial men can do business."

"And what will your role be, eh?"

"Proprietor and hostess."

He grinned wickedly. "I suppose that's how the rich live."

"It'll cost a hundred a year to walk through the door— and I don't suppose I'll see you," she retorted.

She knew she'd made an enemy; the momentary cloud crossing his face signaled a change in him. She scolded herself, knowing that a man who commanded newspaper columns could ruin her. "Unless you get rich," she added cheerfully. "I expect you will. You can start getting rich by selling the lots to me."

"I'll think about it. How do I get ahold of you?"

"At the Palace."

"Oh. Where Daley stays."

She laughed. He was so obvious. "I won't wait for you to make up your mind. It's now or never," she said. "There are lots of good lots."

He looked distressed. "I'll have to talk with my attorney about the warranty."

"No you don't. Here's the clause, all written out."

She handed him a sheet with a warranty clause written in Daley's flamboyant hand.

He grunted, either from the fear he was being skinned or the tragedy of selling something for its market price. "How'll you pay?" he asked.

"State banknotes." She didn't tell him they were on New York and Pennsylvania banks. It was all money.

He nodded and vanished behind the curtained partition, carrying the paper with the warranty language. Sylvie exulted. Nearby, the hired woman worked silently, her eyes averted. Sylvie picked up a proof sheet so she might read tomorrow's edition.

"Potter-Pride Hero of Cashbox; Attorney Smooths Ruffled Feathers in Eviction Case," was the headline on the lead story. She read a sentimental account of the rescue of the Angel of Cashbox by the public-spirited lawyer who had donated a new lot to Regina Maltz after she had failed to rectify her title. The attorney had calmed the distraught new owner, real estate dealer Bass Boehm, who had mistakenly come slightly early to possess his deeded property and was deeply distressed by public disapproval. Attorney Pride had been widely acclaimed by the citizens of Cashbox for his civic conscience and generosity.

What a fantasy, she thought.

Croker emerged bearing some forms with the blanks filled in.

"I print these deed forms," he said. "Here's your warranty clause. A single deed transfers both lots; the copy's for the courthouse. And these are my deeds from the town lot company." Then he pointed to a handwritten warranty clause at the bottom of the deed. She read it carefully, comparing it with the original.

"I'll show it to Mister Daley," she said.

"No, you wanted the lots now. We'll finish now. I don't like to keep a beautiful woman waiting," he said, his face lit in a cheerful leer.

She read the deed again and then dug into her bag and peeled off fifty-dollar banknotes from a wad while he watched like a hungry cat. "There you are: now please sign them. And your assistant here can witness."

He signed with a flourish. Then the woman signed the name of May Goode and hastened back to her work.

"Done. Now you're the proud owner of two lots in bustling Cashbox," he said, scooping up the notes and studying them. "You're from the east. I hope these are sound."

"As sound as I am," she said, tucking the sheaf of papers into her reticule. "Sounder than Cashbox. I was reading your big story there. About kindly Mister Boehm and public-spirited Attorney Pride. It's missing some details, wouldn't you say?"

He cocked an eyebrow. "It looks all right to me."

"It'll amuse the whole town," she said.

The light had blued out of his red-veined face.

May Goode spoke up. "I think we should rewrite it, Mister Croker. It'd only take a little while."

"You just mind your work."

The woman returned to her corrections after a lingering look at Croker and then Sylvie.

"Spell my name right," said Sylvie to Croker.

"What're you talking about?"

"Spell it right and tell it right," she said. "About my club. It'll be called The Exchange Club. I hope to open the door by October. I'll let you peek in."

She chuckled. His affable cheer had deserted him. In tomorrow's issue there would be something nasty about her.

She walked to her lots and wandered through them, dodging sagebrush, enjoying the feeling of ownership. Beneath her shoes was the first bit of this planet she had ever possessed, measured in feet, and marked by pegs in the corners. Joyously she scooped up some of the silty earth and let it dribble through her fingers. She had found her shore, and she vowed she would never step into quicksand again.

CHAPTER 25

· · · · · · · · · · · · · · · · ·

Portia Webb had dressed for dinner. She always did even though Thaddeus scarcely noticed. It was a matter of standards and civilization. This afternoon she wore her pleated white blouse, the one that took her hours to iron and starch after each wearing; a dark woolen skirt of narrow cut, along with a wide black belt.

He was late again, and she feared she must wait again. He had ruined more meals than she could remember because of his indifference to their domestic life and her comforts. All her married life she had competed with the mines, and the mines always won. She had no idea what it would mean when she married the mining engineer freshly graduated from the Columbia School of Mines. She had spent years in one godforsaken place after another. Only Virginia City, Nevada, had offered a life, and that was because she could catch the Virginia and Truckee Railroad and wind up in San Francisco. But the rest—Ely, Nevada; Santa Rita, New Mexico; Globe, Arizona; Cananea, Mexico; and now this wasteland—were sorrows to be borne with fortitude.

The pendulum clock struck seven. She had expected him at five. The potatoes would be boiled to mush and the salad wilted. An idea tickled her fancy. She put the food in the pantry; the beef in her cold cellar. It would keep. This evening, at least, she would capture him. He would not be able to eat and then hasten back to his lamp-lit offices.

In spite of her difficulties, she loved Thaddeus. They had a barren marriage, and now she counted it a blessing. Mostly, the mines preoccupied him, but he renewed his ardor in her arms now and then, and those were her sweetest moments. She had learned not to compete with his ores and tunnels and pumps, but to fashion her own society.

Even that had been extremely difficult here. She could find only nine suitable women, of the hundred or so in this camp of a thousand. And nine was stretching it, she thought wryly. But these had become her circle, and on various days they met as the Woman's Christian Temperance Union, the Cashbox Women's Club, and the Episcopal Church Altar Guild, no matter that the town lacked a church and only four of the nine were Episcopalians. It was a chance to sew and gossip.

She heard his footfall on the gingerbread porch at last, and rose to greet him. Whatever his delinquencies, she never let her feelings interfere with a warm welcome and a hug. He was hers and she was his until death parted them; she would do her best always. She knew it became her, and that he honored her for it. She had married a man whose character was as strong as her own.

"Hullo, dear," he said absently.

"What day is this?" she asked.

He looked stricken, as if searching for an anniversary or birthday.

"It's Thursday. Who's president?"

"Cleveland."

"What's my middle name?"

"Uh, Emily."

"You're all here after all. You're taking me to dinner. I've put away the food. We're going to eat at the Silver Queen chophouse in the Palace. It's been open for weeks and I've never been there. You're going to treat me."

"But the payroll—"

She plucked a tasseled shawl from a chair. "Off we go, dear," she said.

He submitted without further cavil. She felt a little

naughty but altogether pleased with herself. She took his arm and they descended the hill toward the Palace. Their house stood on a slope that commanded a magnificent view, but she felt ambivalent about it. She would have preferred Boston rooftops to wild and terrifying mountains.

The hotel restaurant and adjacent saloon filled an ell in the building and had a street entrance. She felt his arm steering her into the place, which dazzled her with its crystal chandeliers, rosewood pillars and snowy linen tablecloths. Imagine such things in Cashbox. She paused briefly to peer into the saloon. They fascinated her, perhaps because they were mysteries. She had scarcely been in one. This one had an elegant bar with frosted glass ducks on its backbar mirrors. Men lounged along it, a foot on the brass rail, seeming to enjoy themselves in the midst of their awful dissipation.

But then her view of iniquity was eclipsed by her progress through the busy restaurant toward a leather-quilted banquette table in the corner, in the soft light of an oil lamp. It was occupied by a man she knew at once by reputation, although she had never met him.

"Ah, Thaddeus! Won't you and Mrs. Webb join me? I've only just sat down," the man said as he struggled to his feet.

"Why, we'll do that," Thaddeus replied. "My dear, this is Cornelius Daley. He's in Cashbox a while, looking at mining properties."

She found herself the object of an intent gaze, from bright eyes so amiable she liked him at once, even if he was Irish. "What lovely company. Why, this evening'll be a rare treat, blessed by a handsome woman," he said.

What blarney, she thought, not minding it at all. But she regretted not having an evening alone with Thaddeus. Those two would talk about mining, and she would sit quietly and listen to assays and ores and winzes. She eyed the tumbler of amber fluid before Daley, and wondered how many of those he had consumed, and whether his amiability would coarsen as this evening progressed. Unlike most in the WCTU, she wasn't wholly opposed to spirits; she took Communion wine and supposed a proper lady might have a small glass of sherry without ruining herself. But she intended to watch Daley sternly, and if he showed the signs, she would signal Thaddeus.

The men ordered game platters, but she lacked a taste for venison and elk and wild turkey, and chose a small filet instead, accompanied by a red potato in seasoned butter and fresh peas they'd gotten from heaven knows where. Mr. Daley summoned the waiter and pointed to his empty glass. Soon another drink arrived, which he lifted to his lips with relish.

"Ah, Mrs. Webb, now's my chance to tell you how splendid a mining man Thaddeus is. There's none his match in the whole world of mining. He can take the most marginal of mines and wring a profit from it, as he did in Santa Rita and Virginia City. You're attached, madam, to a true American genius."

"Why, I've known that ever since he vanished into his offices," she replied, and wished she hadn't said it.

Daley's gaze caught hers again, and he smiled. "Some day he'll accumulate a fine fortune and retire. Most supervisors get a percent of profit as an incentive." He turned to Thaddeus. "I certainly hope the Hammons are doing you justice."

They weren't. Thaddeus was on straight eight hundred salary, no matter whether the mine poured forth riches or not.

Thaddeus nodded blandly, revealing nothing, and Portia perceived that maybe Daley was fishing as much as he was complimenting.

"All my supervisors get five percent of the profit," Daley said. "It inspires them."

"It doesn't help when there's no values left in the mine," Thaddeus said. "Why, in Ely, at the two-hundred-foot level—"

"Mrs. Webb, how are your lovely ladies coming with the school? That's at the top of your list, isn't it?"

Con Daley astonished her. "Why—we've hardly raised a dime. There's so little interest. All these men—they haven't brought families with them, so there's only twenty-six boys and girls . . ."

"Mining men are afraid the ore'll give out, Mrs. Webb, and they'll be stuck with a costly school just when the town starts to die. But that's not going to happen here. These are great mines—I've rarely seen the like. I tell you what: If your Cashbox Women's Club'll raise half the cost of a two-room schoolhouse—a thousand dollars, I imagine—I'll supply the other half. And then we'll see about teachers."

"Why, Mister Daley!"

That was how the dinner went. Thaddeus and Con Daley scarcely talked about mining at all, and every time Thaddeus turned to the topic—it was all he ever had on his mind—there was Cornelius, turning the conversation to her. She loved the attention, but where was it all leading? She eyed the third glass of whiskey in his hand.

He was handsome in his way, but unmistakable signs of soft living swelled the flesh of his face. It didn't detract from his elegance. She detected the slightest Back Bay inflection in his words, as if he really came from a Boston Unitarian knitting mill family. Maybe he was an Irish Protestant. Whatever he was, a bit of blarney seasoned his conversation. He enchanted her, and the evening whirled by faster than any she'd spent in Cashbox.

After a dessert of crêpes he ordered Napoleon in a snifter, and downed that in small sips while smoking an awful cigar. She listened intently for a slur in his voice; waited for a social lapse or two; studied his posture for any sign of excessive relaxation—and found none. It almost vexed her to see one imbibe so heavily with no effect.

Later, while she slipped her arm into Thaddeus's and they walked up the hill, she thought it had been much the most delightful evening she had experienced in Cashbox—or any other mining camp.

CHAPTER 26

· · · · · · · · · · · · · · · · ·

May Goode hung up her printer's smock and scrubbed her hands with a gritty soap that scraped most of the ink from them, although they looked as if they'd be stained forever. It had been a good day again. She had broken down two whole pages of the previous edition, and created a two-column-by-six-inch advertisement for the Cashbox Freight Company, using ruler lines and display type.

She had started writing small stories without even asking. When someone dropped in with a bit of news, she took notes and then wrote a draft with a pencil. Then she laboriously plucked type until she had her story. She had covered a wedding, a birth and a christening so far, and would do a business opening tomorrow.

She envied Willard, who could compose as he pulled the type from its boxes, his hands working like a burglar's. Her mind raced too fast; she could scarcely remember a sentence in the minutes it took to form its words, spelled properly, with all the capitals in place and the letters right-side up.

She pulled her thin shawl over her shoulders and peered into the late afternoon, fearing that Slug Svensrud would show up again to walk her home. She hadn't realized that there would be about ten or twelve men for every woman here, and she would not be ignored by the males no matter how aloof she kept herself. The constable terrified her, though he didn't mean to. He was only courting. But he was the person she dreaded most.

He didn't stop by this evening, and she sighed her relief. She liked him, which only made her silences more painful when he attempted to converse. She locked the door behind her with the skeleton key that hung on a nail, after making sure the kerosene lamp was out.

Willard Croker was spending less time there now that the work of producing *The Plain Truth* was proceeding without him. She didn't know what to make of him: he would turn his affability on and off like a gaslight, joke with her, rag her a little, only to become obdurate and harsh a moment later. Sometimes he and that Bass Boehm or that slippery lawyer would vanish into the street rather than say things she might overhear. Croker seemed rather devious—but who was she to criticize? It didn't matter. He was paying her, and it was almost enough.

Slug Svensrud had found shelter for her that first day. He had taken her to a Mrs. Flower, who had been widowed a year earlier in an Ophir Mine tragedy. Mrs. Flower took in laundry and lived in a log cabin with a clay floor, along with her skinny thirteen-year-old son, Albert. Her daughter Amy had died of the typhus. Mrs. Flower welcomed the dollar-fifty a week that May proposed to pay for a straw-stuffed tick on the pallet where the girl had bedded. It turned out to be a good arrangement. May had a roof over her head, over fifty cents each day for food and necessaries, and plenty of hot water and orange lye soap to scrub herself and her one change of clothing.

She bought some cheese for twenty cents at Baker's Mercantile—it would do for tonight—and went for a stroll, relishing her leisure. In the lengthening northern evenings she had walked far up the gulch, or south over empty flats, and even up some of the timbered slopes. But this evening she crossed Cashbox Creek and meandered toward the cemetery. Maybe she could find some little grave there that held someone else's Robby. She wandered through the cemetery, studying names and dates. She found a lot of children, their short lives carved into the wooden headboards, the lost infants of other mothers. They didn't interest her after all.

In a corner she found an unmarked grave, with only the mound of gray clay to tell an observer that someone lay

there. It tugged at her in a way that the marked graves
didn't. She sat down beside this sad place and wished she
could know who lay there. She thought to pray for his
soul, but she doubted that God would hear the prayer of a
mother who had killed her own boy.

Still, the grave seemed to fill an emptiness within her,
and she felt glad to sit and eat the cheddar after she had
freed it from its white butcher paper. She wondered what
she was doing in a graveyard, and had no answer. She
simply liked being there, as if the grave itself reached out
to comfort her.

Cashbox had been a good choice. Something wild and
intoxicating welled in her soul here. The sun, which had
fallen behind the high ridges to the west, no longer pum-
meled scents from the sagebrush and pine, but they lingered there along with the subtle scents of alpine flowers,
mixed with an occasional dash of woodsmoke.

From that vantage point above the town, she could see
its first lamps yellowing windows even while the sky
above slid from larkspur to indigo, and the first merry
stars poked through. The slopes blackened but the ridges
glowed with carmine, lemon and copper tones thrown by
the dying sun behind them. She had never seen anything
so enchanting: this rawboned town snugged under the
shoulders of fabulous rock laden with the metals that inspired dreams. She felt its vitality, its lust for life, its rough
hospitality genially offered to strangers—because everyone
was a stranger.

People flocked here to make their fortunes. In every direction loomed mysterious, primeval wilderness, the home
only of catamounts and wolves. Yet here, where no town
had existed only a few months before, men had poured in
to remake their lives, for it was in these raw spots that the
chances of renewing their lives were greatest. She hadn't
planned to remake her life; she had planned to bury herself
in some lost outpost, enduring her life until she died in utter anonymity.

But now she saw things differently. She had come to the

realization that a mortal life won't be buried. She couldn't contain the hungers, the hopes, the swift furtive fantasies that had filled her brim full after she arrived here. Oh, how she hated them, because she could never have them. She would never marry; never bear a child again; never seek for anything for fear of being found out and driven away.

Oh, how she dreaded it when Slug Svensrud opened the printshop door at six o'clock and grinned shyly at her. Three times he'd done that. It threw everything akimbo, and made her want what she could have only at her peril. She didn't know how to discourage him; how to tell him no, not now, *not ever*.

In the space of a few weeks she had learned that Cashbox could torture her more than the stone prison ever had. Here not an hour would pass without longing that verged on pain; there, the days slid by because her very helplessness within those cold walls was the necessary narcotic. She wanted things now. She wanted a new dress of bright blue calico so she might be pretty again. She had no needle and thread, no thimble or scissors or measuring tape or pattern, but somehow she would sew her dress and feel its joyous embrace of her body. She hadn't wanted anything for so long that the yearning astonished her.

She forced herself to think upon Robby, but she could no longer conjure up his image. His pinched face had blurred with the years, and threatened to vanish altogether. She rehearsed again those awful blurred moments when her frayed patience had snapped and a fury had erupted from some unknown chasm within her . . . and the memory of sobbing over his spasming little body while strangers gathered on the muddy street. But even that had blurred, and she could bring it to her consciousness only ritually, as if spoken for the thousandth time in a confessional where no absolution was ever offered and never could be. She didn't want that. She wanted her guilt fresh and painful so that she would know herself. How odd that she couldn't bring it to the forefront of her mind now, the way she had in her cell.

Had she come to the cemetery to renew her guilt? She supposed she had, and yet she could fashion no hairshirt for her heart to wear. Instead she had found a grave that had caught her curiosity because someone unknown to the world lay there. Maybe even Robby's grave would become nameless. She didn't want that.

She would have to find a way to tell Slug Svensrud never, never, never.

CHAPTER 27
. . . .

Sylvie watched raptly as a dozen journeyman masons dressed stone and laid it into the massive walls while ten carpenters anchored massive planks to the floor joists. Ever since construction began, she had spent hours at the site, filled with awe that all this was happening because of her.

It frightened her to think that every cent she had was going into this huge building. Either her club would succeed, or she'd be broke. But she refused to worry about that. Let them see her club when it was done. There would be crystal chandeliers, a walnut bar, a billiard room, a library, a study, a fine dining room with French cuisine, tapestries, overstuffed furniture—every comfort she could think of . . . if she had money enough.

Nearby, a straight and handsome woman watched the builders. Sylvie knew who she was and knew she was about to meet her. She knew also that she had choices to make. She could probably become a part of that woman's world if she wanted to, but it would run against her grain. The woman could bring members to Sylvie's club with a quiet word. Or keep members from joining it, also with a quiet word. But Sylvie knew she couldn't live in the world of sewing circles and altar guilds. She could only be herself.

"You're Mrs. Duvalier, I believe. I'm Portia Webb. Is this yours?"

"Well, I guess so." Sylvie laughed uncertainly. She had a hunch about how she'd fare with the leading lady of Cashbox.

"Thaddeus—my husband—says it's going to be a club."

"That's right. The best club I can manage. For gentlemen."

"How strange. In Cashbox."

"It's pretty strange, all right. There's nothing like it in all the West. They'll turn green in Denver. They'll come all the way from San Francisco, and never go back. I'm going to invite Grover Cleveland. Once you've won over a president, you can't lose. You know how it goes—George Washington slept here."

"Well, it's certainly daring to build a gentlemen's club in Cashbox," said Mrs. Webb. "There aren't ten."

"I wouldn't know. But I want to do it. I like gentlemen."

"I suppose Mister Duvalier will be coming soon to manage it."

"Actually, my husband's Beau Pitt. I use my maiden name. He's in Europe somewhere. I don't expect him."

Sylvie watched Mrs. Webb's lips compress. She knew she was getting into quicksand. It would probably cost her some members.

"You'll hire a manager then?"

"Oh, no. I'll run it. They'll have to get used to me."

"I see. Sometimes I wish I had your freedom, Mrs. Pitt."

"Oh, call me Sylvie. Sylvie Duvalier."

"Is he—are you . . . still married?" She smiled. "I'm being nosy."

"Oh, I'm not sure. We never got divorced, if that's what you mean. I guess so. It's hard to know, though. I never knew if half the people in my family were married."

Mrs. Webb laughed. "You're a tease. I think you're having fun with me."

"No one ever believes it. But it's true. I was never brought up. There was no one around to bring me up except a crazy governess, so I just did whatever I felt like."

Mrs. Webb sighed. "Everything was the opposite for me. I went to Miss Porter's, and they taught me so many rules I can't remember them all. I can't do a thing without wondering if it's right. I sometimes wish I had your daring."

"I inherited it. I come from an explosives family. I mean, the Duvaliers were chemists for the Du Ponts. My father fiddled with dynamite until it blew him into heaven. I think that's where he went. They said so in church. My grandfather ate gunpowder soup—chicken stock, croutons, leeks and black powder—and said it kept him from vice. He always lit a pipe after lunch, and I was always afraid what might happen, but it never did."

"Sometimes I wish I had relatives like that. I come from a quiet family."

"Oh, it gets worse. My aunt is an anarchist. She wants to blow up the whole world, starting with the New York Stock Exchange. My stepmother studied homeopathic medicine. She gives lectures on quinine and hemophilia. My governess studied the bumps on my head and said I'd have trouble with lawyers. When you come from a family that's made gunpowder for a hundred years, you never know how you'll turn out. We're all unpredictable. Only a Duvalier would come to Cashbox and build a Taj Mahal."

Mrs. Webb blinked. "You have more faith in the future of Cashbox than I do."

"It all depends on a railroad. My club'll be so famous they'll build a railroad just to bring the sightseers. I think Mister Webb should join it. He could be my first member."

"Oh, I don't think he would."

"Wouldn't he like a club?"

"He's—not aware of his surroundings. He's perfectly happy in a wooden chair, working at a battered old desk. His mind's off somewhere, ores, hoist cables . . . all that. No, a club wouldn't mean anything to him."

"But I'm going to offer the best food in the Rockies."

"I know, but Thaddeus lacks a palate. He's happy with a bowl of oatmeal. Without salt. Most of the time he doesn't know what's on the table, poor dear. He doesn't even see what I wear—" She stopped suddenly.

"Oh, men are all like that. You send Mister Webb around, and he'll join. Membership's a hundred a year."

Mrs. Webb gazed into some infinity. "No, Mrs. Duvalier. I see him too little as it is. Every second he's in my parlor is precious to me. A gentlemen's club—I'd never see him."

Something buried in Mrs. Webb touched Sylvie. "Maybe there should be a woman's night. On Sundays or something."

Mrs. Webb brightened. "I'm pleased to meet you at last. I'm on my way to the cobbler, and I really must be getting home."

Sylvie watched the woman stroll toward Main Street. Something in her walk suggested she'd spent hours at Miss Porter's with a book on her head, learning how ladies do it. Ladies seemed to float along without a wiggle. Sylvie had tried to walk like a lady when she was a girl. She and Tennessee had lady-walking contests in the upstairs hall, and Tennessee always won. She could walk like a stick. Sylvie's bottom always swished, and at the age of fourteen she had given up.

She found herself liking Portia Webb, and she sensed that the town's grand dame liked her too. She knew she would never fit into the WCTU meetings up the hill but she sensed that Mrs. Webb might become a quiet ally.

She liked men better anyway. Men were always doing stuff that excited her: making deals, buying stocks and bonds, electing someone or other. Men talked about steam engines and electricity and telescopes that could see Saturn's rings, and the yellow press. Women talked about other things: novels, actresses, Paris styles, McGuffey Readers, children, and doctors. That was fine but not for her. Sylvie hoped her club members wouldn't treat her as a waitress. She liked men and wanted to learn everything she could about business.

If she had any members. She had counted heavily on Thaddeus Webb, superintendent of the most important mine, to lead the parade. But now she wondered if she would have any members at all, except for Con. He'd join. Maybe she was building a club just for herself and Cornelius Daley.

The idea amused her. He always made her so comfortable. She felt a great tenderness toward him, and knew he felt that way about her. It had begun as friendship, but now it was more; something she couldn't define. He never manipulated or pressured her, or tried to make her dependent on him. Everything he did announced to her she was a sovereign human being whose will he would respect. If she ever chose Con Daley for a lover, it would be because she wanted to, and not because she was surrendering to him.

Cornelius was just the opposite of a seducer. She never felt any danger in his attentions. Sometimes she wished he would seduce her, overwhelm her, strip away her inhibitions and plunge her into an ecstatic new world. But she knew those pangs were the ancient demons that often demolished women and sucked them into a whirlpool of anguish and fear. A habitual seducer would soon seek other conquests. No. This man was offering her the respect no impassioned seducer could ever give her. She loved him for that, and loved being with him.

Her thoughts disturbed her. And yet she yearned for the day when Cornelius would gather her into his arms and kiss her. She knew she would meet his lips with utter joy.

CHAPTER 28

• • • • • • • • • • • • • • • •

Cornelius Daley studied the assay reports, mesmerized by what he was reading. The six samples that Webb had sent Johann Mueller ranged from fifty to sixty percent silver, one to two percent gold, and most of the rest lead. Those were better than the typical concentrations found in vugs.

He knew the cash value of the ore would depend on several factors, including the way the samples had been collected. So he could only hazard an educated guess. The lowest figure he could come up with was five thousand dollars a ton; the highest around seven thousand. It would take only twenty tons of this incredible ore to put the Giltedge Mine on its feet. And it could be done in a week. The Hammons would never need his capital.

He sighed, feeling his chances of slicing the pie slide away forever. Providence had rescued the innocents. He wondered how large the vug was and whether it would make millionaires of the Hammons. Only some of the bonanzas on the Comstock could equal it. The Hammons would hang onto it for dear life and suck it dry. For once he rued his habit of waiting until a district had started to prove its reserves. This time the ground floor was the place to be.

But he couldn't do anything about that. He could only proceed with the riskier approach. He had to find Ambrose Gill and talk him into selling his property. A trip around the world. A mansion. He'd even offer Gill a partnership. He'd buy Gill out for anything the man asked.

He rented the livery outfit and whipped the surly nag up the gulch looking for his man, stopping at every little camp in the Cashbox district. He asked in Blackhawk and Robinson, and even drove as far as Copperopolis way north of the Cashbox Mountains, asking about Ambrose Gill and hoping he didn't sound too eager. They all seemed to know the Silver Fox, and got a canny look in their eyes as they listened: "Gill, now. I heard of him. Got some fine ore, don't he?"

But a week's hunting yielded nothing. Daley returned to the Palace and settled in. He would spend the summer waiting in Cashbox if he had to. Most evenings he dined with Sylvie, who grew more gorgeous and exuberant each day as she turned herself into an entrepreneur. Every time he was tempted to return to Helena, the thought of her stayed him.

Then one morning Ambrose Gill sat down beside him at breakfast and poured himself some coffee from a pewter pot. Daley set down *The Plain Truth* and waited.

"A man can't walk a mile without ten people tellin' him you're looking for me. I don't want to talk to you; I'm not talking to one that didn't weep a tear for old Ambrose at my wake."

Con Daley didn't reply, though he could scarcely keep his tongue from wagging. Instead he extracted a breast-pocket wallet and laid a fifty-dollar banknote on the linen.

"Bless me, I've not seen a one of those in a while, Daley. Lookit her, sittin' there on that fancy cloth like it owned me. What'm I to make of it?"

"It's an offer," said Daley.

"Ah, for that claim on that slope betwixt and between the Giltedge and Ophir. You never grieved me at my wake. It made me mad. I think I'll try one of these fancy breakfasts. I eat beans mostly out at my ledge. Now what's all that stuff I've never et before?"

Con summoned the waiter and ordered with a wave of the hand.

"How is your ledge? Still paying?" Con asked softly.

"She's holding up, but I can see the end. She's good for about two more trips to Cashbox, and then I'll be skunked."

"You could work in the mines," said Con, knowing he was insulting the prospector.

"I could but I won't," bristled Gill. "You got the wrong feller, Daley."

The waiter arrived with toast and jarred jams on a silver salver, and then brought oatmeal in a china bowl. Ambrose Gill slapped preserves on the toast and wolfed it but scorned the oatmeal. "Porridge. Fancy place like this serves a man porridge. I'd like a lick of sidepork."

Daley smiled. "I suppose you'll be off looking for a new ledge. I'd be willing to grubstake you. I do it all the time. You find something and one-third's mine."

"I don't need your grubstake, Daley me boy."

"It's an offer. I've started a few men that way. They made fortunes; I profited too. A man that knows silver ores is hard to find. You'd be a man to stake, I can see that."

"You got the blarney. That's how you got rich."

Daley smiled. He pulled out his wallet again and extracted a second fifty-dollar banknote and set it on top of the first, beside Gill's coffee cup.

Gill pretended not to see. "This here repast gits better and better," he muttered. "The more I eat, the better it tastes."

The waiter brought a plate brimming with bacon, sausage, and Eggs Benedict.

"Holy Mary, this place even got eggs," said Gill. "I didn't think there was an egg this side of Helena. I don't know what cheese stuff they're swimming in, but I'll have a lick."

Daley let the man eat. Gill tackled the whole array of food, muttering cheerfully to himself. The banknotes lay neglected but Con Daley knew that they weren't really ignored.

Gill patted his stubbled face with the snowy napkin. That it?"

"Sweets," said Daley. He withdrew another fifty and laid it carefully on the two others. "That's breakfast."

"I'm not hungry," said Gill.

Daley plucked his notes from the tablecloth and slid them back into the wallet. "See me if you want a grub-stake, Gill," he said, more matter-of-factly than he felt.

Ambrose Gill swilled the last of his coffee and sighed. "That wake ruint my life," he said. "I haven't got a friend left and I don't want none. I disown them all. Not a one do I ever want to see. They never cared about me feelings. I'm going to live the rest of me days without friends. I'll give 'em me death a little early by leaving the district. Here."

He plowed into his pocket and extracted a rumpled document. "I'm a man of my word. I told you from the grave I'd give it to you, and I'm givin' it to you like I said. Take it."

Daley set his cup down gently and read the mining patent. It was in good order. Ambrose Gill had done the assessment work to satisfy the federal government and had received clear title to the claim.

"Write something that says I'm deeding it to you, and I'll sign her," Gill said. "I'm giving you this out of undying and everlasting friendship. After you make a million, remember how you got it free and clear from old Ambrose Gill, a man of honor lying in his box at his wake."

"How could I forget, Ambrose?"

"I suppose you'll turn around and sell it for a thousand dollars. That's how you financiers get rich."

Con Daley smiled. He summoned paper, ink and a nib from the registration desk and scratched out a deed of the property to himself. Silently he handed it to Gill, who read it carefully, troubling past the words. Daley handed Gill the nib.

"We should have a witness," he said, and asked the waiter to bring Loren Whitmore or Walsh Lake.

The waiter brought them both; Gill signed; both hostelers witnessed; and Daley tucked the patented mining claim into his suitcoat along with the deed. He would probably own the Giltedge after all.

"Do you want a snort, Ambrose?" he asked.

"I quit drinking because I got no friends," Gill replied. "That wake showed me who cared about old Gill and who didn't. Buncha moochers, that's what. That wake was a good thing."

"How about a grubstake? You'll need one to look for a new ledge."

"Well, I could use that, I guess."

Daley retrieved a hundred dollars from his billfold and laid it on the tablecloth.

"You're true blue, Daley," Gill said, pocketing the notes. "You gimme a hundred so you can make a thousand. That's the Silver Fox for you."

CHAPTER 29

· · · · · · · · · · · · · · · · ·

Tonight he would do it. Casper Penrose clutched his fifty-cent hoard and edged through the payday crowds toward The Oriental Saloon just beyond Cashbox Creek. No one would snitch on him this busy Saturday night. All around him he saw boisterous boyos gabbing on the street in the late June evening, slicked up for a night on the town. Oh, they were a fast bunch.

Casper wanted to be faster than any boyo in town. He could hardly stand his parents. All he saw was drudgery and a dirt-poor life with no fun in it. He was going to have fun and be just as sharp as anyone. He had gotten the hang of faro and poker just by hanging around the saloons. They hardly noticed a kid. But he wasn't a kid; he was almost full-grown. Even the girls noticed he was a man. He bought witch hazel so he smelled good, and pomade to shape his sandy hair in a real pompadour.

The time he asked Cindy if she wanted to spark, she giggled and ran away from him. He just laughed. Prissy pigtailed girl. She was fifteen too, but she didn't know her rear from her ear. This time, he'd *do it*. The thought sent his pulse racing. He couldn't wait no more. He hung around the sporting houses, watching the dudes go in and out, peeking through the doors into lamp-lit parlors. A few times he saw some of the ladies all skimpied up and ready for a hot time.

He had tried everyone else. One time he bought some Bugler cigarette papers and snitched some tobacco and rolled one, but it made him sick. He got over it; you had to start somewhere. And a few times he had soaked up lots of booze, too. On crowded nights in the saloons there was always a half-empty glass around. He sipped Old Quaker once, and even some Red Horse mint gin. No one ever cared, except maybe old Constable Svensrud, who chased him out a few times.

He edged through the doors of The Oriental into a smoky cacophony. The miners were all getting rid of their pay as fast as they could. He watched them belly up to the bar and the gaming tables. But what he really studied was the stairway to the second floor. Some dude trotted down the stairs, and then the serving girl after him, and he knew they'd *done it*. He studied the boyo for signs of it, but couldn't see how it had changed him. His pa would never know.

He dodged to the rear and paused before the faro game operated by One-Eyed Jack Wool. Casper had never seen such an awful man. He looked skinnier than a consumptive, and coughed like one as he lipped his crooked cheroot. He wore a black patch over his right eye, but the other one glared maliciously at the world, its gaze skewering everything. He wore a grimy white shirt with a fresh collar, a black bowtie, and a black suit that was shiny at the elbows.

This booming night he had a smirky casekeeper operating the abacus-like casebox where the play of each card was recorded. On slow nights Wool operated the layout alone. But this was tally day. Miners crowded around the green oilcloth, laying their two-bit white chips on painted black images of cards, sometimes coppering the bet with a brass token they placed on top of their wager. This meant they were betting the card to lose. Casper knew all about that stuff.

"Any more money I can skin you outta, gents?" asked Wool in a Vaseline voice. "I'll clean you all out before the night's over. Buck the Tiger!"

It made Casper wonder. Most of the cardsharps he'd watched were flannel mouths, telling dudes they'd probably win, jollying them all the time. But not One-Eyed Jack Wool. He sneered at his victims, insulted them, and still they flocked to his tables. He frightened Casper. On Good Friday Wool had pulled a little Smith and Wesson from that black suit and shot a man dead who accused him of dealing from his sleeve.

Wool drew the first card from a slot in the side of the faro box. This card, the loser, was a king. Men groaned. The next card, a deuce, was the winner. One man whooped as he collected four chips for the four he had wagered. Most of the men had neither won nor lost, and let their bets ride.

Casper studied the casebox and noted that only one trey had been played. Three were still inside the faro bank. Of course any of the three could either win or lose, depending on whether they were drawn first or second, but the trey seduced Casper. He would win. He had to win twice to get the two dollars.

He pushed the stack of five dimes onto the painted three while the others laid their bets. Then Wool noticed, and that fiendish eye stared right at Casper.

"That yours, punk?"

Casper was afraid to speak. The fiend might shoot him. He nodded.

"You'll lose it, punk."

"I'll win."

Wool grinned, the cheroot dangled and spilled ash.

Casper waited impatiently while the bets went down, his

loins already stirring in anticipation of what he'd do if he won. Two greenbacks, that's all he needed.

Then Wool drew the first card—a trey—and the second, a jack. Miners laughed. Casper lost, and suddenly wanted to cry.

Wool snatched up the dimes. "I'll clean you out again, punk," he said. "Now scram."

Casper stared miserably at the empty green oilcloth where his dimes and dreams had rested. Then the faro bank with the tiger painted on it. The gambler had cheated. He wanted to yell it, but that's how the man got killed. Instead, Casper backed away, and fled into the lavender evening.

He stood outside, dashed and grim, watching all the boyos enjoy themselves. Up the hill he heard a piano being pounded by some professor. He felt rotten. Now he would have to cadge a lot more tips carrying valises to the Palace until he could try again. But he couldn't wait any more. The need rushed through him like lava every time he thought about naked ladies.

The first time it happened it had scared him witless. His thing swelled into a pole and wouldn't go down. He'd busted it, that's what. He figured he would spend the rest of his life some sort of freak. He'd pee uphill all his life. He would have to tell his parents something went bad in him. But it finally collapsed like an old wineskin, and he fell to his knees and sobbed to God he'd never think bad stuff about women again. For weeks he had feared it might get busted again. But now he was slicker than grease, and he knew all about that. He just wanted to *do it*.

It was past ten and it still wasn't dark enough. He examined the sporting houses with a connoisseur's eye. Minnie's was up the slope, but it didn't have windows in the rooms. The kitchen in back had windows though, and sometimes ladies would come back there hardly wearing nothing. Maybe he should try The Parlor. It squatted down in the bottom, with Cashbox Creek almost running under its feet. It was nothing but a plank shack with a sod roof,

so badly lit he couldn't hardly see the two fat women and
the Chinee inside. He never liked that one much; in spite
of its name it didn't have a parlor at all, just little cribs
with the green oilcloth shades drawn. And mosquitoes everywhere.

Naw, the best was Charlotte Keiserling's. He eyed the
sky unhappily. The long twilight lingered. He preferred it
pitch black. Hell, no one would notice. They were all too
busy having a skookum time. He scaled the slope on an
angle that would take him above Charlotte's place. It glistened in the twilight like a bar of silver, with yellow light
leaking from all the windows. A red lantern bobbled at the
threshold, caught by eddying breezes.

This joint stood on the edge of town with nothing but
wooded black slopes behind. He liked that. He liked to see
the whitewashed parlor with the piano in it. He liked the
tasseled red velvet drapes in each room, leaking scarlet
light where they hadn't been closed tightly. That was his
idea of a sporting house; lots of red velvet and real nice
furniture and pretty ladies in almost their nothings.

Casper squinted at the fugitive blue still staining the horizon. He edged close and heard voices and music. He
tried one window but the velvet drapes had been pulled
tight. He tried two more, and then found a careless one,
with light eddying from the fringes. He peeked in and saw
an empty bed in the bronze glow of an opened door. This
would be it. He'd see some fast stuff tonight. He'd already
seen everything there was to see. He knew who had this
room; she was a brunette with black hair top and bottom,
and lots of tricks. He wished she'd do her fancies on him.
He crouched and waited, while his pulse climbed and the
swelling began in his groin.

Then she came in carrying a lamp. Some boyo followed
her, grinning like a goose. She smiled and set down her
lamp and didn't waste time tugging that dinky chemise she
wore until it dropped to the floor. Casper got itchy, watching her breasts bobble. Then she was helping the dude

with his union suit buttons, and they were both having a
whale of a time.

The hand clamped the back of his shirt and whumped
him upright so fast and hard he scarcely knew what had
happened. He squirmed like a caught trout, but he knew he
wasn't going nowhere. He finally got a glimpse of the
man; it was the pegleg.

"Peeking without paying, izat it, punk?"

"I wasn't doing nothing—"

He pushed Casper ahead, clumping along behind him,
that massive fist holding a lot of shirt.

"Lemme go! I wasn't doing nothing! I won't come no
more!"

"You come here too much, punk. They're always asking
how come I don't catch you, but you're faster than a one-
leg man."

He was pushing Casper toward the rear, and then up the
stairs into the fragrant kitchen, where Charlotte Keiserling
stood, unsmiling.

CHAPTER 30
• • • • • • • • • • • • • • • • • •

Regina Maltz opened the door of her Majestic range and
studied the four apple pies baking in its bosom, worried they might be burned. She'd had difficulty damping
the fire. But their crusts looked golden. With hotpads she
lifted them out one by one and set them on her white
enameled table to cool. Their intoxicating aromas perme-
ated the kitchen and crept through the boardinghouse.

"There, Kermit. It has to cool for a while and then you
can take it."

Kermit Reilly sighed. "Miss Maltz, I don't know
how—"

"Oh, pshaw. That's what I'm here for." She eyed him

for signs of the dizziness that still afflicted him. "Are you sure you can make it? I can get a wagon. . . ."

"I have spells," he muttered.

"You're welcome to stay on if you need."

"No, thankee, my cabin's lookin' like home to me now."

"Well, you be careful tomorrow. The first day. You quit if it gets hard."

He nodded. She had found him light work that would earn him a dollar a day while he recovered. Emil Aller, the water-wagon man, needed help. Cashbox was growing so fast, he'd told her while he filled her four pails, that he couldn't keep up. He delivered water at a penny for each bucket drawn from the two great casks on his wagon, but now there were plumb too many places needing it. Not everyone had dug a well. He could use another feller until the Cashbox Water Company got its mains into town in a couple of months. So Kermit Reilly had a temporary job until he could go into the pits again—if ever.

It tugged at her to see Kermit off. He'd been like a son to her, smiling shyly and brightening her life with homely talk after his pain began to diminish. Now he was tongue-tied, and she knew how hard he was trying to thank her. So she just shooed him off after giving him a big hug, and watched him slowly labor toward the gulch, with a duffel bag in one hand and a pasteboard box containing the pie in the other. She sighed, feeling as bereft as a mother sending a son off to war.

She undid her apron and hung it from a hook, placed another apple pie in a wicker basket, and covered it with a linen cloth. This one she would deliver herself. The other two would be her boarders' dessert that night—if they didn't snitch most of it first. She pierced into a golden June afternoon, the freshets of air singing their gladness, and walked over to Main Street, and then to the intersection with Pine, and into the gingerbreaded home and offices of Attorney J. Ernest Potter-Pride. These were announced by a small sign with gilded letters on black, dangling from a wrought-iron fixture.

She entered to a jangle of bells and waited in the small reception room.

"It's Miss Maltz," said the attorney, looming in the door. "Oh, I see you've been at it again."

He ushered her into his gloomy office, encased with orange-bound lawbooks and rogue furniture.

She handed him the basket. He lifted a corner of the linen, discovering the pie, and beamed. "You make the best apple pies in the territory, Miss Maltz. I don't know why I'm the lucky cuss who gets them."

"You know why," she said. "And I'll never forget what you did. I can't ever repay. But I can bake a little treat for a bachelor man."

"Well, ah, that town lot was nothing."

"Not just the lot. You asked people to help me and they did. And then you talked that Mister Boehm out of hurting me. I couldn't repay you with a thousand pies."

This exchange had occurred each time she had brought him a pie, scarcely varying at all, as if it were some sort of liturgy.

"Well," he muttered, "they don't last a day. Between torts and injunctions, I'm off to my pantry for another chop of it. It must be the sugar and cinnamon. Makes a man yearn for domestic felicities."

"We all need domestic comforts, Mister Pride."

"Yes, ah, well, thank you, Miss Maltz. Say, is my little act of, ah, civic improvement much talked about at your table?"

"Oh, they talk about you, sir. But they don't call it civic improvement."

"What do people call it, eh?"

"Getting your scabby client off the hook."

"I see. Well, these things meld together. I wouldn't deny, of course, that I had an interest in protecting Mister Boehm from the calumny I sensed was a-building. But of course any shrewd counselor knows that his conduct redounds to public benefit. In the course of our small labors on behalf of a client, we perform a larger public good; a blessing to our commonweal.

"Now, when I was counseling with my client, I saw the chance to be of real service to my fellow mortals; to you, the Florence Nightingale of Cashbox; to that poor injured chap—well, you see, I stepped in. I thought to supply you with a valuable town lot—oh, yes, it was appreciating nicely and worth a pretty penny—as a way of softening the hardness of my client's conduct—but also, of course, to be an inspiration to others. I realized I could make myself a paragon of civic virtue in Cashbox, and encourage others to follow suit by contributing to a new boardinghouse for you."

He paused, jut-jawed, his eyes blazing, his flowing gray locks framing his face.

"You slick-tongued old jasper," she said. "You and your slippery pals were in a jam."

"Why, Miss Maltz, your thoughts are—indelicate."

"That's me. Consarn it, I like you anyway," she said. "And I owe you a thousand pies whether I like you or not."

"I see."

"I like almost anybody. That's the way I am. I had a boarder in Leadville, a pickpocket. I knew it and I still let him board. He stole my rents one afternoon and I never saw him again. I just like people. I even like you."

Ernest Potter-Pride pursed his lips. "I see," he said.

"Now that you're reformed, and a model citizen, there's something I want you to do."

He waited like a crow poised for flight.

"I want you to contact the Giltedge Mine and get Kermit Reilly some money for his injury. They didn't have enough shoring in their tunnels. Everyone says so. They should give him his lost pay at least."

"Under current statutes, Miss Maltz, they're not liable. But they should be. I agree, they should be."

"Well I'd like you to try."

"I presume he has the fee?"

"No, but if you're the man of civic virtue you say you are, you'll donate your time. He's still poorly. Maybe he'll never be able to work in the mines again. The poor boy's so young. How'll he earn his keep? He needs help. It might take only a visit to Mister Webb, or a letter or two."

"But I can't make a living handing out free legal counsel."

"Well, then. Don't talk to me about your gifts to Cashbox. After you take care of Kermit, I've got other tasks for you. The cornet band needs uniforms. They've voted for scarlet. They need them before the Fourth of July. We need a schoolhouse—there's almost thirty children wanting their ABCs. And after that we should do something about licensing those—those brothels. And we should have a saloon ordinance too. But Kermit comes first."

"Ouch! I'm hoist on my own petard. Oh, all right. You're an irresistible force, like a Supreme Court judge. Send him to me and I'll get the facts of the case. I don't suppose I can do much. Webb's tough."

She smiled. "Thank you, Ernest. You're a sweet man after all." She rose. "I'll take the basket and you can return the pie tin. I'll be inviting you to supper in a day or two, if you don't mind eight or ten boarders trying to clean the platter before you get a fork into it. After supper we'll talk about the things that need doing in Cashbox. Just little things. We have six or eight widows that need looking after. We need an infirmary and a doctor. The baseball team lacks bats and gloves, and they want to put a diamond on some of your vacant lots. You've got the only level land."

"Why, ah, certainly. Name the hour and I'll be there. Miss Maltz, you have a way that I admire. You're a force to be reckoned with, like Sitting Bull. If something needs doing in a mining camp, there you are, hectoring people until it happens. No man is your equal. If I resist, you'll stop bringing me pies."

"Oh, the Ivory soap again."

"Won't you let me compliment a lovely lady?"

"Ernest Potter-Pride, I don't trust a word struck from your slippery tongue."

"Well, any smart lawyer would take that for the supreme compliment. It makes me happy," he said, escorting her to the door. "But you should call me silver-tongued, not slippery-tongued."

"Flannel-mouthed, Ernest. You're senator material."

"Senator, am I? Consider me your servant, Miss Maltz," he said.

They laughed on the porch. That silver-haired windbag tickled her. Why did she like the old goat so?

CHAPTER 31

• • • • • • • • • • • • • • • •

Cornelius Daley herded J. Ernest Potter-Pride down a grassy slope to Cashbox Creek, and then leapt the two-foot flow. The lawyer hesitated, and lumbered across also, muddying his patent leather shoes. Daley poked along the brushy slope until he found Gill's tunnel, half-concealed behind chokecherry brush.

"Here," he said gruffly. The attorney annoyed him.

"Ah . . . ," said Pride. "Is it safe?"

"We'll see."

Daley extracted a jackknife from the kit he carried, opened it, and stabbed log uprights and crosspieces the way any timber foreman in a mine would, looking for rot. He found none. These sets were only two years old. He edged inside a few feet and then lit his coal-oil lantern.

"It doesn't feel safe," said Pride.

Daley ignored the man. Long-haired, jut-jawed Ernest Potter-Pride, the terror of stockholders and the scourge of capitalists, looked nervous enough to bolt for daylight. Daley pulled a geologist's pickhammer from the canvas bag and chipped samples of jasper from the mouth of the claim while Pride waited for the roof to fall on him. Daley dropped the rocks in a cotton sack and labeled it Number One.

"Ernest, you can measure it. We need to have the length."

"All the way to the end?" The lawyer peered doubtfully into the blackness. His jaw no longer jutted. "I lack light."

"It angles toward the Giltedge line. Here, let me look." Daley wandered down the horizontal shaft, poking sets with his knife. Only one showed much rot, and Daley eyed the jasper above it suspiciously. Gill had driven a horizontal shaft through steeply tilted strata—not the safest way to tunnel. "It's fine, Ernest," he said. "Note how the jasper slants. It's important. The Giltedge ore slants the same way."

He handed the attorney a tape measure and nodded toward the rear. It wasn't far, really; never out of sight of daylight.

"I can just estimate it," said Attorney Pride.

Daley took the tape from the man's manicured hand and walked the length of the shaft. The jasper at the head looked little different from the jasper at the mouth.

A brief investigation revealed that Gill had quit after about seventy feet. Probably the assay values had declined and he had given up. Daley bagged two more samples, one at the stope and one in the middle. If Mueller found any silver values in these samples, especially the rock taken from the outcrop, Daley would have what he wanted.

The attorney trotted out with unseemly haste. Daley smiled.

They retreated to the rutted mine road and the livery gig, and Daley drove back to town feeling uncommonly cheerful. He had the feeling he owned the whole town.

"You can mine it or you can start a suit," said Pride. "We haven't discussed fees, my friend. I'm willing to handle it on a contingency basis—for only a third. I don't need half."

Daley laughed. "Unfortunately for you, I can pay you."

"Well, my fee'll be rather high, you know. It'll take a

year or two. Eat up thousands of hours. Require a lot of evidence."

"Five hundred a month retainer, a bonus if you win swiftly."

"Ah, sorry, my friend, too low. That's the same as last time. Now, ah, what do you mean by bonus—and for exactly what?"

"I'll decide the amount. It'll depend on how long this drags out, whether I get it all, and my overall gain. Also, how you proceed. I grow weary of bad press."

"Bad press. When's that ever slowed you? Suppose you lose . . . ?"

Daley smiled. "That's where the ore apexed, isn't it?"

"Maybe it apexed on the Giltedge."

"That's what I employ you for," Daley said. "Find out."

"Ah, Cornelius. Cases like this enchant me. I work for the joy of it. I'm a public-spirited man. They're telling me I'm a paragon of civic-mindedness. I believe in sharing the wealth. Would you settle with the Hammons if you have to?"

"Penny-ante poker bores me."

"All right. I'll file in two or three days. It's not going to take long to prepare. You'll claim the entire body of ore that apexed on the Gill property, now in your possession. That'll include everything in the Giltedge and the value of everything that's been removed from it. You'll ask for an injunction halting further removal of ore by the Hammons until it's settled. The Silver Fox has arrived."

"I'm not fond of that name."

"I am hypothetically quoting the Hammons."

"I could just mine it, you know. I've the right to follow that lead straight into the Giltedge. All I'd need from you is injunctions—stop them from taking out any more of my ore."

"You could, but the shoe'd be on the other foot. They'd pepper the court for injunctions stopping you from mining inside the Giltedge claim. Either way, they'll delay any way they can."

"That's what you'll be paid for, Ernest. They've stolen my ore. See that justice is done." Con Daley smiled faintly.

He dropped Potter-Pride at his offices and watched the handsome man spring up his steps with aplomb. Pride would first wipe mud from his shiny shoes and then pour himself a stiff shot of Old Crow now that he had just squeaked past the mortal danger of an abandoned tunnel. About one shot for every twenty feet, Daley figured.

He steered his livery buggy to the barn, feeling empty. He put off the feeling as long as he could, knowing it would catch up to him sooner or later. He was never ready for these moments. In Helena he had simply shut himself up in his twelve-room brick pile on Dearborn for a few weeks.

He had learned that drink didn't help. He had tried to lubricate his dark passage with bourbon a time or two, but it only lengthened his torment. His bleakest moods caught him at the very moment of victory. Let him reap a fortune and he'd slide into a two-month funk.

He thought of going back to Helena to wait out the lawsuit in comfort. But he knew he wouldn't. Cashbox had him in its thrall. Or anyway, Sylvie did. He would stay here, badger Pride on the general principle that lawyers needed a periodic hotfoot if they were to resolve your sluggard case sometime before you died, and explore his other properties—the Ophir Mine and Sylvie Duvalier. Both still in the exploratory stage, with reserves unknown.

He turned in the horse and buggy at the Overstreet OK Livery Barn, and walked into town, resisting the itch to down a few shots at the Shamrock Saloon, in the rare good company of Sourmash Charlie.

Sylvie. He needed her suddenly. She went through bad spells the way he did, but they both brightened when they dined together, as they often did. She always lit something in him with that crooked smile of hers and with her dishabille even when she was immaculately groomed.

Sylvie. He steered toward her lots on Cashbox Street,

where her clubhouse was rising miraculously. Recklessly rising would be more accurate. She hadn't taken his advice about waiting for the railroad. Little did she know mining camps.

He found a dozen masons hard at work on a rectangular building made of dressed limestone—actually slack from the Ophir. They were doing a handsome job of the ashlar masonry, dressing each stone and mortaring it in random patterns.

Great windows with arches and keystones graced the front, windows from which gentlemen of means could watch the traffic from wingchairs. Rock had been her only choice; Helena brick was too far away. Luckily for her, Cashbox had a lime kiln now, and mortar was at hand. Sylvie's Exchange Club would be the finest edifice in Cashbox—and maybe the Territory.

She had seemed upset recently. Money worries, he guessed. He continued to the Palace Hotel, needing her company. They'd been friends for weeks. Whenever he was with her, the whole world seemed sunny. They were still calling it friendship, but he knew it was more than that. He loved her. She had only to bestow her crooked smile on him to melt him like wax.

He plunged into the hotel and found her reading *The Plain Truth* while sipping a demitasse in the restaurant. She saw him coming and waited solemnly, some darkness of flesh under her eyes.

"Look at this," she said, pointing to a front-page item in The Cashbox Till column.

He sat beside her, pulled out his spectacles, and read: "A Mrs. Duvalier is building a fancy club on Cashbox Street. She says it'll be for Gentlemen only, which excludes all the Best Citizens in this burg. Mrs. Duvalier wears a matrimonial ring, but we have seen no sign of a Husband. She does, however, reside at the Palace Hotel, where a certain Mining Capitalist also resides. She seems to have plenty of money, judging from the building being erected by a large crew of masons. We welcome the Lady, and wish we could all be Gentlemen. The nature of her club remains to be seen."

"I should sue him."

"What's there to sue about?"

"The insinuation."

"Just ignore it. That's the price you pay for the life you've chosen."

She sighed. "I guess you're right. Do you pay a price, Con?"

"I do."

"What price? Is that too nosy?"

He contemplated her question. "They call me the Silver Fox," he said.

CHAPTER 32

• • • • • • • • • • • • • • • •

Con Daley appraised Sylvie, who was toying with a chophouse lunch. She was wearing a mood like a shroud.

"What's wrong?" he asked.

"Nothing's wrong."

"Isn't the building going well?"

"It's beautiful. I stand in the street and watch every stone go where it's destined to go."

"It's money, then."

She nodded. He didn't press her. Her pale beauty entranced him so much he could barely throttle the serenades that rose to his lips.

"You're the only member the Exchange Club has," she said. "I've tried every superintendent up the gulch, every merchant. They don't need a club. You were right, Con—I should've waited for a railroad."

"You're especially lovely this afternoon," he said.

She searched his eyes and glanced away.

"I've never asked. Do you need help?"

"I asked if you'd be a partner once—weeks ago. You never replied."

"I'd rather not be a partner. But I can make a loan if you'd like. You'll be charging me a hundred for the suite. How about twelve hundred dollars now—against a year's rent?"

"Could you? Could you?"

"I could. But let's talk about it. I've some ideas. I've lived in mining camps for years. Are you in trouble?"

"I can pay for the building—barely. But not for the furnishings. Or the help. And I'll have nothing left to live on." She sighed. "I hoped ten or fifteen memberships would see me through. That and sales of spirits."

"You could sell the building."

"I like it here, Con. It grows on me." She smiled wryly. Her demitasse grew cold as she toyed with it.

"There's another option. Put your Exchange Club on the second floor. Your private quarters, some rooms for members, a suite for me, and also a club room with a discreet bar—a place for gents like me to meet or play poker."

"And downstairs?"

"A dance hall. A meeting hall. An opera house. Every camp gets one sooner or later. They're lucrative business."

Her gaze seemed to refocus as she considered the idea. He could see in her the pain of letting go of an old dream.

"Put a dais at the back for concerts and lectures. For fiddlers and orchestras. For choruses and preachers. For dance music. For the troupes passing through. The troupes'll come to any camp because the miners love them and flock to the shows. Eddie Foy, Lillie Langtry, Helena Modjeska, Lotta Crabtree—even Sarah Bernhardt. They play in any dance hall. Rent the place. When no one's booked it, bring in lecturers yourself and take a percentage of the gate. They crawl the West, you know. You'll earn more than you dream."

"I guess I could," she said. "I wanted a big club, not some little second-floor thing."

"You'll still have your club—and a good income besides, Sylvie."

"A club with one member? I need a railroad, it seems."

"There'll probably be a railroad in two or three years. Not now."

"Are you sure?"

"There's silver here, enough for a long time. And low-silver lead being stockpiled by the mines because it's too heavy to ship out. Someone'll build a railroad—as soon as the camp seems more permanent. Maybe in two years you could have your Exchange Club on both floors. And lots of members from all over the West."

"Will you build the railroad?"

He shook his head. "Only if it's a sure thing. A line here isn't. About eighty miles of track, including a lot of grades and bridges and one trestle. For what and how long?"

"Cashbox'll die?"

"What's left of Virginia City? Or Tombstone?"

"I must live for today, then." She eyed him wryly. "It's a good idea. I guess I'll build a dance hall. I'll tell the carpenters what I want."

Something seemed unfinished between them. Something tentative and unspoken, different from before. "Thank you for the advance, Con," she said nervously. "Are you—are your business affairs coming along?"

"Sylvie—I'm still huffing and puffing up your mountain. I want you."

She sat immobile, and then a blush crept through her face, rouging her smooth cheeks, burning even her forehead and the lobes of those ears half buried under her rowdy hair.

"Con—did you just buy me?"

"No, Sylvie. I love you. I'm ravished by you."

"Oh, Con."

"I think I loved you when we met on the stagecoach."

"You did? Oh, Con. I never dreamed it." She grinned awkwardly. The blush didn't leave her face. "I've never been bought, but I wouldn't mind." She sighed, and seemed to turn even redder.

"You're treating this as a transaction."

"Do you think I'll be worth twelve hundred dollars?" Something impish lit her face. Then she laughed. He heard silvery tones, unruly chimes in her voice.

"You have the advantage of me, Sylvie."

"Well, you'll know soon," she said. "I think I'm worth twelve hundred at least. Maybe two thousand. I'll ask you in the morning."

It hurt him. "Sylvie—I didn't sit down with you to make a loan—or an arrangement."

"I made the arrangement, not you," she said. "I've never made one, but I intend to now."

He swore her blush had reached her fingertips. She was treading ground few women ever walked.

"Sylvie—you've said nothing of your own feelings about me."

"Cornelius, aren't I obvious? I must be beet red."

"No. I don't know where I stand."

"I'm sure you've had many lovers."

"I've loved twice. Once when I was young—and now."

"Oh, Con, don't."

"My attentions aren't welcome?"

She slid a hand to his face and touched him. "Be my lover, but not my beloved, Con. I came to Cashbox to become my own mistress, not yours. What's this wild place for, anyway? To surrender?"

"Surrender?"

"It's so rare for a woman to rule herself. No ties. No husband. I escaped him. Don't you see? If I'd wanted the other—an affair of the heart—I could have stayed in Philadelphia or gone to San Francisco or anywhere. Cashbox is so raw. It was the only place to try this out."

He didn't see, but something cautioned him to hold his peace. She would have him on her terms. She'd built a picket fence around her heart. He felt loss and solitude creep through him, dampening his ardor. He knew how it would begin tonight; painfully sweet for a little while, but a rapture that would end in minor key. They would feed upon each other, and he would slide into a sadness beyond description.

He had most of what he wanted from life. All the mines he had sought fell into his hands sooner or later. But not this sweetest mine. He thought idly of returning to Helena after all. But he couldn't. The sight of those disreputable lips bewitched him. His gaze slide over her soft bodice, while she watched knowingly.

"It's mid-afternoon," he said hoarsely. "Tonight is an eternity away."

She smiled crookedly and stood. Her face burned. An odd glow lit her eyes. "Well," she whispered, "why are we sitting here?"

CHAPTER 33

· · · · · · · · · · · · · · · · ·

Charlotte Keiserling studied the specimen of awkward adolescence in her kitchen with wry humor. The punk glanced at doors, looking for a way to get past Amos. If he'd been cut any skinnier, he could clean a stovepipe. He eyed her from a narrow, acned face that propped up a grotesque pompadour. She hated that goose grease; it wrecked her pillowslips. There was enough tallow on his head to feed a lamp for a night.

"Sit down," she said, motioning toward the kitchen table.

He did, smarty-like.

"You owe me a double eagle, buster."

"Aw, I wasn't doing nothing."

"Peeps cost the same as the rest around here. I don't care what you like, just so you pay. Everything here's got a price. You've been peeping for a long time. Only this time we gotcha. That's a double eagle, punk."

"I'm not going to pay you nothing."

"What's your name?"

"I haven't got one." He grinned at her, smirky.

"How old are you?"

"Sixteen, going on seventeen."

"You don't have a name, so I'll just have to think one up. How about Casper?"

The kid's cockiness wilted.

"I asked Slug Svensrud who's the kid hanging around here, and he says it's Casper Penrose. Your pa works at the Ophir. I told Slug maybe I'd talk to your ma and pa about you. How old did you say you were?"

Casper Penrose shrank in his chair, the feistiness drained out of him. "Fifteen," he mumbled.

"That's what Slug said, too. He said you're some punk for your age, and heading for big trouble. That so?"

"Dumb copper."

The boy's truculence surprised her.

"I don't care if you talk to them. Ma and pa. I was fixing to get out of there anyway. They're dumb as stumps."

The mazourka someone in the parlor was banging out stopped, and she heard a commotion there. She turned to Amos. "I'll deal with the kid. You keep a lid on the place, okay?"

"The punk'll bolt, Charlotte."

"No, he won't. You and me, Casper, we're going to have a talk, okay?"

The boy nodded. Amos watched silently and then clumped down the long corridor to the front of the building.

"Well, Casper, what's in your pockets? You owe me a lot."

"A big one," he said, and laughed nasally.

She fought back her amusement. The smart kid. "How are you gonna pay me?" she asked.

"I thought whores had a heart of gold."

"Mine's pure arsenic, get that straight. You're going to

bring me a cord of dry firewood, split and cut to stove length."

"Aw, you should be paying me. I'll make you happy. I'll keep your whole cathouse happy. I charge five dollars a shot and make you squeal." The brat leered at her.

"Have you ever been with a woman, Casper?"

"Lots. So many I can't count 'em all."

"Who?"

"Well, half the girls in the camp."

"Well, well. What did they say?"

"They thanked me and got on their knees and begged me to do it again."

"You got 'em all pregnant, too, I guess."

"Yeah, they never can wait for me to put on my sheepskin."

"Big shot," she said.

"I'm the fastest dude in the camp. You gonna let me at them women now?"

She stared at the punk, not wanting to like him. But she was betrayed by her amusement. She'd never run into such effrontery in all her life. He reminded her a little of the boys she had fooled with when she was Casper's age, scared and daring and wildly curious about everything. She came from a more comfortable class, but the boys were still the same. So horny they had just one idea in their skulls. Brazen and daring; egging her on to fool with them. That's what got her into trouble. Trouble! That was *their* word for it, not hers. Life had been mostly a carnival since then, except for a few hard edges.

"You know something, Casper? You're a creep."

"That's what I do, creep in. Lemme have a free one."

"Look at you. That goose grease on your hair. That pompadour three inches high. Do you really think women like that?"

"Gimme a free one," he retorted, but this time she caught some doubt in his voice.

"Do you think we like that grease? You think we like to

run our hand through your slimy locks? You dumb kid. That thing on your head makes you look like a turkey."

"You don't know nothing about men," he snapped.

"They're my business, punk. Look at you. How long since you washed? You think any woman wants to touch some creep like you?"

"They itch for me, dolly."

"Hey." She pointed toward a curtained alcove. "Go in there and wash that grease outta your hair, and when it's clean, brush it down nicely. There's hot water and a basin in there. And a towel. Don't grease up my towel, you slicker."

He snickered. The situation unsettled him. Then his eyes lit and he leered. "Anything you want, sweetheart."

He swaggered into the alcove. It was there for the girls, a place for a spitbath when they needed it, near the hot water reservoir in the cookstove.

He disappeared behind the curtain, smirking at her. She watched him aghast, wondering why she was letting this punk worm into her like some gopher. Had she lost her senses? Would she do it? That memory of fooling around when she was a girl flooded through her, evoking odd pain in her heart. The punk started something unraveling in her, as if he'd pulled the one thread that would strip her bare. Maybe she'd show him a few things. Make a man of him. Teach him to be a lover. Scrub away that cockiness until she found the hungry boy. . . .

He whipped the curtain apart and primped. His hair lay flat on his head, brushed back. "That suit you?"

"You look better."

"I should raise my price. You're itching to try, aren't you. Itching to break me in."

"I thought you were the great lover."

"I am. Only you don't believe it. Tonight you get one free from me."

She stared at him. He stood there leering and ready.

From some place at the back of her mind, fire bells rang. Slowly she pulled herself free, like a drowning woman reaching a safe beach, appalled at her own weakness. "Casper. You go now. Don't ever come here again. Not even when you have two bucks in your hot hand. This place is off limits. I'm telling Slug to keep you out of here. I'm telling Amos to throw you out if you ever walk in. You understand?"

"You're scared of me."

"No. You made me remember some things."

"Maybe I'll just stroll around, see the sights. I want to meet Silver Dollar Annie and The Bobcat."

"Out!"

He smirked. "You see? My pompadour done it. I washed it out and you throw me out."

"Casper Penrose, you're aiming toward a bad life."

"You should talk."

"There's a thing called a double standard. Men are excused for their conduct; women are thrown out. I've made the best life I could." She wondered why the punk weakened her so frightfully.

Amos appeared. "You heard her. Out. Or I'll pound you to pulp."

Casper retreated sullenly, banging the door behind him.

"Thank you, Amos," she said. "I'm having a spell. I'm going to my rooms. You look after things tonight."

CHAPTER 34

. . . .

Baghote announced the arrival of a sheriff's deputy from White Sulphur Springs, but Thaddeus Webb thought to put the man off a few minutes. The incredible vug in the bowels of the Giltedge was maddening him.

The vug ore was too rich for his mill. He couldn't extract the silver from it. He had quietly thrown a chunk of it into the Blake jaw crusher and watched while its iron plates shattered other rock into small bits with a deafening roar. But there was too much metal in it, and it didn't reduce in the crusher, or under the stamps. Neither would his mercury amalgamate with the silver in lumps like that.

He would have to ship every bit of it: tons and tons of ore by ox-drawn freight wagon to the smelter at Wickes. There the Parkes process, in which the lead-silver ore was dropped into molten zinc, would separate the silver when the zinc combined with the lead. The Hammons would still reap a fortune—but at an awful cost.

He had spent hours down in the vug, clawing at ore like a bee after honey. Then his best miners opened the vug wider and fired a new round within it. The result was awesome: the octahedron crystals of almost pure metal lay two feet thick in its walls. He swiftly raised his estimate to a million dollars' worth of silver, plus the lead. But getting it to Wickes without having half of it stolen was taxing his brains.

It would be like hauling money. When Cashbox discovered how rich the ore was, anyone could use it for cash. A fist-sized chunk would have five or six dollars of silver in it. Somehow, he had to ship it to the smelter without losing most of it to crooks. Several times he had watched a rascal teamster who hauled ore for the Ophir. The fellow had a cabin, a family, and four dogs right in the gulch. Every time his wagon rumbled by, his dogs would come snarling out to plague his dray horses—so the feller reared back and fired chunks of ore at the dogs to chase them off. Then his wife and brats swarmed out to collect the ore. Webb sighed. If that teamster were to haul the vug ore, he'd throw a hundred dollars at his mutts every time he passed his house.

Armed guards. He'd try to find some who were honest enough to entrust with a load like that.

"Mr. Webb, that deppity's getting restless," said Baghote.

Webb nodded irritably, and a moment later a broad man with bull shoulders burst in. Webb eyed him dourly. If the fellow's handlebar mustaches grew any longer, he'd have to tuck them under his armpits when he ate.

"Webb. I'm Deputy Grumbach, with some court papers for you," the man said, handing Webb a packet. "It's a restraining order. I'm to wait here and see that it's obeyed."

Webb slid out the thick sheaf of papers. Meagher County District Court, Territory of Montana, Judge Julius Gear presiding ... Docket number 132, in the matter of Cornelius Daley *vs.* John and Henry Hammon, doing business as the Giltedge Mine ... the Gill claim, now the property of Daley ... apex.

Apex. The Silver Fox. Webb bristled. But it got worse.

"Upon plea by plaintiff's attorney J. Ernest Potter-Pride the District Court imposes a fourteen-day restraining order, effective upon receipt, prohibiting the removal or sale of any ores below ground, and any ores or refined ore products above ground. . . ."

A hearing was scheduled ten days hence, after which Judge Gear would decide whether to make the restraining order permanent pending the outcome of the apex litigation.

Shut down. Webb reread it all, rage reddening his face. "Now?"

"Yeah, well, get your men out. I gotta seal the hoist. I've got a chain and padlock here."

"Get my men out? Grumbach, they're probably loading dynamite now. You can't leave dynamite in the rock. Nothing could be worse."

"Yeah, well, you get 'em out. Then I'll seal the hoist."

"The hoist? Grumbach, a mine's a living thing. Even if it's shut down, we've got to go in there and check for flooding. Once a mine's flooded it's almost impossible to pump out. You're not going to destroy our property. I won't permit it."

"Yeah, well I got my orders and I'll haul you back to White Sulphur if you're gonna give me trouble. Just try it, buster."

Webb stood, slowly bringing his rage under control, and

stalked out. The deputy dogged his heels like a rat terrier. Webb found Coke Timmons and instructed him to ring the bells, go down and end it, and to let him know about the dynamite. Timmons looked stricken, but went down as soon as the cage surfaced. Then, after a jangle of bells and some shrill whistles, the miners began to collect around the gallows frame.

Coke Timmons emerged with the last miners, both powder men, and a carload of equipment. "That's it. No one down there. No charges in any holes yet."

"Are you sure?"

"Do you think I'd leave a man trapped?" Timmons snarled.

"What the bleddy hell is this?" asked Hugh Trego.

"Court's shutting this mine down," Webb growled.

"And who the bleddy hell's doin' it?"

"Con Daley and his attorney."

"Would that be Pride?"

Webb nodded wearily. He didn't like being grilled by Trego. It wasn't Trego's mine.

"And why?" The whole world seemed to hang on the question.

"It's an apex suit. Daley claims that the Gill property, next to us, is where the lead apexed and he's a right to the vein wherever it runs—which is over here. That's the 1872 law. Pride's a master at this—he's done it several times."

"Well now, Webb, we'll see. Putting lads out of work, is he? Starving the wee children, hurting the old sons that go down into the bleddy pits, hurting women that have to scrape to keep us fed and dressed. The bleddy capitalist wants to take the wage o' the ones that muck the ore, does he?"

Fifty or sixty angry men stared in dead silence. Then some slipped off toward the company boardinghouse. Several others plucked Hercules dynamite from the ore car and passed the sticks to eager hands, along with fuse and copper caps. The sticks filled them with some sort of galvanic strength. The silence lay coiled and menacing, as large as a hangman's loop.

"You don't want trouble," Webb told them sternly. "We'll reopen in a few days, as fast as our attorneys can stop this thievery. That's all it is. Put that powder back before you blow yourselves up."

But no one did. Several more miners hurried away. Some trotted up the gulch toward the Ophir. Others vanished into the mine sheds and emerged with coiled ropes, thick as sin.

Grumbach chose that moment to wind a chain around a bar of the cage and then through the hoist works.

"I wouldn't do that," growled Trego in a voice so quiet that it could scarcely be heard.

But Grumbach heard it, and reared up, as menacing as a silvertip grizzly. "Want trouble? You want trouble?" he said, eagerness building in his thick face.

"You'll not be shutting this mine, boyo," Trego said. Beside him, Polweal was building a noose.

"Stop that!" snapped Webb. "Stop it or you're done here."

Grumbach grinned and reached for his revolver. Too late. The snick of a shotgun cocking stopped him. He stared into the grim face of a gaunt miner whose twelve-gauge pointed straight at his chest. "I'll throw you in the White Sulphur jail," the deputy growled. "Put it down."

The miner didn't.

"You'll not be closing the mine," Trego said. "You'll be telling the damned jedge you'll not be closing the bleddy mine. Maybe we'll go to White Sulphur and tell the jedge ourselves. He'll listen to a noose, wouldn't you say? A noose talks loud, eh?"

"Trego, you'll obey the court," snapped Webb. "The sooner you obey, the sooner we'll open up again. Now let's settle down. This shift is over. Go home. You'll get pay for the day."

But the crowd was swelling with men from the other mines, hundreds of them, some armed. A lynch mob was gathering around the deputy. Webb suddenly feared there'd be murder done that afternoon.

"Trego, stop this."

The miner ignored him. "Put the little shooter away, depitty. We're going to hike into town and visit the bleddy lawyer and the fat capitalist," Trego growled.

"It ain't over, Trego," said Grumbach cockily. "You're in big trouble."

Someone lifted a noose and shook it in Grumbach's face. Slowly the deputy slid his revolver back into its sheath, hate flaming in his eyes.

The column descended the gulch swiftly, a stern regiment of angry men, their hobnailed shoes cracking smartly along the road to Cashbox. Someone threw a noose over Grumbach. Wildly he tried to pull it off, but a dozen cursing miners swarmed over him, tied his meaty hands behind him, and tightened the noose until he wheezed. Then they dragged him like a shoat going to market. At last Grumbach looked afraid. Thaddeus Webb followed, horrified by the looming trouble. At the edge of town he broke from the crowd and headed for Slug Svensrud's jail. Maybe the constable could halt a lynching.

In Cashbox, some of the mob split off toward Pride's office, and the others marched toward the Palace Hotel, while merchants gawked and shoppers hastened away. Webb didn't find Svensrud in his jail and raced to warn Daley. But he was too late.

Chapter 35

• • • • • • • • • • • • • • • • •

Con Daley customarily spent his afternoons in the quiet comfort of the Palace Hotel saloon, studying mining stocks. But this day his killings were halted by a dozen Cousin Jacks who swarmed into the saloon and surrounded his table.

"What may I do for you, gentlemen?" he inquired, not liking the flinty stares. Much to his horror, several held waxy red cylinders that looked like Hercules dynamite. Enough to blow the hotel—and himself—to smithereens.

"Daley, ye bleddy capitalist, get up. Come with us," said one grim Cousin Jack, who appeared to be the ringleader.

"I'm afraid you have the advantage of me," he muttered. "What's your name, did you say?"

"Come along, damn your fat hide, or we'll drag you."

More of them crowded into the saloon, looking like a pack of wolves. The barman set down a bottle and fled. Daley heard commotion in the lobby.

Uneasily Daley stood, dreading the Cornishmen, wanting some inkling of their purpose. Then he elbowed past them into the crowded lobby. The lobby bulged with silent men waving dynamite sticks like baseball bats. One man carried a roll of Bickford fuse.

They pushed him roughly through the lobby and out into a somnolent summer afternoon, save for a mob that seethed in the street like some rabid pack of dogs. In the midst of them stood Potter-Pride, looking like a man on a tumbrel. "This is an outrage!" the silver-tongued orator cried, but the words sounded like the blatting of a sheep, and Pride looked sick. Daley spotted a captive man with a badge—and a tightened noose around his neck. Then one banged over his own head, and someone yanked it tight, choking Daley momentarily. Shock undid him.

Another noose dropped over the noble head of Attorney Pride. A lynching. Con Daley swiftly surmised the cause of it: the restraining order. The rough hemp bit into his soft neck. He would die.

"But I'm a friend," he gasped.

"No mistake, you bleddy cradle-robber. You're snatchin' bread from poor men; robbin' milk from babes. Robbin' women that work themselves into the grave because your bleddy mines don't pay enough for a family to shift by. You damned blood-suckin' capitalists, scheming to snatch silver and spoils into your fat hands, ye sucking pigs. Not once did you think it'd hurt the poor wretches that muck the bleddy ore out of your hellish pits."

The man had fire in his nostrils. He was speaking for them all, with some raw and mesmerizing gift of invective. Con Daley feared him. His ripsaw tongue could inspire men to murder.

Daley summoned calm from somewhere. "My good man. Listen! I know why you're here. I know how you feel. I've been poor as a church mouse. No one will suffer on my account." He caught them listening, and that encouraged him. "The restraining order can be rescinded. With the stroke of a pen. Mister Pride can draft the paper in a moment. That man—I take it that deputy's from the court—can take it to Judge Gear."

"This deppity devil come ridin' to the Giltedge with your papers and padlocks, and he's going back in a coffin," said the miner.

The deputy sagged.

"Come along, you satans. This talkin's going to stop," the Cousin Jack snapped.

Daley recognized him. Hugh Trego, the one who'd confronted him in the Carbonate Saloon. "Mister Trego—listen, for God's sake. Do you want the matter settled or not?"

A deafening blast shattered the afternoon. Daley thought some madman had shot at him. But there stood Constable Svensrud on the hotel portico, two steps above them all, his double-barreled shotgun pointed at the sky. Even as they gaped, he lowered his piece and jacked in another shell.

"All right, fellows," he said quietly. "All right. You with the scattergun, set it down. All you with the giant powder, step forward and set them down right there." He pointed at a place before the steps.

"We'll not," said Trego. "We'll finish our business."

"If you do your business, you'll hang, Trego. And you, Polweal. Every one of you'll be ashamed of this all your lives."

The miner with the shotgun swung it around toward Svensrud. "You won't interfere, Slug," he said.

But Slug Svensrud didn't flinch. "Let go of Daley and Pride," he said. "And that White Sulphur man."

Daley was hearing the voice of a fearless man and so were the miners. Slowly tension leaked away. The moment turned as slack as an empty noose, and Daley felt his racing heart slow. He clasped the rough rope and the noose and slowly worked it open until he could pull it over his head. Pride looked too sick to attempt it, but the deputy wrestled his free, rage in his face.

Daley worked his way through the sullen miners and stepped up beside the constable on legs that trembled. "I've been a friend of the men in the pits all my life," he said. "We made a mistake and we'll fix it. The Giltedge is going to mine—as usual. You'll be paid as usual. I believe it's my ore, but we'll let Judge Gear decide that. I'll be hiring soon. I'm going to mine here. I'll need good men."

"Ye play with our lives, Daley. Like it's a checkers game."

Daley didn't reply, at least directly. His mind whirled with things to say and unsay. "Mister Pride, go get paper and pen from the desk clerk. Write a rescision of our pleadings for a restraining order."

Pride seemed too befuddled to respond, but after a moment the attorney stumbled into the hotel. Time stalled. Even the puffball clouds froze in the sky. But at last Pride emerged bearing a document in his trembling hand, and handed it to Daley. It was much-blotted.

"You, sir." Daley addressed the deputy. "Take this to Judge Gear. It's our desire to rescind the restraining order."

"All right—but I'm taking these ringleaders with me," the deputy snapped. "I'll file enough charges to put them in Deer Lodge for life. You and you—"

"No you won't," said Svensrud. "You'll get out of Cashbox and forget it."

The deputy snarled at the constable, but the bores of

Svensrud's shotgun swung straight toward him with authority.

"I'll get you, too, constable."

"Neither Mister Pride nor I will press charges," said Daley. "I don't suppose Mister Webb will, either."

"No, Daley, no charges," Webb snapped. "These are good men. And I'll personally make sure your pleadings are thrown out of court. Even if it takes years."

"I'll be hiring soon, and offering a good wage, too. I'm for the miners," Daley said. "I was a poor boy once."

Potter-Pride looked ashen beneath his mop of silver hair. Daley glared at the man. "Mister Pride, before you make any more moves, consult me," he said in a voice laced with swamp ice. "There are other ways."

Pride met Daley's ruthless stare with the old jut-jaw.

"All right," said the constable. "Take that giant powder back to the Giltedge before you blow up this town. Take the rope too. You, Grumbach, get out of here. And take that paper to the judge."

"Yeah, well, I'll be back. It ain't over," Grumbach muttered. "I don't forget."

Con Daley watched the mob break up like river ice cracking on a March day. The moments of terror had drained him of all the animal force in his body; he wanted only to lie down.

"Pride," he said after they were alone. "I'm going to mine Gill's claim. It's safer than getting our necks in a noose. I'll drive a drift right into the Giltedge and get that ore while you litigate. Let *them* try the restraining orders and get lynched."

"That wasn't what you told me last week," Pride muttered. The ashen attorney stumbled off, peering behind him as if he expected the noose to snake over his head again.

Cornelius Daley toiled back to the saloon and sagged into his chair while hotel clerks and the barman stared at him, as they would a man who had returned from the dead. Until this moment he had never thought much about his life. If they had strung him up, he would never see Sylvie again.

PART II

. . . .

1890

CHAPTER 36

· · · · · · · · · · · · · · · ·

The big event in Sylvie's hall attracted more people than Cornelius Daley had expected on a night when the temperature stood at ten degrees below zero. They jammed every seat and lined the walls. All to the good, he thought. Nothing stirred people like a railroad.

Up on the podium sat Old Jut-Jaw, looking more and more senatorial these days. J. Ernest Potter-Pride's wavy locks glowed silver in the lamplight. He wore a black suit with the gold fob of his Phi Beta Kappa key dangling across his expanding middle, the result of eating six hundred of Regina's pies. Next to him, but with an odd psychic distance from Pride, sat the Hammon brothers.

Daley could have joined them but had chosen not to. The Cashbox and Northern was really his own lusty creature, but he didn't want to be publicly associated with it. In any case, it would have seemed odd, given all the spilled blood in Judge Julius Gear's courtroom. He preferred to sit beside Sylvie and watch the show.

The fetid smell of nearly three hundred breaths, mixed at times with blasts of icy air, made him itchy. Sylvie's hall hadn't been designed to provide ventilation for a crowd. But that hadn't stopped Cashbox from booking it virtually every night for dances, speeches, concerts, variety shows, theater, free-silver rallies, church services, and temperance lectures. Only yesterday an earnest young man from the Independent Order of Good Templars had presented a stereopticon show about the evils of the grape, and closed with a verse:

Beware of liquor! Fifty Deaths I died—
Losing in turn hope, energy and pride . . .

I reached that goal of agony and sin—
A drunkard's grave—and blindly staggered in.

Upstairs, in Sylvie's Exchange Club, Daley and other substantial gentlemen had ordered the bourbon or rye she kept at her whorled-grain Circassian walnut bar and planned this evening's event, while keeping an ear on the lecture under their feet.

Up on the dais, Old Jut-Jaw approached the lectern with springy dignity, cleared his tonsils, and smiled benignly.

"Ladies and Gentlemen of Cashbox, we're going to have a railroad," he cried, lifting both arms heavenward.

He smiled while the crowd cheered.

"It's about time," he added, with the agreement of the crowd.

"We won't let the railroad trusts or the malefactors of great wealth stop us," he added, nodding kindly to the malefactors of wealth behind him on the dais. "We deserve the same chance as any other town."

"He's in form," whispered Sylvie. "I swear he's running for office. He's been that way ever since statehood."

"I hope he finishes before these merciless benches of yours ruin my evening," Con replied.

"I scarcely need rehearse for you our crying need for a railroad," Pride continued. "The lack of it steals bread and milk from children, rips coats off the backs of the poor, raises the prices of everything in our fair city—yes, Cashbox is a city. But a city eighty miles from those vital arteries of commerce that make life pleasant, and give mortals hope for the future."

Potter-Pride was playing the jury, Con thought. But this jury would vote with its wallets.

"Now, let me tell you something: the want of a railroad threatens our livelihood. Our jobs. The secure comforts of our little homes and cabins, where American freemen want only to live their peaceful lives and raise their families.

"Friends, every mine in this district has tons of lead piled up. Why, the Giltedge alone yields over five million pounds of it a year. And next to it, the Hangfire Mine produces three million pounds. And no mine gets a penny for it because it's too costly to ship by wagon. We need steam. Cashbox needs to harness the power of steam.

"And that's not all, dear friends: our smelters suffer from the high cost of charcoal, most of which is imported by wagons. Reducing ores here is a costly business that cuts into the profits of the mines, endangers our jobs, and clouds the future of our good citizens. We . . . need . . . a railroad!"

A great applause greeted that. Old Jut-Jaw smiled.

"Now, my friends, our captains of industry have not been blind to these difficulties. They've made every effort to persuade the Northern Pacific to build a branch to Cashbox. But, I'm sorry to report they've failed. The giant railroad would not hear of it. They said there's no profit in it. *Profit.*

"And our business people responded that of course there'd be profit; there'd be freight to Cashbox and White Sulphur Springs; coal and charcoal; supplies for thousands of people; rich ores, lead, and bullion; as well as passengers. What sane man could possibly say there'd not be enough traffic? Especially with the country filling up with cattle, waiting to be shipped?"

A voice rose from the rear. "Well, the NP should know. This sounds like one of them big stock bubbles to me."

"Oh, a skeptic," said Pride. "I'm all for skeptics. They make us prove our point beyond all doubt. I like this man. I tell you what, sir. I'm going to offer you one share of our railroad stock. I'm going to put my money where my mouth is and give it to you. Now I want you to do the same: if you think this enterprise is fruitless, turn it down. If you think there's a good chance it'll bear fruit, grow, pay dividends, why, take it with my compliments."

"One share?" the man shouted. "All right, it's a deal."

"There you are, friends. Our skeptic reconsidered. I want you all to be skeptics and ask hard questions. We love tough questions. See me after I'm done up here, sir."

Daley smiled. Pride had a way about him.

"Now, let me tell you, neighbors. There's something dark and sinister going on. The NP is playing favorites. It's telling the malefactors of great wealth in Helena and Butte that it'll keep their rival, little Cashbox, at bay. Oh, how the cold and ruthless trusts control our lives and destinies.

"But now, several prominent men of Cashbox have taken matters into their own hands. They refuse to roll over and die. They've incorporated the Cashbox and Northern Railroad. One terminus will be right here, and the southern terminus will be Livingston. They've all dug deeply into their private purses to make this dream possible for us all."

"He's got 'em," whispered Daley. "The NP monopoly did it. Listen to that silver tongue."

"I hope so. We need it," Sylvie whispered.

"My friends, the cost of the branch, with its bridges and a trestle, will come to about three hundred and fifty thousand dollars. A lot of money. There's no way around it. If we want our railroad, and the prosperity it brings, we'll have to dig deep. The company has issued twenty-five thousand shares at a par of ten dollars. With a quarter of a million dollars it can complete most of the line, and we'll deal with the rest later.

"Now, listen to this. Mister Henry Hammon, right here beside me, purchased five thousand shares. Mister John Hammon purchased three thousand. Mister Cornelius Daley purchased ten ... thousand ... shares. Yes, you heard me. Ten thousand. His faith in Cashbox is so strong he bought a hundred thousand dollars' worth of capital stock in the new railroad company."

Daley nodded slightly, sensing the stares.

"Yes, and other prominent citizens have purchased an additional thousand shares. That makes nineteen thousand sold, six thousand remaining to be sold. Now you know why we've called you to our bosom this cold evening. I want you all to come forward to invest in your own future. Own a piece of the Cashbox and Northern." He leaned forward, conspiratorially. "Now here's a bit of private news: we will control the rates; it'll be our trackage. The NP has nothing to say about it."

Daley hoped no one would point out the obvious. The Cashbox and Northern might control the rates on its track, but the NP would control the rates from Livingston elsewhere.

"Now, my friends, one final word before I ask you to step to our table at the rear and purchase your stock—I should say purchase your glorious future! Will you lose? Let me tell you, once the Cashbox line proves its merit, the monopolists in the counting houses of the NP will lust—yes, lust—to buy the lucrative line. If you want a foolproof investment, what more could you ask? Don't spend a penny you can't afford—but if you've put a bit by, now's your chance."

More likely, Daley thought, the NP directors would buy the line for ten cents on the dollar.

"Now I know that many of you'll have to dig deep into your purses. But you won't regret it. Oh, think of that day when the first Baldwin locomotive steams into Cashbox, with its whistle shrilling and its big brass bell clanging, and Old Glory waving, pulling a string of cars groaning with good things for us all.

"Oh, you won't regret it when you purchase a rail ticket to Livingston and find it's a quarter the price of the stage—and only four hours—yes, four hours!—away. Oh, you won't regret it when our merchants have fresh fruits to sell us in January. Tons of coal to sell us, and cheaper than cordwood. Oh, my friends, have vision. Believe in the good things to come. May the Good Lord guide you now. Thank you, my fellow citizens of the greatest little mining town on earth."

Cornelius Daley watched the merchants of Cashbox gather at the table. It was going to happen. Luring the Hammons into it had done the trick. It had taken some fancy maneuvering. But that's what Sylvie's luxurious club upstairs was for: deals.

"I'll buy a hundred shares," she said.

"Don't be absurd," he replied.

That crooked smile lit her face again. "He made it sound so good," she said. "He could sell me the Brooklyn Bridge."

CHAPTER 37

* * * * * * * * * * * * * * * *

Sylvie slid her pleated white wrapper over her thick flannel nightgown and stabbed her bare feet into slippers. Then she picked up her skeleton key and eased out of her apartment at the rear of the Exchange Building, into the chilly hall and stairwell, and padded to the door of the Exchange Club. The brutal January cold bit at her through the stone walls. She let herself into the club, enjoying its warmth and the lingering tang of cigar smoke. She loved the musky presence of men in a room. The club had no guests in its two private rooms this night; only Con, in the suite.

She would slip into his quarters shortly, but before that she scuffed about in the dark, enjoying her creation. She plucked ashtrays brimming with stubbed Havanas from the clubroom, study, and billiard room, and carried them to the saloon. She disposed of the butts behind her handsome walnut bar, manufactured by Brunswick-Balke-Callander and shipped by rail and ox-drawn wagon to this remote place. The quilted leather furniture, heavy green velvet draperies, parquet floor, and walnut wainscoting gave this place a cheerful masculine quality, unlike the bright femininity of her apartment.

If she wasn't exactly rich, she had certainly become comfortable so quickly that she still marveled. It had happened because Con had casually suggested she build the dance hall downstairs and a smaller club above. Ever since it opened, the hall had been booked solidly, and her fifteen percent of the gate had made her the richest woman in Cashbox. She smiled, remembering when John Oliver Cromwell, at the Cashbox Bank, had told her that her deposits had surpassed those of the other wealthy business woman in town, whom he discreetly wouldn't name.

At first Sylvie made herself almost invisible, quietly serving drinks and vanishing. But she intuited that once her club members had gotten used to her, they would enjoy having her at hand. Hesitantly, she started to join them. She had over thirty members now, including the Hammon brothers and Potter-Pride. One, a mining engineer, was from Helena.

Done with her ritual housekeeping, she hastened through dim light to his door and opened it. She didn't knock. He would be expecting her. More often he came to her after discreetly waiting for the gentlemen to abandon the club for the night. Then he would let himself in and slide into her bedroom. She would light the lamp, smiling, and wait for him to come to her. But tonight she wanted to go to him.

Apart from Beau, Con was the only lover she had ever had. Unlike Beau, who left her empty and still needful, Con had always kindled fires that released her into a soft peace. Sometimes, when she wasn't inclined toward passion, Con simply slid in between the covers and held her, his embrace balming something painful in her heart. He asked for nothing more.

But tonight he wanted her. She had sensed that in his glances through the evening. She wanted him too. She could barely wait for the last of the men to leave. Joy infused her because she had something important to tell him. Con had awakened something so sweet and strange within her that she was still trying to fathom it. She had discovered love. He was a moody man, sometimes sliding into his own dark thoughts, but whenever they came together the joy of their union dissolved his mood, and his spirit floated into lightness and humor.

She closed his door behind her and hurried across his

small parlor to his bedchamber. She saw him in the dull light, and felt a tingle of happiness.

"Sylvie," he said.

She found the familiar lamp, lifted its glass chimney and lit it with the wooden matches stuffed into the ceramic dish there. Its flare blinded her a moment. Then she slid the chimney back and turned the wick low, bathing the bed chamber in a silvery glow.

He was sitting against the headboard, watching her, his observant eyes alive with delight. She smiled, knowing it lit flames in him. Some instinct in her needed his smile, needed to coax the unruly, half-dangerous inner man out of his shell. Sometimes this inner Con Daley would burst into poetry, verse after verse he had memorized, singing the ballads of storms and sea; hearth and bread and home; mad forbidden lovers in ecstatic surrender; fugitives hiding in bogs and murky fens.

Con Daley could transform himself into a balladeer, a man so opposite his controlled public persona it took her months to plumb the wild stranger whose iron body she drew to her own. It had been Daley the poet who had seduced her, the poet who had furtively stolen her from herself.

"Sylvie," he said, her name soft on his lips.

"Oh, my!" she exclaimed, rivers of delight coursing through her veins. She loved to bask in his attentive gaze. She loved to just be in his presence. It was all she needed. She felt like a cavorting filly. She wanted the firmness of his lips upon hers, and his bold hands attacking her.

She discovered a stray barrette she'd missed in her unruly hair, and pulled it out. She undid her pleated white wrapper and pulled it free. She lifted her flannel nightgown over her head and struggled out of it. He was watching. Her nakedness had always evoked a yearning in his intent eyes. She had celebrated her twenty-eighth birthday, and her figure hadn't changed at all. She had grown into a tall, slender beauty with compact breasts and golden thighs. A thousand times he told her she was the most ravishing woman on earth. She came to sup on his admiration.

"Sylvie. . . ."

"We need each other tonight, Con," she said, sitting beside him on his high fourposter. A happiness as fragrant and thorny as a wild rose caught in her chest.

"Never so much," he whispered, opening the comforter to her.

She sighed, and slid in beside him, discovering his warmth as he clapped her to him. She kissed his scratchy cheek, his eyes and his chest, and slid her hands along his backbone under his nightshirt, while he nibbled her ear, her brow, and then her opened lips. He always took his time. Once in a while she wished he'd be mad with passion, but it wasn't his nature. Given the choice, she preferred this languorous climb up the mountain.

Con had stopped telling her he loved her. She couldn't bear to hear it and had always hushed him. But whenever he spoke her name, just her naked name, *Sylvie*, it sufficed to say the same thing because his lips turned her name into prayer. His poet's soul made a sonnet of a single word.

But her walls had fallen, and tonight she would tell him so. Nothing more important had ever happened to her. She pulled free and sat up, gazing solemnly into his lamplit face, enjoying the moment, wanting Con to know how important her message would be. "Con, I love you," she said.

It arrested him. "Sylvie? I thought—"

"I'm a fool for poets."

"You think I'm a poet?"

"More poet than a businessman. I always thought poets were awful businessmen."

"Maybe I'm not a poet." He laughed softly.

"Where did it come from, Con? The poetry? Why do you hide it from the world?"

"I'm a poor poet, Sylvie. I can hardly rhyme two words. I wish I could write real poetry."

"It's what you feel, Con. A poet feels things more than

others do. Your feelings rule you. Whenever you look at me—I feel your poetry."

"Sylvie, would you say it again?"

"I love you, you big sentimental fox."

He laughed. "Sylvie? I've loved you from the day you sat across from me on the stagecoach. I never thought I'd get to say it. You've been so firm about—keeping feelings out of it."

"Well, I'm weak. Now I'm in trouble. Now I'm foolish. Now I can be captured."

"Captured?"

"That's what you buy when you buy love."

He thought about that for a moment. "Have you ever loved before, Sylvie?"

"I thought so. For a while, anyway. I tried to."

"Beau?"

She squeezed him in reply.

"What changed with us?"

"You analyze too much."

"What do you want?"

"Love me, but don't capture me, Con."

"Don't capture you?" He seemed to be searching for something, wanting something from her.

"Con, Con," she said, kissing him softly. "Do magic things to me."

CHAPTER 38

· · · · · · · · · · · · · · · · · ·

Thaddeus Webb knew this meeting would bring him new grief. In his office stood Hugh Trego, the president of Local 37, Knights of Labor, looking as hard and heavy as an anvil. Webb wondered what the man could possibly want: the Giltedge was adequately timbered now, and the new winze from the three-hundred-foot level to the hundred-foot level had greatly improved the air. Those were the things the union had demanded after it had been formed a year ago; both had been granted. In fact, Webb had wanted the timbering and ventilation as badly as the miners, and only finance and the Hammons had slowed it.

"The Hangfire's given its men an eight-hour day, and we'll bleddy well have it too," Trego announced without preamble.

"Eight-hour day?" The news sent a tremor through Webb. "With a cut in pay, I suppose."

"Not a penny. Con Daley gave it to us. Says he, a man shouldn't have to muck in a hole in the ground ten hours, until he's ready to drop."

"That's a twenty percent raise, Trego."

"I'll tell you what she is—she's daylight, sunshine, time to spend with our wives and children. She's time to have a drink at the Carbonate and not be so bleddy tired we all want to fall into bed. She's a tiny bit o' freedom that makes us better than serfs, is what she is."

"Daley just gave it to you?"

"He did. He says he knows how it is under the grass. Maybe he does and maybe he doesn't. But he's doing it. And we're going to have her, right now."

"You've six months left on the contract."

"We're going to have her, now. I won't have part of the local on eight hours and the rest toiling ten. We'll have her or we'll not be going down the shaft."

Webb sighed. "Trego, a contract's a solemn agreement by sovereign people or groups, each freely committing themselves to its terms. You agreed to it by a vote of your members, acting on their own free will. The courts enforce them when one side or another acts in bad faith. You're acting in bad faith."

"I'm keeping faith with the men, Webb."

"Trego—any court in Montana would find against you, fine your Knights of Labor, and enjoin you from striking."

"You bleddy capitalists, making men work like ants while ye all sit in your overstuffed chairs at the Exchange

Club, and eat fancy steaks at the Palace chophouse, thinkin' about profits you get off our backs."

Webb sighed. "Trego—there are economic realities here, and you know them as well as I do. We're eighty miles from a railroad. This mine isn't able to afford eight-hour days. The smelter's a losing operation because it costs me thirteen dollars a ton to ship charcoal here by wagon. We can't even sell most of the product from these mines, lead-silver concentrate, because it's too costly to ship out.

"The ore's good—I'll grant you that. We're at forty-five ounces a ton at the three-hundred-foot works. But this mine's got a perverse streak in her, Trego. That ore is sulfide now, not carbonate, and it has to be roasted. You know the costs as well as I do. Let's talk profit and loss now. You can break even a rich mine with demands like that. If we had a railroad, I'd consider it. But we don't—and we're two years from one at the earliest. Come back to me in two years and we'll see."

"Eight hours, right now. Beginning at the next tally day."

"I'll talk to the Hammons but I know what they'll say."

"Then we'll shut you down."

"Hugh . . . we've wrestled for years now. And in the end, we've achieved a common good. The Giltedge runs at enough profit to repay its investors and developers the large sums they sank into it with the honest hope of reward for their risk-taking. And between us, we've made the mine better for the men. Our next step is an infirmary. It's budgeted for this year. We're also handling the dynamite in a safer way. *We're making progress* in spite of falling silver prices. Below a dollar an ounce, Trego. We can't control that; if prices go much lower we'll lose money."

"If Daley can do her, you can do her."

"The Hammons are in Helena. It'll take a while to get you an answer. I don't have the authority to make that kind of decision."

"You'll have a bleddy week, and not a day longer then."

"All right, Hugh."

"Don't first-name me, Webb."

"Blast it, Hugh Trego, we're in this together."

Trego glared, and then stalked out like an angry bull. Webb heard the bang of doors. He stuffed a chunk of wood into the potbelly stove to hold off the brutal cold. Mines usually shut down in the Montana winter. Men got sick coming out of their wet tunnels into below-zero air. But this year they had kept on running. They had to, he thought grimly.

He felt weary, as he always did after a table-pounding session with Hugh Trego. There were moments when he wondered why he stayed on. He felt like a general waging war on several fronts: the union, Daley, the Hammons, the competition, the falling price of silver, and the treacherous ore itself. But of all those, dealing with Daley had been the most exhausting.

That pirate had caused him more grief than all the rest put together. An eight-hour day. For two years the mine had been under siege, and for two years the Hammons had been losing ground. There were three parties in this— Daley, the Hammons, and the Knights of Labor, but it was Daley who forged the alliance that could give him victory.

Daley had abandoned Gill's horizontal shaft and driven a new one straight down four hundred feet, getting better values all the while. After that he had driven a crosscut straight across the line into the rich Giltedge ore, which he was mining as fast as possible, carving out huge chunks of the bonanza each day, even including holidays.

This awesome theft had been veneered by the apex law. In vain had the Hammon brothers' attorneys, Arnote and Quinton, pleaded for restraining orders. Salty old Judge Julius Gear had informed them that since the ownership of the ore body was in dispute, he would restrain both sides from mining it if he restrained anyone. The Hammons had retreated from that, remembering with horror how the miners had responded. Maybe old Gear remembered it too.

It seemed to Webb that all he had done for two years

was supply information to the lawyers. Potter-Pride had brought in experts who testified that the disputed ore apexed on the Gill claim; that it was chemically and structurally the same silver-galena in siliceous jasper that was found in the Giltedge claim. Even the stratigraphy was identical. That was bunk, as far as Webb was concerned.

Arnote and Quinton had countered with evidence showing that the ore actually apexed on the Giltedge at the site of the shaft; that no leads crossed the boundary more than a few feet because dikes of porphyry separated the Giltedge vein from the Hangfire's; and that Daley's purchase of Gill's claim was a nefarious act.

But Potter-Pride had been able to demonstrate that the Giltedge ore had been located later than Gill's ore, hence Gill's was the prior and valid claim. And now Julius Gear was mulling all that, while keeping a weather eye on the horizon for mobs of angry miners bearing nooses.

All of it had given Webb clenched-teeth fits. He'd mine, and mine fast, even while Daley's men burrowed like termites. Now and then the Giltedge men at the three-hundred-foot level heard muffled booms thundering through the rock below them, and knew that the Hangfire men were tunneling ever closer and might some day burst into Giltedge drifts and crosscuts. When that happened, there'd be bloody war, crew against crew.

"Baghote, bring me the employment files. I've got to put together some figures," Webb yelled past the open door.

"Oh, hold your horses," Baghote said. "You never give me advance notice. It takes time."

Baghote poked his craggy head into Webb's office. "I heard it. Eight hours. The man's an anarchist. He should be shot."

"No, he's not an anarchist."

"He's a dangerous man. Why, I work twelve hours. Now suppose I was to strike. Go down to eight hours. Oh, then you'd suffer. You don't even know where the employment files are. But I won't. Unlike certain miners, I'm loyal to the company."

"Baghote, I need the files right now."

"Well I'm getting them. Eight hours indeed. Laziness. I work fourteen sometimes and you never hear me complain. Not ever. Not even when I'm sick and you make me work myself half to death."

Baghote's head vanished from the doorway, and then all of him materialized, with thick folders in his hands. "There. Don't you cave in." He squinted about, and quietly closed the frosted glass door behind him. "You know," he said, "there are ways to deal with this."

"I'm busy, Baghote."

"Oh, there are ways. I saw the man in question walking through the sporting district. The very man who was here minutes ago."

"Baghote—"

"Yes, I was standing on the Cashbox Street bridge, but not in that district, and there he was over there. I think you could use that. Just tell him his private life is known, and then you won't have to worry about an eight-hour day."

"Is that so? Thank you, Baghote."

"It's so. I just want you to know that you have at least one loyal and observant man here."

Webb sighed. He had to determine how much production would decline with the same manning of an eight-hour shift, or whether it would require more men—and more pay—or whether they should take a wildcat strike.

CHAPTER 39

. . . .

For weeks May Goode had pined for this night. It would be the most important thing that ever happened in Cashbox. Eagerly she found her way to the front row of seats in the Exchange Hall, with Slug Svensrud at her side.

She doffed her thin coat and settled it under her to soften the bite of the hard bench.

The podium had been converted into a stage, with curtains at either side creating wings. Somewhere just out of sight Sarah Bernhardt waited to open *Camille*, the most famous of her roles. Even though *The Plain Truth* would go to press tomorrow, a hole remained in its front page for her review and for Willard's interview with the Divine Sarah at the Palace Hotel. They would put the paper to bed late this evening.

At eight-thirty, ushers dimmed the house lanterns and lit the row of footlamps whose bright light, thrown onto the stage by reflectors, would limn the great and scandalous actress. At eight-thirty-one, she bloomed upon the makeshift stage in a dazzling white gown, walking as if she had an iron rod down her spine.

May gasped. Bernhardt's frilled white dress fitted her so tightly it looked to be glued on. But not until the French actress turned to face her audience did anyone know that it had been cut below the waist and only the Divine Sarah's rigid posture kept her breasts covered.

"It's so low she could put a leg through it," whispered Slug. "I oughtta pinch her."

May's cheeks burned. She'd never seen anything like that before. Sarah Bernhardt's ivory bosom bulged softly from the slanting neckline. But soon May was absorbed in the great Alexandre Dumas story about an aging Parisian courtesan, Marguerite Gautier, who is rescued from her sinful ways by the penniless and passionate young Armand Duval. Madame Bernhardt's English was almost undecipherable, but the seductive music of her voice, which sounded as if she were in the throes of passion, mesmerized all who beheld her.

How strangely she behaved on stage, May thought. Everything seemed so unnatural, so stylized, and yet so galvanizing that it swept aside May's cares and drew her into the story. It had scandalized American audiences everywhere with its frankness about worldly Continental people.

May thought she'd write about that: this was not a story about Americans, but about a fallen woman of Paris. But she knew she wouldn't: in moments like this her own past haunted her.

Furtively May peered around her at all the rapt faces. Even Mrs. Webb and her temperance women were scattered through the hall, no doubt wrinkling their noses. Maybe the men were waiting for the actress's bodice to fall open; maybe the women were dreading it. But it never did, even when the famous actress, an awful tease, bent over to pick up a flower, using the joints of her legs to lower herself rather than tilting her body. Sarah Bernhardt didn't have a hinge in her backbone.

May sighed when that electrifying moment had passed. She eyed Slug, who seemed vaguely disappointed. Men! Why did they always preach against indecency while enjoying it? Bernhardt's huge eyes seemed to glow like black agates in the fierce lamplight, while her dark hair fell in wild array, adding some kind of electricity to her performance.

When the play came to its tragic end, tears leaked down May's cheeks. The audience applauded recklessly and cheered the Divine Sarah, who acknowledged their fealty with a daring bow.

"Don't you look!" May hissed at Slug.

"I didn't see a thing," he muttered. "She stood up too fast, darn it."

The troupers lit the house lamps and people straggled out. Slug helped her into her old coat and then steered her into the cold blast of night, toward the newspaper office. He became silent, almost dour. She saw through the grimy window that Willard Croker had beaten them. He had donned his apron and was swiftly setting his interview.

"Thank you, Slug," she said. "I loved it."

"May—I want to talk to you."

"Not now."

He paused grimly, and then drew her to him and kissed her. Violently she twisted her lips away and offered only her cheek. He let go, wounded. Then he muttered something savage under his breath and stalked off into the darkness, his feet crunching snow. She watched helplessly as he vanished. He wanted her and she had walled him out. Sarah Bernhardt's seductive daring had inflamed him and made it worse, she thought. She couldn't help it, and she couldn't change.

She sighed. No man had been kinder and gentler. No man had been more persistent, never surrendering in the face of all her rebuffs. Often he had asked her why, frightening her with his intense gaze. Once she had confessed that she didn't want children—which had left him puzzled and despondent.

She hung her coat and donned her printer's apron, knowing it wouldn't keep ink from her only good dress.

"There you are," said Croker. "I thought I'd have to write the review myself. What're you going to say?"

She didn't reply. She still had to compose in longhand and then set her work, even though she had gained speed in her years as a printer's devil.

"Don't you pan her. This is the first time we've seen a celebrity in Cashbox, and we're going to make sure we have more. We're going to fill that hall tomorrow night, too."

"Then it's not a review," she retorted. She no longer worried about Croker's opinions. He could fire her on the spot and it wouldn't matter. There was always work for a woman in a mining camp, and probably at a better wage than eighty-five cents a day, too. She stayed at the paper because the work suited her, not because Croker had made life any easier for her.

Somehow, Croker understood that and didn't push her too far. She had freed him to gallivant around town and play the bigshot while she toiled over type and wrote most of the stories. He didn't want to lose her.

She decided not to let him dictate her review. There had been something artificial about Bernhardt, and she was going to say it. The woman's aura behind those hot footlamps had more to do with the life she led and the gown she wore than with her acting ability. Bernhardt was coasting on her reputation. That's what the review was going to say.

She scribbled furiously on foolscap and then waited for Willard to finish setting his interview, which he would leave for her to proof while he vanished into the cold for a whiskey at the Palace. That was where all the worldly gentlemen would sit around and admire the gorgeous Bernhardt.

May knew little more about Willard now than when she had first walked into *The Plain Truth*. But over the months her intuitions had sharpened. She reported the news more carefully than he, especially when the Cashbox Town Lot Company, or J. Ernest Potter-Pride, were involved. At times he had torn her stories apart and rewritten them, giving her no reason why. But the results were always the same: he had warped the facts.

She had been tempted to protest but she never did because she didn't want anyone looking too closely into her past. She wanted to live. Slug's open caring was tearing her to bits. She wondered how long she could keep her secret from him; how long she could put off the man who was determined to have her. How long she could resist her deepening love for that good man who adored her so much.

She felt an odd panic as she worked, a panic induced by Bernhardt's subtle evocation of the flesh. It had triggered something in Slug and had stirred a hunger in her. She glanced out the window into the bitter black night, fearing he might show up again to take her back to Mrs. Flower's cottage. Oh, God, not tonight.

She swiftly set her review, running the type into lines, and the lines into the almost completed page. She had written too long for the hole he had left her, so she cut her review by seven lines. She locked the form and rolled proofing ink over it. Then she laid newsprint over the inked type and rolled an impression. She proofed swiftly, catching a lot of errors. Willard had been in a hurry.

She was correcting the errors when Slug walked through the door, escorted by a blast of icy air.

"I'll take you home," he said. "It's like unto one o'clock."

"No, Slug. I'll be all right."

"I gotta talk, May. I've gotta ask you lots of things."

"No, Slug, please—please let me be."

"No, I can't any more. You're deathly afraid of something. You're hiding it from me. May, it don't matter who you are or what's happened, I love you and I want you. That show, that fellow Duval, how he loved her; how he loved her so much she was transformed by it. You know, how she stopped being a . . . mistress and just wanted his pure love. That set me thinking. I'm like that play fellow. All I've wanted since I met you is you, May. All I want is to make a home for you, give you my love forever. Don't put me off tonight. That play, May, it got me to thinking I've got to give you more; I've got to let you know. . . ."

May didn't hear the rest through her sobs.

CHAPTER 40
. . . .

In the privacy of his spartan fortress at the back of The Oriental, One-Eyed Jack Wool whirled the combination lock on his black lacquered safe. He heard a muffled click, and then levered the laminated steel door open. He extracted an Eventual Cigar box filled with loose cash, and removed federal greenbacks, state banknotes, eagles and double eagles until he had a total of five hundred dollars and twenty-seven cents.

From a box within the safe he also extracted two decks of busy-back advantage cards sold by E.M. Grandine,

41 Liberty Street, New York. These were available in such back designs as calico, endless vine, stars, marble, perpetuum mobile, and millefleurs, and they had in common a design so complex that the average rube would not see the markings. He always used the endless vine. Brighter gamblers avoided games where the cards had complicated backs. He had four decks left; time to reorder.

He closed the safe and spun the dial. Then he pulled his black eyepatch over his greased jet hair and snapped it into place upon his perfectly sound left eye. He admired its sinister look; it made him a true devil's lieutenant. In his trade, theater was everything. This particular eyepatch, manufactured by Doctor Cross & Co., of New Orleans, was molded to his eye cavity. Its front was covered with glossy silk, giving it a faint shine and concealing the small glassed peephole behind it which permitted Wool to peer through the gauzy silk and see carelessly held cards.

He stuffed the coins and bills into the breast pocket of his black suit, and accoutered himself in a black cape suitable for the mild March weather. He stalked across the Cashbox Creek bridge into the heart of town and turned right on Main, which took him to the Doric pillared portico of the Cashbox State Bank. Within, he snaked past the clerk, Christopher Ravina, straight back to the office of John Oliver Cromwell, and sat down.

"It's that time again," said the banker.

One-Eyed Jack Wool nodded, and emptied the coin and paper onto the banker's desk. The banker counted it, huffing like an idle locomotive.

"Hmmm, a banknote issued by the Merchants and Fishermen's Bank of Georgia," he muttered. "I'll have to discount that."

"It's legal tender."

"Sort of. Ten percent discount. Ninety dollars, Jack. A long way to redeem for gold."

"I'm Wool, only Wool, never anything but Wool."

"That Savannah paper's a risk."

"Take it for face value or be damned."

"Gresham's Law," said Cromwell cheerily. "Bad money drives out good. I'll fob it off on somebody who'll spend it in Livingston."

The banker scratched out a receipt. Then he drafted a cashier's cheque for five hundred dollars, payable to the St. Vincent Foundling Hospital in Baltimore. He slid it into an envelope, addressed it, and attached a two-cent stamp. He dropped the twenty-seven cents into a drawer. "There you are, Wool. Shall I mail it?"

"I will," Wool said, snatching the letter.

"They sent you a reply again," said Cromwell, handing Wool an unopened letter addressed to him in care of the bank. A few weeks after Wool mailed each cheque, one Sister Therese acknowledged the contribution of their rich benefactor with sweet gratitude and the assurance of many prayers from the whole order.

Wool pocketed the letter, pierced into the blustery day, and headed for the post office, as he had always done. When he posted the cheque he had the usual effusion of delight, rather like guzzling a stiff dose of laudanum. It wasn't that he knew a soul at the foundling home. Nor did he have the slightest connection with it. He knew only that it was the oldest orphanage in the United States and operated by nuns. He didn't know a Carmelite from a Sister of Charity, but they all did good works, which is what mattered.

He felt a vast cheer abuilding: his character functioned on the hydraulic principle. Stuff five hundred dollars of virtue into one end, and he'd pump out exactly five hundred dollars' worth of his peculiar vices at the other. With the accounts in his favor, he could be particularly vicious tonight. He studied viciousness the way Southern Baptists studied virtue. He knew all about that because he was the son of a table-thumping Arkansas evangelist and hat passer.

His pleasures included the skinning of every last cent from any sucker who walked into The Oriental, including the stash in the shoe. He preferred to send the rubes into the streets shirtless and shoeless, but Svensrud got upset if he stole their pants also.

He never lacked for customers, and many evenings The Oriental was packed. He had discovered a great truth about human nature: most suckers want to be fleeced. They came into his lair looking for a legendary gulling, something to rue like the clap, something to grouse about for a month to their cronies. They wanted Sin. And he was pleased to offer it to them. With the fierce glare of his brown eye, he intimidated them into betting the wedding ring on their finger or the shinplaster tucked in their belt. He displayed his character like a bishop in his mitre. Not for One-Eyed Jack the gambler's pretense of being a visiting rancher or sewing machine drummer sitting down for a friendly game. Not for One-Eyed Jack the gambler's spiel that promised winnings galore. Oh, no. He'd found a cussed spot in the backside of mankind and bit into it like an eel.

He loved most of all those gents known in the trade as kickers, players who lost badly and yelled cheat. Ah, how they lit Wool up. Let the terrible word flutter from the mouth of a loser and the man would be cold meat. There were always plenty of witnesses to describe Wool's detonation of gunpowder as self-defense if it came to that—which it rarely did.

"This isn't a square game," Wool would say as he recharged the cylinder of his Smith and Wesson and his bouncers hauled away the sidepork. "I'm as crooked as a dog's hind legs." The other gents at the table always hawed and wheezed and shuffled their chips. He'd done that thrice without falling into the snares of Constable Svensrud or the coroner's jury. They were calling a certain pasture in the town boneyard Wool's Park.

Back in his monkish room Wool opened the stiff letter and found an oval photograph mounted in a pasteboard frame. It showed a striking girl of twelve or thirteen, with lustrous dark hair falling to her waist, doe eyes, and the look of a captive deer. She wore a Mother Hubbard that hid everything from chin to toe, but not even that atrocity against womanhood could conceal the child's lithe form. A winsome smile played about her lips.

Puzzled, Wool turned to the letter from Sister Therese, and skipped past her usual effusions of gratitude. "I enclose a photograph of one of our little charges whose name is Marie. She came to us when she was three, abandoned, starved, terribly ill, and nameless. Now she is thirteen. See how she has prospered. Soon she will leave us. We let our children go into the world at fourteen or fifteen, depending on how ready they are. It is a time of many tears for the sisters. When they leave us they are without family or means, and have nothing with which to begin life other than the grace of God and our prayers.

"We have a simple program here that seems to help. We like to give each child a sponsor, a good and loving adult who is firm in the Faith; who can guide our charges into vocations and chaperone them. The sisters are hoping you may do us one more kindness.

"Would you see to Marie's future, see to her life in the Faith, nurture the strength and character that will help her to become a loving wife and mother when that joyous day comes? She is lively and intelligent; she sews and cooks and can do her numbers and read well; she lacks only a strong adult such as yourself to help her cope with a harsh world. Your contributions shine among the sisters, and we have every confidence you are the one to help Marie.

"Surely you understand, Mister Wool, that there is no rush. Pray about it over the next months, asking whether you may be the foster parent of a girl whose real parents no one will ever know. You will receive an answer, we are sure."

One-Eyed Jack Wool snarled an answer that would have scorched Sister Therese's ears. So this is what his money had bought him. There'd be no more five-hundred-dollar donations for the bloodsucking orphanage. Foster father, was he? He laughed nasally, thinking about the shock waves his vocation would send through the sisters if only they knew. Maybe he'd write and tell them to send her out. He'd put her to work upstairs, and get his money back in a year or two. The Little Orphan, two dollars a trick, and all his.

He slid the mounted photograph and the letter into the safe, on top of the rest from the orphanage, and slammed the door shut with a satisfying clank. He'd bought five hundred dollars' worth of hell today, and he planned to spend it all in one night.

CHAPTER 41

· · · · · · · · · · · · · · · · ·

Whenever Con left for Helena to take care of business there, Cashbox wrapped Sylvie like a shroud. Without him, the town shrank into a rough little mining camp as mean as barbed wire. It didn't matter that the silver camp had grown to fifteen hundred; that the old log facades were disappearing behind false fronts and shiplap; that these days one could find two milliners and a tailor, a draper, two bakeries, three furniture dealers, two accountants, and a cobbler all hip to hip along Main Street and its cross streets. The business district had turned itself into brick and stone while a new two-room schoolhouse stood on Robinson and Pine.

It didn't appease her. She thought of ditching Cashbox for some grand and wanton city like San Francisco or Denver, but she was making too much money for that. Better to get rich as Rockefeller before going anywhere. Anyway, she loved her Exchange Club. Her whole life centered upon the gentlemen who whiled away their days in her club. They loved her, and brought her little whatnots. She feared she was putting down roots, even though she hadn't intended to. All she ever wanted was to find the end of her rainbow.

She had a keen business eye. To forestall a rival hall,

she gradually replaced her benches with more comfortable
seating, still movable so it could be stored around the pe-
rimeter of the hall for dances and balls. She built a spacious foyer, which offered a coatroom, a ticket booth, and
a concession stand where—on certain evenings—she did a
lively bar trade. During temperance lectures it offered sar-
saparilla and lemonade.

Her expenses were minimal. The hall consumed nothing
more than a little cordwood and lamp oil. Her Exchange
Club ran itself. She employed a widow named Mrs.
Flower to wash her linens and clean; and the widow's son,
Albert, to supply wood, do chores and run errands for the
members. If Sylvie wasn't at hand, the gentlemen poured
their own libations, usually Old Gideon and branch water,
and kept a tab for her. If they wanted food, they sent Albert around the corner to the Palace chophouse, and soon
a waiter would appear carrying steaming salvers of viands.
That suited Sylvie. It meant no kitchen, temperamental
chefs, pantry purchases, pots or pans or plates. She kept
some minimal service on hand for coffee and snacks, but
didn't bother with anything more elaborate.

All of which made life amiable. One March evening, after Con left for Helena on the three o'clock stage to White
Sulphur and Townsend, she meandered aimlessly among
the members and guests clustered in her leather
wingchairs. Often she sat with them, plucking at strands of
rebel hair and listening. They usually enjoyed it. If their
banter wasn't for her ears, they would smile and wait silently, and she would be cued to wander elsewhere. She always knew what they were gabbing about anyway.

Mostly they debated silver mining stocks, lamented the
price of silver, the costs of mining, and the blindness of
Congress. The Exchange Club, in addition to being the site
of deals, had become a bourse where members bought and
sold shares in local mines, and sometimes even Nevada or
Idaho silver mines.

She poured amontillado for herself one evening and sat
beside Jefferson Grover, the manager of the Ophir, who

was sipping Tennessee charcoal whiskey with half a dozen other mining moguls.

"We hit a new pocket," he told her. "The Cousin Jacks call it the biggest boulder yet. That's how it's been. Just when our reserves look precarious, we strike good values again. Why, we're set for six months with this one. I've made eight thousand dollars in a week. The stock's gone up four points since we announced the new reserves. It'll go up some more, too."

"Eight thousand? In a week?" Sylvie marveled. "What's Ophir stock trading for?"

"Why, yesterday it was seven and a half asked, seven and a quarter bid, Sylvie."

"Does it pay a dividend?"

"Oh, yes, twenty-five cents a quarter—but it was suspended the last two quarters by the directors. It'll be restored, I'm sure."

"I'll buy two hundred if anyone wishes to sell," she said. They stared. She was on new ground, and she wondered how the gents would take it.

"You don't want to do that. Silver shares are risky business, Sylvie," said Lyman Barteau, who managed the Delirium Tremens up the gulch, which was not so shaky after all. "The Ophir's an up-and-down proposition. It's been as low as a dollar a share."

"If the mine hit new ore, that's good enough for me," she retorted. "I don't want to be left out of this little bonanza."

"Well, it happens that I'd be glad to sell some, Sylvie. But I'll tell you, I think you're taking a risk," Grover cautioned.

"I'll do it if you'll sell at the bidding. That'll be fourteen-fifty, right?"

"All right. I'll drop off the shares tomorrow and you can pay me then."

"At the bank at ten."

"Be a little cautious, madam," added Leverett Case, a mining engineer employed by the Belle of Cashbox and the Cleopatra mines in Robinson to deal with a water problem. "Silver's falling steadily. Down around a dollar."

"I have a money tree downstairs, Mr. Case. It drops new fruit each night."

"Well don't count on it. If silver prices drop much more, there'll be no more fruit on your tree."

Sylvie grinned. She had never bought stock before. It tickled her to be privy to so much inside information. She had an advantage. She resolved then and there not to tell Con. He'd try to steer her, manage her, make her decisions for her. Or he would tell her to stick with safer things, the way these gentlemen were telling her. He would never let her spread her wings, let her win or get burnt according to her own shrewdness.

The next day she met Jefferson Grover at the bank, gave him a check, and received two hundred-share certificates of Ophir Mining Company stock, which sported elaborate engravings of bare-breasted Abundance holding up the un-balanced Scales of Success, one of the pans piled high with bars of bullion. At Sylvie's request, John Oliver Cromwell put them into his fireproof safe.

A beginning, she thought. Life suddenly acquired a keen edge. Everything around her looked razor-sharp in the March air. She saw the shabbiness of the Cashbox business district, the intractable wilderness of the ridges, the huddle of houses that would be considered hovels in the east. She inhaled smelter smoke, and watched ore wagons rumble by on the crowded street. Cashbox roared and bawled and licked its young chops, and dropped apples of silver bullion and piles of base metals. She would get rich along with the rest.

From that day on, she began to acquire shares from the gents in the Exchange Club, squandering her dance hall profits faster than they rolled in. On a tip from Case she bought a hundred of the Cleopatra for only three and a quarter. With inside information from other members she bought two hundred of the Belle of Cashbox for only seventy cents a share. She bought ten of the Yellowstone, which went for its par of five, and a hundred shares each of the Silver Star, Iron Chief, Blue-Eyed Nellie, and the Silver Baron. Things would blossom. Soon her nest egg would multiply, and each bar of bullion leaving Cashbox would add to her account.

Con returned in April and got wind of it soon enough. She'd been dreading it. But she wasn't going to let him run her life or wreck her independence.

"Sylvie, how many shares of Ophir?" he asked at the chophouse one evening.

"Lots."

He stared at her, and she couldn't read what passed behind his eyes.

"You'd better sell them. Take a loss if you must. I'll help you."

"Sell them? While you have over half the mine? You just made a huge profit. You're going to take advantage of me."

He sighed, and seemed full of knowledge he couldn't impart. "Sylvie, I have a paper profit, not a real one. That mine—it'll fold one of these days. They never did hit a real lode. They just stagger from one lucky strike to another. When they get past the, ah, geological transition, the belt where granites meet the jasper—that'll be it."

"But you own most of it. Why don't you sell?"

"I can't without driving down the price. Sylvie," he said desperately. "Please sell your Ophir stock immediately. I'll buy it at your cost."

"You'll buy it? You'll get even richer at my expense."

He shook his head. "I'd rather not buy it. All I want is control, and not a share more. Each extra share'll cost me."

"Con, what on earth are you talking about?"

Con Daley stared into the lamplight. "Sylvie, do you know what an assessment mine is?"

She shook her head.

"I thought so. The directors of the Ophir can assess all stockholders any amount they wish to continue development. If a stockholder can't pay it, his shares lose that much value."

"You mean they can charge me instead of just paying dividends?"

He nodded. "That's one way a mine raises development capital. You're in for two hundred shares. If the Ophir assesses you ten dollars a share, you'd owe the company two thousand dollars."

"Two thousand? Oh! Are all mines like that?"

"No, it depends on how they're incorporated. But the Ophir is."

She pondered that. She could be hit hard and it flabbergasted her. "But Con—you own tens of thousands of shares. You'd be assessed a fortune."

Con Daley smiled. "That's right," he said. "Fifty percent plus one share. But I have the controlling interest in whatever comes in from an assessment."

"You mean—you could take everything that comes in?"

"No, but I could direct the way the Ophir management spends it. On risky new properties, for instance. It's a way of using other people's money. That's what finance is about."

She drew a shaky breath. "I'll think about selling, Con. I'm a little impetuous sometimes."

CHAPTER 42

. . . .

May found herself trembling as Slug hurried her through the icy night toward his cabin. It wasn't just the harsh air that made her shiver; it was the looming convulsion that would drive her from Cashbox. She felt his arm around her shoulder, giving her no leeway. She tried to tug free as they passed Mrs. Flower's cabin, but Slug's arm imprisoned her. She resented the loss of her freedom—and yet didn't mind.

She decided to tell him—and leave the next day. She would find some other camp and eke out a life. She knew she would miss him. His determination to win her was flattering. All these months she'd had a gentle friend, even if she hadn't wanted one.

She could tell how bitter the night was from the squeak of the snow underfoot. It would be bitter in more ways than one, she thought grimly. He paused at a darkened log building and opened the door. She entered into icy blackness.

"It'll be a minute," he muttered. He rustled through familiar dark. A coal-oil lantern flared. She gasped. She had expected a primitive, dirt-floored miner's cabin. But the whole interior glowed the color of natural wood. While he built a fire in his cast-iron stove, she marveled at his handiwork. He was a master cabinetmaker. Waxed floors leapt to her eye. He had built a compact kitchen around the stove, with shining counters and cupboards, all brightly shellacked.

Even the furniture had been artfully crafted of peeled poles and slats of wood mortised into them. He had built a dining table and chairs; two easy chairs with red, yellow and orange pillows in them; a long bench, desk, bed and nightstand. She eyed the bed nervously. It had been fashioned from peeled pine poles and was double-sized to accommodate his large frame. Much to her amazement she discovered bright rosemaling on the cupboards and doors which complemented the cushions and pillows that were heaped lightheartedly around the room. Slug Svensrud's place glowed with Scandinavian art.

She grew aware that he was watching her from beside the stove, which was popping and snapping like Chinese New Year, jamming its cheery heat into the room. In all her life she had never been in a cottage that radiated such joy. He watched her as she drew close to the stove and felt its blooming heat pierce through her shabby coat and warm her numb fingers.

"It's beautiful, Slug," she said. "I never dreamed you

could do this. . . ." Even as she said it a certain sorrow slid through her. She had momentarily forgotten why he had brought her here.

He said nothing more until his bright cottage had warmed, and then he took her coat and settled her in an armchair beside the snapping stove, tucking a scarlet blanket about her.

"All right, May," he said.

She sighed, wondering how to begin. She knew she could do it dry-eyed; she had cried a lifetime of tears in prison, and the springs were dry now. He waited patiently, his face utterly blank but his intense blue eyes upon her.

"I'm a criminal," she said softly.

He seemed frozen there in the chair beside her. But his hand clenched.

"I served three years in the women's prison at Shakopee, Minnesota. I killed my little boy. I didn't mean to." She met his gaze. "Now may I go?"

He stared at the stove, at the glowing cat's eyes of light glimmering around its door. He glanced at her and then the stove, as if puzzling things out. "You're not my prisoner," he said. "If you want to go, you can go."

She rose. It hadn't been bad.

"I'd like you to tell me the whole story first," he said.

Why not? She sat down and told him about herself, about Robby, about the afternoon in New Ulm, and the terrible moment she couldn't remember, droning coldly through it all while the stove popped and cracked like rifle shots.

"What did you plead?"

"I didn't. I just told the judge to do what he wanted. He entered that no-contest plea, and sent me away for manslaughter."

He stared at the stove again. "What are your plans?" he asked at last.

"Leave here as soon as I can. Now you know. I'll go somewhere and start again. Unless you're going to put me in jail."

It startled him. "What for, May?"

She shrugged. "Lawmen do that," she said. "Bars. Do you think it stopped when they let me out? Bars and steel surrounding me. Even when no one sees them, I see them."

"Are you still married? That ring—"

"Frank divorced me while I was doing time."

"He deserted you before all this happened?"

"I hadn't seen him in three years. He was . . . a good man in his way. He hired out to a farmer in Mankato, but I didn't know that. He vanished. I guess he couldn't stand me. Then I was on my own, with a little boy and a garden and neighbors that needed things sometimes, sewing, gardening. He never sent me a dime."

"You still wear the ring."

"I'm in a town with ten men for every woman."

"Did you love Robby?"

"Oh, Slug!" She buried her face in her hands, her sobs wracking her slim body and the wetness leaking from her eyes.

He waited until she had snuffled to a stop. "You think it's over? You think it'd happen again?"

"Of course it will!" she cried. "It's a demon in me."

"You don't think you've grown? You know, gotten older—changed?"

"Oh, I don't know, I don't know. Can I go now?" Her words sheared out sharp-edged. "Why don't you put me on the next stage? I don't belong anywhere!"

"Did Charlotte Keiserling try for you?"

"I just wouldn't—"

"She did, but you wouldn't. You cleaned the old geezer's greasy spoon instead, and snitched some vittles. Wouldn't try Charlotte's life even when you were starved to nothing." Some amusement crinkled around his eyes.

She wept again, remembering those desperate hours, and her temptation.

"May, don't cry. Bad things just happen. That's the past.

It's gone forever. You're the finest woman I've ever known."

She peered at him through tears. "Don't you despise me?"

He smiled. "Despise you? I love you. Do you like my house? I did all this for you. I love to work with wood. It's all local pine and ash and birch."

"What?"

"My house. I've a gift, I think. Maybe some day I'll quit lawing and build furniture. I like to come in here when my work's done. I boil up some tea and feel the wood sighing and laughing around me. Wood talks to me when I run my draw knife over it. Wood loves to be shaped by my saws and mallets and chisels. Wood's proud when I dress it with shellac. Wood's God's gift to men with Norwegian souls. Do you think I could sell some furniture?"

"Oh, Slug, you don't care about me." She couldn't understand him. She was talking about a child's death, prison, a condemned life, being an outcast, trying to get past living so she could die; but he was talking about his beautiful cabin with its blond glow of deftly carved and shaped woods.

"Care about you? Listen to what I'm saying. I'm not really talking about wood. I'm talking about us."

"Slug, I'm tired. I'll take the next stage to somewhere. They'll find me out too, some day. Then I'll go somewhere else and keep on running until my life's over. I've got to tell Willard I'm quitting. I've got to pack—"

"You should try rosemaling, May. I think you'd be good at it. Big red hearts and green leaves on twined stems. Yellow flowers. Lots of wood in this cabin to paint on."

"Slug, stop that! Stop that!"

"I'm an artist at heart. That's what I really am. All afternoon and night I'm out pounding on crooks and poking into saloons and misery parlors, but I don't like it none. I do it because I'm big and mean and it pays fifty regularly, at least when I shake the license fees out of the saloons.

Do you like my house? I thought of you when I was doing this. It's all for you."

"I'll go now, Slug." She rose again.

"I wish you'd stay. It's a nice evening, May."

"It's two o'clock. What'll Mrs. Flower think?"

"That you're doing something scandalous." A smile built around his lips.

"Oh, Slug. Would you take me home?"

"The cabin's warm, May. If you insist, but it's below zero."

"I can't stay here."

"There's a nice little bed there. It's got leather straps under the mattress, some elkhide I tanned. I figure if you're tired, you could just slide in there. It's got that comforter, too. You see that wall? In front of it?"

"Wall? What're you talking about?"

"The wall. I see it. It runs from here to there. I guess if I'd try to walk through that wall, I'd just bang my head and get tossed back. But I see it, so I won't go pushing through."

"It'd be scandalous."

"It would? I guess you're touchy about your reputation. I could sleep out in the woodshed."

"You'd freeze."

"I've got pillows and that deacon's bench."

"Slug, don't, don't. Oh, Slug . . . would you just hold me and let me cry? Then I'll go."

He was grinning. She loved him.

He held her until she stopped weeping. Then he kissed her and drew her tight and she felt warm at last.

CHAPTER 43

• • • • • • • • • • • • • • • •

Willard Croker rolled up the proof sheets for the advertisement and hastened to Pride's law offices. The blustery spring wind matched his mood. At last, he'd become a silver king in his own right, and then he could show those fat moguls up in the Exchange Club a thing or two.

The memory still rankled. He applied to that snooty woman for membership, and even laid some cash on her. She seemed reluctant. A day later she walked into the press and said she'd consulted with her members. They expressed their utmost esteem for the publisher of *The Plain Truth*, but felt that an editor's presence would inhibit their confidential dealings. They were, however, eagerly looking forward to entertaining him there. She smiled sweetly and returned the hundred.

So they wouldn't let him in. The rejection still festered in him, and ever since then he'd filled his columns with snide remarks about the Malefactors of Wealth in the Exchange Club. Whenever he had nothing else to fill his columns, he ran something nasty about Sylvie Duvalier. Once he'd called her "the pampered plaything of the ruthless rich." She never responded, which irked him. He wanted her to come storming in—which would give him more fun.

His purse was thin again. He had sold off all the town lots and now he had nothing but the break-even rag for an income. Boehm had come through just in time.

He found Potter-Pride before his mirror, primping his hair with his mother-of-pearl brush.

"Here's the proofs," he said, laying them out on Pride's desk. "Do you have the certificates?"

"Right here," said Pride, handing Croker a sheaf of engraved stock certificates for a corporation called The Aurora Borealis Consolidated Mining Company. These securities were printed on bank paper in money green and black, with a gold gilt-edge. There would be an issue of a hundred thousand shares. Sold at their ten-dollar par, they would yield a million dollars.

"Well?" asked Pride.

"Exquisite," muttered Croker. The engravers had

wrought a spread-winged American eagle perched above wind-billowed flags. Beneath were two pyramids composed of bars of bullion, each radiating stylized sunrays. Wrapped in a banner was the Latin motto, *Monumentum aere Perennius.*

"What's that motto mean?"

"A monument more enduring than brass."

Croker whickered.

Pride hunkered over his desk, proofing the advertisement, which he had written. It would occupy a third of the rear page of *The Plain Truth*. It was a prospectus of the new Aurora Borealis Consolidated Mining Company.

The attorney had cobbled it up. Its board of directors consisted of six Cashbox businessmen. Two were merchants, one a mortician, two were in the drayage business, and one was an ice and coal dealer. None of them knew a lick about mining.

The assets of the Aurora Borealis actually consisted of seven claims that Boehm had jumped, plus the Chollar Mine up at Hawkeye, a promising operation that had flooded at the hundred-foot level and couldn't be pumped out. Now there remained nothing but the shaft, the hoist works stripped of its machinery, and a superintendent's office, occupied by Boehm. The jumped claims were mostly dry holes, but one or two showed good ores. It wasn't much, but the Aurora Borealis didn't need much.

The advertisement asserted that development of promising locations would proceed at once. Rich ores had been located. Assay reports were on file in the offices of the company's attorney of record, J. Ernest Potter-Pride. As for the Chollar, it would be fruitful shortly. Under the direction of the noted New York mining engineer R. Jackson Cain, pumping would be completed by July, and its rich ores, running sixty ounces of silver a ton along with lead and some gold, would be mined beginning in August, upon renovation of the hoist works.

Cain's report was available for public examination, along with the assays. Purchases of the common stock could be made at the law offices, the Cashbox Town Lot Company, and the offices of *The Plain Truth.*

The abandoned Chollar had cost Willard Croker only a hundred dollars. Now it would be the centerpiece of the Aurora Borealis. It did have good ore, and scores of Mueller assays to prove it. But they'd hit an underground river. Now the water stood at the seventy-foot level. The Chollar management had indeed hired R. Jackson Cain to look over the mine. He had concluded that no pump on earth could drain those thousands of gallons an hour.

But neither Willard Croker nor J. Ernest Potter-Pride was intimidated by a mere engineering report. After determining that R. Jackson Cain had removed to San Luis Potosi to run a Mexican silver mine for two years, Pride doctored the report on his new Remington typing machine. When Pride finished, it was Cain's expert opinion that all that was wanting was a larger pump.

"All right, that's fine. Fix the typos," Pride said. "Now let's see your article."

Willard Croker felt uncommonly proud of that article, destined for tomorrow's front page. It was the best he'd ever written. It alluded to Old Glory, loyalty to Cashbox and its sterling future, the new state of Montana, and jobs for miners.

"Willard, this is awful."

The editor was stung. "Why!" he gasped, "it's lyrical. It'll draw them to the stock like iron filings to a magnet. It's poetry. I won't change a word."

"Willard," said Pride patiently, "any trial lawyer knows you can't persuade a jury by ducking the weaknesses in your case. You've got to address the things they've doubts about. If you paint a rosy future for the Chollar and never say a word about its flooding, they'll take you for a bunco steerer."

"But Pride, we can't talk about the flooding."

"Oh yes we can. If we don't, we'll hardly sell a share. Most buyers'll know that the Chollar shut down. We have to deal with it. What'll you tell 'em?"

Croker shook his head. "I don't know."

"Of course not. Take this back and write something with no bulge in the pants."

"Such as?"

"Say that the Chollar's management had been hasty; all that's needed is a larger pump according to the engineers. The directors—name them, Willard, name every sainted soul—all feel there's a great future in the Chollar. They're all deacons under the skin."

The editor stared stonily.

"And Croker—take out all this rubbish. I mean about the future of Cashbox and the virtue of womanhood. Good Lord, Croker: 'If you harken to the music of Cashbox; if you thrill to the Majestic Mountains and the trill of meadowlarks; if you are a man of Grand Vision, able to see the glowing City set on a Hill, a Beacon to the Treasuries of the world; a robust Metropolis with happy denizens, its Womanhood safe and respected, its miners in their cheerful cottages, its booming Commerce, its forthcoming electricity and street cars—if you see the Future, you must open your hearts and Purses. You must invest in the most Fruitful Enterprise ever to grace our fair precinct, The Aurora Borealis Consolidated Mining Company.' Heaven help us, Croker. You've out-purpled William Randolph Hearst."

The lawyer sighed. "No, Willard. Your piece'll have to be about assay values, estimated reserves, the shiny price of silver when Congress acts, the prospect of an adit to drain all the mines up there, the production plans of the Aurora Borealis, the ratio of reserves to investment—you follow me?"

"No."

"All right, Willard. You're not selling this company to grangers. You're selling it to gentlemen of means. How do you sell to investors—by touting the future of Cashbox, or by touting dividends? Returns? Appreciation?"

Croker steamed. "Pride, I've been an editor twenty

years and I've never yet let some shyster lawyer tell me what to write."

J. Ernest Potter-Pride paused, smiled, and waved a milky hand deprecatingly. "Well then, my good friend, I'm out."

"You can't be out. You're sitting here on all the assays, the certificates, the incorporation papers—everything."

Potter-Pride kept an amiable silence.

"All right, all right," Croker muttered.

"Let me see the next draft."

"No," Croker snapped, bulling out the door. "I'll write it the way I want."

CHAPTER 44

· · · · · · · · · · · · · · · · · ·

Regina Maltz waited uneasily in her front room for J. Ernest Potter-Pride to pick her up. She wondered what this was all about. The attorney had never before taken her to dinner, and she couldn't help wondering why he was doing so now.

She perched on the edge of a chair in her old alpaca coat, ready to go. Her boarders would have to shift for themselves. She had laid out steaks and potatoes. Her conscience tormented her. Here she was running a boarding-house and skipping out on a meal. But Pride had been persistent, in fact, overwhelming about it. That old shyster had gushed about the good food at the Palace Hotel chop-house, and how he wanted to treat her to dinner.

She wondered what he wanted. Maybe he was going to try to sell her some shares of that Aurora Borealis Consolidated Mining Company. That must be it. He'd squeeze it out over the meal.

She sighed. She wouldn't buy a thing that jut-jawed Adonis proposed to her. He had all the makings of a politician—a heart as tender as a basket of baby rattlesnakes, the unblinking sincerity of a faith healer, and the look of a Coldstream Guard, much enhanced by stylish grooming. He'd been particularly oozy lately, asking about her life and health.

He arrived at the stroke of six, wearing his chesterfield with its black velvet collar, a homburg perched on his shining hair, and a fine black cape.

"Ah, how grand you look, Miss Maltz!" he exclaimed, surveying her with a trout eye and extended smile.

"I wasn't aware I looked like anything."

"Oh, you are lit with inner beauty, the lamp of fair womanhood forever casting its beams upon the weaker male gender," he replied. He offered her an arm and they plunged into the twilight.

He seemed dapper this evening, fairly bubbling with joy as they progressed down McDonald and Hamilton to Cashbox Street. "It's a splendid little burg," he said. "Just splendid. But there's better, believe me. Think of Washington City, with its electricity. Hotels with running water. Why, think of Gotham. Think of Helena. Cashbox is a bright light, but it's only a candle compared to the great cities."

"I prefer a good mining camp," she said. "One thing about these camps—everybody's living life to the hilt."

"Oh, they live life to the hilt elsewhere, Miss Maltz."

He steered her into the hotel lobby. The Palace never failed to dazzle her. It even had potted palms growing there—a magical bit of the tropics in cold Montana. She wanted to examine the luxurious lobby but he steered her into the chophouse. A gent in swallowtails seated them at a banquette.

"Ah, now, Miss Maltz—may I call you Regina after all this time?—Tonight we'll celebrate."

"Why are you acting so strange, Ernest?"

"Strange? Oh, it's the loveliest of evenings. I'm going to order you a sip of wine."

"I don't indulge."

"Well, I'll order a sip anyway—let's make it something delicate for your palate—so that we can have a toast."

"You're acting very peculiar. Do you want more pies?"

"I always want your pies, Regina."

"Are you selling me mining shares?"

"Oh, any other time, but not tonight. No, my dear, I won't offer you a single share; I won't spill a single tip in your ear. Oh, there're dozens who want my tips. Why, Sylvie Duvalier fastens upon my every word. But no, Regina. Tonight isn't the night for stocks and bonds. We'll be talking about other kinds of blessings."

"Whatever it is, Ernest, I won't buy it."

"Oh, ho, ho!"

"You are certainly in a strange state. Is the moon full?"

"Ah, the moon, pale goddess of night. Ah, night, the moment of bliss and intimacy and everlasting joy."

"Ernest, I'm about to leave. You will not sell me a share. Not one share of that rattletrap company."

He patted her hand. "Now, now, now. I'll order dinner and then we'll talk about serious things. Things that touch the deepest yearnings of the mortal soul."

"You don't have one."

He laughed. "Ah, Regina, we've known each other a long time, across a bridge of pies. Apple, pecan, cherry, peach, plum, pumpkin, quince, huckleberry, lemon chiffon. . . ."

"You're in a ripe mood, Ernest."

"It's a glowing and beautiful world, Regina. Could you imagine a better world or a better time? I relish being alive."

He breathed deeply, sucking in cigar-shot air. Then he ordered for them both: venison and elk, new red potatoes in butter and parsley, cream of broccoli soup. . . .

She listened carefully while he decided what she wanted. A commanding man, she thought. She'd scarcely known a commanding man before. He required the best red wine in the establishment, and two glasses.

"But I don't imbibe," she protested.

"A sip, a sip. We're going to have a toast."

"That's what I'm afraid of, Ernest." She had to admit, though, that the man was in his element. She wondered what on earth possessed him to come to Cashbox. On the other hand, she wondered the same thing about most of those who came here, including herself. The only common thread was that they all loved the wild side of living. A mining camp roared and hooted night and day; even the losers had a grand time losing and went back east full of rich memories.

A waiter uncorked a green bottle and poured a bit into Pride's glass. He sipped and nodded solemnly. "A good bouquet," he announced. "A decent aftertaste."

Regina hadn't the faintest idea what all that was about.

"Now, my little Regina, we'll have a talk," he began.

"I'm not exactly little."

"You are a comely, elegant, surpassingly beautiful woman."

"I have a looking glass and it don't lie, J. Ernest."

He smiled. "I like that. Call me J. Ernest. No one ever has. J. Ernest."

"I'm a maiden lady of forty-nine and if you're intending to have your way with me, let's call it a night right now."

"Ah, my little Regina. You think life's passed you by. But for you it's barely begun." He peered across the lamp-lit table at her. "I need to talk of serious things. From some distant shore of the soul, a small voice has been summoning me across the whispering waters. All these years I refused to listen. I didn't want to hear what the sweet, solemn voice was saying."

"Is this about my boardinghouse?"

"My dear Regina, I'm called to public service on behalf of our republic. I plan to enter the Senate in 1892. I believe I can contribute something of value to us all, in that very chamber where great men—Webster, Calhoun!—have debated great issues. Ah, my dear Regina, I am compelled by some power beyond my ability to resist, to seek public service for the good of Montana and my fellow man."

"Whew! You just go right ahead. You've been running for a year anyway. You're not bashful, J. Ernest. If you can sell The Aurora Borealis Consolidated Mining Company, then you've earned your seat in the Senate."

He smiled. "I'm flattered that you discern some small oratorical skill, Regina. But I'm not running for personal gain. As you know, I'm comfortably fixed. But when I see this fledgling state starving for railroads, roads, silver coinage, people to come and settle ... why, if I've been given a silver tongue, as my friends say, I'd employ it for our commonweal."

"You're truly selfless, J. Ernest."

"Oh, no, Regina. I confess I'd enjoy sharing the councils of power. ... My dear, I've had a difficult time. I lost a lovely wife many years ago. I've come to realize my life isn't complete without my sweetheart on my arm; a beloved lady to host our little parties in Washington; a dear lady to join me during our little get-togethers at the White House. Of course I could think of only one person in that role—yourself. Oh, how the senators would envy me. My dear Regina, I'm proposing holy matrimony."

Regina Maltz gawked. "What? Ahhhhh ... this idea is going to take some getting used to," she muttered.

"Oh, there's no hurry. I won't even be lobbying the legislature for another year or so. But then, my dear, how I'd love to introduce you. ... Do you suppose you could give me some indication of what way your thoughts are running?"

"They aren't running. They're stopped dead in their tracks."

"Are you favorable?"

"You're talking about a real marriage?"

"Why, Regina, no woman is more desirable."

"Desirable! I look like something the cat dragged in."

"I shall place you upon an ivory pedestal. I shall admire your virtue from afar."

"That's what I suspected."

No one had ever asked her before and she should have

cherished the moment. But when it finally happened, it smelled like a business deal. A small, dark bitterness crowded through her.

"J. Ernest, tell me about the new mining company. How did you get those people to be your board of directors?"

"Why, Regina, I asked them. But of course I have no direct interest in the company. I merely organized it, as lawyers do."

"You sure do make things happen."

"Well, let's toast the future," he said, raising his glass.

"To the future," she agreed, and sipped.

CHAPTER 45

· · · · · · · · · · · · · · · · ·

Hugh Trego got his answer when he came on shift. Webb read it to him straight off the yellow telegraph paper. "Under no circumstances will we accede to eight-hour day. We expect compliance with existing contract. Labor disturbance is to be met by lockout at mine, mill and smelter," Webb read. "I was asked to read that to you. Privately, Hugh, they're outraged and disappointed. It's a matter of principle. They negotiated a contract with the Knights of Labor in good faith, and you're not showing good faith."

Heat built in Hugh Trego, but he choked it down. "We'll bleddy well see," he muttered. "If Daley can do it, they can do it. You don't know what it's like to live in the dark and never see the sun. A man goes into the hole before sunup, most times, and comes out of the hole after sundown."

"It's something to negotiate at contract time, Hugh."

"Don't go first-naming me, ye bleddy tool of the capitalists."

"I remember times when I fought as hard as you to get

good timbering and air. And I've kept bringing up the infirmary. I have it on the budget now."

"You didn't do it because you care about the cannon fodder you send down the hole. You did it to balm your mind."

Webb looked grim. "Think what you will. If you're going to strike, be about it. I'm to lock up the place. If you think you can break the Hammons, guess again. They've talked all along of shutting down until a railroad's built. It's hardly worth mining until it comes. They'll close the mill and smelter. Most of the mines in the district'll shut down—they run their ores here. What good'll an eight-hour day do if you're all out of work?"

Trego glared at Webb, who sat in his chair, as immovable as an anvil. "You haven't got a heart. All you think of is dollars. You are made of stone. It's lives you're crushing, Webb, mortal lives."

Webb stared out the grimy window. "You've got five months to go on this contract, Hugh." He lifted a hand. "I'm calling you Hugh because you're my friend, even if—it seems—I'm not yours. Hugh, the Hammons risked everything to build this mine, with the hope of a profit from it. If we hadn't hit the vug, there might be no jobs here. The price of silver keeps sliding. If we don't get help from Congress, we're done for anyway. Not even you expect the Hammons to run at a loss."

"Maybe I do," Trego growled. He didn't want to hear any more company propaganda and stormed out, past a gaping Baghote, down to the yard, clenching and unclenching his fists. He took the cage to the gallery on the hundred-foot level where all his boys waited silently.

"They're not yielding an inch. Time for us to walk out," he said.

Around him men gathered in the darkness, the candles of their lamps pooling light into the gloom. Coke Timmons had tried to stop the meeting on company time, but they ignored him.

"Tell us what she's about," said Tim Trenoweth, one of

the old employees. The Giltedge employed ninety now in two shifts.

Trego did.

"It puts every miner in the district out of work?" asked Fenno. "Not just us?"

"That's how the bleddy fat capitalists fight. I say walk out. Show them we're men."

"We've a strike fund, Hugh?" asked Polweal.

"A little, enough for two or three days. That's enough to show the devils a thing or two."

"What'd Webb say about the contract? Will they call in the law to enforce it?" asked a new man.

"He didn't say. They'll hire scabs. You can count on it. They bring in the army, the sheriff, the bleddy militia to oppress a workingman. They've got the power in their fat white hands. They've got it, and we'll defy it."

"It's a contract we all agreed to, Hugh. That don't sound like oppression to me," said Tim. "We're not far from the bargaining table now. Let's wait."

Trego clenched his fists. "Wait! What's the matter with you, Tim Trenoweth? Do you want to spend the rest of your miserable life never seein' the sun?" He glared at the traitor, but Trenoweth stared back uncowed.

"Hugh, me boy, jist because old Cornelius Daley gives a few lads over to the Hangfire the short day, you're all in a lather," said Fenno. "Daley has his reasons, and it's not that he cares two cents about the men in the pits. It's because it's a way of beating the Hammons. He'd like us to walk out, ye can bet on her. Do ye think maybe ye're being a tool of that other capitalist, Daley, him that's a born pirate?"

"Be you calling me a tool! I'll bleddy well pound you to pulp, Fenno. I'll show you what a doublejack man can do to you."

"Hugh. Stop it!" Trenoweth commanded.

Hugh Trego clenched and unclenched his big fists, the rage boiling through him like lava. He saw how it was going; his own men wouldn't back him. "You bleddy cowards. You haven't any fight in you. There's two hundred forty-three of us. With all the mines shut down we'll put the heat on. Don't you know what solidarity is? Don't you know what all the brothers, of one mind, arm in arm, can do? Are we a brotherhood or not?"

They stared at him unmoving. Trego felt their resistance grow and solidify. There wouldn't be a vote and there wouldn't be a strike. They all looked like whipped curs to him.

"Well, me girlies, let's go back to work before old Timmons docks us," said Trenoweth. "Hugh, we've some drilling to do."

Sullenly Trego watched them disperse. He wrestled with an urge to quit the Knights of Labor, quit the Giltedge; he wrestled down a hunger to smash his fists into the nearest man. Then he found himself stepping into the cage that would carry him down to the three-hundred-foot level.

He picked up his hammer and steels and toiled savagely through the day, pounding steels into rock, his anger hot. At the end of the shift he slid a stick of Hercules dynamite into one pocket, and a copper-sheathed detonator and a couple of feet of Bickford fuse into the other. He rode the cage to the grass, his mind as explosive as the weight in his jumper.

Men scurried away from him this evening, sensing his rage. He stood alone, wondering what to blow up. He thought maybe the hoist works. That would shut down the Giltedge for weeks. Maybe the timber shop. He trudged slowly past the general offices, the lamplight within pouring through its smudged windows. A stick under Webb. Blow the bloodsucking superintendent to smithereens. He deserved it. Trego didn't doubt he would hang for it, and he'd shout at the reporters why he'd done it before they sprung the trap.

But Trego choked back the blast furnace of his mind, and walked quietly to the Carbonate Miners Saloon. The waxy red stick of dynamite filled him with intoxicating power. He ordered a mug of ale and sulked into a dark corner to sip it. He sucked it down and got another, while his brothers, who daily risked their lives to gouge wealth out of hell, eyed him uneasily.

Sam Fenno approached, finally looming over the table. "Ah, Hugh, lad. Come join us. She's not so bad a day. All the lads know you're doing what you can."

Trego grunted.

"Come join us, me boy."

"Leave me, Fenno." The words erupted so hard and final that his old friend stared. Fenno wheeled silently back to the rest.

"Fenno!"

The miner returned.

"Lend me two dollars until tally day."

Sam Fenno dug around in his britches and extracted two frogskins. Trego nodded curtly and stuffed the money into his pocket. He finished off the ale and stalked out, creating a sudden silence in his wake.

The night was young. Anna would be waiting supper. She'd have to wait a while more, he thought.

He stood in the nighttime, staring at the stars. You couldn't see stars in the pits. You couldn't see the sky. He sighed, something as heavy as lead weighing him down, and walked resolutely across the Cashbox Creek bridge, and then left on Granite Street to the red-lit door of Minnie's Sporting House. The dynamite felt heavy in his pocket.

Fat Minnie met him in the foyer; a bell summoned the girls. They stood in a simpering line, cheeks rouged to paint a false and rosy health upon their dead white faces. He glared at them so fiercely they stopped their smirky banter and stared back. He picked a thick Mediterranean brunette, and slapped the frogskins into Minnie's hand.

"Have a good time, dearie," she said. "That's Greek Georgie, ain't she a tiger?"

He followed Greek Georgie to her hot, redolent crib. She eyed him nervously, but he didn't care. She didn't smile.

"Something bothering youse?" she asked.

"Nothing. Get on with it."

"Trust old Georgie. I'll fix you up good."

She hurried, fear in her brown eyes. A few moments later he felt himself detonating, and then fell limp over her while an unwanted peace stole through him. He hated the peace worse than his rage.

"You sure have a short fuse, honey," she whispered. "But I guess that's why you're here."

CHAPTER 46

· · · · · · · · · · · · · · · · ·

Sylvie loved the way the midday sun ripped through the tall windows of the Exchange Club, dazzling the rooms. She subscribed to four newspapers and had them delivered as soon as the stagecoach arrived. A few of her members discovered that the sun-dazzle, warmth, newspapers, and everpresent coffee or tea made the club a daytime refuge.

One of these was J. Ernest Potter-Pride, who often spent his lunchtime there. One bright spring noon the attorney plucked his gold pince-nez from his nose, set aside his *New York Herald*, and smiled benignly at her.

"My dear, what a success you've made of this. Why, in all my acquaintance with fair womanhood, I've never met a lady more astute and wise."

"That's all right, Ernest. I'd vote for you if I could."

He chuckled amiably, loosening a few silver strands from his hair until they fell across his patrician brow. "You won't let a prostrate admirer compliment you," he said. "Why, look at you. A queen of all you behold. Sole proprietor of the most lucrative enterprise in Cashbox. Mistress of this club, so exquisitely decorated that not even a Vanderbilt could fault it. And with fifty men at your feet."

"Ernest, what are you trying to sell me?"

"Why, my dear, nothing at all. I hold that no product should ever be sold by salesmen. The true item will always sell itself without the slightest effort. If something has true worth, why, its merits will become obvious, and folks will line up to get it."

"Ernest, if you're trying to sell me shares in The Aurora Borealis Consolidated Mine, don't beat about the bush."

"Well, I wouldn't want to sell you anything, Sylvie dear. But if you should discover value in the company, I'd be pleased to accommodate you."

She laughed. "Ernest, you're the perfect senator."

"Oh, how I wish I could be there in that august chamber right now. Do you know what they're debating? The Sherman silver bill. Do you know what it'll do for us if it passes?"

"It has something to do with silver prices," she said, wishing suddenly she had kept up with these things.

"Only indirectly, Sylvie. You know how silver people've suffered for years, declining prices, overproduction, the huge output of the Comstock lode flooding the world. Hour by hour the prices erode, murdering our dearest dreams—because of the private greed, the dark design of Eastern money interests."

"Well, I hope Congress acts, so my silver stocks go up."

"We all do. If Congress acts, the Aurora Borealis'll be a bonanza for everyone that got in on the ground floor."

"I don't know, Ernest. Con told me it's flooded."

"Ah, my dear, even the Silver Fox misses his chances. That's because he's looking for sure things. He never gets in on the ground floor. Now I can appreciate that; it's shrewd and he's a master. But Sylvie—the ground floor is where you buy cheap and sell high."

"And where you usually lose," she added.

He chuckled again, appreciation lighting his chiseled features. "If there's no risk, we'd all get rich," he said. "Now, listen: right now, under the Bland-Allison Act, the Treasury is authorized to buy anywhere from two million to four million ounces of silver a year for coinage. Unfortunately, those Eastern interests prevail, and the Treasury buys only the two million ounces. But Sylvie, this great nation produces four and a half million ounces a year. Silver's sound as the Ten Commandments, and a lot better than paper money, wouldn't you say?"

"I'm new at this."

"So the price sags year after year, and the Morgans and Vanderbilts hold us in their thrall. Now, the Sherman bill would compel the Treasury to buy our whole output—four and a half million ounces. Think of it, Sylvie. When it passes—and the word of astute men is that it will—why, you'll be rich. We'll all be rich. The mines'll boom."

"If it passes. If we're fighting Eastern financiers, Ernest, I wouldn't count on anything." She smiled. "I've met a few."

"Well it will. Things have changed. Statehood for Montana, Idaho, Wyoming, the Dakotas—now we have the senators. It's the West's turn."

"It's something to think about," she said. She drifted to the bar and cleaned it, frowning at the scummy glasses left behind by Albert Flower. Out in the clubroom, Pride had restored his gold pince-nez to his narrow nose, and was perusing the papers one by one.

She polished glasses and mulled what she'd learned. She'd heard members toss these names around, the Sherman bill, Bland-Allison, but until now they hadn't made much sense to her. Why, the Sherman bill would be wonderful. Her stocks would bolt upward like startled hawks. She had spent, in all, over four thousand dollars on them, and had lost a little, mostly because the Ophir had declined.

There was a lot she didn't know, she thought. But she could learn. With the meeting hall churning out money, she didn't have anything to worry about. Her members were getting rich, so she should too.

"I don't suppose you have more java around," Pride said, holding a cup and saucer as he ambled into the saloon.

Silently she plucked a speckled blue pot from the nickel-plated potbelly stove in the corner and poured him a cup.

"Ah, yes. It sparks a man to life, coffee does. Corona's a good brand. Now as I was saying about Daley, he misses a few. The Aurora Borealis—Northern Lights. Have you seen the assay reports, Sylvie? They'd knock you flat. Done by Mueller, too. There's none better; a careful operator. Fifty, sixty ounces to the ton, with a little gold besides.

"Oh, yes, they had a water problem—but the old management gave up without half trying. You know why? They looked at the declining price of silver. Rolled over and died, I'd call it. Some managers! Not a bold, visionary, enterprising man in the lot. Oh, it takes courage, daring, vision to win through to success."

"If you'd give me suffrage, I'd vote, Ernest. Women can vote in Wyoming. You'll have to do something about it. Then we could elect the legislators that would elect you."

He laughed cheerfully and sipped coffee. He gasped at the heat and set the cup and saucer on the bar. "Oh, there's a lot in your pretty heads," he said. "I think you should have it. I'll fight for it. We need a little female seasoning in politics."

She had heard that a few times before.

"I came in here to dispense advice, my dear. Privately of course. The company—Aurora Borealis—has a par of ten dollars on its stock. But—get this—we've been able to accommodate the large investor. On purchases of a thousand shares and over, I'm authorized to offer the shares at nine."

"Ernest! A thousand shares would cost more than all my assets put together—this building, my stocks and savings. And I'm not going to buy a flooded hole in the ground. Con tells me there's not even any machinery on the premises."

"Well, there you go. I have to carry my cross against prejudice. Even against my beloved and wise client Con

Daley. The consolidated company's not just the Chollar
Mine; it's seven other promising bodies of ore. And what's
a stock subscription for, anyway, if not to buy the machinery? First of all, a new pump so powerful it can whip the
water out of there."

"Well, he's not buying any."

"Ah, but you should. Imagine, Sylvie. Look to the sunrise. The day you buy a thousand at nine, you could sell
it to buyers at ten. And if the Sherman bill passes—why,
overnight your nine thousand'll rise to twenty thousand."

"Well, Ernest, it can't be. I haven't money like that and
I wouldn't put it all in one basket if I did."

"Oh, but you do. It's simple ignorance to suppose your
wealth consists only of what's on hand. Now, consider
this: you've a flood of money coming in each day, each
week, each month. Use it to get rich."

"Borrow? No, Ernest. . . ."

"Well, mortgage the building. You've got a sure thing
here, enough to pay off the mortgage while you put the
cash to work. Don't use your own money. Heaven will not
help the wretch that uses his own lucre. Use John Oliver
Cromwell's cash to make your bonanza. As Voltaire said,
when it comes to money, we all have the same religion."

"Mortgage the building? The hall?" The idea astounded
her.

"Ground floor, Sylvie, ground floor. When the Sherman
bill is signed into law, it'll be too late."

"When'll that be?"

"They're saying next month. June. You won't see an
opening like this ever again. Not in your lifetime."

"You old foghorn," she said. "I'll think about it."

"Don't think. This time, let your pure, sweet, female in-
tuition rule. You must heed your heart, not your mind."

"I have a cold heart, Ernest, except when it comes to
money."

"Sylvie, you're delicious," he said.

CHAPTER 47

. . . .

Thaddeus Webb stared irritably at the daily reports. For the twelfth straight day, ore production had run several tons below normal. The decline showed up in the carload count at the mill and in the decline in silver bullion from the smelter.

The rounds fired each day remained the same. Theoretically the amount of ore blown loose hadn't changed. But why wasn't it being mucked out? One of the exasperating things about the Giltedge was that its rich ores didn't yield the sort of profit one would expect. The Hammons had become so irritated about it that Webb feared they would start looking for another supervisor.

He sighed. It would make Portia happy to leave. It galled him to think that his job hung in the balance because no railroad reached here and the ores were hard to reduce.

A slowdown. That was it. Hugh Trego's revenge. There had been that trouble about the eight-hour day, and not long after that the mine's ore production had declined. That had to be the answer, but how to prove it? How to persuade the miners that red ink could cost them their jobs?

This wasn't something he could solve from the comfort of his desk in the mine offices. Grimly he withdrew a jumper from his closet and donned it. He plucked up a carbide lamp and charged it with calcium carbide and water to generate the acetylene. Its reflector would throw a terrific beam.

He would start at the hundred-foot level, which had been opened into a giant gallery. The answer would probably be simple. There might be a lot of ore just lying around that hadn't been mucked out. Or maybe the trouble was at the three-hundred-foot level, where the gallery was smaller and the mining more intense because the ores were better. Somewhere down there he'd find Coke Timmons and ask the shift foreman some hard questions.

His descent into the mine would slow production. No Cousin Jack would so much as lift a hammer when a supervisor was in sight. Every man would quietly stop and wait in the time-honored fashion for him to leave, as if the mine were their private dominion—which, in a way, it was. Well, that would be the price of this trip. He intended to get some answers.

Webb took the cage down to the hundred-foot level, along with empty ore cars and the cage man who rode with them. He walked the crosscut to the gallery, entered a vast chamber in the neighborhood of the old vug, and looked around at the several crews working stopes in their own pools of light. Rising blackly about him were the cubical timbers, brilliantly designed on the Comstock lode to create a sturdy framework that would support even a huge cavity like this one. They comforted him.

His presence somehow became known immediately, and a silence settled over the whole chamber.

"Is Timmons here?" he asked one crew.

A man shook his head. "Down below, sir."

Webb studied the stope where the doublejack crew was working. They had completed three of the seven holes for the next round. Muckers had cleared almost all the ore from the previous shot. Quietly he studied each of the faces being worked, while men watched him. He found nothing amiss. He wandered into the abandoned part of the gallery, his carbide lamp the only light, looking for rubble that had never been mucked out or anything else that might signal a slowdown. He found nothing.

He surveyed every dark corner, his beam probing into small drifts that followed leads out from the gallery. Nothing. He retreated from that gallery, and rode the cage down to the three-hundred-foot level. Timmons was waiting for him at the vestibule.

"You looking for something?" the foreman asked.

"Yes I am. Ore production's been down a few tons a day for almost two weeks. I want to know why."

"How do you know that, Mister Webb?"

"Carloads at the mill. Less silver bullion. Less argentiferous lead."

"That could be lower values, sir."

"Our current assays are the best ever. Timmons, is this a slowdown? Are they making war on me?"

"Not that I've seen, sir. Trego, he's a firebrand, all right. But his men stopped him on the eight-hour day. Trenoweth, he says it ain't right to bust the contract. Most of them, they ain't grieving anything. They want the shorter day, and they'll strike for it—but not now."

A strange boom shivered the rock beneath them. A Hangfire crew had fired a round.

"How close are they now, Timmons?"

"Right under us, sir, maybe seventy, eighty feet. My powder men don't like it. They hate to have those rounds go off when they're loading their own rounds. It makes 'em sweat real bad. They hate that outfit."

Webb sighed. "I'd stop them cold if I could. It's piracy. It's in the hands of lawyers, and we're being eaten alive while they wrangle. Judge Gear says he won't shut them down unless we shut down too."

Webb explored this smaller gallery, examining stopes, looking for heaps of ore that hadn't been mucked out. Men stopped their work and waited quietly. Hugh Trego stared sullenly. Webb found nothing in the part of the gallery being worked, and wandered toward the abandoned portion.

"Timmons, are they firing smaller rounds, by any chance? Five or six holes instead of seven? They're working gallery faces—does that change things?"

"No. I'm often around when the powder men are setting up. Nothing like that. Sometimes, when they've drilled high up the face, they fire a smaller round on a longer fuse so the powder man can get out of there. He's got to go down some ladders to get out. But that's the way it's been for a year now."

They paused under the ventilation winze that connected the two levels and Webb shined his carbide lamp up it. "Good draft," he said, feeling the steady flow of it. "This mine's got air."

They probed through the abandoned part of the mine, seeing nothing. Webb's beam played over jasper, over cubical timbers running several sets high to a distant ceiling.

"Sir, there's too much air around here," said Timmons.

"What do you mean?"

"I mean there's draft here."

"I don't feel it."

"You mind letting me poke around with that lantern, sir?"

Webb handed it to Timmons. The foreman headed for the dark edge of the gallery and began probing the rocky floor. Bits of rubble lay about, ore that should have been mucked up. An ancient wheelbarrow lay belly up.

Timmon's beam paused. "Here." He pulled the wheelbarrow away to expose a small winze that dropped sharply into blackness. It was pumping air into the chamber. "The bastids."

Thaddeus Webb froze. He peered down the shaft, which seemed to drop about twenty feet and then expand into something cavernous, with debris on its floor.

"That's ladders, I reckon," said Timmons. "Lying down there. There's where it's going, sir. They're mucking it out in the night."

Webb swallowed back his rage. The two Giltedge shifts ran twenty and a half hours, with the half hour between. For three and a half hours in the deeps of the night the Giltedge had no crews in it. That's when Hangfire's crews were mucking rock and dropping it down the winze into their own workings.

"I should have known; I should have known," he muttered. "With the labor trouble I never thought of this."

He stood, staring at the perfidious winze. "Timmons,

they needed measurements to do this. They needed to know where to drive it, what was abandoned up here."

Timmons lifted his felt hat and scratched. "Hard to feature, sir. There's a man I'm thinking about. A loner."

"Who?"

"Chap named Jarvis Jones. Him that's in Trego's crew. He's an old-timer here."

"Why do you suspect him?"

"I don't have a reason in the world. I just do, that's all."

"I'll talk to him. Timmons, pull a turning sheet over this and then fire a round on top of it. And after that, watch this one every day. Check this whole abandoned area every day."

"I sure will, sir."

"I don't know what I'm going to do. Something. It's bad enough that Daley steals our reserves. But this. . . . This is the work of a scoundrel."

"Mister Webb, sir, we'll have to find out who's doing it. Maybe we should post an armed guard and try to catch some of 'em before we seal it. Get 'em red-handed."

"Maybe we should. I've got to talk to the Hammons and a lawyer first."

"The bastids," Timmons muttered. "Mucking our ore."

CHAPTER 48

. . . .

John Oliver Cromwell seemed almost to ignore Sylvie. He steepled and unsteepled his hands and peered through his office window, which afforded a spectacular view of the mountains. She waited patiently, knowing that Cromwell was a deliberate man. She admired it in him. She wouldn't be comfortable with a hasty banker.

He turned at last toward her, and peered from soupy eyes, almost leached of their original blue. Some vast dignity attached to him, not only from his funereal clothing but also from the puritan iciness he exuded.

"I'd have to wait a few weeks," he said in his oddly piercing voice. "I'm not lending much until I see how the Sherman silver bill goes."

"But then it'll be too late."

He blinked. "There are always opportunities, Miss Duvalier."

"But it'll probably double if it passes."

"And if it doesn't pass?"

"Why—everyone says it will."

"And what would happen to your hall if it doesn't?"

"Why—it'd just go on the way it is."

He shook his head. "The Sherman bill, Miss Duvalier, is essential to Cashbox, and all silver-mining towns. That ought to be obvious. Have you been keeping up with silver prices?"

She nodded.

"You should know, then. No. I'd be happy to make the mortgage once conditions are settled. Just how much I'd lend, and at what rate, remains to be seen. I'd say I could lend six or seven on your building and lots—they're worth eleven. But that'll depend. Come back when we all have good news."

"No, Mister Cromwell—then I wouldn't need the loan. If I buy the stock now, I'd probably double my money."

Cromwell pushed his gold-rimmed half-glasses up his nose a notch. "I trust you've gotten expert advice about such a—radical purchase."

"Why—Mister Pride showed me the engineering report—some New York man. And the assays."

"That wasn't my question."

She shook her head sullenly. She wanted to do this on her own. Why did men think a woman couldn't make a good investment without their help?

"It's not for me to recommend or condemn any offerings of the local mines, of course. I bank for them all. But I'd urge some caution, Miss Duvalier."

It irritated her. "Everything I've heard, without exception, is that the Sherman bill would double the value of the mines. Now you won't let me take advantage."

He steepled his pale blue fingers again. "Oh, I'm not stopping you from taking advantage. No. I'm considering only the prospects of the Exchange Hall if the bill fails."

"You're saying Cashbox would die?"

"Not at all. The future is burning-bright. There's one inexhaustible mine and many other good ones; there's a potential timber industry; there's a settled retail and trading business for the ranches that're starting up."

"Well, thank you. I seem to be confined to my cage," she said tartly, rising.

He nodded amiably.

He wouldn't do it. The thought irked her. He hadn't joined the Exchange Club. He hardly ever showed up in the hall, either. He didn't imbibe spirits, play whist or poker, or dance, and the only occasion he had entered the hall was to hear a dull Chautauqua lecture. He was inhuman. His stupid caution would keep her from an easy bonanza.

Well, she'd have to tell Ernest she couldn't manage it. They would all get rich while she just ran her club, like a prisoner in a gilded cage. Men! Maybe she would start importing Susan B. Anthony and the others from the National Woman Suffrage Association. They'd give them an earful.

She found J. Ernest Potter-Pride wolfing apple pie.

"Ah, Sylvie. Would you like a piece?" he asked, bolting up from his padded swivel chair.

"No, Ernest. I just stopped to tell you I can't do it. Cromwell says he won't lend until the silver bill passes. After that I could get six or seven thousand."

"Oh, oh, a pity, Sylvie. You've been culled out like a bum steer. You've been thwarted from reaping the sweet rewards of your intelligence."

She smiled. "You don't have to run for office, Ernest."

He certainly cut an impressive figure. Towering behind

his enormous desk was a gilt-framed mirror, so that his clients were forever staring not only at themselves, but at the bun of hair at the nape of his neck and the silk back of his waistcoat, perfectly tailored to his patrician form.

"A pity, a pity. I'd so wanted you to share in this opportunity, Sylvie. There'll never be one like it. As God is my witness."

"Well, I'd better get back—"

"No, no no—" He waved her to a seat. "Let me think. There must be a way. Some way for our beloved Sylvie to reap her reward." Frown lines ridged the alpine slope of his brow. "Yes, yes, I'll do it. It's a sacrifice, but I'll do it."

"What, Ernest?"

"Sell you a thousand of my own shares."

"But I can't pay—that's the whole point."

"Why, Sylvie, I'd take a mortgage on your building, even if that silly goose won't. Why, you've a sure thing here, a money tree."

"You would? You have shares?"

"Oh, yes, quite a few. A man who sells them to the public really ought to own it himself, wouldn't you say? Oh yes. I could do it. I've the certificates right in my files."

"But then you'd be cheating yourself out of profit when the bill passes."

"Oh, some, some. But mind you, the thousand shares I'd sell you privately would have to go for the full ten dollars. I couldn't duplicate the company offer. That's my security. I'm sure you understand. But I'd do it—we'd all want our dear Sylvie to share one of the great moments in the history of silver."

"You'd—give me a mortgage?"

"Why of course, my dear. Who could resist an earnest plea from so lovely a woman?"

"You'll make a good senator, Ernest."

He chuckled, a twinkle building in his eyes. "Ah, Sylvie. I already have my reward, just seeing the joy that flushes your smooth cheeks."

She sighed. "Well then, what're your terms?"

"Why, what do you need?"

"I'd like ten thousand dollars against my real property. I have some other silver stocks but I'd rather not sell any—not with what's going to happen. I think my building's worth about eleven. That's what Mr. Cromwell said. I'd like annual payments for, oh, five years. And the best interest you can give me."

"Yes, surely, it can be done. Not cash, of course. In exchange, you'll receive from me a thousand shares of the B series stock, at par, of The Aurora Borealis Consolidated Mining Company."

"B Series?"

"Yes, that's the common stock being offered by the company. We hope the whole hundred thousand shares will be subscribed."

"Is there another series?"

"Oh, yes. The A series is just about the same. Common stock. Not preferred."

She wished she had Con at her side to explain all that. But she pushed it out of mind. This would be her deal, and hers alone. She decided not to say a word to him. She was going to make her own life.

"All right," she said.

He glowed. "Oh, Sylvie. Oh, my, dear woman, what you have done for yourself. For Cashbox."

She smiled. "It's not for Cashbox. It's for me, all for me."

"I understand the sentiment, my dear. Sometimes I'm possessed by the same feeling, but I try to stamp it out. A man seeking high office must school himself to the needs of the whole state, eh?"

"That's noble, Ernest—"

"Oh, I suppose it might be. Well, my dear, you'll have your mortgage and your stock."

"Do you need anything from me?"

"I'll need your deed. That'll go into escrow. And I'll need your signature as soon as I draw up a simple little agreement, Sylvie. When I'm done, later this afternoon, I'll drop over to the club and we'll go through it clause by clause. I want you to understand each and every word. And I'll bring along an interest-rate schedule as well, the kind that cold-hearted bankers use, and we'll set the exact amount. You'll have some choices, of course. The longer your mortgage, the lower your payments. You sure you won't have some pie? I'm connected to the world's foremost pie factory."

"No, Ernest. I'll see you at the club."

"Very well, my dear. You won't be sorry."

CHAPTER 49

. . . .

No woman ever approached the marriage altar with more dread than May Goode. Slug had patiently talked her into it, worn down her resistance like a grinding wheel on a knife, and finally achieved her numb surrender.

It would all start over again: the marriage bed, the child, the anger . . . the death. She couldn't understand why she had let herself be pressured into this. She wanted only to live out her life in utter privacy. She tried to think of poor little Robby, but she couldn't. She seemed years removed from that.

Slug's gentle and encompassing love had done it; awakened hungers in her, dreams of a sweet life in a rosemaled cottage brimming with warmth. She wished she had never seen the inside of that place, which reflected the inside of Slug's happy soul.

She waited in the vestibule of the only church in Cashbox, a small frame building painted white and shared by several congregations. Slug had gotten some circuit-riding preacher to perform her doom over her, and now it was too late to escape, though her frightened soul fluttered and battered the cage that trapped her there.

She wore a gentian blue dress that she and Mrs. Flower had sewn for this moment: a small coronet of white velvet, with a veil, and in her arms she carried a bright splash of daffodils. But the gaiety of her attire didn't match her heart.

Slug took her arm and led her gently into the nave. How joyous he looked, his every glance adoring her and conveying peace and assurance. This would not be a formal affair. She glanced fearfully out to the pews, and saw only a few of Slug's friends, Mrs. Flower, and Willard Croker.

Almost as if there were a conspiracy to marry her off before she fled, the minister plunged in.

"Dearly beloved: we have come together in the presence of God to witness and bless the joining together of this man and this woman in Holy Matrimony," he said in a booming voice that sounded like ten tubas tooting.

He certainly threw himself into his labor, she thought as she listened to him discuss the nature and purpose of marriage. She listened afraid, and there was only Slug across from her.

And then the man was saying, "Into this holy union Sven Svensrud and May Goode now come to be joined. If any of you can show just cause why they may not lawfully be married, speak now; or else forever hold your peace."

She wanted to cry out: I have a reason! But Slug's steady gaze prevented it.

"May, will you have this man to be your husband . . . ?" the minister boomed.

"I will." She fought back tears.

Numbly she listened to Slug, and then the minister's elaborations of Christian marriage, and then Slug repeating his vow: "In the name of God, I, Sven, take you, May, to be my wife, to have and to hold from this day forward, for better for worse, for richer for poorer, in sickness and in health. . . ."

Then she said it too and wept. Those few spectators would think hers were tears of joy.

"I pronounce that they are husband and wife, in the

name of the Father, and of the Son, and of the Holy Ghost. Those whom God has joined together let no one put asunder."

She had become May Svensrud. She was no longer May Adamek, May Carlson, or May Goode. She had traveled westward into a new name. The minister beamed. Slug's arm caught and held her, and something in his eyes melted May's heart.

A few hours later, in the dark of the April evening, they closed the cabin door behind them. Slug's little home glowed with light and warmth, but she was afraid. He saw it in her, and gathered her gently to him, lifting her velvet coronet from her hair.

"Make this evening yours," he said. "Whatever you want is my wish too, my sweet May."

"Oh, Slug."

She wished desperately she could be anywhere else. Why didn't someone in the pews rise and condemn this union? She had killed her own son. She was not fit to be a mother.

But no one had. No one knew.

"Slug—I . . . can't."

Tears welled and tumbled down her cheeks. He was expecting a wedding night. Expecting the union she had committed herself to, joyous and tender.

"I'm not in any hurry, May. We can wait until you're feeling better."

"Don't you see? I can't. I can't be a wife, Slug."

He released her and plucked out the handkerchief that had been neatly folded into his breast pocket. He dabbed her cheeks and her eyes, wiping away her terror. She tried to smile at his tenderness, but dread possessed her.

He fussed at the woodstove, making tea from the hot water there, and then brought it to her in a chipped cup and saucer. She took it gratefully and sipped. It was something to do; something to delay what would come. It felt hot in her throat.

He sipped from his own cup, surveying her amiably.

"May, you're not a prisoner here," he said softly. "If it was a mistake, we can walk back to Mrs. Flower's cottage and I'll leave you there. If you'd like to stay here—I hope you will—you need not become . . . intimate with me." He smiled ruefully. "I can endure—I think. For as long as you want."

"I can't do that to you, Slug."

"If it's something I accept, then you're not hurting me in any way, May."

He seemed so earnest. His blue eyes glowed with such warmth and kindness. How could this strong, good man, so used to the roughness of the streets, be such a tender spirit in his own home? She ached to leap into his embrace, to share his passion, to fling the past aside forever and grasp the future, the West of a new life. Her tears came again, an ever present funeral wreath upon her soul. "I don't know, I don't know," she mumbled.

He led her to the parson's bench he'd made, and sat beside her, his arm making a nest for her to slip into. "It's the past that's gripping you," he said. "It's the fear of having a child and what might happen. I know that. Look, May. Back then, you were abandoned and desperate. You'd worn yourself down. You saw no future. I won't ever abandon you. I won't ever let you get worn down. Count on me."

She wept softly, craving the release that eluded her.

"You see a demon in you. It's not there. It never was there. It just happened, and it won't happen again."

She buried her face in his shoulder and felt the wetness of her tears leak into his scratchy suitcoat. He held her that way for a long time, until she calmed.

"Come on," he said, "let's go for a walk."

"Now?"

He smiled and slid her cloak over her. They plunged into a cool spring night. He led her up a path that clung to the hillside, higher and higher until her heart pounded. What madness was this? He annoyed her, traipsing up the mountainside on their wedding night. But at last they

topped the ridge and he stopped on its thin spine, surrounded by rock and juniper. Other, higher ridges lay
about them in the starlight, but from here they could look
down upon Cashbox, its lamps glimmering in the restless
air far below, a magical village in a black wild. She could
see the snug homes dotting the slopes, the dark hulk of the
businesses along Main, the brightly lit saloons, the glow of
the Palace Hotel radiating light from its arrayed lamps.

"There now. We have to be able to see the future," he
said.

The night seemed alive with stars and aching distances.
She clutched the hard hand of the man beside her and
peered across vast spaces.

"You have to get up high to see it," he said. "The
future's pretty frightening, and if you want to enjoy it you
have to be pretty daring. You've got to catch a star and
hang on tight. Be daring tonight, May. Dare to make a
wish. Dare to live a dream. Dare to want anything your
heart desires, and wish upon a star. And I'll wish too, for
whatever you dare."

"You want me to dare?"

"Dare everything. Dare your life. Dare to believe."

She snuggled against him, and felt his arm draw her to
his side. Here, with the world at her feet, she felt hope.

"This is the West, May. It's the place where people
come to start over. It's a place where you can just shuck
the past. It's a miracle, all this country just waiting for
folks to try themselves out. Some fail—but you know
what? They don't regret that they came here and tried.
Some succeed and make a new home in a new land. And
make themselves new, too. . . . May? Come out of the
East. Leave the East behind."

Minnesota.

He turned to face her. "You've a new name if you want
to keep it. You can leave the old ones in the East where
they belong. Come west with me, west toward the setting
sun."

The West. A new name. She pulled Slug to her and

kissed him. "I'll dare," she whispered. "I'll dare. Oh, Slug, help me to."

CHAPTER 50

• • • • • • • • • • • • • • • • •

Thaddeus Webb didn't relish the small hours of the night, but he wanted to deal with the mine rats personally. He waited at the headframe while it disgorged the weary second shift. With him were Coke Timmons, up early, and Big Bull Focher, staying on an extra hour. Each carried a shotgun.

The three rode the cage to the three-hundred-foot level, and waited quietly in the vestibule. Acrid fumes seared Webb's throat. It couldn't be helped. They had to be in place before the mine rats showed up.

Focher led them along the crosscut and into the long gallery, where the fumes worsened. He motioned Webb and Timmons toward a wall where they could see the rathole. Then he turned off the acetylene lamp. A frightful blackness clamped them. In spite of all the years he'd been around mines, that terrifying blackness still pierced Thaddeus.

They crouched in the bowels of the rock so long that Webb supposed the rats weren't coming that night. But he knew the way time stood still in the dark. He worried that something might go wrong; that the two double-barreled shotguns wouldn't be enough.

But then they heard noises. A scrape of wood, perhaps. It lifted Webb's pulse. Timmons' elbow gently nudged Webb's ribs.

They watched a faint light blossom around the overturned wheelbarrow, its dimensions limned by the edges of the winze. It brightened as someone ascended a ladder. Then a mine rat pushed the wheelbarrow aside and crawled out, bearing a candle lantern. Another followed. Light and shadows bobbed crazily.

Webb heard the soft rush of air expelled by Focher. The man was itching for a brawl. Focher wasn't called Big Bull for nothing. The mine rats left a lantern burning at the winze and took the other with them to the nearest pile of rock, perhaps seventy yards distant.

"Wait," whispered Webb under the squeak of the barrow wheel. "Let them dump one load down the winze first. Witness it."

They didn't have to sit long. In a few minutes one of the rats returned with a laden barrow and dumped ore down the winze.

Webb and his foremen rose, shadowed the man back to the ore, and waited until he and his companion mucked rock off the turning sheet again. They were big bruisers. Webb wished he had armed himself.

He could see fairly well. A single candle had an amazing reach in a pitch-black pit. Webb said nothing but touched each man's arm, a signal to go ahead.

Big Bull took the lead. "All right, lay down them shovels," he barked.

The rats whirled. The bigger one threw his shovel at Focher, missed, and raced for the winze. Focher took after him. The smaller one kicked the lantern. Glass shattered. The candle blued out. Blackness rolled down again.

Webb heard scuffling. Timmons was wrestling with the smaller one. Webb snatched a lucifer and scratched it. Light flared long enough for him to see Timmons on top of the mine rat, his shotgun pressing the man's throat while the rat kicked and bucked.

The match died. Webb scratched another, this time reaching for the candle. He lit it. His heart hammered. Timmons had the smaller one, but Webb had no idea whether Focher had nabbed the other. He heard commotion, and then Focher materialized, pushing the bigger one before him. The rat was bleeding from both nostrils.

Timmons wound Bickford fuse around the wrists of the

man he pinned, growling every time the man resisted. The big one tried to bust loose from Focher's grip, but Big Bull twisted him to the rock and trussed him like a hog.

"Let's get out of here," Coke said.

Webb agreed. He collected the acetylene lamp and lit the way back to the hoist. His foremen prodded the rats into the cage with their shotguns while Webb belled the engineer.

Moments later they emerged into a chill night. His foremen jabbed their prisoners into Webb's office, where he lit a couple of lamps. He wanted to see what these mine rats looked like. Both were bruisers. Neither was the worse for wear.

"What's your names?" he asked.

The two didn't respond.

"Well, Svensrud'll find out. You've stolen ore. We'll press charges—but maybe we won't if you talk. Who ordered this?"

The rats looked at each other and decided silence was the best policy. Webb eyed them flintily.

"Our production's been down seven or eight tons a day for weeks. That means a lot of silver. Enough to make it grand larceny. A good stretch at Deer Lodge."

The pair stared sullenly at him.

"Bull, it's way past your quitting time. Put in for the overtime and let the hoist engineer go. Coke'll take care of things."

Big Bull smiled. "Haven't had such fun since New Year's."

"I don't have nothing to be ashamed of," said the younger one. "I'm Muddy James. The boss, he said it's the Hangfire's ore. He says it's okay to get it. He says the court'll okay it soon."

"Who said that, James?"

"The shifter in the Hangfire, Egor Doppler."

"Did anyone else tell you that?"

"No, just Doppler."

"Who cut the winze up to our mine?"

"Doppler had a crew working on it."

"How'd he know where to drive it?"

"They just followed the ore up."

Webb turned to the other one. "Have you a name?" The other stared back stonily. "It'll go easier for you if you talk."

"The Knights'll walk out on you," the nameless one said.

Webb sighed. "We'll see about that. We'll press charges, I assure you, walkout or not. You both could have refused this. All men have to make moral choices. You had a choice. All right, Coke, padlock them in the toolroom. I'll go wake up Svensrud."

Webb watched them shuffle out, the rancor in him barely under control.

Five hours later, Webb walked down the gulch through a heady spring morning, aiming straight for the Palace Hotel chophouse where Daley would be having his usual leisurely breakfast while reading half a dozen papers and stock market reports.

He was there, all right, in his corner banquette, coffee steaming before him on the padded linen tablecloth.

"Why, Thaddeus, it's a fine May day. Have some coffee."

Webb preferred to stand. "We caught your robbers."

Daley set aside his *New York Herald*, looking puzzled.

"We're pressing charges, Daley, and if I could prove you'd given the orders I'd charge you, too."

Daley stared blankly. "You have the advantage of me, Thaddeus."

"We found the winze and we've caught the crooks and we're going to court."

"The winze?"

"The winze into our bottom level."

"I'll have to talk to my people to find out what this is about. Of course we believe all the ore's ours; we're perfectly confident that Judge Gear'll rule for us."

Webb curbed his instinct to ball his fists. "I'm taking this to Gear and asking him for an injunction."

"Perhaps you'd better explain, Webb."

The man was feigning innocence. Webb detailed the matter anyway, while Daley sipped and listened.

"Why, I'll put a stop to it. We can't have that," Daley said quietly.

"It doesn't matter what you do. I'm laying boiler steel over that winze and blowing a round onto it."

"That'd be a pity, Webb. The air's good for the men."

That was true. Miners cherished fresh air more than anything else but good timbering. "I'll think about it, Daley—but no sewer rat'll ever crawl out of that winze again."

"Have some coffee, Thaddeus. This is something we can work out. I've told them many times it's my ore, but they've gotten a little enthusiastic." A nod of his head brought a waiter with a pewter pot of coffee and a cup and saucer.

Webb sat down, wondering why he was supping with the devil.

"How's Mrs. Webb?" Daley asked.

"Portia?"

"A lovely woman. Without her, we wouldn't have a school."

"The world's falling apart, Daley. Business isn't business any more. It used to be production. Men working together to create something of value. Now what is it? It's the Hangfire, boring ratholes into my mine. It's Jay Gould, Jim Fiske, Daniel Drew, and you. It's getting rich cheap, by hook or crook."

"But it's not your ore, Thaddeus. . . . You know, Portia's an organizer. That's one of her loveliest qualities. She's been after me to build an infirmary. There's no resisting her. She governs Cashbox, Thaddeus. We're all better off for it."

"What good is theft, Daley? I'm from a long grim line of Puritans. I've got it in my blood. If a man defies the laws of God, he'll pay the price; right in his soul, Daley. He'll peer inside, and loathe what he sees there. He'll see a robber when he could be a giver, helping all who need him."

"Why, Thaddeus, Portia's been writing doctors, and she tells me she's found one, a Rochester fellow. He likes the Wild West. He'll come just as soon as the mines give him an infirmary. I told her that as soon as the silver bill passes, we can do it."

"I'll tell you what I believe, Daley. I think there's a Justice in the universe, slow but sure. I think this Justice takes its time, and gives a mortal every chance to better himself, to heed the laws of life. But when a man shows no inclination, then this Justice lets the man go to his appointed fate. His own appropriate fate, fashioned from the fruits of everything he did. That's when he heads for an early grave. Or a stroke takes his mind from him. Or the people he loves hate him. Or he ends up in the poorhouse. Or in prison. Or shunned by everyone. Or mad as a rabid dog, seeing demons tormenting him where none exist. Or maybe he's lied so much he can't see reality any more. When Justice comes you can't escape."

"You know, Thaddeus, Portia is the fairest blossom in Cashbox. You're a lucky man. You really ought to pay her more heed. I suspect she's alone too much, with you at the mine night and day. She's a brave soldier, though, never letting on that her life lacks something. . . . I think you should read her some poetry each evening. All the truth of the world's in poetry. I've never met a woman who didn't enjoy it."

"Daley, you know the cruelest thing of all? To win at everything and still have nothing. To make every dream come true, and discover they weren't good dreams. What have you got, Daley? Nothing worth having. Empty mansions. Nothing but bad dreams."

"That's all fine about justice, Thaddeus, but it's not your ore. Now you'll look after Portia, won't you? She needs you."

CHAPTER 51

. . . .

Cornelius watched the June zephyrs tug at Sylvie's straw boater, threatening to pluck it from her chaotic hair. How he loved her. The playful breezes had pounced on them when they'd topped a long rise. Con tugged the lines to stop the matched bay trotters so they could enjoy the breathtaking view.

Off to the west loomed the pine-thatched slopes of Elk Peak, the slumbering volcano that had poured out its wealth upon these fastnesses eons ago. Except for the two-rut road, the whole country lay in primeval glory, not yet wounded by man. The volcano had left geologic chaos in its wake, its granite and diorite shoulders uplifting and demolishing beds of shale and limestone that here and there outcropped into colorful stone monuments.

"It's so beautiful it's almost frightening," she said. "Something in it makes me want to huddle in a city."

"It's the last of the wilderness, Sylvie. Only a few prospectors have poked through here." He pointed at the great mountain. "That's what brought us our silver out of the core of the earth. Do you feel its power? It's asleep now, but maybe sometime after the last mortal has died, it'll come to life again."

"You frighten me, Con."

"Ah, Sylvie. This is the last of the unexplored, except maybe in South America. Look at this and memorize it. Soon there'll be cattle grazing here. The game'll be shot away, and roads'll pierce it. It awakens something in me. I love the unexplored. After this continent is no longer a mystery, I'd like to plunge into the Andes and conquer the mysteries there. We need mystery beyond the horizon."

"Oh, Con, why are you such a mystery to me? I never heard you say anything like that."

He chuckled softly. "Under the skin, I'm an explorer. I don't want the world's mysteries to end. Before we know it, there'll be only Antarctica left." He slapped the lines over the rumps of the bays and they trotted smartly toward his destination, the country around the little mining camp of Blackhawk.

The June day seethed with life. Puffball clouds raced across the vibrating heavens, plowing shadows across the broken land. The new-minted grasses bent under the caress of the wind. He steered the gig around miry holes, souvenirs of the recent snows, and sometimes slogged through them, feeling the gumbo tug at the wheels. The horses loved the day as much as he did, and pulled eagerly in their collars.

"We'll picnic soon. But first I'll do a little business."

"Even on a picnic," she said, wryly.

He nodded. He had more planned for this outing than the gorgeous feast in the wicker basket behind them, prepared by the chophouse. "How would you like to look at a few claims?"

"I wouldn't know one thing from another."

"That's why I brought you," he said.

She eyed him seriously, sensing that something lay behind his words. Which it did.

He drove the trotters another half hour, scaring up a wolf and several mule deer. Great shoulders of rock eclipsed the view of Elk Mountain, and their world became much more intimate, hemmed by shattered rock and gloomy trees. Con spotted signs of mineralization, the rust of iron oxides, the blacks and oranges of igneous rock.

"This isn't as beautiful," she said.

"It's richer. We're only a couple of miles from Blackhawk."

He stopped the bays and withdrew a topographic map from his briefcase. He had overlaid it with claims, and brief notes about the assays of each. He drove another half mile and then stopped.

"We'll take a little look, Sylvie," he said. "Time to stretch."

He helped her down, loving the warmth of her hand in his. She wore a loose white cotton today, blousy at the bodice and full-skirted, a perfect complement to the straw boater with its scarlet ribbon. She had taken to wearing tailored, stiff suits in the Exchange Club, thinking that the suits were emblematic of the club. But now she seemed gloriously freed. The breezes whipped her loose skirts about her legs, and kissed her cheeks and threatened to undo the rat's nest of her hair.

He found a rock cairn locating a corner of the claim, and soon found the other corners. He poked through grasses to a color-stained bluff and found a small glory-hole there, long abandoned. It poked into the shattered igneous rock a few feet and stopped.

She stooped to peer in. "Is there something here, Con?"

"I don't think so. This claim assayed a little bit of copper and some iron and a showing of silver and gold."

"Were you thinking of buying it?"

"No. It's probably worthless."

"Whose is it?"

"It belongs to The Aurora Borealis Consolidated Mining Company."

She eyed him sharply. "Oh," she whispered.

"Well, let's look at a few more, and then we'll picnic," he said, leading her back to the gig.

He drove another half mile, stopped, and began looking for stakes or cairns. He didn't find a corner, but the shaft was obvious. It poked into a rocky facade about halfway up.

"Are you game to get up there? Might be snakes."

She nodded. Her gaiety had fled.

They toiled up a steep grade, clambering over detritus until they peered into an up-slanting shaft that stabbed into gloom. It was well-timbered. Some mining debris lay about: a corral and manger for a mule, some rusty iron rail, and an ore car on its side. A small heap of tailings lay below the shaft.

"This looks more promising," he said.

"I wouldn't know."

"The assay reports show some low-grade silver ores, maybe one or two ounces a ton, declining in value at the head of the shaft."

"Could it be profitable?"

"Not now. This one's a tease. It kept them digging only to disappoint them."

"I suppose it's owned by The Aurora Borealis too."

"Yes, I'm interested in the company."

"I see."

"Their main holding is the Chollar, up the road a mile. They've some other claims, but they're not accessible from the road. Three are in a gorge five or six miles west of here. It's so narrow and rock-strewn that you can't get in by wagon. Only with a packtrain. It's doubtful even a good claim would be profitable—at least until there's a railroad. To work them profitably, there'd have to be road laid to them, and a local mill and smelter. It's over ten miles to Cashbox. Who knows? Maybe they're good claims. One shows some good values—ten ounces a ton of carbonate ore."

"What if the bill passes?"

"Silver's a dollar five now. It'd have to go much higher than that to get bullion to the railroad at a profit. I doubt that the silver bill would help much here."

"I see."

He led her back to the gig, sorry he was forced to wound her day. He snapped his lines over the croups of the horses and headed for the Chollar. They pushed up a vast gulch, meeting some teamsters walking beside ox-teams that were dragging heavy Murphy wagons.

They rounded a bend and discovered the Chollar, occupying the only level ground. A weathered hoist works and gallowsframe hulked across a weedy flat, along with a sagging building consisting of side-by-side offices, each with a doorway and ancient wooden steps.

A sign said "Keep Out."

Con turned in, following a trace of a road hidden by weeds.

"It doesn't look very active," Con said. "No machinery. Not even a piece of scrap metal. This one flooded a while ago. A good mining engineer, Jackson Cain, took a look and decided no pump on earth could handle that water. I was very interested in this one until I read the report. It's a good mine if it could be drained. But there's nowhere to drain it. We're in a cupped valley. There'd have to be a three-mile adit, and it's not worth it."

"This man said it couldn't be pumped?" she asked, something bleak in her face.

"He's the best, Sylvie. Columbia School of Mines. Off in Mexico now."

"I see."

Armed men boiled out of the sagging superintendent's office. One came trotting toward them, shouting. Con stopped the bays and waited.

"Git out! Can't you read?" the man bellowed.

Con recognized Bass Boehm, and wondered if Sylvie did.

"Turn around and git," Boehm said.

"I'm Daley. I'm interested in the property. I learned of it from Mister Pride."

"I don't care who you are—git."

"Now, we'll just take a quick look. I want to see a few things."

"Mister, you set foot off that gig and you'll be carried outta here on your back."

Several of Boehm's thugs had gathered now, eyeing Sylvie.

"Let's go, Con," she said.

"I suppose you could always shoot buyers," Con said calmly. "Then you wouldn't make a dime. You're a bright man, aren't you?"

"I'm just guarding the place."

"I imagine you are. I checked with the secretary of state. There's ten shares of class A common stock. It has voting rights; the class B doesn't. Willard Croker's down for five, and Bass Boehm's down for two and a half, and the other two and a half are held by a Greentree Trust, for a party unknown. It looks interesting. Maybe you'd like to persuade me to invest."

"Get the hell out, Daley."

"All right, sir. I'll tell Pride I'm no longer interested."

"Wait." Boehm smiled through yellow teeth. "You bring me a permit from Pride and I'll let you look."

"No, I don't think so, Boehm. You lost your chance." Con wheeled the bays around and drove out, his wheels slaying weeds until they hit the road.

"We'll go back to that ridge with the view of Elk Mountain," he said. "There's a good place for a picnic there."

But Sylvie was lost in thought.

CHAPTER 52

• • • • • • • • • • • • • • •

Regina Maltz had come to enjoy her occasional dinners at the Palace Hotel chophouse with J. Ernest, but she suspected that tonight would be the last one. He'd been pressing her for an answer to his proposal, and this evening she would hand him one he would not like.

Her decision had surprised her more than it would surprise him. The more she'd thought about it, the more she thought she just might do it—under certain conditions. This would be the only proposal she'd ever receive. He was moderately crooked, but being a senator's wife certainly would be something. But best of all would be to reform him. Oh, how she'd love to roll up her sleeves and knead him like bread dough, let him rise and then knead him again.

She wore a new dress for this occasion, a summery pleated pink cotton that softened the angular lines of her big-boned figure. It was an extravagance. But the boardinghouse yielded a good income now, and she could afford to get herself gussied up if she felt like it.

She met him in the lobby. He breezed in, looking like John L. Sullivan after a three-round victory, fixing her with his innocent blue eyes and then beaming.

"My goodness, Regina, pink. A lady in pink's just like an orchid."

"I'm not exactly an orchid, J. Ernest."

"You are to me, Regina."

It flustered her.

He ordered for both of them, selecting mutton and fresh asparagus. Then he ordered two glasses of sparkling wine.

"What're we going to toast this time, J. Ernest?"

"Why, Regina, that's for you to tell me—isn't it?"

Her pause was pregnant. "Well, J. Ernest, you want an answer. All right. I hope you like it. It's yes—I'll marry you—if you agree to certain things."

"Oh, I'm sure I could agree to anything you'd ever want. Would you like a monthly allowance?"

"No, Ernest. I'd like a little contract. My boardinghouse is a great comfort. The rents give me a good, steady living, around two thousand a year. And it's always full. The property's appreciated, too. Why, they tell me it's worth over six thousand. Imagine it. I've been able to put something back, it's over a thousand now, and Cromwell pays me two percent on the savings. Now, Ernest. The boardinghouse is mine. I'd like a contract that says what's yours is yours, and what's mine is mine."

He looked stricken. "Regina . . . don't you love me?"

"Well, I do, all your exterior parts."

"If you loved me, Regina, you'd say, 'Everything I have is thine, my beloved.' And I would say, 'Everything I possess is thine, my beloved.' Now I'm smitten with sadness."

"Well, don't be. I'm just an old mining camp lady that's seen the elephant."

"But that's not true love. Love is giving. Love is surrender. Ah, Regina, this holding back . . . it's like saying you don't quite trust me. Is there any way—words fail me, I fear—is there a way we can pass this awful hurdle?"

She shook her head.

He sighed. They slid into silence while the waiter set a covered pewter salver before them, and began slicing and dividing the meat onto two china plates. When the man had finished, they ate quietly.

She knew it would come to this. J. Ernest fancied her boardinghouse, her cash, and her annual income. He had plans to squander it on his lobbying for a senate seat. Her plainness had been a mercy, she thought. It gave her a grip on reality. She'd have to forget her plan to reform him.

He paused in the middle of his chop, his knife and fork raised upward like pikestaffs. "I'm not peaceable with it," he said. "This holding back. Actually, I'd be a little ashamed to have the wife of Senator J. Ernest Potter-Pride cooking and drudging and keeping a boarding place for rough mining men. It'd say to the world that I can't support you. But I can. I'm quite comfortable."

She smiled and added some sauce to the pungent lamb. She'd never been much for lamb, but J. Ernest loved it. A thousand sheep must have been massacred to feed him over his lifetime.

"I have an idea," he said slowly, his bold blue eyes fixing her. "A capital idea. My dear Regina, you can do better. There are sound investments that'll yield far more than your boardinghouse—and save you the drudgery besides. Surely you don't want to spend your days washing dishes for boarders.

"Now, as it happens, I'm an authorized sales agent for The Aurora Borealis Consolidated Mining Company. They've floated an issue of common stock to raise development capital. Ten dollars a share. Why, not long ago I sold a large quantity—the number's private, of course—to

Mrs. Duvalier, who was quite taken with the prospect of getting in on the ground floor before the silver bill goes through."

"Poor dear. That's what happens in the camps."

"Well, Regina. How'd you like to have shares in this promising venture? Some common stock equal to the value of your boardinghouse? Why, it's likely to double almost overnight. This is no ordinary stock. This is a succulent, juicy lamb on a spit. This is roast pork on a platter, served with yams. This is the standing rib roast of all investments, juicy and rare.

"The risk—it's minimal; everyone says the silver bill's on the brink of passing. We would work out a little trade. We could put it in a special trust for you, so it'd always be a comfort. You'd double, treble, quadruple, your boardinghouse income."

"J. Ernest, it just so happens I've lived most of my adult life in mining camps."

He looked puzzled.

"J. Ernest, Tombstone mines are flooding."

"Oh, you're talking about the Chollar property. That's just one of several the company's earmarked for development. I have in my office a report—"

"No reports. I'm like Con Daley. Nothing but working mines earning a profit. I've bought a few shares of those, and most turned out all right. I lost a little in Tombstone, The Lucky Cuss . . ."

Pride wolfed lamb as if it were dog food. But she wasn't going to budge. If the old goat wouldn't let her keep her boardinghouse, that would end it. J. Ernest wasn't the first who'd tried to separate her from her hardwon property. Each camp had produced a few friendly leeches. Fortunately, she had learned before some conniving jackass had swept her off her feet. That's what they'd all been—jackasses. J. Ernest was a dashing old jackass, though.

"I'm wounded to the quick," he muttered.

"I'm sorry. But I'm keeping my boardinghouse."

"I thought you loved me as dearly as I loved you."

"Everything except what I don't know about, Ernest."

"I don't follow you."

"You've never shared what's in your soul. What are you?"

He bridled. "Why, Regina, I'm what I am. I'm transparent. There's nothing inside that's not worn on my sleeve for all to see."

"I don't know you very well. But what I don't know I can always reform."

He laughed. "Well, my dear, you're an original."

"How about the contract, J. Ernest?"

"Well all right. I'll draft a little agreement."

"What's the agreement going to say?"

"It'll say that what's yours is yours. It'll go into a trust and the trustees will act in your behalf as long as you live."

"Oh, no. There'll be no trust. I'm keeping what I own. And my estate won't go to you unless I will it."

He looked sulky. "You'll just throw away all you've acquired, Regina."

"That's going to be my privilege. What do you think I came west for? To let some old goat run my life?"

He winced. "You drive a hard bargain."

"A moment ago you were talking about surrender. All right, J. Ernest. What are you going to surrender to me?"

"Why, my dear, my utmost love and loyalty and esteem; my most treasured hours; my intimate moments . . ."

She sort of liked that. "Let's toast it, J. Ernest."

"Toast what?"

"The arrangement. You'll pledge your love, loyalty, esteem, treasured hours, and intimate moments. I'll pledge to sit beside you at boring Helena dinners, and wave at the crowds on the Fourth of July."

The unblinking gaze didn't surprise her. Then the old lantern-jaw relaxed, his noble brow crinkled, and he chortled. His slender white fingers plucked up the wineglass filled with blood-red juice.

"To our arrangement, my dear. May it always be blessed."

She clinked his glass with hers and sipped.

"When shall we set the day, Regina?"

"None too soon," she said. "I'm still gonna think this over. I read the fine print."

CHAPTER 53

. . . .

Sylvie broke out a bottle of Dom Perignon. Jubilation filled the Exchange Club that evening of July 14th. Little Ben Harrison had signed the Sherman Silver Purchase Bill into law. It wasn't everything the free silver forces wanted, but it did provide that the Treasury would purchase, at market prices, four and a half million ounces of silver a year—roughly the national output—and issue paper money against it.

The West had won. There'd be easy money now. There'd be cash in the pockets of western people. No longer would the unblinking eastern financiers and their gold standard strangle the new states. It was the time to whoop and laugh and buy drinks for everyone.

Most of her members gathered in the cool of the July evening to celebrate. Their net worth had just increased by hundreds of thousands. Their future was secure. Cashbox sat on a bonanza. The West was an El Dorado. She opened the tall windows overlooking Cashbox Street to release the sullen summer heat. Then she sat down beside Con, who was off in a corner, not sharing the excitement.

"Will my stocks rise?" she asked.

"No, not much, Sylvie. They're at the top now."

"I don't understand."

"A market anticipates events. If your stocks went up these past months, it's because speculators bid them up, expecting this to happen. Are yours up?"

"Some are. All my smaller purchases."

"But some didn't make it."

"I thought they'd all double. Everyone told me they would."

"Not everyone."

She slid her hand over his, acknowledging it, and he smiled.

She plucked up her champagne bottle and poured the rest of it into emptied goblets.

"Well, Sylvie, did you get rich?" asked Henry Hammon. "I'm a lot richer today than I was yesterday. The Giltedge. . . ."

"I'm not a silver queen," she said. "The rising tide missed me, I guess. The Ophir stock actually went down . . . along with another stock I have." Suddenly she felt blue.

Con had never said a word during that picnic. All that day he acted as if he were just trying to inform himself, but she knew he had done it for her. She had let herself be gulled. And Con understood her too well ever to say a thing. He'd quietly shown her stark reality without appearing to. Never in her life had she met a man who'd given her that respect. If she wanted to be on her own, she would have to make her own mistakes. Including this one, which was so bad it could ruin her.

She had hoped the passage of the Silver Purchase Act might bail her out. But now, only hours after the word flashed in on the telegraph, she knew it wouldn't. She had nothing left to cling to. Suddenly the whole celebration turned sour, and she had to choke back her anger.

The attorney was here, with that scheming editor Willard Croker as his guest. The editor had gotten the wire news; then Potter-Pride had invited him up to celebrate. She eyed Croker with some interest; maybe she could sell her shares to him. She'd sell at a loss if she had to. But she'd have to find the moment to catch him alone.

She tolerated Ernest, no matter that he was as fishy as a carnival barker. But the booming, gregarious, wolfish Croker she could barely abide. His newspaper had become almost two-faced. The stories composed by Mrs. Svensrud always seemed to be right on the mark, while Croker's own stiletto work would slice one victim and then another, including herself.

Her chance came late that evening. Con had retired to his suite but Croker and Potter-Pride still sipped their drinks and talked with feverish joy, the smell of money intoxicating them more than the ginger beer in their steins.

"You seem pleased, Ernest," she said, settling beside them.

"Ah, my dear Sylvie, I never expected it from the Republicans. Whatever inspired Little Ben?"

"Votes, I guess."

"Western votes. The Omnibus States—the ones that came into the Union last year, that's what."

"They tell me we didn't get everything. No free coinage."

"It's good enough. It'll make you rich, Sylvie."

"Will it? Can you really promise that?"

"Why, Sylvie, the future's a dream come true. Wait until the Aurora mines start humming. A fountain of wealth."

"Has my Aurora Borealis stock gone up?"

"Why, it's a bit early. But I'd say it'll bloom like a rose. Why, Sylvie, the act'll push silver stocks through the roof."

"I don't hear anyone talk about the Aurora Borealis. Why's that?"

"It's because they're afraid. They all sit here wishing they'd had the courage to seize the day. Oh, yes, the Chollar has to be pumped out—and they're afraid. But I'm not. It'll be done. Modern pumps, good engineering."

"When?"

"Any time now."

"Ernest, I don't like that purchase."

"You don't? Why, Sylvie, that's like worrying about volcanoes erupting under you. Put it out of mind."

"How can you be so sure?"

"Why, if the Aurora stock doesn't double soon, I'd call

it a weak investment. I think it'll triple by year's end. The Sherman Act's on the books."

"What's it worth now?"

Croker chimed in. "Why, it must be fifteen or sixteen, wouldn't you say, Ernest?"

"At least that."

"Does it sell at that?"

"Oh, I'm sure it could."

"Well, that's good news. You know, Ernest, I'm not good at speculating. I just want to run my club. I've been thinking: I'd like to get out of the deal—give you back the thousand shares and tear up the mortgage."

"Why, Sylvie. I wouldn't consider it. Depriving you of such a golden opportunity."

"Well, Ernest, I want to. If the shares are worth fifteen, then you'll make fifty percent."

"That's a theoretical price. I'd say they're worth all of that, but sometimes the market misses the slumbering giants for a while."

"Well, then, I'm sure you'd love to take back the shares at ten and be ready for the rush to buy your slumbering giant. I just want to keep my club and the hall."

She waited, fighting back the fear stabbing through her.

"I wouldn't think of doing it, Sylvie. You don't quite grasp the complexities of finance."

"Profit, Ernest. I'm offering you a fifty percent profit."

"No, no, no. I can't do that just now. I have financial obligations that prevent it."

"Prevent you from making a fifty percent profit—without even spending a dime? Just by tearing up a mortgage? Imagine that." She glared at him. "I guess I'll offer the shares to my Exchange Club members for whatever they'll pay."

"Oh, I don't think you should do that. Bad timing. Let the shares grow in their little cocoons and sell them after they've become beautiful butterflies."

"This building's all the butterfly I want. The hall and the club are my only support. They've earned me a good income from the moment they opened. I don't want to lose them. To make my payments to you, I'll need help from that stock. My income alone won't do it. But I suppose you knew that."

"Why, Sylvie, everything'll be fine."

"Will it?"

He patted her hand. "You need vision."

"My vision improved when I saw the Chollar—and some of the claims."

He seemed taken aback for a moment. "How . . . ? Oh, I see. That's what they all look like before they're developed."

"Claims with no ore in them?"

"Lady," said Croker, "don't trespass. Don't you mess around on company property or we'll have you in court."

"How does swindling people feel, Mister Croker?"

"What?"

"Oh, now, Sylvie, tut tut," Ernest said.

"Knowing you, I suppose it feels wonderful."

"See here now, Sylvie. *Caveat emptor.* Buyer beware. That's the ancient law of the universe. You're jumping to unwarranted conclusions. I hope you watch your sharp tongue when it comes to confidential matters."

"Ernest, I'm going to sell my shares. You're going to buy them back. I'll exchange them for the mortgage."

"Mrs. Duvalier, he's not gonna do it. Now you just don't bother your pretty head about it," said Croker.

"Not bother my pretty head. Thank you for the compliment, Mister Croker. I think you meant empty head. But I will. This happens to involve ten thousand dollars of stock, virtually every cent I possess. So I'm going to bother my empty head about it. Perhaps you'd like to buy them, Mister Croker? A moment ago you told me they were worth fifteen. You could make quite a killing."

"I'm extended to my limits, sweetheart."

"Well, Willard, it's time to be off, eh? How about a late feast at the chophouse?" Old Jut-Jaw stood, and Willard Croker sprang up like a jack-in-the-box.

"Adieu, my dear. You just remember what I said: wait quietly while the seeds sprout; wait until you see the mighty oaks."

From her club window she watched them scurry into the darkening streets. She couldn't sell her worthless stock. She stood at the window, thinking of ways to fight back.

CHAPTER 54

....

Charlotte Keiserling knew from the look on Calliope's face that something bad would transpire this afternoon. The girl had barged into Charlotte's rooms unannounced, while Charlotte was pouring six drops of laudanum to float her through the evening.

"I'm leaving, and right now," said Calliope.

"But you can't. You owe me money. You have little habits that I've paid for."

"I am. Try and stop me."

The sullen raven-haired beauty stared defiantly at Charlotte. "I'm going to Minnie's place. And I'll tell you why. It's that brat."

"Casper? But he's just a boy."

"He's no boy, and he's wrecking this dump. Now he wants a frogskin a night from each of us. If we don't give it to him he says he'll cut us up. I'm gonna vamoose."

"Casper wouldn't do a thing like that."

"Oh, you think not? Wake up, Charlotte."

"But I give him. . . ." She had been giving Casper Penrose two dollars each night. She didn't want to, but he told her he'd take it anyway if she didn't. He'd been scooping up anything he could find until she'd bought a small safe.

"I won't let you go. Not until you pay for your powders."

"How can I pay for it when that brat takes everything from me? Tough luck, Charlotte."

"But Calliope—I'll make a deal."

She didn't want to lose her. Whores were hard enough to find, but this dolly earned more than all her other girls together. She shrilled like a circus parade in bed. There was hardly a man in Cashbox who didn't want to try out her whistles. A dozen times a night her steam pipes would shatter the peace, stirring the men in the parlor. They came clear from Blackhawk, Copperopolis, and White Sulphur Springs just to try Calliope. On a summer's night when windows were open, men all over Cashbox paused, with faraway looks in their eyes, at the sound of Calliope's music.

"You stay, dearie. I'll deal with Casper when he comes. He'll never bother you again."

Calliope didn't respond.

"Dearie, I'll write off what you owe me. Just stay. We'll raise your price again."

The steam seeped from Calliope's boilers. "Charlotte, if he ever bothers me again, I'm sailing. And that goes for all the girls. They're all ready to quit you."

"They are?"

"You bet. That's all they talk about. You and that brat." The girl stormed out, slammed the door.

Charlotte sat on her bed, shocked. She hadn't realized how close she was to apocalypse. She downed a quarter of a teaspoon of laudanum and waited for the thrum of peace in her blood vessels. That was a huge dose. She settled back on the coverlet, letting the narcotic rub away the pain. Whenever she couldn't deal with something, the laudanum helped. Some girls bought cocaine or hashish, but Charlotte's paradise came in dark blue bottles.

Casper Penrose. He had always amused her with his cocky ways, his awful pompadour, his sharp-edged nastiness that reminded her of the cut-ups she'd known. He had hung around, lipping off to customers and girls until she finally took him to her own room and showed him the ropes. He had bleated like a calf that first time, his fifteen-year-old body trembling and bucking.

Now he was seventeen and he didn't tremble any more. It hadn't taken him long to try out the others—he wanted them for free, and when they refused he got nasty. So she slipped him two dollars now and then just to quiet him down and let him think he was a man of the world. She'd get a dollar back anyway.

But somehow it all fell apart. That cockiness in him wouldn't stop pushing. She'd known for months that he plagued her parlor house; known it would get worse. He was driving away customers, threatening the girls. And yet whenever he sauntered in, she melted like ice in hell. She hated her own weakness. Never before had she betrayed herself. Why did she let him? What on earth was the matter with her? Her own softness toward the punk kid shook her.

Now she had to curb him or quit. Maybe she would ditch Cashbox. Take the next stage to Butte. She still had Amos, but Casper had turned brawny and could whip the peglegged man without half trying. Maybe she'd try Constable Svensrud, but he didn't like to mess around the houses unless he had to stop a brawl. She knew a dozen miners who'd love to hammer Casper—but she couldn't bear the thought.

The evening trade often started around five, but she didn't feel like greeting the gents. The girls could do that. She lay quietly in the twilight, not knowing what to do. Nothing made sense. Time drifted by, hazed by the dope in her veins.

She heard him in the kitchen at dusk, and then watched her door spring open. He stood there leering at her.

"You ready?" he asked.

"No, not tonight, Casper."

"You don't say no to me, sweetheart."

"Casper, how old are you?"

"Less'n half your age."

"That's right. You need a girlfriend your age."

"I got a dozen."

"We have to talk."

"Yeah, I know. You ain't giving me enough moolah to spit on. It's gonna be ten a night now."

"How do you even spend two?"

"Buy stuff. Like this here suit. And look at this." He plucked a nickel-plated revolver from the breast pocket of his white suitcoat. "What a dandy. I'm heeled. It's a little thirty-two, five-shot, hardly makes a bulge."

"I don't want that in here."

"Tough, ain't it."

"I gotta talk, Casper. You're costing me trade. My customers don't like your smart lip."

"Too bad for them. They bitching? They can say it down the barrel of this little baby." He waved the revolver.

"That's what I mean. They're going to other houses. You're costing us lots of trade, dearie."

"Well, I'm going to fix them other houses too. I'm going to run the whole show."

"Calliope's going to leave if you bother her again."

"She said that?" He laughed nasally. "Guess I'll have to mark her up. Then she won't earn so much."

"Casper!" A dread infused her. "Don't even talk like that."

"All I need's a broken beer bottle, sweetheart. I'll mark 'em so's they never work again except for two-bits with a Harvest Queen sack over their head."

"If Calliope leaves, I'll go broke. I can't afford you unless she's here."

"She ain't leavin'."

"Casper—I'll give you something if you promise never to come in here again."

"You what?" He laughed. "Never come in again? How about a thousand a month? That's what I'm worth."

"I'll put two hundred dollars a month into an account at the bank if you never, ever come here again."

"Don't you like me any more?"

"That's more than I can afford."

"You old slut. I like it here. Now gimme ten bucks."

Ten a night. Three hundred a month. That was sometimes more than she made after feeding the girls and paying the quarterly license to Cashbox.

"I can't do that, Casper."

"You gonna resist me? You want to get sliced up?"

"I don't make that much."

"Then you'd better get out and hustle—like I do."

"No, don't, Casper. Be a good boy."

He bleated, and sat beside her on the bed. "That's what my ma tells me. Casper, you be a good boy."

"Look, dearie, I'll give you a real good time."

"You old bag. I want moolah."

She shook her head.

He landed on her, driving breath from her lungs. His forearm slammed across her throat, crushing her windpipe. She gasped, trying to suck air into her lungs. She squirmed and fought but his forearm pressed like an anvil, choking her. Distantly she heard him cackling. Her lungs burned, but his forearm pushed downward even harder. Then suddenly it lifted. She gulped air, sobbing.

"Now you know," he said.

She sucked air, sucked life back into her wounded body. Her throat ached. He'd damaged her windpipe. She wondered if she would ever feel right again.

"Open it," he said. "Unless you want more."

Wordlessly she struggled out of the bed and staggered to the green safe. He bounded along behind her, watching over her shoulder as she spun the dial. Her safe wouldn't be worth a damn any more. Numbly she worked the dial right, left, right again, and pulled the handle. The door squeaked open.

"Holy cow," he muttered, seeing the five hundred in small bills she kept there for emergencies. He snatched them all, stuffing some into a money clip, and the rest into a breast pocket.

"Don't hold out on me, you old slut, or it'll be worse next time. I'm good with a toadsticker."

She nodded mutely as he sauntered out the door, heading for The Oriental, where he'd lose it all to One-Eyed Jack and count it a good evening.

Charlotte knew only one thing: she was doomed.

CHAPTER 55

• • • • • • • • • • • • • • • •

There were moments when Portia Webb felt cheated by life. On the day she had married Thaddeus, she had believed their wedlock would be a loving partnership, a sharing of hopes and dreams forever. But it had never been like that. She refused to succumb to self-pity though. She'd been wrought from finer steel than that. She knew herself to be a strong woman filled with courage and optimism.

But this hot August day had tested the limits of her courage. It was their twentieth anniversary, and he was oblivious to it. More and more he seemed oblivious of her, married to his mining. She had become a useless thing, like a vermiform appendix.

He had said he would be home at seven. She'd been tempted not to cook; to meet him at the door with an accusation and let him feel such guilt as a stiff New Englander might feel. But she was made of better stuff than that. He might not remember this day was special, but she did. She had dressed herself in her best summer frock, the canary one, even if he wouldn't notice. She would cook a sumptuous feast, a standing rib roast, just because *she* would celebrate and keep the occasion sacred. If love was giving and marriage a sacred pledge, then she would remember all her vows.

She did love Thaddeus so. Once in a while—how she wished it would be more often—he returned to her like a black sheep, his face filled with fondness, his love manifest in his gaze. Then, for a while life would be nectar. But it never lasted, and soon his concubines, the mines, captured him again.

He walked through the door at six, astounding her. She had just repaired to the kitchen to complete the meal she'd started earlier, and there he was, kissing her warmly. Eagerly she embraced him.

"Did things go well, dear?"

"Oh, yes. Ever since the Silver Act, things've hummed." He peered about him. "These things'll keep, won't they? I had dinner at the chophouse in mind."

"Oh, Thaddeus." She stared, fighting back the impulse to weep. She would never weep if she could help it. But the turmoil that swept through her caught in her throat. Wordlessly she restored red potatoes and asparagus to the pantry, the rib roast and hollandaise sauce to the ice chest, the roasted coffee beans to their canister, the lemon meringue pie to the pie safe.

"It's a lovely eve," he said, the faintest smile building crow's feet around his eyes.

She closed the draft on the Majestic kitchen range to bed down the fire, hung up her apron, and turned to him with an odd tremble she hadn't felt in more years than she could remember.

He offered her his arm and gravely led her down the sloping clay streets to the Palace Hotel, past raw buildings built higgledy-piggledy on sagebrush-choked lots. Cashbox had grown, but not in beauty. Most of the year its miry streets threatened to swallow horses and children. But this moment Cashbox seemed utterly radiant and endowed with uncanny grace, like a city gilded with silver.

He had, it seemed, reserved a banquette at the Palace Hotel's Silver Queen chophouse. A gentleman in swallowtails beamed at them and escorted them to a private corner. But he did not hand them menus. Instead, a waiter appeared with a bucket of crushed ice containing a bottle of Bordeaux. He opened it with his corkscrew, and poured a sip into Thaddeus's crystal wineglass. Thaddeus sipped and nodded. The waiter filled both glasses exactly one-third full.

"But Thaddeus, I'm the president of the WCTU," she said.

He nodded amiably. The waiter vanished.

"I'm not very good at this," he said. Nonetheless he lifted his bright wine, and she found herself doing so too. Around her the pewter service glistened in the lamplight. He paused, as if trying to remember something he'd rehearsed a thousand times which had vanished from his mind. And then it came to him and he smiled, fixing her in his innocent gaze.

He seemed tongue-tied, and she wished she could help him.

"Just twenty years ago, my dear, we pledged ourselves to join forces for a lifetime, for richer for poorer, for better for worse. Well, here we are. A bit richer perhaps, but for you, I know, a bit for the worse."

She swallowed. She couldn't speak. Around her the chophouse hummed, but in this banquette she experienced only his slightly gritty voice and his intense gaze.

"These hard little towns haven't been easy for you. Nothing much to do. None of the comforts. Nothing like what you expected from life; nothing like what your parents provided. I've always known that and grieved it. And yet my calling drew me on, at the sacrifice of your dreams and hopes. . . ."

She felt panic build in her soul. She didn't want him to say these things. They ought to remain buried.

"We weren't blessed with children, though we yearned for them. You've often had time on your hands and scarcely a thing to do with it. And there's been a certain lack of society, too. And yet you've endured. It occurred to me yesterday that I've never heard you complain. Never a word, even when the narrow life in these remote places crushed you. You endured; you fell back upon your fortitude, and made do with whatever was at hand—in rural

Mexico, in remote places like Silver City and Virginia City. Ah, yes, you made do."

"Thaddeus, don't. . . ."

"Oh, I must. There's things that need saying, and certain moments when they must be said, Portia. I've known my lacks—and yet I've not done what I might to overcome them. For that reason I'm humbled whenever I think of your resolute love all these years. You're the finer partner in this match."

"Oh, Thaddeus—"

"Ah! Let me talk or I'll jump the rails. I thought perhaps this would be the moment to change things. Oh, yes, there're things that need changing, Portia." He lifted his glass. "I wish to toast two things."

"But, Thaddeus, you don't need to say—"

"Bear with me. Mining engineers don't know how to be poets, but I'll just fumble along. Here's to twenty blessed years, to your courage, to your abiding love. And here's to a better life to come, a time of joy for you; a time of fulfillment for you; a time when we are drawn ever closer. I love you."

He touched his crystal wineglass to hers, the ting a sweet and flawless note in the breathless quiet. He sipped, and she did too, feeling the wine catch in her throat.

"I've two things for you, Portia. One is this." From some recess under the linen cloth he withdrew a package wrapped in tissue and tied with a sky-blue ribbon. She discovered within it a red morocco-bound edition of the poems of Alfred, Lord Tennyson.

"Tennyson! Oh, Thaddeus. How did you . . . ? It's—lovely."

"That comes with a little something more. I'll read them to you each evening."

"Oh!" She could no longer see him clearly, or see the gilded letters on her book of poems by England's poet laureate.

"Now, the rest of it is . . . simply an offer. Portia, Cashbox has been the hardest of all for you. A rough, raw little town. A boring town miles from a railroad, and hundreds of miles from anything resembling a city. My darling Portia, here's my offer. Any time you wish to leave, we'll leave. I'll resign. We'll go to some gentler place. Would I regret it? Not a bit. Why, I'm proud of the Giltedge. I built it up. I've made it safe. I've gotten what can be gotten from it. I've achieved something. But I don't need to stay here. Portia, whenever you want to pick up your heels and run, we'll run."

"Oh, Thaddeus, I couldn't ask you to do that. . . ."

"Oh, you're not. It's my gift. We'll move whenever you want to move."

"I love that," she whispered. "You're so dear. But Thaddeus, I'll never ask. Wherever thou art, there will I be."

He absorbed that quietly, as was his wont. "Things are getting better here, Portia. Daley tells me the railroad's under way. It'll come within twenty miles, this phase. The engineering's done, right-of-way purchased. He's contracted with the Northern Pacific. They waited—wisely I'd say—until the silver bill passed. Next year you'll have a way out any time you want. Twenty miles to the railhead won't be so bad."

"Thaddeus—I love you so."

"I'm yours, Portia." He fumbled about. "I'm not good at these confounded sentiments."

"Yes you are," she said. Tears were ruining her composure but for once she couldn't contain them. She placed her slender hand over his and squeezed.

"I'm going to read poetry to you tonight, Portia. Ah, a little birdie told me you'd enjoy that."

"I would!" she cried. "How did you ever know?"

CHAPTER 56

· · · · · · · · · · · · · · · · ·

May Svensrud hung up her printer's smock a little early that Saturday afternoon. As long as she had her work done, Willard didn't seem to mind. He was rarely around anyway.

She had completed three of the four pages, as usual, leaving only the front page. She had created the advertisements, many of which she had sold earlier in the week. The inside pages she had filled with national and foreign news copied from other papers. The front page she always left half done, so that the latest material could be stuffed into it on Mondays, just before she and Willard put the paper to bed.

This issue, the top story would be the construction of the railroad. She rarely found a story as good as that, and she had already written two sidebars for it, one on the anticipated cost, and one about its economic impact. Mr. Daley told her that the last twenty miles would cost as much as the first fifty-seven, because of the trestles, grades and bridges.

She scrubbed her hands with gritty soap, the only thing that would scour off some of the inkstains. Her fingers had gradually purpled from their daily dyeing. It was worth it. Croker was paying her a dollar a day. She had said she would quit if he didn't, and he had grudgingly surrendered, grumbling that the paper wouldn't support a field mouse. If it didn't, that was his own darned fault, she figured. It earned enough so he could rent an apartment over a saloon. He hardly came around any more, except on Mondays and Tuesdays. He even left the advertising and subscriptions to her. She wished he would give her a paid vacation too, but he said printer's devils never got one.

Whenever she took a day off, he groused about it for weeks.

She stepped into a vicious August sun, only to run into the mayor, Hiram Claflin, and Mrs. Webb.

"Ah, we caught you, Mrs. Svensrud," said Mrs. Webb. "Could we have a word?"

She nodded, puzzled, and opened up the offices again.

"We're alone, aren't we?" asked Claflin.

"Himself's not here, if that's what you mean," May said.

"Good. Mrs. Svensrud, we're here to offer you a job."

"Me?"

"Yes, you, my dear," said Mrs. Webb. "You know, for many months now, *The Plain Truth* has benefitted from your skills. Oh, it hasn't escaped us. Every one who reads the paper knows it. Your stories are beautifully written, easy to pick out. I never see an error. And of course every merchant in town knows how well you sell advertising; how quick you are with your arithmetic. You're uncommonly well schooled, Mrs. Svensrud."

May waited tensely, wondering about all this.

"Something has happened. Our dear Miss Rice at the school house has been called east, and had to submit her resignation. It's just a month before the new term. She was our elementary teacher, first to eighth grade. The committee got together, and your name came up. In fact, it's our unanimous choice. The pay is fifty dollars a month for the nine-month term. Would you be interested?"

"School? Teaching? Teaching little children?"

"Why yes. We'll hire you without further ado if you're interested. You're so perfectly suited."

"Little children?" May felt a terror whirlwind through her, sucking away her composure. "But you don't know. . . ."

"Of course we know. You don't have the usual normal school credentials, but we haven't the slightest doubt of your abilities."

"But I can't, I can't." She felt a roaring in her head. She clenched her fists until her knuckles whitened.

"You can't? Are you sure? We'd be so disappointed. You're just the one, and we haven't any other very adequate choice. . . ."

"Mrs. Webb . . . Mister Claflin . . . I don't . . . know. I . . . wouldn't . . . be . . . good with children. . . ." She felt tears welling up and she couldn't squeeze them back. On this awful Saturday, her whole past had tumbled down upon her head.

They stared at her, dismayed.

"We didn't mean to upset you, Mrs. Svensrud—" said Claflin.

"It's a shock, isn't it?" said Mrs. Webb. "A surprise. Why, I think you should go home and talk it over with Mister Svensrud. We don't need to know right away."

"Yes . . . yes . . . I'll do that," May said. She managed a smile. "It's a nice offer."

"Well, you're the ideal one. We're sure of it."

May laughed shakily. "You're more sure than I am. Forgive me. I was so—surprised."

"Why, I'm surprised you never thought of it. You'd make a perfect teacher. It's a good profession. A chance to nurture and inspire our children. You've the Three R's, and a nice knowledge of civics and history and morals. We see it in the paper each week."

"Oh, thank you. I didn't know anyone noticed."

"We all do. Well, until we hear from you, then."

She saw them to the door and then sat down, dizzy with dread. It took her a long while to compose herself. She wandered home in a daze. She knew she couldn't accept. A child-killer couldn't be a teacher. If they had known, they wouldn't have asked her. And if she taught, she'd live in daily terror, not only of having her past exposed, but of doing it again in a bad moment. If she couldn't cope with the whining of one little boy, how could she cope with a dozen children?

And yet . . . the pay increase would be nice. She and

Slug struggled and had so little to show for their long hours. He welcomed her income because they had so little. And the free summers would be glorious. Days like this with nothing in the world to do but soak up the sun and breathe in the sage-scented air.

But she couldn't think of it. If she had even one responsible bone in her body, she couldn't accept. She would thank them, refuse, and put it out of mind.

Slug walked in early, even before she'd had a chance to put a meal together. "Not much doing," he said. "Strange Saturday. Even the dogs are asleep."

"That's what I want when you're out there," she said. "Every night you go out, I worry. Especially Saturdays."

"No need for that. This's a real peaceful town," he said. "We haven't had a shooting in two years. Just some theft, drunk and disorderly. Not like some mining camps you hear of."

"I just worry. Because I love you."

He smiled, and something gentle passed between them.

"Slug? Something happened."

"Bad?"

She nodded. She could see it only that way. Swiftly she recounted her encounter with the mayor and Mrs. Webb, the offer and her decision.

He sat quietly, thinking about it a while. That was his way, to reflect before opening his mouth.

"You'd make a good teacher, May."

"I'd be haunted every second by the past."

"Remember when we walked up to the ridge on our wedding night? I just wanted you to face west. Forget the east. Follow the sun. It's always heading west into the future. May, you'd enjoy the teaching. This is here; this isn't Minnesota. You've got a man that loves you, sittin' here. It's not the same now."

"I can't forget it, Slug."

"You could teach—you'd be good at it. And you'd never get ruffled up, not any more. And you could kinda look at it in a good way, helping children grow up good.

All those little tigers, they'd be boys you could help raise up into big tigers. May, don't you be in such a rush to turn 'em down. You gotta look west again."

"Oh, Slug. . . ." She leaned over his chair just to hug him. "That's only half of it. The other half's the secret. My years in prison. I couldn't do it without telling them. Don't you see? They've got to be told. I couldn't teach and live with that secret every minute I'm in the classroom with all those children. It'd tear me to bits, Slug."

He nodded. "You up to doing it?"

"No."

"You think maybe just talkin' to one person—Mrs. Webb—would do it? She'd keep a secret. Lady like that probably invented the Ten Commandments."

"You don't know what you're asking, Slug. Don't you know why I came here—to hide?"

He grinned. "That notion's passed between my ears a time or two."

"Oh, Slug, how could I? Go to Mrs. Webb and tell her I did three years in prison for killing my own boy? My God!"

"Take some doing," he said. "But you got time to think on it."

"Slug, tomorrow take me up to the ridge—please?"

"Sure, May. We'll go up and have a gander. You can do what you set your mind to. There never was a sweeter gal than you."

CHAPTER 57

· · · · · · · · · · · · · · · · ·

One-Eyed Jack Wool watched Casper Penrose settle on a stool at the faro layout. The punk had been rolling in frogskins, and One-Eyed Jack considered it his civic duty to separate every last one of them from that dimwit. Dumb twits like that shouldn't be allowed to keep their boodle. The whole human race benefitted whenever punks were skinned.

Wool fixed his fierce and imperious gaze upon the brat, surveying his double-breasted, chalk-striped suit, the callow pimpled face, the pulpy lips and above them the loathsome pompadour, a four-inch erection of grease-slicked brown hair that gave the punk the look of a gobbler.

"Beat it, punk. I'm going to clean you out again."

The punk licked his fat lips and laid twenty dollars on the green oilcloth. Wool snatched it up and slid out a stack of dollar chips.

"You dumb puppy, you'll lose it again. I'm not going to let you get up from the table a winner. You're gonna sit there until it's all gone."

"I got more where this come from, Wool."

"That's for sure, you pimp milk-sucker."

"Watch your mouth, Wool. I don't have to take nothing no more. You'll get worse'n you give. I'm warnin' ya."

"Play, sucker. So I can clean you out again. As long as Charlotte's donating to my business."

All this was observed with amusement by the four others at the faro layout. Wool was keeping his own cases this Wednesday night. Only on paydays did he hire a lookout and casekeeper.

Wool shuffled the deck and turned the soda card under. He slid the deck into his casebox and waited for the gents to lay down their bets. Some sports liked faro because the the house odds were small. Wool liked to run a faro layout because the saps thought it was the most likely to reward them. There were ways to cheat, but he didn't bother with them. It was so much easier just to wring their necks. The punk was easiest of all. Let him get ahead and show signs of pocketing his winnings and Wool simply shouted at him to sit down and play like a sport. Which the punk always did.

It took only a half hour to clean the punk out. The rat kept coppering bets that won and scattering Charlotte's cash around the table until it was gone. One-Eyed Jack sighed. It'd been easier than ever. He was almost tempted to toss five dollars to the kid. Which reminded him he should send another five hundred to the foundling home. He was feeling the uneasy pressure of too much indulgence.

He clawed the last of the punk's chips in, musing on the delights of fate, when the punk caught him.

"You cheat!" cried Casper Penrose. Wool saw a flash of nickel plate, heard a deafening report. Something stung his left ear, twisting his head as the second report blasted through The Oriental. That one bit Wool's arm, even as Wool's own spring-loaded thirty-two-caliber piece came to hand.

Wool aimed and fired, putting an innocuous little hole one inch under the pompadour, just left of the bridge of the nose. The punk's eyes crossed and he slid to the wooden floor. Not a drop of blood leaked from his empty skull. Not a hair loosened from the oily pompadour. He looked sort of cute.

It had happened so fast. His ears rang from the reports. The punk's arms moved, his carcass shuddered, and then he didn't move at all. Gunsmoke boiled toward the lamps, the smell of it acrid in Wool's nostrils. The prick was unquestionably dead.

Wool stared, dumfounded. No man had ever gotten the jump on him before; no man had ever wounded him. The punk had done both. Wool swung his piece toward the other players. They looked thunderstruck. "None of you moves. You're my witnesses." He glared at the shocked crowd. "Get Svensrud."

It took a few minutes. Then Constable Svensrud pushed through the staring mob, eyed Casper Penrose, and eyed Wool. The constable knelt beside Penrose and tried to find a pulse at the wrist and the throat. He gave up and stood.

"Poor loser," said Wool, clutching his bleeding arm.

"That's a seventeen-year-old kid, Wool."

"Looks twenty to me."

"You shot a boy."

"Punk lost, shot me first. Twice. You gonna tell me I can't defend myself?"

Svensrud grunted. He picked up the punk's shiny piece and opened the cylinder. Two rounds had been fired. Svensrud sniffed, muttered, snapped the cylinder back, and pocketed the piece.

"Let me see yours."

Wool slowly handed it to the constable, who examined the cylinder, sniffed it, and pocketed it also. Wool extracted his handkerchief and dabbed blood from his ear. Then he wrapped the handkerchief around his arm and twisted it into a tourniquet.

Svensrud eyed Wool's bloody arm and ear. "Too bad he only got half an ear, Wool. I would have preferred your other eye, myself."

"I perform a service, Svensrud. I keep the rat population under control."

"You shouldn't of let him in here—a minor. I'll cite you for it." He pushed the punk with the toe of his boot. "I wish this town had a doc."

Wool shrugged. "Looked twenty-five to me. You should give me a hero medal."

Svensrud ignored him. "All right, I'm going to get your stories. I'll start with you four."

The players at the layout stared back uneasily.

"I think I'm going to question you separately," he said. "I want your names." He pointed.

"Octave Few."

"Denver, Walt Denver."

"Jacques, Beau Jacques."

"Alexander Hamilton."

"I'll deal with you later. All right, you." He pointed at Few. "The rest of you stay put."

"I'm bleeding. I need to get a patch," said Wool.

Svensrud nodded at one of the sluts. "Fix him up," he said, and disappeared into the back hallway.

Wool let Venus de Milo—her business name—cut open

his shirt and soak a bloody flesh wound in his upper arm
with popskull. It stung, but not so much as being
outgunned by a punk. She bound toweling around his arm,
and they watched it turn red. His perforated ear had quit
dripping. Wool felt nauseous.

Svensrud returned Few and took Denver out of hearing
range.

"What'd you tell him?" Wool asked Few.

The Belgian smiled. He'd opened up a photography stu-
dio in town recently. "What do I say? That this idiot swine
of a boy had a shiny little gun in his hand under the table
even before he called you a . . . certain word. He'd shot
twice even before you got your own weapon out. It was
pure self-defense. He was planning to murder you before
he walked in."

Wool grunted.

One by one Svensrud questioned the others privately,
and then collected stories from two sluts and three barflies.

It all amused Wool. The constable was itching to make
arrests, but couldn't. The man wandered around looking
for someone to pinch. The dollies were smirking.

"All right, Wool. I got four witnesses that say Penrose
shot first twice. I can't do nothing with that, but a coroner's inquest might. I've got a dead boy here, and I'll tell
you what's gonna happen. Cashbox—it's gonna close you
down. It's gonna clean up this district. You might have an
excuse this time, but a dead seventeen-year-old kid's not
good for your business. Why don't you get out? You do
that tomorrow and I'll drop the charge."

"Charge?"

"Letting a minor in here. That's all I've got, but I'll
stick it to you. I'll hang around in here until your trade's
ruined."

Wool yawned. He hurt in too many places. "Go ahead.
I like the town. I'm a bottom cleaner, like a big carp."

"Can I go now?" said Few.

Svensrud nodded. "But don't leave town."

Wool eyed his customers. "I'm closing the faro layout. Rest of the place stays open."

"Wool, you're coming with me," Svensrud said.

"Why?"

"I'm pinching you, that's why."

Wool shrugged. He lifted his black coat with his good arm, and followed the constable into the night. They walked silently to the jail. Every step fired pain through his arm. His ear throbbed.

"Get in there, Wool," Svensrud said.

"Beg pardon?"

"I said get in there."

"You mind if I get a shyster first—bail me out?"

"Get in there."

"Why?"

"I got a dead kid, that's why. Shot by a tinhorn. You know what that adds up to? A mob. We got a lot of no-nonsense miners around here. You're safer in my custody."

Wool hastened in, and heard the door clang behind him.

"I'm double locking the place. I've got to get Hildebrand to pick up the body. And then I've got to tell the kid's parents—good folks—that you put a bullet into his face."

"Be sure to tell Charlotte Keiserling. Tell me whether she laughs or cries."

But Svensrud was padlocking doors, and missed Wool's wit.

CHAPTER 58

• • • • • • • • • • • • • • • • •

Willard Croker had a sensational story. A tinhorn gambler shooting a seventeen-year-old boy had stirred up Cashbox more than anything had in months. Willard intended to fan the flames and sell a lot of papers. It didn't matter that the kid had crawled out of a sewer; it didn't even matter that it was an airtight case of self-defense. What mattered was that One-Eyed Jack Wool had plugged a boy from a nice Cornish mining family and was getting away with murder.

Cheerfully, Croker composed his story, his hands whipping in and out of the type case with practiced speed. He had interviewed two witnesses, Beau Jacques and Walt Denver. He'd talked to Svensrud. He'd gotten some nasty comments about the punk from two of Charlotte's girls. Oh, it was a corker. He would spread it across the front of *The Plain Truth* and keep it on the front page for five or six issues. He'd write some editorials lashing Svensrud for doing nothing. All the constable did was charge Wool with having a minor in his dive. The paper would make hay.

But not much hay. Croker figured he could hawk an extra hundred copies of several issues at five cents a copy. That came to an extra five dollars. The cold reality washed through him. His pockets would still be empty.

He examined May's front page, and decided to pull some of it to make more room for the murder. She'd done a piece on the impending strike at the Giltedge. The Knights of Labor were demanding an eight-hour day, a paid one-week vacation, and rest breaks. The union boss, Hugh Trego, was threatening a strike if the Knights didn't get everything. Superintendent Thaddeus Webb had offered an eight-hour day but none of the rest.

It would have been a good lead story if the murder hadn't come along. News always came in bunches, he thought. May had done a good job on the strike story, but Willard wasn't going to tell her so. He'd become more and more dependent on her and hated to let her know it. If she got the notion she was useful, she would want more money.

"You certainly are cheerful today, Willard," said May, who was doing bookkeeping.

"I don't see a story like this but once in a blue moon," Croker said. "I can flog this for weeks. Tomorrow, we'll get some brats to hawk papers. I'm printing up an extra hundred-fifty. After that it's good for a few editorials."

"Against Slug."

"He's not doing his duty."

"And what is that?"

"Charge Wool with murder."

"Slug wishes he could."

"Well, what's stopping him?"

"The facts of the case. Four witnesses, Wool's own wounds, and—"

"Slug's in too tight with all those sports. We need an inquest."

May stared, stood, removed her printing smock, and collected her lunch pail.

"What're you doing?"

"I'm quitting."

"You can't do that. You—"

He spoke into a closing door.

Good riddance, he thought. The woman had taken over his paper, and most of her stuff wasn't worth the powder to blow it up. By God, he'd just saved twenty-five a month. And if she came whining for the pay she was owed, she could just keep on whining. He'd hire some new devil for fifty cents a day. He'd just gotten his paper back, and he was going to put some heat on Svensrud. He'd make *The Plain Truth* into something.

The Aurora Borealis shares hadn't sold. Someone— probably Daley—had put out the word. Maybe that was something for *The Plain Truth* to editorialize about— malefactors of great wealth, manipulating markets. Sinister deals struck over poker games in the Exchange Club by men who didn't give a damn about the public. *The Plain Truth* would be a stick, and he was going to swing it.

There came to him, as he locked up the front page, an epiphany. The more he thought of it, the more it excited him. *The Plain Truth* could become a bucket of gold after all. Swiftly he reopened the front-page form and threw more of May's stuff out until he had freed two columns.

Then he plunged into an editorial. He described the far side of Cashbox as a cesspool of vice that corrupted young boys like Casper Penrose and ruined the town's men. Its gambling robbed honest citizens of their hard-won wages; its scarlet women corrupted youths and men. Predatory vicemongers plunged innocent girls into lives of misery and degradation. On he went, sentence after purple sentence bursting into type.

He finished the long editorial, proofed and corrected it, and ran off a copy of the front page. He thought he'd start with Charlotte Keiserling and then try One-Eyed Jack Wool. Cashbox supported seven bordellos and two gambling dives. At twenty-five a month from each, he'd pocket two hundred and twenty-five dollars. That was better than peddling town lots.

He arrived at Charlotte's joint just after five, and caught her in the kitchen. He heard that she had grieved the punk kid in her rooms for two days and when she emerged she scarcely talked to anyone. She eyed him with stony indifference.

"I got something to show ya," Croker said, laying the page over the table.

Wordlessly Charlotte disappeared into her rooms and returned with gold-rimmed spectacles. She read silently, studying the murder story first and then Croker's long editorial.

"Well?" asked Croker.

"You write like a rutting rat."

"You should know, sweetheart."

"You're going to push us out. That's nothing new."

"It don't have to happen, Charlotte. You could buy white space, fill up this space here." He fingered the two right-hand columns. "I'll sell ya space right there—two columns by four inches, for twenty-five a month."

She stared at him. "Advertise? I don't need to advertise." She laughed. "Try the latest French fashions? In big type?"

"No, just buy space. I wanna sell these two columns.

There'll be eight or nine sporting joints that'd buy the space. You could put patriotic mottoes in it. God Bless Meagher County. Building America. The Stars and Stripes Forever. Stuff like that."

"Get out, Willard. Stay out. You bust in again and I'll have you thrown out."

He laughed affably. "I figured you had more brains than that, Charlotte."

She shrugged. "So we move. So Cashbox doesn't get its license fees from us. So everyone has to pay property taxes. There's lots of places, Croker. I was getting tired of here anyway. Maybe we'll go to Butte."

"You'll be sorry, Charlotte. You'll be paying lawyers and facing lots of fines."

"Get out before I bounce you out."

"Well, we'll see," he said, rising.

"That punk kid was better than you," she yelled at his back as he hastened out the door.

It hadn't gone the way he'd planned. He would try Wool, who had the most to lose if *The Plain Truth* kept the heat on.

He pushed into The Oriental but didn't see Wool at his faro layout. That meant Wool was back in his room. He ignored the saloon girls, plunged into the rear hall, and pounded.

Wool opened, and surveyed Croker with two good eyes. The tinhorn's flesh looked pale green. The room stank of suppuration. Obviously the arm wound had putrefied, which seemed entirely suitable. Maybe Wool would rot to death.

"Make it fast, Croker," Wool snarled. "I'm going to my layout in sixty seconds."

"Here's the story, Wool." Willard thrust the sheet at the tinhorn. Wool didn't take it.

"Read it, Wool."

"Why should I read your rag?"

"Because it concerns you."

"I shot the punk."

"Yes, and I'm going to crusade to clean up Cashbox."

"That's fine. You do that."

"You'd better read this editorial. I'm proposing that the sporting places be shut down."

"Good idea. I back it. Now I've got to open up my faro bank."

"Look, Wool. You buy some space in *The Plain Truth* and there won't be room for my editorials."

Casually, Wool slid a hand into his breast pocket and extracted a black revolver. Croker stared into the bore aimed right between his eyes. A sweat broke around his neck.

"What did you say, Croker? But some space?"

"Ah, no, I didn't mean that. Ah. . . ."

"It's reloaded. The punk cost me a round. I should send a bill to his parents."

"Well, I'll be leaving."

"You do that, Croker. Say what you want. I'll enjoy the story." Wool slid the revolver back and then pulled his eyepatch over his left eye, smiling faintly. "I can see through this one—skin the man on my left in a poker game."

Croker gulped and then backed out of the door uncommonly pleased to be alive. He'd come west to make a killing; not to be killed. When he reached daylight, he knew *The Plain Truth* was no pot of gold after all. He'd have to find something else.

CHAPTER 59

· · · · · · · · · · · · · · · · ·

May Svensrud gathered courage. No matter how hard it might be to bare her secret to Portia Webb, she knew she could do it. She knew she had to or live in the shadows of the past, haunted and afraid.

Slug had wormed it out of her, and the result had been

release and relief. He loved her, and didn't consider her secret an obstacle to his love. She had gotten from that an inkling that truth is something to be embraced, not feared; that our worst sins find forgiveness; that our darkest acts don't keep us from being accepted by others.

She loved Slug for releasing her. In his rosemaled cottage she had discovered a sweetness so intense that it intoxicated her. It had been built on truth and love. He knew about her and it didn't matter. But she had not yet reached that stage with the rest of the world. No one else in Cashbox knew—and because they didn't, she bore her ancient dreads.

On the ridgetop Slug had shown her once again that all lives head west, out of the past and toward the future, like the everlasting sun. She made up her mind then and there to try for the teaching position.

She knocked on the Webbs' door, and Portia admitted her.

"Ah, you've come to tell me your decision, Mrs. Svensrud. Have a seat. I've some hot water on, and we'll have tea."

May seated herself in the lovely blue parlor, which exuded an easy grace and comfort. In a moment Mrs. Webb returned with a laden tray and began her pouring ritual. May watched, unafraid and calm. She felt protected by truth rather than threatened by it. Truth and Slug's love.

"Really, I'm going to leave the decision to you, Mrs. Webb."

"Call me Portia, dear."

"Thank you, I'd rather not. I'd like the position, but after you hear what I'm going to tell you, you may wish to withdraw your offer."

That puzzled Portia, and she settled herself on a silk settee to listen.

The only problem with telling her story was deciding where to begin. May chose to begin with Frank's desertion. From there, she could describe all that followed in a way that would make sense.

"I grew up on a farm near New Ulm, Minnesota, and was married at age nineteen to a man named Frank Carlson," she began, wondering at last whether she could bear to tell the story she'd buried for years. Tendrils of dread slid into her mind after all, making her voice quiver and her narrative lose its coherence. And yet she endured.

She described her struggle; her efforts to raise her children; her Robby. Then she came to the terrible moment in New Ulm, and she described that too, her voice involuntarily cracking. She described the aftermath, her sentencing, her life in prison, her education there. Then it was over. She sipped cold tea and waited.

Mrs. Webb sat in stunned silence. Her parlor windows afforded a grand view overlooking Cashbox, the receding hills, the black bulk of the Crazy Mountains on the horizon, and there she gazed.

May sensed she'd made an awful mistake. Here was no merciful auditor like Slug, but a woman sitting in judgment, a woman whose strong character kept her from the pit May had fallen into. A woman like that would never understand. Suddenly May knew she'd just destroyed herself. A rush of despair crowded her mind. She'd leave Slug; she wouldn't embarrass him; she wouldn't shame him. She'd slip away as fast as she could. She felt tears welling, and angrily wiped them back.

"Thank you for telling me, Mrs. Svensrud. Under the circumstances, I don't think the school committee could risk employing you."

May sighed and stood.

"Wait."

May settled herself again, waiting for the worst.

"Why did you tell me?"

"Two reasons. You should know the sort of person you're hiring. I wanted to be fair to you. The other is that I would have been miserable, teaching children each day while I was hiding something terrible from the world."

"What did you expect me to tell you afterward?"

"About the job? I don't know. I had to tell you for my sake."

"Is it a secret?"

"It was. Once something's out, it spreads like an ink-blot. I'm sorry. I made a mistake. I've ruined Slug, too."

"Why do you say that?"

"How can a constable explain a marriage to a woman who killed her child and did time? It'll destroy him."

Mrs. Webb sat quietly, registering that. "Do you think it'd ever happen again?"

"I live with that every minute of every day. I think not. I am so—blessed. I'm loved. I'm supported. Before I met Sven—that's his real name—before I met him I used to go to the cemetery. There's an unmarked grave there. I used to pretend it was Robby's—and I could talk to him. I told Robby I could never undo what was done but I would try to pick up the pieces. I wished him joy with God. He was such an innocent boy."

May dabbed at her eyes with her handkerchief, hating it, hating that it was happening in front of a woman who never lost her composure.

"I must go," she said.

"Please don't."

"I must." May didn't sit down this time.

"You have courage, Mrs. Svensrud. There is no greater courage, no harder thing to do."

"You have it just reversed, Mrs. Webb. It took all my courage to live with a secret, terrified I'd be found out. This was easier."

"You have courage. I could not do it."

"You couldn't?"

Portia Webb shook her head, ruefully. "I'd be doomed to live with my secret."

"You? But you're so strong."

"I've not had to face what you've faced. I admire you. I've never met anyone so brave. But that's not all of it. I've never met anyone so conscientious—telling me because it was the right thing to do. You must have splendid parents."

"I must go now."

"Please don't."

May sat down, bewildered.

"If it were in my power, I'd employ you as a teacher, without the slightest qualm. It's not in my power. There's five people on the school committee—the mayor, two merchants, the minister, and myself. They might be pleased to employ you. Do you want me to tell your story to them, along with my recommendation?"

There it was again, a widening ripple that would spread through all of Cashbox eventually.

"I don't know. Do what you think best."

Portia Webb smiled tautly. "What I think is that your secret should stay with me. In a perfect world, people would forgive and forget your past, and think of what you are now. It's not a perfect world. Some people are very good at shunning other people. Hurting you because they enjoy it and think they're doing the right thing."

May nodded. "Thank you," she whispered.

"May I ask you an impertinent question?"

May nodded, dreading it.

"Are you and Mr. Svensrud hoping for a family?"

It took the breath from May. She responded slowly. "Yes . . . I have decided to believe in myself. We would like that. I want to . . . try. . . ." She couldn't finish it.

"I hope God bestows little ones on you. I've always yearned for them."

"You?" May stared at the woman, as if seeing her for the first time. "You?"

"I would have given anything for a Robby."

May swallowed. She had just told her story to a woman who had yearned through a lifetime for children.

"I hope you're blessed," Mrs. Webb continued.

"I must go—"

This time her hostess didn't stay her. "Come for tea. Come often and we'll talk."

"I—I'm not—"

"Oh, I insist on it. Just the two of us."

"Thank you. I will if you want me to."

"I certainly do. Mrs. Svensrud, I'm not privileged to meet women of your character very often. You have much to teach me—and others."

May escaped into a bright day, and wept all the way back to her cottage.

CHAPTER 60
•••••••••••••••••

Attorney J. Ernest Potter-Pride sprang from the Helena and White Sulphur Springs stagecoach and hurried straight to the Palace Hotel chophouse. He ignored the sultry evening heat, the layer of alkali dust the journey had deposited on his suit, and his gouty leg. He barged into the restaurant and found Cornelius Daley at his usual table, having dinner at his usual hour.

The attorney slid into the banquette uninvited.

"We won," Pride said.

Cornelius Daley mopped his lips with the linen napkin, abandoned his medallions of beef, and smiled.

"Julius Gear ruled that you own the ore in the Giltedge claim. Gill's claim stood up."

"And?"

"You won't have to pay the Hammons anything for ore you've taken out of the Giltedge. He ruled that under the 1872 act, it's yours."

"And?"

"Well, he ruled against us in one respect; he won't grant you compensation for ores removed from the Giltedge by the Hammons."

"Why?"

"It was a matter of equity. He ruled that you bought the Gill claim only after the Giltedge was a proven success, and that the Hammons should have the fruits of their investment. That was the equity argument that opposing counsel made—that you had simply moved in and appropriated ores to yourself long after the mine was proven. Oh, they used such nasty words. I had to object. I wore Gear down objecting. He ended up muttering in his beard."

"What else?"

"All Giltedge ore above ground belongs to the Hammons; all unmined ore belongs to you. The Hammons retain possession of all their works and equipment, and have a month to remove whatever equipment is underground. All stockpiled concentrate belongs to them; they're free to sell it when the railroad arrives."

"Is there more?"

"Lots. There were twenty-three points of contention. You can read it here." He waved the twelve-page decision at Daley.

"What was Gear's frame of mind?"

Pride smiled. "Gear didn't like it. He said he was *compelled* by the mining act—and my demonstration that Gill's claim was filed first, and our expert testimony—to rule for you. He sympathized with the Hammons but couldn't do a thing about it."

"It's a pleasant evening."

"You won almost everything. The richest silver mine in the country. Oh, it's a star-spangled day, a heaven-sent jubilee day, a day to defy the force of gravity; a day to send you soaring on gossamer wings—"

"Pride, button up. You sound like a politician. When I win, I am always reminded that someone loses. I'll pay my respects to John and Henry."

"You don't seem as happy as I'd expected."

"Ah, but I am. Life's entertaining. I've not done a day's work in my life. It's amusing to make a fortune without working for it. It's so easy just to pluck up anything I want."

"You'll make them an offer for the mine works, I suppose."

"Why should I? Let them come to me."

"If I do say so, you were well represented."

Con only smiled, which irritated Pride. Daley tackled the medallions of beef again, and then some squash puddled with butter.

"When must the Giltedge close, Ernest?"

"Midnight Saturday. That's payday. Whatever ore they can get out by Saturday is theirs. It'll throw a lot of men out of work."

"It can't be helped."

"The Hangfire could hire some."

"I'd rather mine the Giltedge. It sits right on the ore. Its costs are lower than the Hangfire's. Webb's a phenomenon."

"The Hammons don't have to sell anything on the surface if they don't want to, Con."

"Then they'll be left with only salvage to sell, at about ten or fifteen cents on the dollar."

"They've no use for the works now. They'll make an offer."

"Tell me—will Arnote and Quinton appeal?"

Pride shrugged. "I doubt it. Why should they? The Hammons came out all right. They get to keep everything they've taken out of it, including their profit from the vug. They still own about two hundred thousand dollars' worth of concentrate they can sell as soon as the railroad arrives. And Gear dismissed your suit against them for appropriating your ore. They're ahead. They're giving up a mine that won't earn much until the railroad comes."

"Maybe I'll appeal."

"But why?"

"I didn't get what I asked. The Hammons got the profits from the vug—my vug."

"But Con—they hit that vug before you'd even bought the Gill claim. Gear simply acknowledged that. That was

Arnote and Quinton's argument—that your actions were predatory."

"Ah, Ernest, I never compromise. You'll prepare an appeal."

"Look, Con. An appeal's risky. The appellate court might find for the Hammons. My counsel is—"

"I am never cautious."

Daley sipped from a wineglass, and tackled a baked potato smothered in chive sauce. "It's getting cold," he said. "I never like to talk business at meals. I tell you what, Ernest. Prepare an appeal. I want full compensation for every ounce of silver stolen by the Giltedge. Gear failed to uphold the law. Once he ruled that the ore belongs to the holder of the Gill claim, he should have awarded me for the loss of that ore. Let the Hammons know. Then let them settle if they choose. I want it hanging over them. A bargaining lever."

Pride exhaled hot air. "All right. You're the Silver Fox."

Daley smiled, and masticated rare beef. "Won't you join me, Ernest? You'll want to celebrate."

"I could use a dust-cutter. That was a hot ride."

Daley motioned to a waiter, and Pride ordered a bourbon and branch water, and the plat du jour. The attorney downed the whiskey in two gulps and ordered more fortification. Good work required good compensation, but asking Con Daley for it was like asking a duke for his mistress.

"My dear Cornelius," he said, after the spirits had ballooned his courage. "We've a great and famous victory. We've climbed Mount Everest. This is what you came to Cashbox to do. Today was the silver lining on your rainy life. This is the premiere day in your walk upon earth. You now possess one of the richest silver mines in the world, a bounty, a cascade, a fountain of silver. I take no small pride in my achievement. It's the fruits of years of diligence at law, burning midnight oil, polished courtroom conduct, and no small skill. Oh, I'm perfectly at ease saying it."

Daley smiled. He was forking in some cheesecake.

"Now, I've my sights set upon high office in 1892, and from that prominence in Washington I ought to be of no small value to you. The eastern gold interests are still prowling. Oh, I will remember and cherish my Montana friends when I am in the sacred precincts of the Senate. . . ."

Daley smiled.

"It costs a tidy sum to lobby a senate seat. Now I remember, my esteemed friend, that when we first negotiated the matter of, ah, compensation for my professional services, you put me on a retainer—and said there'd be further pleasantries if I brought the matter to a successful conclusion. Well, I did."

"Oh, I don't know about that. I got half of what I wanted."

"But you own the mine. A great victory. Now, as I was saying, there was a certain promise given."

Daley speared the last crumb of cheesecake and licked the fork. "You're quite right, Ernest. I haven't forgotten. In fact, I've decided to give you my controlling interest in the Ophir."

"The what? Not cash?"

"I'm always strapped for cash. But I have ten thousand and one shares of the Ophir, which gives me the controlling interest. It was capitalized with twenty thousand shares at a par of ten dollars. It's worth rather less now, of course."

"Less. I hear the ore's pinching out."

J. Ernest Potter-Pride seethed. Daley was about to fob off some almost worthless stock and call it the bonus he'd promised. Betrayed!

"Quite right, Ernest. This time it looks like the end. They've hit an angling dike of diorite, and the jasper's narrowing down. It'll be all over in a month. But I'd suggest you take the stock. You might find it quite lucrative."

"Ten thousand shares of a dead mine."

Daley shook his head. "No, no. The controlling interest in an assessment mine."

Pride licked the news as if it were ice cream. "Assessment, did you say?"

"Assessment. Most of the shareholders are in California. They've never laid eyes on the mine. It trades on the Pacific Exchange mostly. It'll be all yours. The way it's set up, shareholders who don't pay the assessment keep their shares, but their value drops by the amount of the assessment."

"Ah, an assessment mine. Why, my dear Con, that's sterling. A private mint."

"I thought you'd like it, Ernest. We each got a mine today. Have some cheesecake. It's delicious."

CHAPTER 61

Hugh Trego wanted solidarity. He wanted brotherhood and the absolute loyalty of every man. When it came to the strike vote, he had been unable to force a public show of hands upon his miners. They wanted a secret ballot. Like most Cornishmen they were a stubborn lot, and they often resisted him. Foolishly, he thought.

He glowered over the ballot box in the Carbonate Miners Saloon, daring the men to defy him. If the Knights of Labor were going to get a workingman a fair wage, there could be no traitors. The night shift had come in to vote on their way to work; now Trego's own day shift was trickling in slowly and stuffing their votes into the box, under Trego's heavy glare.

Quietly the miners nursed nickel beers. Scarcely a one ordered a second mug, not with a strike brewing. There was enough in the strike kitty to put bread on tables for only a few days. Kitty or not, Trego itched for the strike. He would show Webb a thing or two about how wealth is

really created. At the meetings, he had shouted down a
few fools who wanted to keep on working no matter what;
and then no one had resisted him any more.

An uncommon quiet laced the saloon as pensive miners
waited for the tally. Their food and drink, rents and clothing, were on the bargaining table. At midnight the contract
with the Giltedge Mine would expire; at midnight Trego
might call the night shift out of the hole and shut down the
Giltedge mine and mill. It would paralyze the district; paralyze Cashbox. He enjoyed the power.

He heard the Giltedge whistle wailing down the gulch,
and knew the next shift was starting. No more men pushed
open the double doors of the Carbonate Miners Saloon to
vote. He knew some had not voted, and these he would
deal with down in the hole some time, maybe with fists.
He waited a while more, and then stood.

"We'll count," he said, daring anyone to dissent.

He overturned the box, dumped ballots on the bar, and
began his tally, neither asking nor wanting anyone's help.
The question was whether the Knights should accept
Webb's offer. Trego tallied the Nay votes with grim satis-
faction, twenty, then thirty, then—a Yea vote. He set it
apart, a cursed thing. In a few minutes he had a final
count.

"There's one bleddy traitor in our brotherhood," he announced into the silence. "I'd like to wring his neck. It's
one hundred seventy-three against; one for. That one for,
he stinks up the local; I'm going to find out who he is, and
I'm going to teach him something he'll bleddy well not
forget."

Tim Trenoweth set his mug on the bar. "I'm the man,
Hugh."

"You, Tim?"

"I'm the man. Do what you have to do, then."

Hugh Trego clenched his fists and hulked toward
Trenoweth, a white heat building in him.

"Hugh, you'll not be pounding on a sixty-year-old

grandfather from Padstow with miner's lung," said Sam Fenno.

"Who're you to say," Hugh snapped. But he stopped short of old Trenoweth. "You! You!"

Trenoweth seemed unabashed. "We're asking too much, at least until the railroad comes. I voted to keep a pasty in our lunch pails. Bleed a company too far and there's naught but grief and suffering and wee children's tears. There's a line, and if we breach it, everything lands on our ears—like a cave-in."

"You're a bleddy fool. They're rich as Midas."

"I voted as I voted, and that's how she is, Hugh Trego."

"You didn't vote at all, Tim." Trego ripped the ballot to shreds and stuffed it into Trenoweth's beer mug. "I'm telling Webb the vote was solid against his offer."

"If ye do, Hugh, ye'll give the man a lie."

"I'm putting you out of the Knights, Tim Trenoweth. I'm putting you out of the mine, too. We'll have no weakness."

Trenoweth didn't reply. Hugh almost wished he would. He glared around the saloon, daring one silent man after another to say a word. None did.

"All right, then. I'm going to Webb and tell him. He's waiting for me. He'll either cave in or take a strike."

"I'll come with you," said Sam Fenno.

"No, I'm going myself. I know how to deal with that bloodsucker. I want a strike kitty. When I get back, I want every nickel in your pockets. You pass the hat, Fenno."

Trego bulled through the screeching doors and straight up the gulch to the general offices of the Giltedge Mining Company. He relished the moment. He'd dreamed of this hour for months. Thaddeus Webb was going to sweat. Trego plunged with springy steps past old Baghote and straight into Webb's lair, not bothering to knock.

He found the superintendent studying documents, looking curiously grim. He looked up, startled. "Trego?"

"You're bleddy well going to take a strike, Webb. Every last man in the Knights rejected your offer."

Webb stared out the window, his gaze on distant shores. It made Trego uneasy.

"Ye didn't hear me. I said we're walking out tonight. Have you got a new offer, or do you take a walkout?"

"It's too late, Trego. We're shutting down."

"Oh, a lockout is it? Well, Webb, we'll wrestle you to the ground. You'll never make a bleddy dime off our backs again."

Webb shook his head. "No, Hugh. The Giltedge isn't locking you out. It's shutting down. We'll shut down on Saturday."

"I'm not Hugh to you, Webb. I've told you that a hundred times. Is that your final word, then?"

Webb swiveled around. He plucked up one of the documents and handed it to Trego.

"Some bleddy paper, is it?"

Trego read: *District Court, White Sulphur Springs, County of Meagher, State of Montana. Judge Julius Gear presiding.... In the matter of Cornelius Daley, plaintiff, doing business as The Hangfire Mine vs. John and Henry Hammon, doing business as the Giltedge Mine, defendants....*

Trego studied the sentences and paragraphs, page by page, a tightness building in his chest. He reread portions, scarcely believing what he was reading. A wildness built in him. He wanted to shred the document. He wanted to march on White Sulphur Springs and hang the judge from the nearest tree. He clenched and unclenched his giant fists as the reality of all this hit him. Hunger, heartache, broken dreams. Finally he threw the document down on Webb's desk.

"You bleddy capitalists, hurting workingmen, taking bread from our mouths."

"I don't think that was our intent, Hugh."

"What's to become of us?"

"That's a question to ask Con Daley."

"We'll be out of work, that's what. Because of your bleddy quarrels, we'll all be out of work."

"Maybe not. The Hammons are throwing in the towel. They've made an offer to Daley—everything on the surface. The hoist, the shops, the mill, this building you're standing in. Daley's countered with a lower offer. I think the Hammons'll accept. If they sell, I'd guess that Daley would keep the Giltedge running."

Trego mulled that. "Maybe that's a good thing, Webb. Maybe Daley'll give us what we want."

"Maybe he will, Hugh. It's not for me to say."

"He gave our men at the Hangfire the eight-hour day. That's more than you gave us."

"I've offered it. But you want more. Daley's mining better ore at the four-hundred-foot level. Fifty-five to sixty ounces a ton. We're mining forty a ton. Somewhere in all this, Trego, profit and loss are going to play a part."

"All you do is stuff your fat butts into soft chairs at the Exchange Club and figure ways to beat us down, Webb."

Webb sighed. "I don't recollect ever looking for ways to beat you down. Quite the opposite. If I could give you more I would. Well, what'll you do? Strike tonight? Obviously I have no new offer. On Saturday I'll be out of work, like you."

"You could give us what we want, right now."

"I could. You'd have a contract that would last four days."

"We'd have a lever on Daley, is what we'd have."

Webb thrummed the desk with his fingers. "I'm a peculiar duck, Hugh. I'd do it if I knew it was right for the mine. But I don't. I'm sticking with the offer for an eight-hour day—the rest'll have to wait for the railroad. That's break-even for any owner of this mine. Strike if you must."

Trego felt robbed. For months he'd maneuvered and schemed. He'd pounded on stubborn heads down in the hole. He'd begged help from the national labor federations. And now the whole bleddy bunch was out of work.

He waved his massive fist at the superintendent. "Damn you all," he cried. "There's no justice in all the universe for the poor slaves that go into the pits. Trade places with us one week and you'd find out."

He stormed back to the saloon, his eyes glistening with tears.

CHAPTER 62

· · · · · · · · · · · · · · · · ·

Thaddeus Webb's visitors were the last people on earth he would expect to walk in together. John and Henry Hammon and Cornelius Daley shook his hand and seated themselves on his tailbone-torturing wooden benches that were intended to hasten visitors through their business. They were all smiling, as if two years of bloodletting had never happened.

"Thaddeus," said John, "we've some good news. The Giltedge Mining Company's being reorganized. The partnership's over. We've reached an agreement with our colleague, here, to create a new stock company. Cornelius will hold eighty percent of the shares, and Henry and I'll hold ten percent each. We've a letter of agreement, and our lawyers are drafting the articles."

Webb wondered whether he liked that or not. Once he got past his astonishment, it seemed logical enough.

"We're contributing the entire surface works—hoist, shops, tram, mill, smelter, offices, outbuildings. We're also contributing our underground works—tram, ore cars, hoist, and so on. Cornelius is contributing the Giltedge ore reserves, and the entire Hangfire Mine works. That mine's not as economical to operate as the Giltedge, and we'll phase it out as soon as we can bore down to the four-hundred-foot level from here. With an ore body like this, we expect the Giltedge to turn large profits for years."

"I see," said Webb, wondering what would come next.

"Of course we're keeping our silver-lead concentrates," Henry broke in. "That's not part of it. And we've got several runs of ore going through the milling. We'll ship our lead when the railroad arrives."

Webb turned to the man who had said nothing, and found nothing he could read in Cornelius Daley's face. "Do you intend to continue production after Saturday, Con?"

"Yes."

"You've a strike pending."

"They've no contract with the new company."

"Try to explain that to Hugh Trego. They've taken a strike vote. The contract's expired. They could go out any time. They decided to work through Saturday. Then it'll be your problem."

"That's what these gentlemen and I are here about, Thaddeus. We'd like you to continue as supervisor."

Things were happening too fast. "I'll take it under advisement. I'm not sure I want to. Portia doesn't like—"

"I'll need a decision in twenty-four hours."

"Portia doesn't particularly like Cashbox. I'm thinking it's time to move on."

"Why?" ·

Daley's question startled Thaddeus. "I don't quite know," he muttered. He wasn't sure he wanted to work for a man as ruthless as Daley, but he couldn't say that. "I'd like a month."

"It'll have to be tomorrow. You're the man who makes this mine work. You've turned a profit eighty miles from a railroad, and that's a feat I've never heard of. If you leave, we'll simply shut down until we get the railroad. There's no point in running a mine at breakeven just to keep miners employed. That's how it is. If you stay on, we'll offer your Giltedge crew an eight-hour day, but that's it."

"I'm sure they'll strike, Con."

"Then we'll wait for the railroad."

Webb realized the fate of Cashbox rested in his hands. Fifteen hundred people. Miners and their wives and children, merchants, tradesmen, woodcutters, teamsters. . . . It seemed too heavy a burden to place on one man's shoulders. For an angry moment he glared at the Silver Fox, wanting no part of the man.

"Would I operate the mine as I see fit?"

"You'd consult with me about major things."

Thaddeus eyed the Hammons. "I've always consulted with the owners. There are things I won't compromise. Safety is the main one. There'll be adequate shoring, good air."

"It's not politic to kill or wound men."

Daley's answer seemed odd to Thaddeus. "Build the infirmary. We've gone three years without a place to treat the wounded."

"We all want one. But we all deal with reality."

"The Knights want six days of paid vacation."

"They can't have it. Later, maybe. Thaddeus, I'll talk with them. Tomorrow, bring your decision to us at the Palace. We'll have lunch at noon."

Daley's tone seemed peremptory but Thaddeus wasn't going to be intimidated. "What'll you tell Hugh Trego? It affects my decision."

Daley shrugged. "They'll get the eight-hour day. And they'll wait for the railroad."

"And if they strike?"

"Then we'll all wait for the railroad. There's three miles of track down, and seven miles of roadbed done. We're hoping to finish the first fifty-seven miles by April, if the weather permits. The rest is mountain work, which takes time and money. But we can ship ore fairly cheaply by April, even if it's a twenty-mile wagon haul to the railhead."

"It'll be a long winter for Cashbox," Thaddeus muttered. "All right. I'll see you at noon tomorrow. I've things to talk over with Mrs. Webb."

"Things'll work out," said Henry Hammon. "That's how it is in a new land. We're building the country, and things are tough sometimes."

The superintendent watched them file out. It had been

an oddly unpleasant interview. Daley the entrepreneur was plainly not the affable Daley the speculator who lounged in hotel restaurants and clubs. The Hammons seemed elated. They had gotten a piece of the Giltedge mine and its fabulous ore after all.

He peered out a grimy window upon the great mine. Smoke billowed from its chimneys; steam from its pipes. The mill thundered. Soon it might be moribund. It would depend on Trego—and on himself.

He particularly loved this mine. It had driven him to his limits. Its complex ores, its distance from the rails, its peculiar geology, had all succumbed to his gifts. He loved it as a man loved a difficult woman. He had brought it this far, and hated to let go. So many things remained. So much ore. . . . Leaving now would be like burying a wife.

He knew what he had to do next. He had to surrender his every dream. For once he would go home early. He would astonish Portia, and not because he would walk through their door at three in the afternoon.

"Baghote. I am taking the rest of the day off."

The clerk eyed him suspiciously from under his green eyeshade. "Are you ill, sir?"

"I'm quite well, thank you. I'm simply taking the afternoon off. I'll be here in the morning. And you know how to reach me."

"I don't think you are well."

Webb stepped into a bright sun and blinked. The noise struck him. Steel clanged against steel. Slack racketed down a chute onto the pile. The stamp mills thudded like heartbeats. All his. A surge of sorrow flooded through him. Like all things, this creation of his would die. Maybe on Saturday. Who would ever know all the innovations in his blueprints, all his engineering, all his chemistry, all his midnight hours seeking economies? Did Daley know? Did the Hammons know? No. They saw only results, and not the ways and means.

He found Portia abed, hiding from the burning sun.

"Thad? Thaddeus?" she said, startling up from the coverlet. "Is something wrong? The strike?"

"No, nothing's wrong." He sat down beside her and took her hand. "We're at a crossroads. We can do whatever we choose."

"You've been discharged."

He laughed. "No, not at all. In fact I've been offered the same position in a brand-new Giltedge company."

He recounted the afternoon visit, enjoying the squeeze of her hand as he described what had transpired.

"Well, now: how would you like to leave Cashbox? I thought this might be the time. You've borne this town for years. Now you don't have to anymore. The decision's yours."

She looked panic-stricken. "Oh, Thad, I don't want a decision like that."

"Yes you do. You just have to get used to it. Say the word and we'll pack up."

"Thaddeus, I truly don't want that kind of decision thrust on me."

"Well, all right, I'll make it if I must. But what do you dream of doing? Where'd you like to go? I need to know."

She laughed, uncomfortably. "Why, dear, all these years I've dreamed of escaping these awful little towns. To anywhere. New York. Boston. San Francisco. But. . . ." A tender smile lifted the corners of her lips. "Now I'm not so sure."

"I could become a consulting engineer, Portia. Offices in New York. I'd travel a lot. I could join one of the engineering firms, or start my own. Would you like that?"

"Before I came here I would have loved it," she said, clenching his hand in hers. "Do you suppose I'm getting old?"

"You're as young and beautiful as the day I married you."

She looked at him gravely. "Thaddeus, if I told you the unexpected, would you promise not to think I'm being self-sacrificing?"

"Huh?"

"If I told you I've come to love Cashbox and its brave people—that I want to stay ... would you believe me?"

He nodded, reluctantly.

"I want to live here," she said. "This is a place where people come to renew their lives. Why, just a few days ago I talked with a remarkable, brave woman. . . . I'd never thought of it. But all these people are building something. Creating their lives. Living their dreams. What a beautiful land this is, where people can reach for the stars. People chasing rainbows—I love that. We all need to chase rainbows. Let's stay, Thaddeus."

CHAPTER 63

• • • • • • • • • • • • • • • • •

Sylvie stood in the middle of Cashbox Street watching her doom. Masons swarmed the scaffolds, laying up the walls of the new opera house while carpenters laid the flooring and fitted windows. Her new rivals, Gleason and Magee, had announced that the Grand Opening, on November 1, would feature that all-time miners' favorite, Lotta Crabtree.

She recognized her new arrival, Erasmus Gleason, approaching.

"Well, how does it look, Miss Duvalier?"

"Like an empty cashbox."

"Oh, there's room in this town for our theater and your meeting hall. We're not going into the dance hall and Temperance trade."

"That's all that's left for me, I'm afraid."

"The opera house won't be fancy. But we'll have a complete stage with wings and flies, an orchestra pit, and the most advanced lighting. Arbuthnot—that's my colleague, Arbuthnot Magee—he's cutting every corner. No marble. Nothing like the one in Leadville."

"It sounds grand. You'll get the cream, I'm sure."

He smiled like a cat licking his chops.

She would get the dances, balls, and weddings; the fiddlers, brass bands, lecturers, and reformers; anyone who couldn't pay the stiff opera house fees or wanted a dance floor. But the cream of her business had always been the stage and variety troupes. Their engagements earned her more than the rest put together. She had just had Eddie Foy and his troupe for a week. Her share of the gate and the concessions had netted almost four hundred dollars in just seven days.

Soon that would end. She planned to fight back with lower gate fees. But she knew the palmy days were over no matter what she did. A theater like that would attract not only Miss Crabtree, but also Lillie Langtry, the Great Modjeska, Ada Rehan, John Drew, Otis Skinner, Maurice Barrymore, and other big names—especially when the railroad came.

At the post office she picked up a letter from the directors of the Ophir Mine, assessing each share two dollars for development work. The assessment was signed by Potter-Pride. She hadn't even known he was the chairman of its board. She read it again, dismayed. Ophir stock was sitting at two dollars, and an unpaid assessment against it would reduce it to almost nothing—even if she could find a buyer. She felt miserable. Fourteen hundred dollars gone. Well, she'd been warned.

She continued on to the bank and deposited her cash. Her account looked slender. She still lacked the means to make her first annual payment on Potter-Pride's mortgage. For months she had scolded herself for buying the Aurora Borealis stock. She knew about Potter-Pride. Everyone knew about him. And yet she had let herself be gulled by that silver tongue.

She had run her business right into the ground, she thought. She wasn't accustomed to melancholia, but for once it subdued her spirited nature. Well, she had come west to try her mettle. She had tested it, all right—and lost. Maybe she would lose everything. But not if she could help it.

She had never lamented being a woman the way some did. In fact she believed her womanhood gave her advantages that men lacked. She could fold herself into Con Daley's arms and accept his protection, but she hated the idea. It amounted to a surrender. He understood that, and she blessed him for it. She had come west to see what she could make of her life. If the west knocked her down, she would just get up and try again.

From John Oliver Cromwell she got the Aurora Borealis shares she kept in his safe and stuffed them into her reticule. Then she walked to Potter-Pride's chambers on Pine Street. She had gotten into the mess by herself; she would get out of it by herself. Sylvie figured she was married to herself, for better for worse, for richer for poorer, till death did them part. The figure of speech amused her, but it had also become her credo.

She stormed his veranda and pushed into his foyer. He appeared at once, as coiffed as a Shakespearean actor with a noble profile. She wondered if he wore a hairnet to bed.

"Ah, my dear Sylvie. Come in, come in. What brings your sweet visage to my parlors this chilly day?"

He turned a chair for her to sit in, but she declined. Standing said something.

"Business, Ernest."

"Now what might that be?" He peered at her from behind his glued-on smile.

"We're going to undo our deal. Here are your Aurora Borealis certificates. We're going to tear up the mortgage."

He paused, his smile widening slightly. "That's not how things are done, Miss Duvalier. Of course I wouldn't expect you to understand that."

"I understand that—and you're going to do it."

"Have some pie. Regina baked a sublime cinnamon apple. We're tying the knot on September thirtieth, you know. The Reverend Prowell. Reception at the hotel. A little coochie-coo at Chico Hot Springs. Have you ever tasted a nobler pie?"

"The Aurora Borealis stock isn't worth the paper it's printed on."

"Oh, I wouldn't say that. But you know the doctrine in law: *caveat emptor*, buyer beware. I'm sure none of us had an inkling, but that's how things turned out. It happens every day. Stocks go down. No one gets excited about it."

"*Caveat emptor* doesn't apply to fraud."

Only a clock-tick went by, and he smiled again. "I'm afraid you don't understand," he said patiently. "What a pity we must endure a moment's unpleasantness. It's like a migraine."

She pulled the mortgage contract from her reticule and laid it on his polished desk. "Write Paid," she said.

"I haven't seen a dime, Miss Duvalier."

"With these shares."

"I'm so sorry. It was good of you to stop by—"

"Is that final?"

"I'm afraid so."

"All right. I'll see you in court."

That caught his attention. "In court?"

"Meagher County District Court. I'm suing you for fraud. I'm going to tell the judge you knew perfectly well that the stock was worthless when you sold it; that you misrepresented it to be extremely valuable; that your design was to take my building from me. Well, I'm keeping my hall."

"I see. Well then, we'll meet in court."

"That's right. I'll have it placed on the docket just when you begin lobbying the legislature for the Senate seat."

That time she caught the small startle.

"And there'll be a second suit. I'm a stockholder of the Ophir Mine. I understand its ore is exhausted. That suit's going to be about the assessment. I'll make sure it's well publicized in Helena."

"Why, so will I. We have great plans to build the mine's reserves."

"There are no reserves. The crosscut's up against a dike."

"Oh, a mining company doesn't look for reserves in a dead mine, my dear. It examines new properties. We'll need capital to probe for new pockets of ore."

"That's right. Your pockets," she retorted.

"I wish I had your razor tongue," he said. "I'm rather bland by nature. It hurts during disputation. I enjoy people so much I lack the inclination to say some things."

"There'll be a third suit," she added, relentless now. "About irregularities in the Cashbox Town Lot Company. I'll file it during your Senate lobbying campaign."

"Why, that'd be fine. I'm proud of the way I licked the scoundrels."

"Licked them or protected them."

"My dear, you'll feel better in the morning."

She managed a smile. "Well, Ernest. I'll give you a couple of hours to think it over. The stock for the mortgage. We'll see about the rest." She restored the shares and note to her reticule. "See you at the club," she said. "The suit'll be of some interest there. I'll expect an answer this evening."

"I'm perfectly delighted that you paid me a visit, Miss Duvalier. Delighted. I'm for suffrage, you know. I'd love to have your vote. Wouldn't you like some lascivious pie?"

She laughed. She couldn't help but laugh at that reprobate, even if he had ruined her. That was the paradox of Ernest Potter-Pride. He was a likable crook. But the minute she stepped into the autumnal afternoon, the chill reality of her situation hit her. She decided she would spend every cent she had on the suit instead of trying to pay the mortgage. The next step would be a trip to White Sulphur to find a bulldog of a lawyer. She would do that tomorrow. It would let Potter-Pride know she wasn't making idle threats.

CHAPTER 64

. . . .

J. Ernest Potter-Pride beckoned Sylvie into the billiards room of the Exchange Club. She had a hunch what this would be about, so she grabbed her reticule. It still contained her mortgage and her thousand shares of The Aurora Borealis Consolidated Mining Company.

He set his briefcase on the green baize, right under the three-lamp chandelier.

"Yes, Ernest?"

"Ah, my dear Sylvie. I've had time to reflect. You know, once in a long while, sublime opportunity knocks, and if we're not quick we lose our chance forever.

"Now, take the Aurora Borealis. It may be moribund to the casual observer, but slumbering in those claims and shafts lies a fortune that would satisfy King Midas. Ah, yes, unheard-of wealth. I have faith."

"Is that what you came to say?"

"No, no, no. I've been meditating about your generous offer, and the more I weigh it, the more it tickles my fancy. I've been casting around for something grand to give to my dear Regina, a wedding gift truly worthy of her. I thought to myself, why not give her these thousand shares? That'll affirm my everlasting love."

"That'd be a truly unusual wedding present, Ernest."

"Indeed. Now, I have the mortgage. You have the shares. Are you up to a swap?"

"I am." Her spirits soared. Could it be? She extracted the stock certificates from her bag and laid them on the baize.

"I'll write 'Paid' on these, and you'll assign these shares back to me," he said, extracting a nib pen and ink bottle from his bag.

"Make it 'Paid in Full,' Ernest. Sign it and date it." She handed him her copy. "Both copies."

"As you wish, Sylvie."

He scratched the words on the contracts and blotted them, and she gave him the certificates. He plucked them up and stuffed them into his pigskin portmanteau, while she claimed both copies of the mortgage.

"Ah, Sylvie, this is a sublime moment in my life," he said. "A perfect wedding gift. I presume, that, ah, our business is complete in all respects?"

"No, Ernest. I'm going to sell you two hundred shares of the Ophir Mine at two dollars a share. It's a bargain you'll not want to miss. I bought them at seven and some."

"Oh, I see. Two hundred shares. Four hundred dollars. Well, now." He paused to contemplate. The lamplight tinted his silvery countenance with gold. "Why, it happens I have quite a few shares of the Ophir. But I could add these to them and give them to Regina. It'd endow her with a competence all her life. It'd be a worthy gift to lay at her feet. I'll do it. Four hundred dollars. I'll write a draft on my account at the bank."

"They're in the bank vault, Ernest. You can run over there right now and give your draft to John Oliver Cromwell for my account. I'll write a note asking him to give you the shares. All right?"

"Perfectly suitable. Regina will be thrilled." He stared at her rather glumly. "Does that conclude our business?"

"Yes, Senator," she replied, and suddenly beamed.

He nodded. "My dear, I won't forget it. When I assume my duties in Washington, you'll be in my mind. No matter whether we're debating war or peace, my thoughts will return to Sylvie Duvalier. You'll always be just as important to me as the national debt. I want you to know that if ever you need a favor, large or small—"

"Please, no more favors, Ernest."

She scratched a note to Cromwell and handed it to the attorney. He pocketed it, snatched his bag, hurried through the club and out the door, as jaunty and cheerful as ever. She leaned over the billard table, feeling giddy. The building was hers again. She looked about her, relishing its solid comforts, its familiar dimensions.

All hers. The hall downstairs wouldn't pay as well now, but that didn't matter. She'd come west to chase rainbows, and this was still her pot of gold. She had made some bad choices, she'd lost, she'd learned, and she'd come out on top. That mattered. Sylvie Duvalier had conquered J. Ernest Potter-Pride.

Her giddiness faded into quiet elation as she wended her way into the clubroom. Everything she saw was hers.

The club was empty save for Con, who sat at a window chair reading the *New York Herald*. She sat down beside him.

"You look happy," he said.

"I am. Ernest just bought a thousand shares of Aurora Borealis stock from me—at its par value."

"You don't say."

"He's going to give it to Regina for a wedding present."

"Really. That's a thoughtful gift."

"Oh, there's more. He's giving her his shares of the Ophir Mine, and two hundred more he just bought from me."

"That's rare. I've never heard of a wedding gift like it."

"Neither have I, Con. He must love her a lot."

"Regina's the apple of his eye. She'll be flattered."

"Ernest likes extravagant gestures."

They laughed quietly.

"Ten thousand dollars of Aurora Borealis stock," he said. "You must've made him an offer he couldn't turn down."

"I did. I offered him a seat in the Senate."

"You have amazing powers."

"I think so, too. I'm taking you to dinner at the chophouse. We're going to celebrate."

"Now that's a novelty. What kind of cigars do you prefer?"

"Oh, Con, why can't a woman take a man to dinner?"

"What're we celebrating, Sylvie?"

"We're celebrating my passage. I've arrived at the life I want."

"You have the advantage of me, Sylvie."

She glanced around her. They were alone, except for young Albert Flower washing glasses in the saloon. She leaned across and took his hands in hers.

"Con," she said gently. "This isn't the moment for repartee. This is too important. I realized a moment ago that this is my most important day. Not much happened—all I did was get out of a jam. But I did it by myself. That's important to me."

He smiled. "Getting out of jams can be the most important things we do."

"I'm going to bore you, and talk about me. I came west on a lark. Looking for something I couldn't even name. Just wanting something good to happen."

"Did it?"

"Oh, yes, Con. I wanted to govern my own life—and now I do. I'm free. I work for myself. I'm not a wage slave. I'm not tied to a man's will. I'm independent. I'm— sovereign, if that's the word. Not many women achieve it."

"Regina has."

"Yes, and I admire her for it. She's made her way without anyone's help. I'd like to be like her. She's wiser than I am. I made mistakes. I bought bad mining stock. I didn't want your advice. I hid those things from you because I wanted to do it on my own. I let Ernest smooth-talk me into something. But today I fought my way out of trouble. All by myself. That's what I'm celebrating. It's not as grand as making a million dollars, or buying a mine, or getting control of a railroad or a steamship company. All I did was recover what I lost. For me, that's having my every dream come true."

"Are you happy, Sylvie?"

"Yes. I'm independent. I'm comfortable. I do as I wish.

I've learned to cope with a rough world. If I am happy, it's because of you, Con. You've always known what I wanted. Sometimes I think you knew what I was seeking even before I could put it into words. I cherish the things you didn't do. You took me on a picnic and showed me things I needed to see. But oh, Con, you never said a word. You're the most wonderful man. I've never known a man so—careful of me."

"Sylvie—would you marry me?"

It took her aback. "What? But darling. . . . I thought you understood. I'm married."

"Would you end that and start fresh?" He was as earnest with her as she had been with him.

A tenderness flooded her. "Con, must we talk about it now? When everything is so perfect?"

CHAPTER 65
· · · · · · · · · · · · · · · · ·

They were alone at last. Regina peered about the two-room suite in the Palace that J. Ernest had rented, suddenly shy. But no amount of shyness could dispel her joy. She had waited a lifetime for this. She had believed it would never happen. But it had. As of about four o'clock that afternoon, she had become Mrs. J. Ernest Potter-Pride.

She had decided against a wedding gown. From the time of her girlhood, when she'd studied herself in the looking glass, she had known that she would look absurd in one. Her big, rawboned body just wouldn't fit. She had chosen, instead, to have the milliner sew a lovely street dress of pale pink, a puffy dress that would soften all those bony angles.

She wore that now. How dashing he looked. As if he'd been born to wear clothes well. He wore a swallowtail coat of dove gray, pinstriped black trousers, a white shirt starched into an instrument of torture, and a floppy black bowtie that made a little joke of all his formality. He smiled at her from eyes that exuded innocence. What a handsome devil! She'd come to admire his noble profile with its long straight nose and jut jaw, and the wavy silver hair. He was the very model of a senator even if he wasn't one yet.

"Ah, Regina. A perfect wedding. Old Prowell read chapter and verse like a trial lawyer. And a perfect reception. There's nothing like the Palace for a thousand miles."

"It's what I've always dreamed of, J. Ernest."

"Well, here we are. Cozy in our little nest, eh?"

She nodded. For years, she had wondered what this moment might be like. She had wondered what sweet mysteries would happen, and whether she might enjoy them. Now she would know. A coil of doubt gripped her, and she couldn't make it go away even when she told herself all was well. Would J. Ernest be gentle and kind, and help a woman going on fifty?

"My dear, now that we're alone, I cherish the chance to give you a nuptial present. I've thought much upon it. I wanted to do something memorable, something that would express unwavering devotion, love that would pass beyond the grave into foreverness." He paused, kindliness building in his chiseled face. "I'm going to give you a trust fund. A trust for your everlasting security and comfort."

"Why, J. Ernest—"

"Others may give temporal gifts, practical and beautiful, but I have chosen something eternal."

She hadn't expected this, and it brought her to the brink of tears. He had depths she had never suspected.

"This trust is richly endowed with good mining stocks, my love. I'll be its trustee. I'll buy and sell from time to time, to refresh it and expand it."

"Mining stocks? Are they eternal?"

"Why, they'll live longer than we, my dear. For starters, there's a thousand shares of The Aurora Borealis Consolidated Mining Company, a powerful hold on the future; and over ten thousand shares of the Ophir Mine—"

She began chuckling. She couldn't help it. She whooped and wheezed.

"Regina, what's so funny?"

"Nothing, J. Ernest. I have strange humors. Your trust fund's lovely; a perfect expression of your devotion."

His eyes kindled. "Ah, how I adore you."

"J. Ernest, it's lovely but not terribly practical. Here you are, running for the senate. The only way to get in is to woo the party whips in Helena. You know, Porcullus Ralph; Big Mike Dillon. Isn't he the one who decides? They've got the power; they're the ones who'll line up the legislature."

"Oh, I'll get to that—but this mining trust is for you, Regina."

"Now, dear, let's not worry about me. We're running for office together, you and I. You've got half a dozen men in Helena to win over, and that takes gifts. J. Ernest—you just give each of them a token of your esteem. A few hundred shares of Aurora Borealis. Then they'll bow and scrape. Then they'll dance to your tune. No, J. Ernest, this treasure's not for me; it's for the party whips."

"That's unthinkable. It's all for you, Regina."

"J. Ernest, you can give me gifts later. After we get to the senate. We'll get rich in the senate; everyone does. If you want to give me a wedding gift, you just make yourself a senator."

"Ah, Regina. How thoughtful you are, looking after my interests. But no, this fine portfolio's all for you."

"All for me?" She laughed. She loved J. Ernest. She almost hated to reform him.

He laughed too, but with puzzlement.

"All right. I accept. Thank you for the trust fund. You're sweet."

"I'm delighted to give it to you. And how noble, how self-sacrificing you are to want to donate it. I always knew I'd picked a special woman."

They slipped into silence. She wondered if he would kiss her. He'd scarcely ever kissed her, and that was only to buss her cheek. She wanted to be kissed on the lips the way she'd always dreamed of being kissed.

She waited for him to come to her, but he didn't. He stood like a Greek statue, as if the next thing required deliberation.

"Ah, Regina. We're not young, you and I."

"I feel young as a filly. I'm ready to kick up my heels. How about you?"

"Oh, I'm fine, never happier."

He was shy, she thought. She felt shy too. She hardly knew what to do.

"Why, let's have a toast!" he cried, as if fleeing from a guillotine. He hurried to the table, where a bottle of red wine nested in a sweating pewter bucket of ice. "This is the beginning; we'll toast it."

Hastily he uncorked the wine and decanted it into goblets. It was the first time she'd ever seen his hands shake.

"Here, my dear," he said, with a sweet smile. He'd never looked so alert, so kindly, so handsome.

She held her glass. It caught and shattered the yellow lamplight. He held his high. "To us; to wedlock perfect and spiritual and free; to wedlock ethereal and soulful. To your sublime spirit and tenderness and pure womanhood; to the nurturing soul and comforting word and sacred devotion that transcends mere fleshly matters. To the perfect union of souls, my dear."

He drank. She stared.

Then she examined the room. Here was her new steamer trunk, the gift of her boarders, with all her things. In the other room were his valises, his coats on hangers, his briefcase.

"J. Ernest, hug me."

"Ah, of course." But he didn't move.

"J. Ernest. I've been a maiden lady for thirty years. It wasn't easy to say yes, but I said it. It took all my courage. I'm really rather frightened. I don't know much about these matters—but I'm going to find out. I've always wanted to be married. But . . . I'm learning I'm not really married."

"Why, my dear, I've tried to be sensitive—"

"I want you to hug me. I want a real honest-to-God hug and a real kiss. And then I want all the rest."

"Why, Regina. . . ."

She eyed him skeptically. "J. Ernest, aren't you able? Is that it?"

"Why, of course I am. Most certainly. But I'm no Adonis. My waistline—I just thought you'd rather not. . . ."

"Well I'm no Venus. But I'm married—I think."

"Oh yes, married without a doubt."

"Then hug me. I don't want an alderman's hug, either, or a two-bit mayor's hug. That's not enough. I don't want a state senator's hug, either. That's not big enough.

"We're going to do some federal hugging. J. Ernest, I want the real McCoy. I want a United States Senator kind of hugging, and nothing less. A senator gives hugs that make a lady's heart leap and dance. He makes a lady laugh and cry. I want a Senate Majority Leader hug if you're up to it. Nothing less'll do."

For the first time in her memory, J. Ernest Potter-Pride was speechless.

"Move your stuff in here, Ernest, we don't need that other room. You're going to make me a senator's lady."

CHAPTER 66

. . . .

Charlotte Keiserling drew her mink-trimmed alpaca coat around her and stepped into the night. She picked her way down an icy slope, buffeted by an arctic gale, wondering why she even bothered. Her girls had all left earlier. She didn't want to go with them and listen to their maudlin singing, and watch them weep and pretend to have a good time. She'd seen enough whores' Christmases to last two lifetimes.

Still, she would visit a few saloons and hoist a few drinks and drone out a few carols. This was the only evening of the year when a professional lady was welcome, and she'd make the most of it. She always dreaded Christmas, and none more than this one. No frail ever did business Christmas Eve.

She crossed the bridge over Cashbox Creek and scaled the slippery grade to Main, wondering what compelled her. It wouldn't lift her spirits any. She paused at the Carbonate Miners Saloon, suddenly shy. She wished she had gone with the girls after all; they were planning to visit One-Eyed Jack's, sing carols, get drunk on slivovitz, and go home weepy. But that was the one place she didn't want to enter. The place where the kid had died.

What the hell, she thought, and pushed open the doors, letting in a blast of icy air. She stood just inside, smelling sour beer and cigar smoke. The bachelor miners would be here; the family men in their cottages. She spotted men she knew, looking as miserable as she, sipping from sudsy mugs and trying to put some gloss on the holy night. She saw some feeble attempts at decoration. Popcorn strings looped around a scraggly jackpine.

She pushed through a male throng toward the bar. They were courteous, she'd give them that. Sometimes, when she sashayed into a place like this, conversation stopped. She saw her customers here and there, and they acknowledged her with an amiable glance or a wink. It would be all right. She unbuttoned her coat in the moist heat. Let them see she was dressed as respectably as a parson's wife.

"Merry Christmas, Charlotte. What'll your pleasure be?" asked Joe Wales, the keep this night. He smiled.

"Panther piss, Joe."

Beyond the billard table an impromptu chorale was assembling. Someone passed out sheet music, and then they plunged in.

"O holy night, the stars are brightly shining, it is the night of our dear Savior's birth. . . ."

How sweet was the harmony of a dozen male voices, and how marvelously the tenors, basses and baritones blended. She listened raptly, stirred by some unfathomable sorrow. Why should a frail celebrate Christmas?

"Joy to the world, the Lord is come; let earth receive its King. Let every heart, prepare Him room. Let heav'n and nature sing, let heav'n and nature sing . . ."

She downed her panther piss and ordered another, suddenly wanting the booze to dull her pain. Dammit, she hadn't asked to become a whore. She'd been thrown out back there for foolin' around, just for foolin' around like everyone did anyway. She'd always insisted she was having a great ol' time, just a great ol' time, but now it rang hollow. It had never been a great ol' time. She wished she didn't feel like crying. Why did Christmas do that to her?

"It came upon a midnight clear, that glorious song of old. . . ."

Damned men. They all wanted her. They all wanted what she had to sell. And they threw her out because she gave it to them. What the hell was the matter with the males of the human race? She stared about her, eyeing men who'd visited the girls, visited her, all of them singing holy songs celebrating a Christian feast. She leaned into the bar and waited for them to talk to her, but none did. They didn't boot her out and they didn't talk with her.

She downed three more drinks, listened to a dozen more carols, and grew more morose with each one. That's why she always dreaded Christmas. It was a lie. She had to get the hell out before she burst into tears. She buttoned her coat and pushed through the mob and into the bitter night.

Only to run smack into the Cashbox Cornet Band gathering around the doors, bravely sporting their red tunics on a bitter night, and lipping the frozen mouthpieces of their instruments.

"Of come, all ye faithful, joyful and triumphant, O come ye, O come ye to Bethlehem. . . ."

The brass rang sweetly in the crystal air, bold in the quiet night. She stayed, fighting back grief. The brass chorale was achingly beautiful. She wept. Miners boiled out of the saloon to listen, mugs in hand. They cheered and smiled at the end of each carol. It was cold. In the midst of "Angels We Have Heard on High" she slipped away, hiding her frozen tears, fleeing across the little bridge to hell, scraping and sliding up the slope, back to her goddamned quarter.

Only to be accosted yet again, this time by carolers. They were mostly miners' wives, bundled in scarves, muffs and thick mittens. Their breaths steamed the air. Carolers on her very doorstep. Bringing sweet Christmas to soiled doves. She quelled her instinct to dash inside, and made herself stand quietly.

Women's voices, soprano, alto, crystalline as glass in the hard air, sweet as silver bells. "Round yon Virgin, mother and child, Holy Infant, so tender and mild, Sleep in heavenly peace, Sleep in heavenly peace. . . ."

"Thank you, that was beautiful," she said, and they smiled. "I'm very cold," she mumbled and slid into the forlorn quiet of her parlor.

Her house was empty. She felt it creak in the deepening cold. She shut out Cashbox, and instantly felt better.

She closed the door to her room, grateful to escape the caroling world. She would hear no more of frauds. She'd had wild times enough. But not real happiness, the kind that comes from a life well lived. Her days had been spent in desperation, looking for things she couldn't have, laughing at the world's carolers.

Everyone told her she was better off with that punk kid dead. That was for sure the whole damned truth. He'd bled her of everything, chased off her girls, wrecked the trade. But that was just the public stuff. He'd grabbed her hair and twisted her to the floor. He'd pounded on her until she'd had to powder her blue and purple bruises. He'd pulled his knives and threatened to carve her flesh. He'd looted her. She sure as hell was better off with him dead.

She sighed, knowing something about herself so awful that she couldn't bear it. She didn't want the kid dead. Everything Casper Penrose did to her she somehow invited—no, not invited. *Let happen.* She could, at any time, have gotten help from a variety of sports. She knew a few miners, big as bulls, who could've pulverized Casper into a yapping puppy, and done it gladly as a public service. Even Constable Svensrud. All she'd had to do was ask. But she let the punk invade and ruin her, invade and ruin her house. It was a weakness. No, not a *weakness.* It was an abyss.

Too late to worry about that.

She opened an aromatic cedar chest and withdrew a white wedding gown and all the lacy underthings that went with it. She'd had it made long ago against this time. Many of the girls had one. Every whore buried in the Cashbox cemetery wore one. The white silk and Brussels lace smelled of cedar. She hoped it'd still fit. She eyed it fondly, admiring its puffed sleeves, tight bodice, full skirt and train. It had taken a Denver seamstress a month to sew.

It spoke to her of things lost and things hoped for, better things to come. She would be a virgin in white, looking the way a bride should look. Slowly she undressed and hung up her woolen suit, then her petticoats. Naked, she washed herself in cold water scented with lavender, shivering. Then she donned the underthings, which had never before been worn. She admired herself in them; they were so delicately wrought they delighted her. She wrestled the wedding dress over her head and buttoned it slowly, right up to her neck. It barely fit but that didn't matter. She slid her feet into white slippers, and anchored a silken wreath to her hair.

She stood before her looking glass, admiring herself in the radiance of the coal-oil lamp. She looked ravishing. Her heart leapt out to herself. She would make a lovely

Christmas bride, entering the new world of sunlight and springtime and nightingale songs.

She paused, wondering if she could manage the rest. But she knew she could if she tried.

It was time. She supposed most families would be going to midnight services now. They would sing their carols and rejoice, and bid the Christ child welcome. Then they'd go home to snug beds and dreams of sugarplums and fairies.

She was not afraid. She didn't even feel bad. She had known she would do this ever since she'd discovered that she was so vulnerable. She sat on her bed. She uncorked the rectangular blue bottle of laudanum and poured a teaspoon full. Six drops was a normal dose. Six or seven teaspoons would suffice. Quietly she swallowed the tincture of opium. Then again. And again. Even before she finished she felt the upwelling peace creeping through her limbs.

"God forgive me," she muttered. "Like you forgave Mary Magdalen. You're all I have."

Then she lay back on her bed, adjusted her dress so as not to crush it, and waited for a better world.

PART III

....

1893

CHAPTER 67
· · · · · · · · · · · · · · · ·

Promptly at the appointed hour of one, Old Jut-Jaw appeared on the bunting-draped platform of the observation car, accompanied by Regina, decked in mink. The new senator from Montana was on his way to Washington.

He waved cheerfully at the throng, saluting friends with the arm that wasn't around Regina's waist, enjoying himself in the soft breeze of a January chinook that had scoured away the snow and lured most of Cashbox's four thousand residents out to see him off.

"Doesn't the old rascal look grand," Sylvie said to Con. "He probably practices being senatorial before his looking glass every morning."

But what fascinated her more was Regina, who had blossomed into a handsome woman, her angular lines and heavy bones somehow magically transformed into a middle-aged glory one never would have suspected in her. Sylvie hoped that she would look half as lovely in her fifties.

When the Cashbox Cornet Band, in silver-trimmed red plumage, concluded "Semper Fidelis" and "The Washington Post March," Senator J. Ernest Potter-Pride lifted his arms upward, stretching his fingertips higher and higher, as if to touch the sky. Somehow the magical gesture quieted the crowd that had gathered at the new railroad station to see the senator from Cashbox begin his public life.

Something electric lay in this moment. Sylvie thought it marked the passage of Cashbox into a great city that would endure for generations. It had its own senator, duly selected by the state legislature. It had its railroad, its rich mines, its rows of large houses, its lawns, its young cottonwoods along its streets. And Main Street was even cobbled. Somehow all these things seemed to collect into a glow surrounding Senator Potter-Pride.

Old silver-tongue waited a moment longer, almost too long, she thought. But he knew this crowd, and the stretching moment only riveted the attention of the gaily dressed people who crowded the track. Why was it, she wondered, that she utterly forgave him for bilking her? Why was it that the old reprobate had won the hearts even of those who know precisely the sort of fraud he was? Maybe it was Regina. Somehow that formidable woman had transformed him, even as he had transformed her. Those who had gathered around the observation car that afternoon were seeing not one, but two dreams fulfilled.

"My dear friends, my fellow Montanans, my neighbors from the grand city of Cashbox," he began, in a Vaseline voice. "I've come to say good-bye, at least for the moment. Oh, my, I'll miss you all. When the queen of my universe and I are off to that noble capital in the East where our Republic is seated, we'll remember each of you; this fair city; this place of dreams—and, of course, our obligations to you and the people of this great state, whose motto is *Oro y Plata*, Gold and Silver. . . ."

"Still a spellbinder," Sylvie whispered. The chinook hadn't quite swept away the bite of January, so she drew her ermine coat tighter.

"He's spreading it pretty thick," Con muttered.

"I am now, and always will be, a silver man," cried the senator. "Silver now, silver tomorrow, silver forever!"

The crowd clapped politely. A baby wailed.

"From the moment I repeat the oath of office on the Senate floor, my friends, I shall fight the sinister moneymen who want to starve us with gold. Must this great state be held in thrall by hard-souled men who worship gold, who hoard gold, who buy votes with gold, who crush the upright workingman under a steamroller made of gold? I say no. I say, let there be free and unlimited silver coinage. Let there be easy credit so that humble men, people like you and me, can begin our lives anew, here in the sweet, spacious West."

Senator Potter-Pride paused, letting his words sink home. Sylvie became aware of the quiet chuffing of the locomotive up ahead, poised like a racehorse at the gate. The crowd had become quiet, too. Silver was serious business.

"Now, let me tell you something: we're in for a fight. They've got us on the ropes. Those malefactors of great wealth, men with countinghouses where their hearts should be, are trying to repeal the Sherman Silver Purchase Act. Oh, how close they are. They say they've got the votes. They say they want sound money. Sound money! They call it sound, but we call it something else. We call it poverty, rags, starvation, sickness, and the death of our dreams. Well, my dear friends, here's one vote they don't have—and never will have."

A few miners whistled. Some businessmen cheered.

"String him up!" yelled a miner. "He's talkin' too long." The time they almost hanged J. Ernest Potter-Pride had not been forgotten in Cashbox.

The Senator laughed, his sincere blue eyes focusing briefly on the miscreant.

"Oh, my young friend, there's so much to talk about. But let me just tell you how things stand. We've a new president who's a gold man. Yes, Grover Cleveland's been listening to the wrong side. Well, I plan to tell him the silver side, the side of progress and justice. I'm going to make a westerner of him if I can. He's a man of my party—the Democracy—and he'll listen.

"This republic's heading for trouble. We need unlimited coinage of silver at a ratio of sixteen to one with gold. It's fallen to twenty-three to one, and that's where the trouble is. My friends, I intend to fight for these things. Oh, there's clouds on the horizon, but I'm going to put a silver lining on them all. Thank you and God bless you."

Senator Potter-Pride lifted his arms once again, higher and higher, reaching for something Sylvie couldn't see, even as the whistle shrilled joyous blasts, and the brass bell on the engine bonged. He drew Regina to him. She smiled and blew a gentle kiss to her friends. A conductor flagged the engineer. Then the gilt-trimmed Number 999, one of the two engines owned by the Cashbox and Northern, spat steam from its valves, thumped and creaked to life, and wailed down the track.

Sylvie sighed. "I'll miss them," she said.

"He'll do some real good there, Sylvie."

"He's too slippery."

"He's got to do something, fast, or we're lost."

She stared at Con. "You're exaggerating."

"Silver's down to eighty-seven cents. There's hardly a mine that can make a profit at that price." He sounded bleak to her.

"What'll he do?"

"Sponsor a free silver bill. The mines are producing a lot more silver than the government's buying. The Treasury should coin all the silver—not just four and a half million ounces a year."

"Are you going to be hurt—the Giltedge?"

"We're still profitable—but only because we're getting sixty ounces to the ton. A little gold, too. That's incredible ore. If the price drops any lower, Sylvie ... not even Thaddeus could squeeze a profit out of silver. You'll see a different Cashbox. Half the mines up the gulch have laid off men, and it'll get worse."

She felt chilled, and knew it was more than the January cold. "But Con, this is a big town. Stages twice a day to Helena. Businesses everywhere. The brick company. They all employ people. Why, I employ two people. Timbering and ranching. . . ."

"They exist to support the mining, Sylvie. If the mines close, everything closes."

"It'll never happen," she said. They were walking through a burgeoning city with brick buildings that had replaced the frame or log ones. *The Plain Truth* was boasting that there would be ten thousand residents by the end of the century. The Cashbox Water and Power Company had announced plans to build a generating plant and contract for coal. In the fall, her lecture hall might have electric lights. The club, too. Why, her club had ninety-one members, and kept on growing. "It's the railroad. We're a *place* now."

"The railroad. I hope you're right," Con said, but she sensed he wasn't saying all that was on his mind.

"Con—are you still a stockholder?"

"Of the Cashbox and Northern? I don't own a share. I took a small loss, but I'm out safely."

"You didn't tell me." She felt the cold spread through her. "Why, Con?"

"The price of silver."

She drew her silk scarf tighter around her neck. It had been his gift. The ermine-trimmed coat, too. He had found things to buy her and with each gift his earnest eyes searched her, seeking her pleasure, delighting to please her. She had never been so loved, nor had she ever known a man like Con Daley, whose deepest joy was to surprise her with something more.

At first she had resisted, feeling she could give little in return. But the gifts kept coming, month after month, as if he were determined to spend his profit from the Giltedge upon her. When cornflower-blue sapphires were discovered in nearby Yogo Gulch—stones that rivaled the finest sapphires of Ceylon and India—Con bought a two-carat stone from the British who were developing the mine and had Tiffany cut and set it in a ring that shattered light into blue dazzle.

But as much as she loved these costly things, she loved the other gifts more. Some nights when they were alone in her quiet rooms, he hooked his new gold-rimmed glasses over his ears and read one of the sonnets he had written for her. They spoke of dreams. They plumbed her spirit. They transported her to the only solid shore. No gift of stones could match that.

"Oh, Con, everything'll be all right," she said.

CHAPTER 68

. . . .

C on was going to have fun. He steered Sylvie up Hamilton Street, enjoying the riotous April day. The warm sun was pummeling the last of the snow, while cottony clouds plowed shadows across the world. They reached the top of the hill, puffing a little from the climb, and Con guided her to the new brick house on the corner.

"Oh! It's delightful, Con."

He smiled. The red brick house stood at the highest point in Cashbox, not far from Thaddeus Webb's place. The contractor had finished it a week earlier, and now the drayage company was done with the moving. The house had generous proportions, a steep roof, a handsome bay window, and spindle gingerbread enameled white to soften the brickwork. At the rear of the lot Cashbox Mountain vaulted upward, but the front afforded a breathtaking view of the city.

The house was so situated that it seemed to rule this corner of the universe. That was why he had chosen this lot. He had bought it not only for its aesthetic qualities and its view, but for something else, intangible, mysterious, that he couldn't define. Whoever lived in this house would, in a sense, own Cashbox.

"Let's go in," he said. "I want you to see the view from the bay window."

"It'll be perfect because you wanted it to be. Oh, Con, I'm glad you're staying. For as long as I've known you, I've dreaded the moment you might return to Helena."

"So have I," he muttered.

They ascended the enameled wooden steps to the recessed porch. He thrust the skeleton key into the chased brass lock, and swung open the white door. He wondered how long it would take her to grasp the meaning of this.

They entered a foyer with a white-banistered stair leading to the rooms above. On the right was the parlor; on the left the dining room, and behind it the kitchen. But he guided her into the parlor, which glowed like burnished gold in the light of the noon sun leaping through the bay windows. Gauzy white curtains in loose folds gently subdued the glare. A yellow silk settee, matched by two yellow silk wing chairs, a table lamp, and escritoire filled the room.

"Oh! It's gorgeous. Why, Con, I didn't know you liked my colors."

He smiled. She exclaimed at the view. From that window they could see all of Cashbox, which sprawled down to the business district, the railroad terminal on the south edge of town, and the sporting places clustered on the east slope across Cashbox Creek. Everywhere below them stood ornate homes, built to last forever, each created by craftsmen. Some were red brick; most were whitewashed wood. Many had carriage sheds, root cellars, and outhouses behind them, but the newer ones boasted indoor plumbing.

He took her through a door with fluted molding into the study, less well lighted but filled with feminine furnishings, scatter pillows on the gold sofa, lacy curtains, a Brussels carpet of gold and teal, built-in shelves for whatnots or books.

She stopped cold, stricken with amazement.

"Con?"

He laughed.

"Con? What is this?"

He captured her hand, and pressed the skeleton key into it.

She stared at it, at him, speechless.

"Want to see the rest?" he said, the glow inside of him so bright he could barely speak.

"Con. You've got to tell me. . . ." Her words trailed into nothingness.

He took her hand again and felt the tremor. "It's cold in

here. We ought to build a fire," he said. "Each room has a stove. But let's look at the rest. Do you like it?"

"Like it?" She sounded rattled. "Oh, I think so."

He took her hand and tugged her up the carpeted stairs and showed her the two cheerful bedrooms. One contained a shining brass double bed with ruffled skirts and a white cover, the other a bed with a massive walnut headboard and footboard. She peered at the room uncertainly, glancing nervously at him. He showed her the complete lavatory, with claw-tub, running water sink, oak-seated commode with a pull chain. A kerosene-operated water heater stood in one corner.

"It's nicer than the one at the club," she said, nervously. "This is the fanciest house I've ever been in."

He smiled.

Downstairs, he showed her the dining room. It had a cut-glass chandelier, and a heavy oak table that could seat eight, along with matching ladderback dining chairs. A beeswaxed sideboard glowed under a window. He led her into the kitchen and showed her the shining nickel-plated range, cupboards with built-in flour and sugar bins. He opened the door of a commodious pantry and let her gawk. He knew she wasn't much of a cook. He could hardly imagine her with an apron on, kneading dough or peeling potatoes. But he wanted her to see everything. He opened the rear door, and took her into a screened summer kitchen and laundering area.

"What a kitchen. I guess you're planning on doing some entertaining," she said too lightly.

He didn't answer. From his capacious breast pocket he plucked a thick document and handed it to her.

She peered into his eyes uncertainly, and read it. He had deeded the lot and the house to her. She read it again, and he watched her struggle with it. He had known she would struggle, and waited quietly.

"Oh, my dear Cornelius. Let's go sit in the parlor," she said. "I love the light there. Build me a fire, Con. It's so cold in here."

He caught a tremor in her voice. She stood in the middle of the room while he stuffed *The Plain Truth* and kindling into the nickel-trimmed parlor stove. He scratched a match, and watched yesterday's news and the sticks of pine turn to ash. But his attention was on her. She watched rigidly, mute and dumfounded, emotions passing across her face like those puffball clouds outside. A tender heat began to build in the parlor, and as it did, she relaxed.

"I love you," she whispered.

Of all the words she might have spoken, she had chosen the ones he most wanted to hear.

She pulled him to her and hugged, melting into him with all her body. He drew her even tighter, his arms encircling her, banishing aloneness. She hugged him as if she would never let go, her hands forming thank-yous, her lips finding his. Her kiss was gentle, not sensuous. It spoke of things that transcended flesh and desire, all the most important matters of the soul. Then, at last, they separated. He felt his aloneness again.

"I thought you'd like a private place. Your life's hardly your own any more. All those new members. Poker games all night. People coming in for a nightcap after the show at the opera house. It's like a railroad station." He left unspoken the rest of it: the success of her club was robbing them of their private moments. It had become harder and harder to be lovers. He had always been discreet. She had, too. She could no longer slip into the club to tryst in his suite. He could no longer pad through the building in robe and slippers, en route to her door.

"Are you—going to live with me?"

He shook his head. "I'll keep my suite. This is for you, forever. . . . But I'd like to come visit."

She smiled crookedly. How he loved that odd twist of her lips. "You're always worried about my reputation."

"Sylvie—you could divorce Beau. Desertion. We could get it through a court in a week. Then you'd be free."

"Is that a proposal?"

"Everything I say to you is a proposal, Sylvie." He

wanted to marry her more than anything else on earth; but she was the one thing he could not have. She had kept her independence. Her club and hall afforded an income. Her dead marriage formed a maddening barrier that left him with one foot in paradise.

"I've never been so loved," she said. "You would do this for me. Why ... you even knew my favorite colors. You know me so well. This house is like a sonnet you've written for me."

"I'm glad, Sylvie."

"I think this is the happiest day of my life. I think years from now, when I'm old and reminiscing about life—whether I lived it well, and found what I wanted—I think I'll always turn to this day, this place, this parlor. I didn't even know I wanted this until you gave it to me. Do you know you're a poet of bricks and mortar, too? You're such a contradiction. Yes, this is the day, all right. I didn't even know we're allowed to have moments like this. I thought they were just in fairy tales."

"Does it mean that much?"

She nodded. "Now I have everything. But even if I had nothing at all, I would still have everything." She squeezed his hand. "I'll love you forever. We don't need to be married, Con. We have everything now. This is better than marriage."

"It's less than marriage, Sylvie. Everything I am, everything I possess, is yours. I live only for your happiness. My own joy springs from that. My love, my life, my possessions, my dreams—they're all yours."

"That's beautiful, Con. I'll always remember."

"Remember?"

"Yes, the happiest day of my life. The end of the rainbow. I never thought I'd find it."

CHAPTER 69

· · · · · · · · · · · · · · · · ·

May Svensrud hurt more than she could ever remember hurting. Dr. Kratz had given her a little chloroform, but not enough. It had only made her dizzy without sponging away her hurts. Pain is good, he explained, and chloroform is dangerous. She had been too weary to argue.

She lay sweat-drenched and sundered, but it was over. She had delivered, but she felt so miserable it didn't lift her spirits. She wondered at the delay, but then she heard a smack and a sharp yowl, followed by a soft whimpering. Something tender flooded through her pain.

She waited, too tired even to ask the question. But then he presented the cleaned infant to her. "A good, healthy boy," he said. "Seven and a half pounds and hungry as a hog."

She took the child with leaden arms and guided it to her breast. "Oh, thank you," she muttered. She struggled up a little so she could see her boy, and was content. He looked flawless, tiny but active, with a hint of silky blond hair. She felt a sudden gratitude.

Waterford Kratz examined her further, while she lay embarrassed, wishing doctors could be women. "I think you'll be all right. This isn't your first. You're not torn up."

"It's the first . . . ," she began, and retreated from that. "It's my first with my present husband," she mumbled. Doctors knew everything.

"Well, you could have a dozen more. Some women are like that. You're one of the lucky ones."

"I guess I am." She felt the tug of the child's gums.

"Your milk's down? He's nursing?"

"Yes," she whispered. She looked down on the quiet infant, liking the touch of his silky flesh upon her own.

"You'll be all right. Fetch me if you bleed. Even a drop. Have Slug get me, day or night."

"I will. Where is he?"

"I'll find him. Husbands are worse than useless during childbirth. He's probably hiding in the outhouse."

"I don't want to be alone."

He poured some carbolic in the washbowl, mixed it with water, and then scrubbed his hands thoroughly. She watched dreamily, as if he were a mile away. The only reality was her pain, her dizziness from the retreating anesthesia, and the light, soft, silky infant on her chest.

He scribbled something on a pad with a pencil, ripped the top sheet off and laid it on the table. She wondered what he had charged. He snapped shut his Gladstone bag, sternly straightened his bowtie for the effrontery of being cockeyed, slid into his black suitcoat, and patted her arm.

"Nice little rascal. Easy birth, no complications. What'll you call him?"

"I—don't know. I haven't thought about it." She wondered why she had said that. She had done nothing else but think about it. She had desperately hoped for a girl, so she wouldn't have to think about it.

"Well, I'll fetch the happy father. I can see him out there splitting kindling as if he wanted a year's supply."

"Thank you," she whispered.

"You're strong as an ox. You can get up any time you feel like it."

She nodded. Men didn't understand. She felt too weak even to sit up, much less walk.

He banged out the door into a spring morning. She clamped a hand around the firm little body on her breast, hoping she could love the boy. Oh, she had so much wanted a girl; a child who wouldn't remind her of Robby. But now she had another little boy, and it tore her to pieces. What would she do to this innocent baby? She drove the thought from her head. She had to resist it.

Slug entered, closed the door softly behind him, and stared across the shining room at her and the baby.

"May—are you all right?"

"I guess so."

He sidled closer, as if afraid to come near. "Are you sure? Is he all right? It's a boy?"

"Yes. He sucked and went to sleep."

"Is there anything you need?"

"Well, you could come over here."

"But I might hurt him. I'd better stay back—"

She laughed, each spasm shooting pain through her. "You're afraid of him."

"No, I just don't want to get too close. He might not like me."

"He's armed and dangerous, Slug." She couldn't help it.

Slug looked sheepish. He walked to her bedside as if on stilts. "That's him. Hard to believe."

This child was his first. She could almost read his mind; the memory of their union, and now the child they had conceived, there before him. He looked like he'd rather be in Argentina.

"Hold him, Slug."

"What? Me?"

"He's yours."

"I'll drop him."

She smiled, and lifted the child to him. He took it gingerly, studying this infant they had wrought in a moment of clinging.

"Put your hand under his head, Slug. Hold it up. It's still very soft, isn't it?"

"Ain't he cold?"

"You could wrap him in that flannel there."

"Oh, no. You do that." He deposited the boy on her chest again and snatched the small white blanket. She wrapped it around the infant. The nameless boy.

Slug seemed itchy, but finally drew a chair to her bedside and sat. "You sure you're all right?" he asked.

She nodded uncertainly. How could she be sure, with such a bone-deep ache pervading her whole body?

The child yawned.

"He's some little Norseman!" Slug exclaimed.

"He's also English, German and Dutch, Slug."

"May, are you gonna name him?"

She hadn't wanted this moment to come. She loved the little unnamed boy because he had no name. If she gave him a name, he would be a person—a person she could destroy.

"You name him. I can't."

He scratched his head mightily. "You don't want Robby, do you? You could, you know—try again."

She felt tears welling up and leaking down her cheeks.

"I'm sorry," he said. "Shouldn't've asked. A new family, that's what we have."

He was trying, but he couldn't repair the moment.

"Well, do you want one of your family names, or one of my family names, or nobody's family name?" he asked.

"Let's start new. This is a new land, a new life."

"All right. I like Tim. There was a kid named Tim I used to beat up every day after school, and whenever I could catch him all summer. Then we got to be pals and he started to beat me up. Do you like Tim?"

"Yes."

"Timothy Svensrud. How does that sound?"

"He's a Timothy."

"Well, Timothy he is. You got a middle one?"

"I'm too tired. Maybe tomorrow."

"Well, Timmy, you got named," he said. "What'd Kratz charge?" He answered the question himself by fetching the bill on the table.

"Twenty-five. Why that's half a month's pay. How'm I—"

"I saved a little, Slug. I have seventeen dollars put by. In the sugar jar."

He smiled suddenly, and the blue light sparked in his eyes again. She closed her eyes a moment.

"Town doesn't pay me enough to keep body and soul together. You'd think with almost four thousand people they'd pay a decent salary. I'll tell Mrs. Flower to look in on you. I gotta go to work."

"Please stay a little, Slug. I—don't want to be alone yet."

"Something wrong?"

She shook her head. "Hold my hand, please. Just hold it while I rest."

"But—"

"Just this morning. Your beat can wait. No one's going to rob the bank at nine in the morning."

He settled into the chair, and took her hand, and it comforted her. "May, are you pretty blue? You afraid again?"

She nodded. "I'm always afraid of myself. What might happen I mean, if I'm alone. But as long as I have you, Slug, I'll be all right. We'll have a family. Oh, Slug, I don't know what I'd do if you weren't here. If you left me—if something—Slug, don't ever leave me. When I'm with you I feel secure. Safe. It's a new life, and you're so strong. . . ."

"I'll never leave you, May."

Chapter 70

· · · · · · · · · · · · · · · ·

Willard Croker figured he was going to solve his financial problems once and for all at the court house in Livingston. *The Plain Truth* didn't earn much, and his schemes to rake in the cash of Cashbox had all failed. In recent months things had gotten worse: merchants had fallen behind on their payments for ads, and subscriptions had fallen off in spite of the burgeoning population. It puzzled him. Cashbox seemed wealthier than ever. Its restaurants were so busy one had to wait for a seat. But money had vanished from sight. People lived on credit. No one saved a dime. Wages were lower than ever. Even the Knights of Labor didn't press for more money. John Oliver Cromwell was issuing bank scrip to help the merchants because he had no cash on hand.

Some weeks *The Plain Truth* hardly took in a silver dollar, but Croker had staved off disaster. Beside him stood a roly-poly little lady, dressed in something that resembled a gold-tasseled brocade opera curtain. It was a wedding dress from Kansas City, and it had cost a young fortune. The happy bride was Minnie, the proprietress of Minnie's Sporting House, to which Willard had repaired after the death of Charlotte Keiserling.

Miss Minnie—he had found out her last name was alleged to be Smith-Jones only minutes before, when they had applied for a license in the court house at Livingston—had consented to become Mrs. Croker, provided that Willard perform certain tasks. Most important of these was crusading against the high license fees for the sporting houses that Cashbox was imposing on innocent fun-loving people. Willard had promised to fulminate against them for as long as he and Minnie were united in sacred matrimony.

It would be a good arrangement, he thought as he adjusted his fresh white shirt. She would have a champion in high places. He considered an editor the occupant of a very high place, and also one who rubbed shoulders with others in high places. He would enjoy her comforts for free. More important, she had vast reserves of cash—he didn't know how much—that he would tap, eventually. He need never fear starvation again.

In moments it was over. Park County Justice of the Peace Sax Baer, who had even shaved for this occasion, led them through the vows of eternal love and devotion and then pronounced them husband and madam, which the abominable Baer considered a fine joke. Willard paid him two silver dollars and a brass token from Minnie's house, redeemable any time the JP felt like catching the train up to the mining town. Willard intended to get his paws on more of those brass tokens. They would make him uncommonly popular around Cashbox.

He kissed Minnie gallantly. Then Baer kissed Minnie. Then the clerk of court, who had served as witness, kissed Minnie. Then Minnie hunted around for anyone else to kiss, but she could find only old Mrs. Petersen, who cleaned the courthouse on Friday afternoons.

After an enthusiastic honeymoon in Butte, where Minnie checked out market conditions and possible employees, they returned on the evening passenger train to Cashbox, to begin life in a spanking new cottage that Minnie had erected next to her Sporting House. Willard was grateful not to pay the usual forty a month for his digs over the saloon on Main Street but he wasn't happy when Minnie proposed charging him for the chow and spirits he consumed in the sporting house.

Willard intended to say nothing of the match in *The Plain Truth*. It was nobody's business but his own. He had employed a string of printer's devils after May Goode left, but most had lasted only a few weeks, and since then Willard had run a one-man weekly newspaper. There were compensations. Each edition included exactly what he wanted in it, and excluded anything he chose not to run.

No sooner had he returned from his May honeymoon than he received another of Senator Potter-Pride's epistles. The senator had been mailing one to Willard each fortnight, expecting Willard to print them. Other weeklies would reprint the letters, giving the senator statewide coverage.

But they posed an awful dilemma for Willard. The senator had lost his marbles. He didn't know enough to keep his yap shut, or rather his pen under control. Willard hated to run letters that would erode the confidence of Cashbox even further. For months he had censored the letters, running whatever was hopeful while cutting the things that might start a panic. But the senator's letters had become more and more gloomy, reaching the point where Croker quietly rewrote them.

Willard scanned the senator's latest letter. Potter-Pride's calamity list was frightening. Stocks had been plummeting ever since May fifth. Foreigners were unloading American securities and siphoning gold from the Treasury. The McKinley tariff was so punitive that it was throttling trade and reducing government revenues. But worst of all, the gold interests had become a thundercloud that threatened to wash away the Sherman Silver Purchase Act.

But all was not lost, the senator added. A young Nebraska fellow in the House named William Jennings Bryan was a fiery silver man, whose tongue could summon angels. Between Pride in the Senate and silver-tongued Bryan in the lower chamber, they would try to stem the tide.

Potter-Pride said he'd do it by filibuster if all else failed. He would begin by reading the entire Bible, repair to Webster's dictionary, switch to an encyclopedia, work through Boccaccio's *Decameron*—except for certain tales; read the U.S. legal code, tackle Caesar's *Commentaries* in Latin, and retreat to the daily newspapers of a dozen American metropolises if he must. If he still had his tonsils at the end of several weeks, he would defeat the sinister gold interests.

Bad news, the senator concluded, but he and Regina, the queen of his universe, devoutly believed that the tornado would have a silver lining. And of course he and Mrs. Potter-Pride sent their love to their dear friends in Cashbox.

Willard Croker read and reread the blasphemous letter, loathing every word of it. He decided he would not print one nasty line. Nothing but financial avalanche would result. The paper might die. Minnie's business would reach its climacteric. Better indeed to manufacture a pleasant little letter from Pride, something to restore confidence and get some cash moving around Cashbox. He had ceased printing national news, and had concentrated for months on the simmering Venezuela Boundary Dispute. In almost every issue, *The Plain Truth* had urged Grover Cleveland to get tough with the British. Because of Croker's crusading, the grade school children had sent the president a letter.

He sighed, knowing he couldn't hide the deepening financial crisis from Cashbox. Each day a bundle of newspapers from all over the United States arrived in the Cashbox and Northern's express car, destined for Sylvie Duvalier's club. Worse, the telegraph had reached Cashbox. The town was no longer isolated, the way it had been in the early days.

Willard balanced the letter on an inky finger, wondering whether to relent. The old fraud was probably exaggerating just so he could fashion himself the white knight who would rescue the Free Silver interests. Sadly, Croker folded the letter from Washington and slid it into his pocket.

That evening Croker's honeymoon cottage became the scene of domestic strife.

"I thought you were going to crusade for lower license fees," Minnie said.

"I'll get around to it. That's a delicate issue."

"Delicate is it? Well, Slug Svensrud came today and wanted three hundred dollars for the city. That's twelve hundred dollars a year. I'm tired of forking it out. I can hardly stay ahead."

"Well, Minnie, it's the nature of your business."

"Nature of my business? They all want to jump on me and get their money back? You just march right down to your stinking newspaper and tell them it's going to stop."

"It's a little touchy, Minnie."

"Feely is a better word, Croker. You're not climbing onto me until you write that editorial."

"All right, all right. I think I know a way."

"What way?"

"Well, ah, word's gotten out we're married. I can't exactly go crusading to lower the license fees on saloons and brothels and be taken seriously. Newspapers are supposed to be sort of independent. But I can come at it from another direction."

"You sure are one to come at things from a new direction, Croker."

"Yeah. Well, the city of Cashbox gets these license fees from all you sporting people so it doesn't have to levy property taxes. That's the way it is in every mining town. I'll just start saying it's time for the city to levy a property tax."

"What good'll that do my business?"

"Well, I want to shift the tax base. Let the property owners pay something. The merchants. The rich people with big houses. Why, I'd love to see the Exchange Club pay. Why should Sylvie Duvalier not pay a cent in taxes while you pay a fortune? See what I mean?"

"I'll end up paying a license fee and property taxes too, Croker."

"Well, I could write about the Yellow Peril if you want. We've got seven of those Celestials in town, working so cheap they steal jobs from decent citizens. We could tax them. A head tax on Chinese."

"Oh, do what you want. But you sleep on the couch until you get my license lowered."

Croker grinned. "A newspaper's always good for something or other," he said.

CHAPTER 71

• • • • • • • • • • • • • • • • • •

The weariness that afflicted Thaddeus Webb was one of the soul. For months he had tried to keep the Giltedge profitable in the face of plummeting silver prices. At eighty cents an ounce the mine was still in the black, but that was only because he was cutting every corner he could. His biggest savings had come from not driving the shaft to the six-hundred-foot level. They were mining at five hundred twenty feet, below the crosscut at the five-hundred-foot level, which meant that every pound of ore had to be lifted twenty feet by muscle power.

He would keep going as long as he could for the sake of his men. The temptation was to shut down and wait for better days. Why mine when there was no profit in it? Somehow, even Hugh Trego sensed Webb's desperation and the old lion of the Knights of Labor had settled into quiet rumbling, like a distant thunderstorm.

Coke Timmons appeared in the office door, looking grim. "You'd better come down," he said.

"What's the trouble?"

"You'd better come look."

Webb stared sharply at the shift foreman and reached for his jumper. In a few minutes they were descending to the five-hundred-foot level. Coke had been dead silent the whole descent, which puzzled and finally alarmed Webb.

"There's been no injury, has there?"

Timmons shook his head.

They walked the long crosscut, their carbide lamps bouncing light off the timbering. Because of the sixty-degree slant of the ore body, they had to walk three hundred yards from the shaft. Webb saw no activity along the way; no ore cars on the tram rails. They burst at last into the gallery currently being worked, the most recent of many that staircased upward toward the surface. They descended wooden ladders until they reached the face, where a dozen men stood around, their lamps leaking pale light. They were waiting for something.

"Well?" asked Webb.

"Look," Timmons replied.

Webb crawled over rubble toward the face. None of the mountain of rock left by the previous shift's blasting had been mucked up. He lost his balance, teetered, and scrambled down to the slanting rock. Then he lifted his lamp—and knew.

Before him bulged a solid boss of granite, the igneous mass that had thrust upward and tilted the nearby sedimentary rock to its present angle. Most of the rubble behind

him was granite. A sinking feeling slid through him. He
stumbled to the right edge of the gallery where the ore
ended at a dike of porphyry. Then he checked the other
side, where the ore petered out in limestone.

He returned to the face that had just been blasted and
studied the material at its foot. There the ore had narrowed
into a thin pyritiferous vein. He could hardly come to grips
with what he was seeing. Desperately he studied the side
of the gallery bounded by the porphyry dike, wondering if
ore lay beyond it.

Around him stood men with long faces, radiating black
thoughts. They were waiting for word of their doom. Waiting for the word that would send them to their cottages to
pack up and leave. If this was the end—and Webb believed it was—the Giltedge would close. There was still
ore in the upper galleries, most of it in the floors under the
complex timbering, but it would be difficult and dangerous
to mine, and could not be touched while silver was eighty
cents.

"Coke, let's pull back to the crosscut and drive through
that porphyry dike. I want to see what's on the other side."

"Is she closing, sir?" asked old Trenoweth, who had
been a good, hard-working man from the beginning.

"I wish I could give you the answer. It doesn't look
good."

The rest listened silently. Thaddeus knew their thoughts.

He pocketed some samples of the granite, the pyritical
rock, and a bit of ore, and stuffed them into his jumper.
There still might be a few days of mining along the wide
face. But that was no consolation. He stood there helplessly, feeling the desolation of his men, who looked to
him for hope he couldn't give them.

"Maybe we can find more. Rich mine. Best ore. . . ."
His voice trailed off. He was giving them false hopes.
"Well, anyway, let's cut through that dike."

Timmons nodded. Silently men gathered shovels, wheel-
barrows and drilling steels, and clambered up the ladders.
Webb watched, filled with an ache he couldn't define. Ev-

erything he had built—the works above, the mill, the smelter—was crumbling.

He fumbled along the crosscut back to the shaft, wondering what to do. He would have to tell Daley and the Hammons. Perhaps he'd missed a trick. He should get the opinion of a good geologist. He ascended in the rattling cage, without the usual company of filled ore cars, and burst out upon the grass, blinking at the harsh light.

Well, he thought, he and Portia might be packing up. He wondered where they would go. Some Nevada mines were producing still. The Idaho silver mines still looked good. Maybe they would end up in Kellogg. Maybe Mexico. Maybe Chile. It felt odd not to have the faintest inkling of one's destiny.

He found Cornelius Daley in the Exchange Club, reading William Randolph Hearst's *San Francisco Examiner*. Webb had long since come to some grudging conclusions about Daley: the man left Webb alone to run the Giltedge as he saw fit and even supported Webb at key moments. Pirate he might be, but a man with some business acumen too.

Webb sat down beside Daley, dreading to begin.

"Why, Thaddeus, what an odd time to see you here," Daley said.

"The Giltedge died last night," Webb blurted. He was not a man to soften blows.

Daley put down the paper and registered that a moment. "Poor ore?" he asked at last.

"No ore. We hit granite—an uplift. Part of the Elk Mountain igneous stock. It's what tilted the sedimentaries to sixty degrees."

"What level?"

"Five hundred and twenty feet."

"How do you know?"

"The vein shrank like an axehead down to an edge, a two-inch seam full of pyrite. The only thing I can think of is to cut through the porphyry dike on the west and see what's beyond it. But I haven't any faith in it."

"What's above? Can we still mine higher?"

"There's some ore in the gallery floors, supporting timber. At eighty cents an ounce. . . ." Webb's voice trailed off.

"I see."

Daley sat unmoving for a long time, until Webb wondered if his mind had wandered. He looked around the comfortable clubroom. They were alone. "Cashbox will hurt," Daley said.

"That's been on my mind. I've done everything I could to keep going while prices fell. Everything. For us, but also for Cashbox. Maybe you'd better come down and have a look."

"No, I'm not a geologist. Tell me, are you confident that you're right?"

"I'm pretty sure. Everything I know says I'm right." Thaddeus felt oddly guilty, as if the doom of the Giltedge and the wound to the city were his fault.

"Is there any ore still to be removed?"

"I can keep going a few days. That was the first round to reach granite."

"I'm thinking to bring in a man I admire, R. Jackson Cain, from New York. He's a legend, you know. He's the one who rescued the Potlatch Mine in Unionville. They'd reached a blank wall, the ore stopped as if it had been sliced off with a knife. Cain wandered around the hills above, and a mile or so south of the Potlatch he discovered an exposed fault that gave him some clues. The fault had shifted the matching strata about two hundred and fifty feet on the west side. So he advised the mine to run a crosscut two hundred fifty feet to the left, and then bore west. They did, and hit the vein again, just as Cain said they would. There's none better, Thaddeus. I'll wire him right away. We can have an answer inside of a week. Meanwhile, try to keep the lid on this."

CHAPTER 72

· · · · · · · · · · · · · · · ·

Standing on Main Street one taut morning, Sylvie beheld a strange sight. A black lacquered barouche and a wagon were wending their way down the slope of the sporting district. Jammed into the opposing seats of the carriage were six women, each severely dressed and veiled. Some wore veils of net or chiffon suspended from their hat brims, but the one woman she could identify wore a black lace mantilla over her blonde hair. It hid her face.

The wagon, following behind, carried numerous steamer trunks and other luggage. Young men from Overstreet's OK Livery Barn and Feed Store drove the vehicles, but seemed separate from the women and their luggage. Sylvie knew the blond woman only by her first name. She was Lotta, the proprietor of Lotta's Resort. Lotta had moved into Charlotte Keiserling's building in January of 1891, along with the other women in that lurching carriage.

They turned south on Main Street, confirming what Sylvie suspected: they were catching the morning train to Livingston. And they wouldn't be back. She watched them roll by, the procession oddly funereal, the veils a signature of their profession. How curious that a respectable woman could travel without a veil if she chose, but one of their kind could rarely step aboard a Pullman without one.

Sylvie peered up the hill at the old log building that had just been vacated, wondering who had bought it, and how much had been paid. Prices had fallen and it would be a bargain. Probably some other sporting woman, she thought. She put the disturbing image behind her and walked up Main, comforted by the solid mercantiles, restaurants and hotels. The cobbled street and plank sidewalks spoke of enduring life and vitality.

The street was deserted but that didn't surprise her. It often was, especially in the morning. Her walking shoes tapped hollowly on the sidewalk planks, somehow loud in the hush. She needed a new ledger, and she wanted Willard Croker to do some job printing for her. Her dance hall business had declined, and she wanted to take an advertisement announcing lower rates. She had also booked the Cashbox Cornet Band for a summer concert and wanted to promote it with posters.

She pushed through the double doors of the Hammon Brothers Mercantile, enjoying the pungence of the drygoods store. Its manager, Birney Cooke, materialized out of the shadows, rubbing his hands as he always did.

"I need a new ledger, Birney," she said.

"Certainly, certainly," the old man said, scurrying off to a half empty counter that displayed office things. "This is the last one," he said. "That'll be cash, of course."

"No, put it on my club account."

Birney shook his head. "Sorry, Mrs. Duvalier. They tell me it's cash only."

"Birney! Put it on my account."

He shook his head dolefully. "These are hard times," he said.

"Why, Birney, I've carried you for six months. Your club dues were owing in January. Now you can put it on my account."

He looked as if he wanted to be anywhere else. "I wish I could, but the Hammons won't let me."

She stared. "Why won't they let you?"

He blinked. "Because things are so—uncertain."

"Of course they're uncertain. These are hard times. We'll get by. We can help each other by buying and selling."

"Well, there are rumors—"

"I've heard them. Do you think Cashbox is going to dry up and blow away?"

"Well, of course not, but, ah, my hands are tied."

She didn't have cash. No one did. She sighed. "All right. I'll try Baker's."

"I'm sorry, Mrs. Duvalier."

She stormed next door. Baker's had been in Cashbox from the beginning. They wouldn't let her down.

And they didn't. Claude Baker sold her a thirty-cent ledger and charged it to the Exchange Club account. "Things are sure hellacious, Sylvie," he said. "You know anything about the Giltedge?"

"Con says it could be bad news. He's getting a geologist in to look at the five-hundred-foot level."

"Ah, I mean about the company's long-term plans?"

"Claude, they're mining six days a week."

It didn't satisfy him. "Sylvie—if you hear anything, would you let me know? If I can hear something early, ahead of the rest, why—a man's fortune depends on things like that."

"Well, I'll tell you. But it's a huge mine, Claude, and the ore runs every which way."

He nodded. "You know how it is in mining towns," he said.

It annoyed her. "Claude, this whole district's full of ore. Some mines have hardly gotten started."

"I wish I had your optimism, Sylvie. I'm here alone now. I couldn't pay my clerks. Look at this." He waved a hand at half-empty shelves and counters. "I can't afford to restock. I'm eating the seed corn."

"We'll endure, Claude. We'll all make it. Just hang on."

"The Cousins Jacks—they come in here and want their groceries on account. They're the only ones with cash—payroll—but they want it on account, as if they're socking cash away. It burns me up. One of 'em, he told me there's nothing but granite down there, five-hundred-foot level. I've got this place for sale, one thousand dollars plus inventory at cost."

"A thousand dollars? Why, Claude, it's worth ten times that."

"Yes, if there's a buyer. It could also be worth nothing at all."

"Don't you dare leave. Stay and fight," she said.

She crossed Main, dodging manure, feeling a stiff summer breeze flatten her linen skirts against her legs. She had been putting off dealing with Willard Croker until last, because it was going to be bad.

She entered the grimy log building, an anachronism in modern Cashbox, and found Croker breaking down type. He looked up and leered.

"You've come to complain. People always whine when their ox is gored."

"No, I came on business. I want to place an ad, and I have some job printing for you. A poster. But if you don't want it—"

He wiped his stained hands on a gray rag, and approached the counter. "Oh, I'm always open for business."

"You can have it if you stop picking on me and my club—and my personnel."

"Ah. I knew you'd get around to it. Sorry, sweetie. The heathen are the cause of our troubles. Cheap labor. They take jobs away from real Americans. We should ship them back to the Celestial Kingdom."

"The Lees have been excellent help. They do more than anyone else I've employed."

"And you pay them less. Which means everyone in town suffers. The Chinee never spend a cent. They send it all back to their tong lords, and they import more of the yellow devils."

"Willard Croker, there are exactly seven Chinese in Cashbox. And you're blaming the whole trouble on them."

"They'll do it every time," he said.

"I can see you're not interested."

"Oh, I didn't say I'm not interested. What've you in mind?"

She hesitated. "A two-by-six ad with new rates for the Exchange Hall. And some posters for the Cornet Band concert."

"Cash?"

"On my club account, same as everything else in town."

"I can't eat credit."

"Then you don't get the business. I'm good for it. I have assets."

"Ya sure do, sweetheart. Make me a deal."

She didn't like the insinuation. It had been that way between them from the beginning, but she would never get used to it. That didn't deserve an answer, so she turned toward the door.

"Hey, sweetie—I'm looking for stories. I hear rumors about the Giltedge. It's all horse apples, though. Who started them—Daley?"

She saw no reason to say a thing, and didn't.

"Well, here's how it is: all your scheming moneybags in the Exchange Club are putting the squeeze on the town, and I'm saying so in the next issue. Your old pal Daley, he's the worst. You know what all this is? A way to bust the union. A way to cut everyone's wage in half. Do you hear Trego hollering for a strike these days? Webb and Daley, they've cornered him at last. What a bunch of bloodsuckers. Silver prices down—ha! That little deal's been put together on Wall Street. Lower the price of silver. Then cut wages in half. Then raise the silver price again. They get cheap labor, so they all make a few million more clams. But meanwhile people like me go belly-up. There's not a dime in town. Your moneybags hid it all. Between the moneybags and the Chinese, it's a wonder any decent white man can live. That's what I'm saying in the next *Plain Truth*, sweetheart."

"I'll have my printing done in Livingston, Mister Croker. Don't say I didn't try to keep the business in Cashbox."

She banged the door upon the sound of his heckling.

CHAPTER 73
. . . .

The recipient of Thaddeus Webb's unbelieving scrutiny seemed more like a Continental dandy than a world-famous mining engineer and geologist. The apparition in Webb's office, R. Jackson Cain of New York City, wore a spotless double-breasted white suit, white spats, two-tone shoes the color of taffy, a brown bowtie with enormous polka dots, and French cuffs with links made of Mexican gold coins. He had the mournful brown eyes of a mortician, black hair slicked straight back, and a pencil-thin mustache.

It was plain from the look about him that he had experience handling terminal cases, and before it was over he would put the Giltedge in a winding sheet. He was the physician of last resort, only his patients were ailing mines. Like doctors in similar specialization, he had discovered that terminal disease is big business. His fee would be ten thousand dollars. In exchange for that fee, the owners of a mine could be well assured that the corpse was truly dead—or in the case of the Potlatch and a few other diggings, the heart still beat.

Con had brought him from the railroad station. Webb studied Con's face, looking for some reaction to the legendary Cain, but Daley's expression was pure poker. Old Baghote abandoned his clerking entirely and shamelessly gaped through the doorway, clucking to himself.

"Ah, Mister Cain. We've been waiting. Good of you to come."

"Goodness had little to do with it," Cain said in a silky voice. "It's all money."

"Well, if there's ore to be found, we're confident you'll find it."

"Usually there isn't."

"Well, what do you need? I've some diagrams of the works here."

Cain extracted a monocle from his pocket and twisted it into his right eye socket, where layers of bags propped it up. Then he studied the schematics of each level and the vertical cross-section charts, absorbing it all with one satanic eye. Webb swore that Cain ticked like a clock, but it was only imagination.

"All right, let me see some ore from each level, especially if there's gangue in it. And the assays."

An hour later, his homework done, Cain restored his monocle to its leather slip. "I need a place to change," he said.

Webb directed Cain to the water closet across the building. Cain hefted an enormous portmanteau, and vanished.

"Do you suppose his soul's as white as his suit, Con?"

"He spent years in Mexico. They all wear white down there."

"What do you think?"

"Undertakers should wear black."

"He's a man of few words."

"I admire it," Con said. "I talk too much. Make promises I can't keep."

"He didn't exactly proffer hope, did he?"

"That's why he's a legend. No flimflam. He's telling us the odds of rescuing a dead mine are a hundred to one."

"How'll we pay him? I'm spending about thirty days ahead of receipts."

Daley smiled thinly. "Salvage."

Cain reappeared in an outfit that made Webb think of hunting tigers in Siberia. Dangling from his shoulder was a compact canvas sack filled with mysterious items.

"It'll take a few hours. Will you gentlemen be accompanying me?"

"If you want us to."

"I'd rather prowl on my own. There's a crew down there?"

"We're cutting through a dike on the five-hundred-foot

level. I thought there might be values on the other side of it."

Cain nodded. "All right, then. I'll see you in a while. Tomorrow I might want to do some hiking. I can tell more from the surface indications. And maybe I should go into the Ophir."

"It's been closed for two years," Webb said. "Out of ore and flooded now. It was a pocket mine—they never did find a large body of ore."

Cain nodded. "Mines like that run on faith. They blunder from one pocket to another, and each time they hit ore they say they've finally come to the main body. I suppose you gentlemen are bursting with faith. Cain'll find more ore with his divining rod, which'll dip when the emanations strike it." He peered at each of them from his mortician's eye. "Faith is a bug that needs crushing. All right, then."

They escorted him through the shed to the gallowsframe and left him in charge of Coke Timmons. Moments later the earth gulped him.

Feeling apprehensive, Thaddeus walked back to his office. It surprised him that Con Daley kept pace. Webb sensed that Daley wanted to talk, or at least wanted to wait at the mine for news, like a member of the family waiting for the doctor's verdict.

"Well, now we wait," Daley said. "If you'd prefer, I'll leave you alone. I can pester Baghote."

"No, Con, stay." He really did want Con to stay, for some reason. "You don't need to go to town."

Daley nodded. "Misery loves company. I suppose the Giltedge has had its day. Of all the mines I've owned. . . ."

"I know, I know . . ." Webb muttered.

"My own thoughts embarrass me, Thaddeus. I'm sentimental. Of all those mines, the Giltedge was my favorite. I was drawn to it. I couldn't resist. I had to have it. I would have sold my soul to the devil for it. I had an ache, the kind of ache a man has when he suddenly sees the woman of his dreams, radiant, joyous—and happily married to someone else. Did you have favorites?"

Webb pondered it. "None was more difficult. None had richer ore. None was more rewarding. Most lasted longer. It's like dying at age thirty-five."

"Yes, a beauty dying young. That's why I can't bear it. Any other mine I'd shut down without a second thought. This one ... why, I'd pump my last cent into it just to keep its heartbeat going. There're times when I'm not a businessman at all. You know who told me that? Sylvie."

Thaddeus Webb stared at the man, discovering something tender in someone he had always regarded as a buccaneer. How could he like a man who had ruthlessly used a fluke of law to steal the Giltedge from its rightful owners? For years, he'd recoiled from Daley as one would from a leper. But in this moment, on these hard wooden seats, waiting for the death sentence, he felt a tentative affection for his employer.

"I still stand at that window and look at it, Con. I stand there, knowing I designed it, and much of what you see out there wasn't anything I'd learned at the Columbia School of Mines, either. It came from hard experience, from being humbled and frustrated, from—" He stopped suddenly, embarrassed.

Daley seemed amused. "Not even a puritan need be ashamed of pride, Thaddeus. I think you're grieving as much as I am. Only you have better reason to. I was inspired by—lust. Yes, and adultery. She was married to the Hammons. I lusted for her and I took her, only to have her die in my arms a few days ago. But you're a builder. You came here when there was nothing but a ten-foot gloryhole in that slope. Nothing but wilderness for leagues in all directions. And out of it you built the finest silver mine in the country."

"Con—you don't have to apologize—"

Daley laughed comfortably. "You didn't hear me apologizing. What's done is done. I made my choices as a young man. I chose to live by my wits. I thought it beat working. Everything's there for the taking. I was wrong, you know. But I'm not sorry about anything. Are you?"

Webb nodded. "Men died, and I could have prevented it. We bored down to a hundred feet and begun a crosscut to the ore—and a lot of rotten limestone trapped them. We couldn't get them out. They sat in there, alive but eating up the oxygen, waiting for us to break through. We were a few hours too late.... I didn't put enough timber in there."

"Thaddeus, my friend. Let go of it. I admire you. There are two kinds on this earth: producers, and takers. You're the rare kind. People like you create wealth. Your kind adds to everyone's comfort."

"You're bucking me up. You don't need to do that, Con."

They slid into silence while the clock ticked on, discovering kinship in the hour of doom. "I suppose we should talk about how to shut this down, Thaddeus."

Webb sighed. "Saturday's tally day. They'll be through the dike by then, I think. If there's nothing on the other side—that'll be it. Put the pink slip in the envelopes."

"And?"

"Salvage. But I hope to leave before then. I don't think I could stand dismantling what I've been building for eight years. Of course I'll stay if you insist, but—"

"I'm hoping you can manage a week or two more. Just to take bids on machinery. After that, Baghote could do much of it. If you get out soon enough, you'll be spared the sight of Cashbox dying. It's not pretty."

"Not much about mining's pretty. See how ugly it all is? The earth scarred, the slack pile that poisons the creek every time it rains, the rails and wires and rusting iron? Well, I don't apologize for it. That's what I built. I'd like to build another one, even better. I've learned from this devil, and I'll do it differently next time."

"There'll be a next time. There always is out here."

The whistle blew, and men began spilling from the cage each time it erupted from the earth. R. Jackson Cain stepped off the lift along with the others. Soon Webb and Daley would know.

CHAPTER 74

· · · · · · · · · · · · · · · · ·

Thaddeus Webb waited impatiently while R. Jackson Cain eased into one of Webb's bone-killer chairs. Cain shuffled assay reports until he had them arranged by depth, from surface to the five-hundred-foot level, and then perused each one, sometimes reacting to something with a mutter.

Webb fiddled with pencils. Daley stared. Outside, the gulch filled with afternoon shadow. Cain studied a topographic map of the area, and jotted some notes with a blunt pencil. Then at last he stretched in his chair and smiled.

"The Giltedge is a dead duck," he said.

Webb suspected that Cain was enjoying himself. "No ore?" he asked.

"Oh, there's some ore above, but it would all be mopping up. And not at seventy cents an ounce."

"And below?"

"You've run into the igneous stock of Elk Peak. That granite boss is what uplifted the sedimentaries. The porphyry dikes trailing off it are igneous intrusions. At higher levels, you're moving farther into sedimentaries and away from their junction with the igneous stock. There won't be ore there. You could drive an exploratory crosscut west at the three- or four-hundred-foot level. I wouldn't risk it myself."

"Should we continue our bore through the dike?"

"It's probably several hundred feet wide, with decomposed granite on the other side. Like the ones in the old Gill claim—the Hangfire part of your works. You cut through two dikes there, and I measured them. It's true that the ore in this district is located along those dikes. But I'd say no."

"Continue the bore when the price of silver rises?"

"There are always faith healers, aren't there? Once in a while they're right."

"What about a new shaft higher on Cashbox Mountain? Say, five hundred yards west of the present one?" Webb asked.

Cain grunted. "According to your assays, your ore got better as you went lower. The salts were deposited by aqueous solution, percolated upward from the igneous stock. Of course you may enjoy squandering money."

"Is that it?" asked Daley.

"Oh, I'll poke around for a few days. It might give me some clues about future exploration. This is some of the most complex structural geology I've seen. Ore's a real possibility. But it won't change my verdict about the here and now. All it'll do is suggest whether to hang on to the property or sell it."

Webb sighed. "Thank you, Mister Cain."

"There's the matter of my embalming fee. When I locate ore, I call it my surgical fee."

"You'll be paid, sir," said Daley.

"Of course I will, but will I have it before the turn of the century?"

"Sixty days."

"That's about the usual. The salvage price of a few steam engines. I'll have a report written for you before I leave. Perhaps you'll let me borrow your clerk's typing machine. I'm a two-finger whiz. I can leave copies for you and the Hammons. Death certificates, that's what they'll be. Pity, isn't it? Nice little burg."

"There are scores of good mines here," Daley said.

Cain smiled. "And together they produce less than a quarter of the ore in the whole district. This mine produced three-quarters of all the ore. Most are closed because of seventy-cent silver. But maybe you know something about Cashbox I don't know."

Daley sighed. "It was wishful thinking, Jackson. Is that how you wish to be addressed? You have the advantage of me."

"Call me Mister Cain. I've the devil's own time fighting familiarity. It's a western vice." He smiled. "I'll be dining at the Palace chophouse. I hope you gents and your ladies will join me. We'll talk about happier things."

They agreed to meet him at seven, and watched him hike back to Cashbox. A heaviness pervaded the office. Webb studied the hard, mean room from which he had directed a great enterprise for so long. He grieved. Everything seemed different. The solid office building had turned into rice paper. Those great structures out there had been transformed into scrap.

"I suppose we'd better make plans, Thaddeus. Not that I feel like it. But the sooner the better."

Webb rubbed his eyes. "I know. I've been thinking about it for days. We've three days to payday. Time enough to get everything out of the hole. I'll have Coke hunt for any profitable ore at each level. Then we can pull up the ore cars, tools, and anything else. I'll have Baghote make out the pink slips. I'll cancel some orders. Tell our firewood suppliers and the charcoal makers. We've got some pump parts on order in Colorado, the Pueblo foundries. I'll cancel by wire. You'll need to tell me what to do about services—insurance, bonding, all of that. You'll have to tell me what you want done with everything here. The records. Desks, safe, chairs."

"That desk of yours will make good firewood if anyone's left in town to burn it."

Webb laughed. "I saved sixteen dollars by having it made in the shop."

"We'll have to get bids on the heavy equipment. Baghote can do some of that. Oh, we'll work it out. I hope you'll stay on, Thaddeus. I need you for a fortnight."

Thaddeus sighed. Duty, again. Why did he always respond to duty? Other, happier men ducked it and did what they pleased. "A fortnight," he muttered.

"Two weeks to bury your mine, eh? It's yours, top to bottom."

"It's more than a mine, Con. It—it was hope and steady wages. It was wealth. It was silver to eat with, or coin into dollars. Silver to make light-sensitive plates for photographers. Silver to make mirrors. Teapots. Jewelry. And the lead, why it's used everywhere. Newspapers. Electrical batteries. Foundries. White lead's a pigment in paint. Lead and tin make solder—how could we get along without solder? Shot and bullets. Pipe—think of all the lead pipe.

"Why, this mine made a town, a city. It made neighbors."

"I hadn't much thought about it."

"The need won't go away, you know. This mine's dead but the world'll need lead and silver. Con, it's not just for this generation. We're building a good life for all the generations to come."

Daley stood restlessly. "The pair of us are avoiding the main thing. We've got to tell them." He gestured downward.

"They know."

"We still have to say something. The second shift starts in a few minutes. Shall we go out there?"

Webb sagged. "Do we have any reason to keep it a secret? Hold off until payday?"

"None that I know of. The men may as well have as much notice as we can give them."

"But Cashbox, Con. The whole town. . . ." He didn't want to think about how people would take the news.

"We have to do hard things sometimes," Daley said. "Are you up to telling them?"

"No, but I will. It's a duty."

"I'll come with you. Maybe that'll help."

"It'll help."

They walked to the shed and then to the headframe, where miners were waiting for the whistle. Men stared, and Webb knew what they were thinking. He spotted Big Bull Focher, the night shift foreman, and drew him aside.

"It's dead. Cain's verdict was negative," Webb said.

Focher sighed. "That's no surprise."

"I'm announcing it. We'll keep on until tally day. That's three days to clean out everything, even tramrails if you can. But I want you to look for stray ore, every level, and go after it with one face crew."

Focher nodded. "I'll do it. Some may quit right now."

"Tell them they'll have to wait until tally day for pay, and they'll simply lose three days. You'll keep track?"

"You bet. This ain't gonna be fun."

"No, and telling them's not going to be, either. But it's better than handing them an envelope with a blasted pink slip in it."

"They'll like that—that you told them in person."

"It's been less than an hour since we got the news from Cain."

Focher nodded. "I'll hold the lift. You waiting for the whistle?"

"That's when they'll all be here."

They stood for another five minutes in the somber light. The night shift men looked unusually solemn.

The whistle shrilled. Then Thaddeus Webb, standing at the headframe, told them.

"We've run out of ore," he said, his voice cracking. "We'll keep going until tally day. I'm sorry."

CHAPTER 75

● ● ● ● ● ● ● ● ● ● ● ● ● ● ● ● ●

Hugh Trego couldn't bear Anna's tears any longer. Neither could he bear the solemn stares of his girls, or Anna's question: "Oh, what'll we do now?" She had asked it twenty times, and he had no answer for her.

What he would do now was flee to the Carbonate Miners Saloon. He banged the door behind him and stalked down Granite Street. An awful silence gripped the city.

Behind all those doors frightened people were wringing their hands, praying, trying to make some plans—and wondering where their next meal would come from.

It wasn't a normal July night, with doors and windows open, children and dogs caroming through the streets, and the band practicing in the schoolyard. It was hushed and mean, as if everyone had just received the Last Judgment and been given a few hours to straighten their affairs before descending to the Pit.

He pushed through the battered doors into dead silence, but not the quiet of an empty room. All his friends stood there, and many miners he didn't know well. They had gathered unbidden, a last meeting of the brotherhood who braved the bowels of the earth and darkness six days a week. He sensed they had been waiting for him, as if he alone could give voice to their hopelessness and grief.

He would try. He stared tenderly at them all. Why, there was Polweal at the bar, clutching a five-cent beer as if it would be his last on earth. And old Trenoweth, weakened with miner's lung but made of oak. And two Penroses from the other shift. And not just the Cousins, either. Why, there was O'Rourke, McCarthy and Carney. And down at the bend stood Hans Doppler and Serge Krivitzky. Even Kermit Reilly, who had become a clerk in the Hammon mercantile.

Joe Wales drew a mug of draft beer and handed it to Trego, dripping foam. Hugh dug in his britches for some change.

"Ah, no, Hugh. For you it's on the house."

Hugh lifted his mug and sipped, even as he discovered fifty men he knew, most of them Knights of Labor, the men of the pits. The men who always suffered the most.

"It's a bad time," he said, but his words were sucked into a void. A few men were doing some serious guzzling. Wales was refilling mugs as fast as he could settle the foam in them.

"I couldn't stand the old lady," Hugh said to no one in

particular, and then felt bad that he had said it. He treated Anna badly and didn't know why. "She was carrying on so."

"She's thinking about empty stomachs," said Trenoweth. "She's thinking maybe she'll have to give up her girls. Damme, we all should be home comforting them."

"No, we shouldn't. We should be right here," said a miner from the Delirium Tremens. "We've business."

Trego wondered what business the man had in mind.

"Where be you going, Hugh?" asked Sam Fenno.

"Butte, I guess. Where else is there?"

"Nay, there's not a job in Butte. Every miner in the state's gone there. Copper they're digging, but there's not a job."

"Butte it is," Trego said stubbornly. "Butte's a union town, and the union'll look after us."

"Well, damme, old son, that brings up a little something that needs sayin'. There's a bit in the strike fund," said Fenno.

"Oh, no you don't, me beautay! That all goes to the Knights. It's in our charter. They've a need for every cent, and if a local dissolves, they get the loose change."

"But it's ours, Hugh." Anger laced Polweal's words.

"You'll bleddy well forget it."

"Hugh—what's a union for, anyway?" It was Tim Trenoweth this time, Hugh's old nemesis. "Is it for us, or is it for the big shots? Now, Hugh Trego, you'll get it out of the bank tomorrow and you'll divide it up. There's mouths to feed, and places to get to, and tickets to buy."

Trego felt the old heat building in him. "It's a strike fund, and it'll stay a strike fund, and it's going to the Knights."

"Well, me beautay, I feel a strike comin' on. It feels like the ague. Don't you?" Trenoweth was grinning like a fox. "That Giltedge, I've got some grievances. It's turned around and quit payin' us. After Saturday we'll not see a nickel in the brown envelope. Makes an old boy mad."

"Makes me plenty mad," McCarthy yelled from across the room. "We got enough here; let's vote."

"Ah, now, you'll bleddy well forget it."

"Oh, no, you don't. This here meeting of the Knights of Labor's in session," said Fenno.

"Do I git to vote?" asked Wales.

"You've been a member since you spilled the first foam, Joe."

"All right then," Fenno yelled. "Seein's how we got grievances, all in favor of striking the Giltedge—"

"Hold up. Not jist the Giltedge. Every mine in the district," someone yelled.

"Good idear. All in favor—"

A chorus of yesses and a few hoots and whistles drowned out the rest.

"Opposed?" asked Fenno.

They all stared at Trego. But Hugh only sipped his beer.

"Damme, we're on strike, Hugh. You can fetch her out of the bank."

Hugh laughed. "You'd hang me by me bleddy neck if I don't," he muttered. "All right. I'll visit John Oliver Cromwell first thing, and we'll hand it out. Let every man know."

Something hard dissolved in him, as it always did when he was among his kind; men he loved, men he would die for. "It won't be much. Maybe ten or twelve dollars a man. But it'll buy a ticket to Butte. If the Cashbox and Northern's still running. I want to say—" A rush of feeling swept him. "I want to say I'm bleddy proud to know all you beautays."

"Where's everyone going, eh? I hear there's gold and silver mines running in Colorado," someone said.

"Sure, and every laid-off miner in Leadville's applying."

"There's diggings all over Nevada."

"How about the Homestake? That's a gold mine big enough to hire us all. And just over in Dakota, too."

"Old Hearst, he's a moneybags, and he's partial to miners. I'd say that's a place to go. Black Hills, why, they're nice as Cashbox."

Cashbox. The name retrieved them from imaginary excursions. They huddled in a wounded town, a city with a cobbled street and more promised, brick buildings, an opera house, a dance hall, fancy hotels, and a good school.

"I'm not going anywhere," Trenoweth said. "I've got me a snug cottage. I can't make a payroll any more anyway, not with miner's lung. Why, this'll pass. Cashbox'll be prettier than ever. You boys just remember to come back and see how pretty she is. I'm going to sit on my porch and take the sun each day."

"Who's staying?" Trego asked. "I'm thinking, the ones that stay can look after the houses of them that go, taking care of things. Maybe these cottages'll sell some day. All it'll take is some ore. Lots of mining towns, they start to die but never do."

"I paid twenty-five for the lot, and two hundred for the house, and now it's not worth a plugged nickel," McCarthy grumbled.

Trego counted a dozen men who were planning to stay on and scrape by. There'd be a lot of salvage a man could live on for a while.

"All right, Tim," he said. "You see who they are. Maybe we can send you a bit if you look after our places."

"Ah, Hugh, they'll go to pieces in a few months. A place has to be lived in. Vandals—"

"They're not worth saving," someone said.

"This is a tough city," Trenoweth said. "Good times will come again."

They drank deep into the evening, as if to stave off the reality that would smack them when they stepped into the darkness outside. In many of their cottages wives waited, their lamps extinguished to save oil, for their men to come home and tell them what their fate might be.

No one knew. The New York Stock Exchange had crashed on June 27th, sending a shiver even through distant Cashbox. Banks were failing. Businesses were dying.

The Philadelphia and Reading Railroad had failed. Where would a good powder man get a job? Where could he get some other work? How would a man feed his bleddy family?

Trego walked to his cottage that night feeling as helpless as he had ever felt in his life. Things ganged up on workingmen. The bleddy capitalists would survive; but a man with no job and a family to feed—why, he was alone in a mean world.

He felt the strangest ache in his heart. In a few days, everyone he had known for eight years would scatter to the winds. It was as if they had never shared the dangers of the pit, or rejoiced in squeezing something out of old Webb, or celebrated a new contract, or quaffed beer at a Fourth of July picnic or spun a waltz at the Exchange Hall, or listened to the Cornet Band play good Sousa marches all summer long.

The anger boiled in him, and the old tension too. He glanced at the sporting district up the slope, wishing he could bury himself there. But it lay solemn and quiet, half-deserted.

He swallowed his rage and walked resolutely back to his cottage, where Anna would be waiting.

CHAPTER 76

C ornelius loved the way sunlight seemed to gather around Sylvie in that clubroom. She and her Exchange Club had become bonded into some sort of mysterious unity. The club completed her and made her whole. It had become her most important part. And that was worrying him more and more.

"Well," she said, "you've other mines."

"None like the Giltedge. That was the best of them all. I just didn't expect it would be a shallow one." He sighed.

"Optimism is a weakness. It feeds on hope. Realism is the only strength a mortal can possess."

"But Con—you're diversified. You'll be all right."

He nodded. "My gold mines are prospering. The ones where silver's a byproduct are surviving. But not the silver mines. I own two and have a controlling interest in three others. Sylvie, three-quarters of my holdings are in trouble."

"I know. A hundred percent of mine are."

"There's still the future, though. Cain spent a day hiking above the mine. He believes the dike that lies alongside the Giltedge runs for miles toward Elk Peak. He thought there might be more ore along it. He suggested that we hang on to the property and even buy claims above us. But that's not for the here and now. We're too strapped to do anything."

"Oh, it'll all come back. It always does."

There it was again. He'd never known a person to dismiss trouble the way she did. It was the ultimate optimism. "Sylvie? No. I don't think you're grasping—"

"Cashbox isn't going to die, if that's what you're trying to tell me."

"It could. Look out the window and see what your eyes tell you."

She set down her teacup and did exactly that, studying Cashbox Street below her. The way the window light played over her slim form transfixed him.

"What do you see?" he asked.

"Horses and wagons and traffic."

"And what's in the wagons?"

"Oh, Con, so a bunch of people leave. They're ones with no roots. The first moment something goes wrong, they throw everything into their wagons and go somewhere else, like—tumbleweeds."

"Sylvie—" He wanted to help her face the reality of these times. "Sylvie, is the club making money?"

"It's making money, but lots of members are in arrears."

"How about your bar tabs? And the hall rentals?"

"Well, those'll pick up after this panic is over. I'm scheduling the Cornet Band."

He grunted. He had seen three band members roll out that morning, their creaking wagons overburdened with furniture and trunks.

"You might not sell many tickets."

"Something's better than nothing. They've always loved the band."

"What about dances?"

She shrugged. "I'll get some in the fall. People spend the summers outside."

"The Opera House shut yesterday. Gleason and Magee didn't make it."

"All the better for me. The fall tours'll start soon. Maybe I can get Lotta Crabtree. She's touring."

"And who'll come, Sylvie?"

"Cornelius, just because the Giltedge is laying off a couple hundred miners doesn't mean that the whole town is collapsing."

Daley knew he was getting nowhere, but he had to try. "Every seat on the morning train was sold. They're running an extra coach tomorrow. As long as they have the traffic. But after that. . . ."

"After that they'll run trains three times a week instead of each day. That's what you're saying. When it gets better they'll run daily again."

"The Cashbox and Northern's lost forty thousand in six months."

"How do you know?"

"Henry Hammon told me. I don't know how to say this, but you've got to consider moving. We all do."

"How can you say such a thing?"

"I've seen mining towns decline. Virginia City, Nevada. Tombstone, Arizona. The ore gives out and that's it. People just walk away from property. What else can they do? I'm sorry. You've got to face it."

"But Con—" She walked to the massive stone wall and

touched it, and the gold-tasseled damask drapes, and the wainscoting. "This isn't paper."

"That's right. It's built to last centuries, and maybe it will."

"I can't get the price I want for it, so I'll wait it out. Is anything wrong with that? Maybe I'm wrong. I don't know. I don't have any crystal ball."

He paused, wondering how he could tell her what it was worth. "Coming back here a while ago, I wanted to get a haircut from Ike Cobb. But the door was locked. I rattled it, and looked in. It was dark. He's got a marble counter where he kept all his bottles and combs. Not a thing on it. He's got a big barber chair, fanciest one made, Emil Paider and Company. You sit in it and feel like a duke while you get a ten-cent trim. It swivels and tilts, and there's a foot lever so Ike could raise or lower it. Big plush seat, black leather. A nickel-plated foot pedestal. That thing cost a lot of money. Then I found a little sign on the door. Closed, won't be back, it said. He left it. That chair must run three hundred pounds and he didn't have a dime to ship it out."

"I think the club should have a tonsorial parlor. I'll get one."

Con laughed. Sylvie would always be Sylvie. "That was a long way of saying that things are bad. I don't think you could sell this building for a hundred dollars now. I don't think you could sell your house at all. Look at it this way, Sylvie. There's not a soul in here. It started weeks ago, with the stock market crash. I could name a dozen members on your books you haven't seen for two months. The books, Sylvie—nice numbers in columns, receivables, payables—it's all illusion."

"Oh, the books may be but the city isn't. Look at it. All that's wrong is the lack of cash."

"Lack of cash is like lack of blood. Your heart quits beating without it. I talked to Loren Whitmore today. They're thinking about folding up the Palace. They used to get a lot of trade from the drummers, people doing mining business. It dried up. Not one customer last night. No one in the restaurant, either. He and Walsh Lake are hoping to auction it. They think maybe a big auction'll give them some getaway cash. But they didn't know who'd bid. Maybe someone in Bozeman for the salvage."

"Maybe I'll bid on it. I could afford it. I don't know what I'll do. Oh, this is so confusing."

"Sylvie . . . there's no ore. That's all you need to know. *No ore*."

"You just told me there might be lots of ore."

He didn't reply because it was futile to speculate about the ore. He wished he could know. Some camps did revive. Leadville had bounced up and down a few times. "I hope you're right, Sylvie. I hope that someone strikes gold. Or copper. That's what happened at Butte. It started as a silver camp and ended up a copper town. Sylvie, you're certainly an optimist."

"Oh, I'm just me. When you come from an explosives family, you aren't very regular. My grandfather ate gunpowder soup. That was after daddy was born. I start gentlemen's clubs. You've got to make allowances for the Duvaliers.

"Con? Do you remember the first time we met, in the stagecoach, coming to Cashbox? You asked me what I was doing, and I told you I was chasing rainbows. Well, here's the end of the rainbow. Cashbox, Montana, of all places. I've had such a happy time. Why, I've been to more plays and variety shows here, Eddie Foy, Sarah Bernhardt, right downstairs in this building. And I got some of the box office.

"I've had more fun. We've had more balls downstairs, oh, grand balls with string orchestras and wearing all those beautiful things you gave me. I've been more successful than I ever dreamed I could be. Why should I leave? I'm going to weather the bad times."

"You may not be able to some day."

"Well, I'll cross that bridge—"

"Sylvie. Come to Helena. Let's make a good life there.

I have everything. You'll have everything, and especially my love for as long as I draw breath."

"Oh, Con. . . ."

"I would have gone back long ago but for you. I've kept two domestics all these years. I didn't need to be here, especially with a man like Webb running the mine. In fact, it's much easier there than here—banks, contacts, mining companies, brokerages. The governor, the state offices. But I stayed here, Sylvie. Being with you is worth more than anything else."

"I know."

"Ask what you will, and I'll give it to you. But come with me. I've wanted you for as long as I've known you. I'll not be complete until we say our vows. There's more to life than things and wealth. Sacred pledges, trust, shared dreams. . . . Sylvie, those things are worth more to us than a hundred good mines. Is there anything richer than a shared life?"

"You're so dear, Con. I just burst."

"Would you think about it?"

"Of course I will. And if Cashbox springs back, would you stay here? I want you here."

He smiled. "You couldn't keep me away."

CHAPTER 77

• • • • • • • • • • • • • • • • •

The clock ticked toward four. Thaddeus Webb stalked the offices like a man about to be executed. From time to time he glared out the grimy windows, seeing what he didn't want to see. Both shifts were stowing the last of the rails ripped from the bowels of the mine. Then the cage popped from the earth. Coke Timmons and Big Bull Focher stepped off it, looking solemn. The two foremen had made a final sweep of every level of the old mine.

There was nothing more to do. Ore cars, rails, tools, explosives were above ground and locked away. Men gathered silently around the headframe, waiting for the tick of the clock. The mill had run the last of the ore and had fallen silent.

The minute hand pointed straight up. The mine whistle blew, the shrieking of a dying animal. It never stopped. It wailed its dirge into the afternoon, echoing down toward Cashbox where it would raise goosebumps on the flesh of all who heard it. It blew and blew, never stopping, steam boiling from its throat. Its howl set his teeth on edge. It pierced his flesh. But it never stopped. It echoed up the mountain, a lamentation before the throne of God, and down the mountain to the gates of hell.

And then, slowly, it died as the last of the steam in the boilers escaped its throat. The Giltedge Mine lay silent. Something had passed away, like the mortal soul. Men lifted their hats in some unconscious gesture of respect for the dead. The moment passed, and they shuffled toward the pay window, where Baghote waited to hand out 177 brown envelopes filled with greenbacks and coin from the company safe.

Baghote somehow knew them all. As each silent man reached the window, the clerk pencilled a check beside a name and handed the man his envelope. No one spoke, not even a farewell. A few proffered a fleeting smile, sometimes to Baghote, sometimes to Webb, who stood by, watching. Seventy, eighty passed the window, and then Hugh Trego materialized.

"Mister Trego, could I see you a moment?" Webb asked.

Trego glared. "Gonna shake my lunch bucket, are you?"

Webb didn't respond, and a moment later the Cousin Jack stepped in. Webb nodded him to his office and closed the door.

"It's a bad time," Webb said.

"Bad for us. Not bad for you. I don't suppose you'll miss a bleddy meal."

"That's what I want to see you about. Mrs. Webb and I,

we've decided to do what we can. There are people in trouble. We know that. No money, no place to go, and not even enough to buy a ticket."

"I don't want any of your bleddy capitalist charity, Webb."

Webb was not put off. "It's something that Mrs. Webb and I decided to do. We need your help. Is there anyone in Cashbox who needs a hand? We can spare something."

"Trying to salve your damned consciences, are you?"

A faint irritation built in Webb. "I don't feel guilty about running out of ore, Hugh."

"Don't you first-name me, Webb. It's the bleddy system. You'll walk away fat and comfortable, and these men out there'll walk away desperate."

"I'm not good at reforming the world, Mister Trego. But I can help a little. I want to."

Something died in Trego, as if a lit fuse had pinched out. "There's one comes to mind. Mrs. Flower. She lost her man in the Ophir years ago, and she's been scraping along, barely putting food on her table."

"I know her."

"She hasn't even a dime. Her boy's gone off to Butte, but he don't send her anything."

"Has she kin back east?"

"She does, but she told me she wants to go to Seattle. It's better in the West, she says. She wants to see the ocean. I was going to give her a little from the strike fund, but that bleddy John Cromwell was off fishing yesterday. When you need cash you can't get it from your locked-up banks."

Webb slipped some greenbacks into an envelope and wrote her name on it. "This'll get her and some baggage to Portland. With some to spare. I'll want you to deliver this, and keep it anonymous. Say it's from your union fund if you wish. Now who else, Mister Trego?"

Hugh Trego thought of six more, all mine widows who lacked the means even to leave Cashbox. Quietly Webb slid bills into envelopes and wrote names. Then he handed the seven envelopes to Trego.

"Well, Trego. Good luck wherever you're going. You'll look after your own, wherever that'll be."

But the lion of the Knights of Labor didn't reply. Tears leaked from his eyes. Webb thrust a hand out, and Trego shook it hard and then fled.

The tally had ended, and Baghote was putting away his records. For two more weeks Webb and Baghote would occupy these offices, arranging for salvage. But the Giltedge Mine was history. Webb slipped outside and wandered through the works. The sheds stood black and solemn. The cage stood above ground, padlocked there with a chain. How many times, he wondered, had it descended into the darkness with its load of brave men? How many times had it ascended with rich ores?

He walked to the mill amid a strange hush. The giant ore crushers stood cold and dead, the California stamp batteries silent, their half-ton hammers poised to pulverize anything under them. The tanks had been drained of their lethal chemicals but a man walking inside of them could still die from the fumes.

He exited into afternoon sun, and walked out the trestle to the slack pile which formed a stupendous mountain. Every pound of it had been mucked out by miners. Another mountain of tailings lay beneath the mill and smelter. One could find good ore in the waste, and he knew that in a few days the Chinese would slip in and mine the slack piles patiently to make a few cents an hour.

It all seemed so strange. But the sight didn't oppress his spirit. There would always be more mines to build. The world had barely begun to mine the treasures in the earth. He walked through the slack afternoon to the offices and found that Baghote had left. He locked up, wondering uneasily whether anything would be vandalized.

He walked home, thinking about Portia. She had been a good soldier. In a fortnight they would be free to go anywhere. Take a holiday. They had scarcely had a holiday since they were married. And after that . . . he didn't know.

She was waiting for him. The door opened even as he set foot on his veranda.

"Thaddeus, dear."

"Why, Portia. . . ."

She looked lovely, and the realization of it sent a small pleasant awareness through him. She closed the door behind him, plucked his eternal briefcase from him, and then slid her arms around his neck and drew him to her, holding him as one infinitely precious. Holding him in the woman's way that heals a man's wounds and releases him from his cares. He responded, feeling the warm pressure of this woman who had chosen to share a life with him. She was saying something without words, and her message buoyed his spirits.

"Tea, dear?" she asked, and without waiting for a reply, drew him into the parlor where everything was ready. She filled a Wedgwood cup and handed it to him.

"Did it go well, Thaddeus?"

"As well as could be expected, I guess."

"Did Mister Trego—"

"He did know of some. He was grateful."

"What did he say?"

"Well, he didn't really. You have to know him. But he was grateful."

"Thaddeus, you must be blue."

"No, not really. Empty. I'm full of hollowness, if that makes any sense to you."

"That's what I knew you would be. Each mine fills you up. But the Giltedge emptied you. I've been thinking about you, dear, and I found just the thing in Tennyson that I want to say to you. But I didn't have the words."

She opened the morocco-bound book to a page she had selected, and read:

Oh yet we trust that somehow good
Will be the final goal of ill,

> To pangs of nature, sins of will,
> Defects of doubt, and taints of blood;
>
> That nothing walks with aimless feet;
> That not one life shall be destroy'd,
> Or cast as rubbish to the void,
> When God hath made the pile complete;
>
> That not a worm is cloven in vain;
> That not a moth with vain desire
> Is shrivell'd in a fruitless fire,
> Or but subserves another's gain.
>
> Behold we know not anything;
> I can but trust that good shall fall
> At last—far off—at last, to all,
> And every winter change to spring.
>
> So runs my dream; but what am I?
> An infant crying in the night:
> An infant crying for the light:
> And with no language but a cry.

"Thaddeus, there's good in everything we do; good in all you've achieved. Good in the sweet life you've given me."

Thaddeus withdrew a handkerchief and blew his nose.

CHAPTER 78
· · · · · · · · · · · · · · · ·

Hugh Trego stood numbly before the Cashbox Bank, desolated by the sign on the door. Closed until further notice. He wasn't alone. Half a dozen others stared mutely at the perfidious sign, announcing the death of hope and dreams. He wanted to withdraw the strike fund. That bank still had two thousand dollars belonging to the Knights of Labor, and he would bleddy well get it even if he had to wring Cromwell's neck.

He rattled the door. He pressed his nose to the glass and peered into the gloom. The bank was as quiet as a grave. Wild rage. built up in him. Scores of miners were counting on the miserable bit of cash to help them leave. For some, who had been laid off for months, it was all they could hope for. But now the doors were locked and that rich swine had locked their money inside and walked away.

"It failed," someone said.

"There was a run on it Thursday. Maybe he'll open when he gets more cash in," said another.

"Naw, once they fail, they're done. He had a lot of bad loans. You can't keep your doors open when nobody pays back a loan."

"You're giving him too much credit," muttered an old man. "It's just a polite way to rob poor people like you and me. He should be strung up."

Which expressed Trego's views perfectly. He needed something to kick. Something to blow to smithereens. He could almost feel the waxy paper of a stick of dynamite; almost feel his muscles tapping through the red brick and planting a dozen sticks inside that rotten bank; almost feel himself touching off the Bickford fuse, and watching it spit into the bank, until the pile of bricks erupted into the sky.

He unclenched his fists and stalked up Castle Street toward Robinson, where Cromwell was hiding in his fancy frame house. Trego would have it out with the banker. A few minutes later he banged on the door. Mrs. Cromwell opened it, looked him up and down, took alarm and vanished inside. Then John Oliver Cromwell materialized.

"Look, Trego, I'm as sorry as anyone—"

"You bleddy crook, stealing loaves from the poor, taking the last crust from the hungry."

Cromwell sighed. "There's nothing I can do. There's not a cent in that safe. We had a run Thursday. There wasn't much anyway. Eighty percent of my loans were failing, default, nothing coming in. The bottom dropped out."

"I've got two hundred miners waiting for their money, and you're going to get it for me."

"I guess I'd better go there and show you the safe. There's not a cent in the bank."

"You'll get it right now, you bleddy—"

"Mister Trego, listen. From one end of this country to the other, there's been a collapse. The stock market. The government. It's got only eighty million of gold left in the Treasury to back our currency. No one has any money. There isn't any. Five hundred banks failed this year. Thousands of businesses."

"It's the system. You bleddy crooks, you've found another way to cheat the poor."

"Well, I agree with you, to a degree."

Trego stopped, astonished.

"This is called deflation. Prices have dropped steadily for several years. The eastern bankers call it sound money, but it isn't sound. Sound money keeps its value over time. If its value changes it isn't sound. Inflation cheats creditors. Deflation cheats debtors. They have to pay back loans with dollars that are worth more than the dollars they borrowed. Yes, I agree, sir. The debtor West has been broken by the financiers of the East, you and me along with the rest."

"I don't follow this stuff you're talking about. But you and your kind, you'll roast in hell. I promised a bit of cash to hungry men to buy a bit of bread for starving children, and you give me fancy words."

Cromwell looked shaken. "Starving? Is that so?"

"Starving," Trego said.

Cromwell sighed. "All right. I have a hundred dollars. Mrs. Cromwell and I, why, we hoped to go somewhere, start over. God knows where. I've lost eighty thousand of money entrusted to me. *Eighty thousand.* And I'm responsible for all of it. I'll keep on owing it until I pay it. The law says I owe it, and so does conscience, even though it isn't my fault. I owe your Knights over two thousand. I'll give you the hundred. It's a start." He wheeled into the room, and reappeared with five double eagles. "Buy bread for the children, sir."

Trego stared at the white-faced banker, took the coins and stalked away wordlessly. He'd be damned if he would thank the man. He stalked back to Main Street, seething with emotions that crawled like lice. He stormed into the Carbonate Miners Saloon—or tried to. The doors didn't yield. He kicked a door, but only stubbed his toe. Cursing, he swung around to the window and peered in. The Carbonate had died. Wales wasn't there. Neither were there bottles on the backbar. He could make out the billiard table in the dusk at the rear.

"Damn you, Wales, you couldn't wait one day!" he yelled.

He had a hundred dollars to give to the men. He could give a dollar to a hundred men. He stalked up the gulch to the Giltedge boardinghouse, where fifty bachelors bunked. The solemn quiet of the gulch scraped his nerves. It was usually choked with ore wagons and people. He eyed the Giltedge, feeling itchy again, hungering to break a padlock and steal a box of Hercules and some fuse. He'd blow up half of Cashbox, starting with the bank, then the Palace Hotel, and then that bleddy Exchange Club.

He stormed into the boardinghouse, into a wall of silence. The doors to the cubicles stood ajar. He peered in, discovering desolation. "Where are you?" he roared. "Where are you bleddy miners?" But he found not a man. It shook him. The brave men he had known for years had dispersed into a void. They had vanished on the morning passenger trains, or walked, or hitched rides with teamsters, or bummed in a freight car. "Fenno! Polglase!" he cried, hearing only echoes.

But they were bachelors. All they had to do was load a trunk or a bag and go. There would still be Knights in their cottages; the family men who needed the money the worst. He stalked out of the gloomy building, and was amazed by the sun. He blinked. The world hadn't changed. Cashbox Creek purled by. The eternal mountain vaulted upward behind the Giltedge. A dozen birds soared above him. A quieter mood filled him, and he walked pensively toward his own neighborhood, where humble cottages stood cheek by jowl.

He tried the Polweals first. They were packing. Mary's face was tear-smudged. Hugh pulled Tom aside and showed him the gold. "It's a bit. Two dollars is yours."

Polweal shook his head. "I can't make change. Why, Hugh, I don't have a wooden nickel."

Trego cursed the gold in his hand. He knew that not one of the miners in his neighborhood could make change. "All right, I'll think of something. I'll get some change. Take heart. We'll all take heart. We're brothers of the pits."

Wearily, Trego trudged back to Main Street. He tried Baker's Mercantile, but old man Baker had no cash. He tried two dead hotels and a dead restaurant. He rattled doors that were locked. He turned onto Cashbox and tried the Palace. Surely those rich bloodsuckers would have a bit of change. But the door didn't yield. He peered in upon blackness. He kicked the door, defeated. He had a hundred dollars in gold that he couldn't even break.

Then it came to him. He walked down the long slope to the railroad station and the yards and roundhouse of the Cashbox and Northern. The railroad would make change. Around the station baggage lay in heaps, destined for the next express car. But he saw not a soul. There wouldn't be a train until late that night. His boots echoed hollowly as he approached the grilled ticket window, and then his heart leapt.

"Kermit Reilly, you're selling tickets?"

"I am. It's fifty cents a day, but it buys me chow."

"Well, I'm glad to see you. Kermit, boy, I need change. Dollar bills, for this." He thrust the gold coins across the counter.

Kermit looked dismayed. "I can't do that. I don't have it here, and they don't let me into the safe."

"Can you do a little? Break a twenty?"

"I—we're so short. . . ."

Defeat clutched Hugh Trego. And then inspiration. "Look, boy, I'm going to give you this. It's for the men. It's union money. Any miner that wants a ticket, you take it out of this. Any miner, his wife, his children, his baggage. You use this up until it's gone."

"I don't know . . . ah, Hugh, I will. I'll make it work."

Trego laughed, and Kermit did too, though the young man scarcely knew why. "I'll be seeing you, boy. Give it all out, to the last bleddy cent."

"Count on me, Hugh Trego."

"I'll tell any miner I see. So they know."

"I will, too."

Trego stumbled home, too weary to think. He had done all he could. The town reflected his weariness back upon him. No one was on the streets. He wondered how many had left, and where they had gone. Somewhere. The world seemed impossibly large and lonely. Men he loved were vanishing into it; men he loved would soon be memories.

It was time to pack and leave for Butte. He didn't have it in him to console Anna.

CHAPTER 79

• • • • • • • • • • • • • • • • •

Minnie had absconded. Willard Croker stared numbly at the naked rooms. The plump madam and her four nymphs had hopped the morning train while he was toiling at the paper. Summary divorce, that's what it was, Croker thought. And without benefit of the courts.

They had contended the night before. Minnie proclaimed that Cashbox was a dead rat, while Croker counseled patience. He agreed that Cashbox had cashed in, but he saw the possibilities of salvage.

Willard sighed. He lacked even a dime. And now his meal ticket had vanished, along with his pneumatic consolation each night. He didn't grieve. The hitching had been pure business, and when Cashbox died, wedlock died with it. He trudged back to *The Plain Truth*, where the curtained alcove would shelter him again, as it had before. He had spent a tedious day breaking down the previous edition, never dreaming his very own bottled-in-bond tart would crassly abandon him.

The grubby little dump depressed him. From these inky precincts he had waged countless struggles to corner some little bit of the fabulous fortunes that had made Cashbox a legend in all the West. Here he had connived, snatched town lots and resold them, floated the Aurora Borealis, manipulated the news, censored Senator Pride's letters, drummed up phony crusades—and all for what? He'd squeezed a few months of flashy living out of it, but he was poorer than when he had arrived in town.

He stared wearily around the plant. He still had newsprint. He could publish his four-page rag a while. He wasn't sure he wanted to continue, but on the other hand he had no way to leave, especially if he intended to take his flatbed press and type fonts with him. If he walked, he'd end up working for some swine.

May Svensrud walked in, surprising Willard. She was carrying her child.

"What do you want?" he asked truculently.

"I—I wanted to thank you for the editorial, Willard. Slug wants property taxes too. He hates collecting licenses from all those awful places. A city shouldn't be financed that way."

It astonished him. "Why—that's what a newspaper's for. Do some good. If there's anyone left around here."

"Well, I just want to thank you. I don't like to see him collecting license fees from those people."

"It's all politics, sweetheart. Get someone else to pay the taxes."

She hesitated, as if gathering up courage to say something. And then she did. "Willard, you could save Cashbox if you try. You don't help by attacking Slug. He's working for nothing now. The city hasn't paid him. But he goes out each day to keep this town safe for you and me."

"You're still telling me how to run my paper."

She turned to leave. "I suppose I shouldn't. It's yours. But Cashbox needs a real newspaper now. I just wanted to encourage you to write one."

With that she left, not waiting for his sarcasm.

A certain disgust stirred in him, the faint prompting of conscience. He had prostituted *The Plain Truth* and himself, and for what? For nothing. Cashbox had laughed and gone about its business. The people who counted, Portia Webb and those about her, had long since dismissed him and his rag.

Willard Croker felt shame, an emotion he found unfamiliar. He wished he could numb it with spirits, but he lacked the boodle to buy a pint. For some reason his mother sneaked into mind, especially the way she harped on the virtues she held dear; the things he had joyously scuttled as soon as he was old enough to take a hike. She had been right. Too hard on him, but right.

This small epiphany didn't make him feel any better, but it did awaken something vaguely pleasant. What if, at this late hour, he were to transform *The Plain Truth*? He asked himself why he would do something so nutty, and decided he would because he wanted to. He was tired of being laughed at and ignored.

He donned his printer's apron. He had been the biggest sucker of all, thinking he could get rich by snookering people. He couldn't redeem his reputation, but he could, in the few issues left, create an honest paper. It became a need crying out in him. Maybe he could help Cashbox.

Excited, he mapped out a new edition. There would be the story of Cashbox's crisis. And an editorial asking those who remained to pull together and see whether a splendid town could be salvaged. And he would run Senator Pride's last three letters verbatim. Even as he shaped the new edition in his mind, he found himself sobbing. He didn't know what had bludgeoned him; only that he desperately wanted to do something sweet and beautiful, just once in his rotten life.

He forgot he was hungry. His fingers began plucking type from its boxes, composing a lead story about the closing of the Giltedge, the collapse of the bank, the exodus of miners, the lack of money, the demise of services—no barbers, no bakers, no cobbler in town; Doctor Kratz and three dentists gone, all but one hotel shut, undertaker gone. But four mines up the gulch still ran, and probably half of the citizens still remained. Baker's Mercantile was open, the railroad still running.

Why was he weeping? He couldn't answer that lousy question. Was it for wounded Cashbox, or for himself, or both? Was it only because his own shame-filled soul bled, stabbed by an ancient memory of his mother? He didn't know. But his fingers set type, and his burning mind leaped ahead of his fingers, adding one item after another. It took him until midnight, but he never faltered.

He slept fitfully, his mind feverish. If he could do but one thing, redeem himself, he would accomplish much. He could never win the esteem of those who knew him for what he was. It was too late. But he could begin a new life. There would be plenty of places to start over. As long as there were young towns blooming in the West, he would have a third chance. He could be a gypsy printer until he found the right shop, and then his journeyman skills would help him to become something new and clean.

The next morning, ignoring the convulsions of his empty belly, Willard set Senator Pride's last letters from Washington. Pride wrote that Grover Cleveland had called Congress into special session, which began August 7th. The express purpose was to repeal the Sherman Silver Pur-

chase Act, which the gold party was blaming for the
Panic. Things boded worse in the House than the Senate,
but William Jennings Bryan was a lion, and maybe he
could stem the tide in the lower chamber. Whatever the result, it would split the Democracy into two parties, the
populists of the West and the gold men of the East. Cleveland was doomed. Let no one wonder where the heart of
Senator Pride rested.

Done at last, Willard packed the type into the form next
to the lead story. He had to eat. Then he had to do some
sidebars. He hastened to Baker's Mercantile and cornered
Baker.

"Look, Claude, you owe for six ads. You haven't got a
dime and I'm not asking for cash. But I need vittles. I
haven't eaten since yesterday morning. Anything off the
shelf. I'll write off the ads if you'll stake me."

"Well, Croker, I don't know that advertising's done me
a lick of good—"

"I have to eat."

"Oh, well, we'll settle up a couple of the ads, then. This
blasted business, it's the wrath of God on this town. Greed
everywhere. I look for the Second Coming."

Willard carted a burlap sack full of chow back to his
digs. Most of it was flour and pinto beans, but a man
could survive on such for a while if he had to.

That afternoon Willard interviewed a railroad clerk, several mine managers, a few businessmen, and dozens of
out-of-work miners. Their agony shocked him. He'd been
so absorbed with himself he had barely grasped the tribu-
lations of others.

But in the midst of his interviewing, he heard another
kind of story. A widow, Mrs. Flower, had received an
anonymous contribution. So had several others. The
banker, it was said, scraped up a little to help people leave.
Out-of-work teamsters and freight outfits were helping
families that couldn't buy a railroad ticket. Scores of people had heaped their worldly goods into the huge Murphy

wagons, and then walked beside the merciful freighting men, to Livingston or Helena or Butte.

Willard wrote those up too, for it had come to him that people's nobility was as much a part of human nature as their venality. Besides, people needed something to lift their spirits.

He came at last to the part he dreaded. He wanted to write an editorial that pierced to the heart of things. An editorial that would confess past weakness and pledge *The Plain Truth* to public service for as long as it survived.

It would be an open *mea culpa*. It surprised Willard that he would do such a thing. And yet he knew he had to. It would be a confession, but it would also be a purging of something he wanted to wash out of himself. And thus he began, fearfully, to set an editorial in twelve-point type that apologized for his shabby little rag, and pledged *The Plain Truth* to something finer.

Every time he set a line he reproached himself for being a fool. But then he examined the emptiness of his years in Cashbox. He had succumbed to mining camp fever, the wild hope that he could make a fortune in weeks. He hadn't been alone. But he alone had twisted a newspaper into a lie.

He touched lightly on that. Just enough to let people know. There wasn't much point in groveling. The rest of the editorial dealt with prospects. Cashbox could survive as something else. Perhaps as a logging center, or a ranching supply center. And meanwhile, the paper would encourage people to help each other.

That done, he proofed it and ran off two hundred of his strange edition, wondering if anyone in Cashbox would bother to read it. After that he scrubbed and scrubbed with abrasive soap until he had scoured the ancient black stains out of his hands, along with a lot of skin. For the first time in years, Willard Croker felt good.

CHAPTER 80

· · · · · · · · · · · · · · · ·

One-Eyed Jack Wool didn't know whether he was making a killing or wasting his stash, but it didn't matter. He was having fun skinning miners, and he relished that more than the boodle he kept in his safe. If Cashbox wanted to croak, he would be glad to squeeze its windpipe.

His Oriental Saloon was the last dive in town, and he was doing a booming business. He had bought the bar stock of every saloon that shut its doors, usually for about ten cents on the dollar, and he was peddling Valley Tan and Medora Busthead at a dime a shot and coining money. His profit was nine and a half cents a glass. His two floozies were the last in town, and they weren't suffering from anything but the clap, while his three mixologists were hustling drinks so fast they needed rest breaks and milk of magnesia.

But that was nothing compared to the little game he had invented, one that wrung the last juices out of the miners. He simply offered to buy any lot in town for one dollar. That was one clam more than they could get for it anywhere else. But there was a hitch. He paid them with one of his house chips, and they had to take their turn at the roulette wheel to convert it into cash. A few won a few bucks; most walked out empty-handed.

And in they came, men who'd never been in a sporting house before, toting their deeds while he leered at them from his bright eye and studied their documents. At times he actually had a line of suckers waiting to be gulled, which filled him with such ebullience that he accidentally offered a free Cub cigar to a sore loser.

"One dollar!" cried a big anvil of a miner. "Why, it's worth a hundred fifty, lot and cabin."

"Don't waste my time."

"I can sell it for a dollar somewhere."

"Well do it then. I'm busy."

"Won't you give me five?"

"Sign here, sucker. Then I'll give you a chip and you can lose it on the roulette."

The man signed, took his chip and lost it.

"Ow! I just lost a good house and lot; one damned house with new shingles on the roof, and a hundred-foot lot for one whirl of the wheel," he said, dumfounded. "Why did I do that? What'm I gonna do now?"

"Have a seegar, chump."

That's how it went. One-Eyed Jack traded a chip for a deed. Then he spun the wheel and dispatched the ivory ball around its track while the suckers placed their bets. They could convert one chip into two by winning a bet on odd or even or red or black. Or win two chips if they bet on any third of the thirty-six numbers. The most they could win their dollar chip was thirty-five, if a single number came up. But it rarely did.

He had snatched a hundred thirteen lots so far, along with two wedding rings, a gold watch fob, and three pocket watches, with an outlay of eighty-nine dollars. If he kept it up he'd own Cashbox. One lucky idiot had put his chip on the nine and won thirty-five chips plus the one he bet when the ball landed in the nine pocket. The idiot had cashed them and walked out with thirty-six frogskins. Good advertising, Wool figured. That sucker would bring him more business than he could handle.

But he really wanted the mines. It was worth hanging around just to see if he could cop them. He had picked up a few claims, but no mines. Running a gyp joint required patience, and he would wait.

He had six suckers at his table. They had descended upon him like manna from heaven. The ball dropped into the thirty-four. He paid off two reds, pocketed two blacks, an odd, and a bet on the first twelve. He fingered the stacks of chips, feeling cheery.

"My God, that was my house! I ought to kill you," bellowed one.

The man found himself staring into the bore of One-Eyed Jack's cannon. "Try it," muttered Wool.

"Yeah, well I mean, I gotta go."

"You're evicted. Don't go near my property."

"But I gotta get my stuff."

"You're dead."

That one and three more dudes slinked off, terrified of a bullet in the back. One-Eyed Jack snickered and slid the deeds onto the heap behind the wheel. It would cost him dough just to register them in White Sulphur Springs, if he didn't unload them on some chump first.

Business got even better as the days passed. He began giving each loser a brass token, "Good for One Lay at Minnie's Sporting House," and they all heehawed. Wool had a whole box of them he found after Minnie vamoosed. He even began doling out golden-leaf Cub cigars, too, at terrible cost to his reputation. And finally he gave each loser a drink chit, which reduced the sucker to babbling his lifelong, everlasting gratitude to a purely noble citizen of the metropolis.

Wool thought of himself as a buzzard, feasting on the carrion of a city, a figure of speech that took his fancy. He even looked like a buzzard. His prey wandered into his rookery eager to surrender their flesh and blood to him, and he was happy to oblige. The only trouble with all this was the daytime hours. He had to get up at noon and stand at the roulette wheel, which was inflaming his hemorrhoids.

But the nights had become nightmarish excursions into hell. He dreaded to shut down because he would have to face that lonely cubicle again. When he closed the door behind him he always remembered he had no place to go. The unruly West was dying. There no longer was a circuit, the regular tour a sporting man could make from camp to camp, each an isolated town surrounded by primeval wilderness. The ploughmen had arrived, along with wives, deacons, teachers and temperance lecturers. It chilled him to think of it.

After Cashbox, what? Creede, Colorado. New Mexico. Hawaii. There wasn't much left except a few dull outposts. Nothing like Cashbox when the silver ran. Oh, this burg had been a corker. He remembered paydays, when the whole district lit up like the Fourth of July sky and the professors hammered ivories against cantatas of busting glass. Those were the evenings when wild gaggles of miners guzzled coffin varnish, blew their payroll bucking the tiger, and ended up laughing and addled, their grins still pasted to their faces as bouncers tossed them into the sagebrush.

Cashbox!

He metered out that much sentiment in the blackness of his lair. It annoyed him that he would miss this place. He lit the lamp, knowing he needed to indulge once again in a habit that he considered a great weakness. He opened his safe and pulled out the photograph of the orphan the sisters at the foundling home had sent him, and stared at the adolescent girl in the Mother Hubbard. Marie. She smiled brightly back at him from within the oval matting.

That photograph, along with the request that he shepherd her into the adult world, had come to him years ago, and he had never replied. But every time he was tempted to toss it out, some tug of emotion stayed him. Whenever he gazed upon that sweetness, something he supposed was love filled him. A tenderness, at any rate. She became the might-have-been of his life. She was the angel of the never-never life: if he had not run off; if he had settled into quiet respectability. That is why he considered it an indulgence to gaze upon her, and let her sweetness undermine his chosen life.

He gazed a while longer, wondering what had become of Marie. She would have left the foundling home long since, and be making a life somewhere. He hoped it was a good life. Then, annoyed by his own sentimentality, he stuffed the portrait back in the safe and slammed the door.

He had no friend on earth, no confidante, no lover, no mate, no standing in the community. His youthful rebellion against his hell-and-damnation father had taken him to this: to skinning suckers, murdering men at cards, devouring the world around him with barracuda teeth. Oh, it had been fun sometimes. It had been a carnival, parting miners from their lots and houses. He didn't care if Cashbox died and the lots weren't worth a nickel. He was in it for the carrion.

But there was no place to go any more.

CHAPTER 81

May checked on Tim, who slept in the crib Slug had built for his son. He was cooing and pawing air. Love melted her every time she gazed at the rosy-cheeked infant. But Slug was waiting for lunch, so she slipped back to her shining kitchen and put cheese and bread she had baked and new Jonathan apples on the table for him.

"I can't stay; got more rounds than ever," he muttered. "Near as I can tell, hundred-fifty more left yesterday. I got twelve more houses to watch, and the Silver Queen Hotel. There's not a body in any of them. I could use two more men."

"And some pay," she added. City funds had vanished even before the failure of the bank, and Cashbox couldn't raise another nickel anyway.

"We can last a while. Don't know what we'll do next week," Slug muttered. "I stopped to see Old Man Baker. I said, if you want a constable in this town, you'd better put me on credit, because I'm not getting a wooden nickel from no one. But Baker, he just shook his head. He said they all want credit and he's going broke, too. He said he's got a twelve-gauge under the counter and that'll have to do if I leave."

Fear laced her. How would they live? She could nurse Tim a while more, but she needed eggs, milk, flour, salt, butter and beef for Slug—and for her own nursing body.

"Where'll we go, Slug?"

He shrugged. "West. I guess. We can homestead, maybe around Dillon or Missoula. That Bitterroot Valley's got some good grazing land. The best land's all took up, but we can scratch by on something. Give me a mule, a harness and a plow and I can turn sod as good as any of 'em. Maybe we can buy some beeves somehow. Or I can try some lawing in some town that's not broke. I've been watching the dodgers coming in—you know, the wanted-man flyers. There's a wild place called Creede, in Colorado. They might need a copper."

"I don't like wild places. Cashbox—it's always been quiet."

He grinned. "Give or take a One-Eyed Jack or two."

She watched him devour a pound of Wisconsin cheddar, the last of the cheese. He sawed off a massive slice of her bread, carved some butter from the crock and laid it on thick. He needed lots of food; he was a huge man. She would bake more bread this afternoon between feeding Timmy and washing diapers.

"Is it quiet?"

"Yeah, but I don't like it. All them houses with stuff in them, just waiting for someone to bust in. I look into the windows to see what I can see, but that's all the time I've got. Anyone wanting to get all that stuff, they could sure get to it when I'm on the other side of town. It's mostly furniture, though. Stuff too expensive to ship." He sighed. "It's impossible. One man can't look after a mess of houses with no one in them. No neighbors around to keep an eye on things. There's gonna be vultures around here."

People had been coming to the Svensrud cottage for days, asking that he watch their property. Sometimes they left keys, which he tagged and kept in a pasteboard box. She had written down over a hundred names and addresses in a ledger from his office.

"Slug, it's not fair. You're doing this for free."

He stared at her mildly. "Someone's got to. There's good and bad folk out there. I want to hang on a bit. But if it gets to where we can't, why ... May, I hope you're good at walking because we can't afford a ticket."

"I know," she said softly. "Slug, let's not do it in cold weather."

He grinned. "You're tougher than you think." He stood. "Gotta go. Take care of that little squirt for me." He lifted the double-barreled scattergun he had been carrying on rounds the last few days.

But a knock on the door surprised them. Slug opened it.

"Mister Svensrud? May I talk a moment? I've some business."

"Why, yes sir."

May wondered who it might be. Someone Slug called sir. Someone who used good English. The man stepped in and she recognized the superintendent of the Giltedge. He smiled at her, and briefly examined their bright cottage. But she thought he didn't really see its beauty.

"Thank you, Mister Svensrud. I'm Thaddeus Webb, the Giltedge."

"Yeah, I know."

"Mrs. Webb believes you haven't been paid and might be leaving. We've been wondering."

"Well, I sure haven't seen a dime."

"Are you leaving?"

"We're staying as long as we can. But I won't have much choice if the town won't come up with something. We haven't even got a mayor any more."

"Constable, that's what I'm here about. I've got tens of thousands of dollars of mining equipment up there. Except for you, it's unguarded. I'll be leaving in a few days. And after that—no one. I've been selling it, mostly by wire. It'll go to Colorado. But it's going to take three months to get crews in and move it out on flatcars. And that's what's bothering me. Cashbox could be defenseless by then. A lot of people gone."

"Well, I don't reckon to stay three months, that's for sure. A week or two, maybe. I can't even buy vittles."

"No one can. It's frightful. There's valuables in Cashbox, and the town's becoming a husk. I've talked this over with the Hammon brothers and Cornelius Daley and we've pretty well agreed that we have to protect our property. That means two things: a hired guard at the mine, living in our boardinghouse; and we're prepared to support a constable in Cashbox so vandals can be arrested, charged and detained if necessary by a proper officer of the law."

May listened quietly, aware that this might mean salary, food, security for a while.

"Well, that makes sense," Slug said.

"One of our foremen, Focher, is willing to stay. We'll offer him thirty a month for three months. Not a lot, but we've a failed mine and times are hard. We'll offer the same to you, cash, if you'd stay three months too. Let's make it December the first."

Slug grinned. "That sounds like a fortune to me."

"It's not, and I'm sorry to offer so little. I can do it either way. Cash or a credit at Baker's Mercantile. With the bank gone, I'd suggest credit at the store for safety's sake."

"Well, I'd like to have some folding money in my britches and some credit too. I forget what a dollar bill looks like these days."

"All right, constable. How about thirty in currency, and sixty at Baker's?"

"That sounds about right. I'll work out something with Focher so we keep the mine covered pretty well. Maybe I can get up there by daylight, while he sleeps."

The superintendent eyed him sharply. "Constable, do you have any reservations about accepting private money to continue a public service? I have none. Am I out of bounds? If you think this is some sort of private inducement, or worse. . . ."

"This is nothing but manna from heaven to me, sir. You're not asking me to do special favors. No, don't worry about it. You're helping everyone. It'll help keep a lot of property safe. I've hated the thought of just walking out. Especially after telling people I'd keep an eye on it as long as I can."

Webb looked relieved. "Good. I don't want to do anything improper. You come up and I'll show you what's under lock and key. I'll have inventories for you. Big Bull Focher'll tell you when crews are dismantling and shipping machinery, so you know." Webb peeled thirty dollars in greenbacks from a roll in his pocket and handed them to Slug.

"Holy cow, it's folding money," Slug muttered. He immediately handed ten to May. "In your sugar jar," he said.

"One more thing," said Webb. "Have you heard whether Bass Boehm's around?"

Slug shook his head.

"Well, he may come back. Some mining people I've been in touch with say that he's been hanging around Granite, over on the other side of the state. We're worried that he might come around here just to clean the flesh off the bones."

Bass Boehm. A dread filled May. Oh, why didn't they just leave right now? "Slug? Let's just go. . . ."

Slug scratched his head. "I wouldn't want to meet up with him, that's for certain. You know how many men he travels with?"

"I have no idea."

"Could you find out?"

"I'll wire Sherman Branson at the Lucky Strike and find out more. Boehm's dangerous. He stays out of trouble, more or less. But he'll do anything he thinks he can get away with."

"I don't know if I can handle a whole gang of his kind, sir."

"I have no idea whether he'll come. But we want protection."

Slug saw Webb out the door.

The baby whimpered. May raced to Slug and threw her

arms around him. "Oh, Slug, let's go. Please let's go somewhere right now. Return his money, darling, and let's go."

She felt his powerful arms encircle her and crush her to him. It felt good.

"Ah, May, it'll be all right. I hear rumors like that twice a week. It'll be all right."

She buried her face in his shirt, drawing strength from his. "Be careful, Slug. I need you. Oh, God, we've money enough, but every day'll be hell until we go."

"May, I live for you and Timmy. I'll never leave you," he whispered in her ear, and she took comfort.

CHAPTER 82

· · · · · · · · · · · · · · · · ·

Portia Webb couldn't bear to watch the draymen tear her rooms apart. Some were nailing lids on kegs and crates while others dollied the furnishings of her lovely home out to the waiting wagons. She knew she should be used to it by now; she had dismantled several homes in her peripatetic life. But these moments always rent her in two. Her comforts, her decorating, her little pleasures vanished one by one, leaving cold heartless rooms behind.

She especially loved this house, with its bay windows that afforded the view of the surrounding highlands. She had transformed it into a home that brimmed with sunshine and peace. Not all her houses had been like that. But it wasn't just this house, it was Cashbox, which had grown upon her until she had surrendered to it, finding bliss where she had least expected it.

She watched Thaddeus in his waistcoat and shirtsleeves, directing draymen like some emperor. They didn't like it, and Thaddeus had no idea that his tones were imperious. She smiled. It was only eight. At ten they would catch the Cashbox and Northern passenger train to Livingston, and then take the Northern Pacific and New York Central east, where they would visit his father and her parents. After that—she wasn't sure.

Their furnishings wouldn't follow them east, nor would they be put aboard the train they were about to take. They would be warehoused in Denver for the time being, until Thaddeus decided which of the offers from Creede, Cripple Creek, and Telluride to accept. She knew only that she would be high in the mountains again, this time in Colorado.

She couldn't bear standing there, watching her nest vanish into barrels, her presence keeping the draymen from using the expletives that lay trapped behind their silent lips. She needed to do something.

"I'm going for a walk, dear," she said, and received a grunt in reply.

There would be time enough to say good-bye to a city she had come to love. She hurried down to McDonald Street, eyeing the cottonwood saplings that had been planted along it at her prompting. Some day they would shade the street magnificently.

Yesterday Thaddeus had watched draymen cart the last records and furnishings out of the Giltedge. He shook hands with Baghote, locked the door of the administrative offices, and handed the key to Cornelius. Then he walked home, settled in a wingchair in the torn-up parlor, and stared out the window for four hours, until dusk hid his view.

She hadn't disturbed him. She understood perfectly. She knew he was saying good-bye to the Giltedge. He sat there remembering assays and tunneling, headframes and shops, the vug, the Knights of Labor, the cave-in, the timbering, the long courtroom battle between men who became joint owners, Hugh Trego pounding on his homemade desk, the collapsing price of silver, the jubilation when the Sherman Silver Purchase Act passed, the faces of hundreds of men, who, with their families, found daily sustenance in the profitable working of the Giltedge Mine.

She knew he was reminiscing, fighting old battles, loving, and letting go, so she never said a word. She brewed tea and brought him some. He sipped it without even knowing he had it in hand. The dinner hour came, and she laid out food for him, and then put it away, nibbling on a little.

Then at last, when the dusk lay purple outside, he returned to her. "It was a good mine, darling," he said. "The best I'll ever build."

Now it was her turn to say good-bye. She turned on Robinson and walked two blocks to the red brick school. She discovered children caroming around the schoolyard, and Miss Prescott still at her post, even though she hadn't been paid. A dozen children of stepladder sizes remained, all gathered into one class. That school was still teaching a new generation of citizens.

She stood across the street recollecting her struggle to build the school. Mining communities paid scant attention to such things. She remembered looking at the plans, approving this and opposing that. She remembered raising money from her women's circles and from merchants. She had dragooned two hundred dollars out of the Giltedge just by pestering Thaddeus. She had raised three thousand dollars, and the rest of the cost had been assumed by the city of Cashbox. And then she had struggled to find the right teachers and pay them fifty a month.

She watched the schoolchildren, wondering how much longer they would enter Miss Prescott's classroom when the bell rang. How long it would be before cruel winds and snow sifted through shattered windows, covering the little wooden desks with debris? But all things died, she thought. The school might die; but there were over a hundred youngsters who could read and write and cipher, who knew the history of the Republic and its great men, who would grow up better and richer for their education in that little schoolhouse, and pass something along to their children too.

She strolled back toward the center of town, pausing at

the dark and somnolent Palace Hotel, feeling loss. She remembered when she had corralled Thaddeus, just after the chophouse had opened, and made him take her to dinner. What fun that had been. And how many splendid evenings since then they had sat in the plush chairs there and enjoyed fine food and fine company. She wondered if it would ever, like the phoenix, rise from its own ashes.

She passed the shabby log shop of *The Plain Truth*, and saw a stack of papers with a brick pinning them. She found a nickel in her reticule and bought one to read on the train. She noticed the front page featured letters from Senator Pride. Oh, Willard Croker, that affable, devious man. She would read it in the coach and not believe a word of it.

She toured Main Street, admiring the flat paving stones set in fan patterns for four blocks. That had been something every woman in town begged for. They had all grown weary of dirtying their skirts and shoes in the muck of the business area. And the merchants had wearied of swamping out their stores every time it rained. Everything seemed so quiet. But as she walked from store to store, she realized Cashbox was alive. Baker's was doing a trade. She saw a man in the town lot company office. The usual knot of old codgers surveyed their world from the bench in front of the post office.

She passed the bank, disturbed by its silence, its betrayal of a lot of people, including the Webbs. Yet it wasn't Cromwell's fault. She knew that. But the place radiated something dark, and she hurried past that thief of hope. She strolled past the Carbonate Miners Saloon, dark and silent, knowing that it had been the place of friendship for scores of miners. It had never been a dive devoted to wanton drinking, the sort of saloon she and her WCTU opposed. She glanced briefly at the abandoned sporting district, slumbering across the creek. She had heard that only The Oriental survived. Where had all those women gone?

She had better go back, or Thaddeus would have a fit. She walked past The Exchange Club, rock-solid and handsome, but a mysterious place to her. Soon she was passing fine homes, some of them with a dozen rooms. She hoped Cashbox would prosper again, and these splendid homes would soon house happy families.

She found a livery buggy and driver parked before her house, beside the drays. Thaddeus stood on the veranda, his suitcoat back on. She expected him to scold her, but he didn't.

"Are you ready?" he asked. "Your bags are in the buggy."

"In a moment," she said, hastening past him to survey one last time her gorgeous rooms, needing one last look in every cupboard. Then she was ready.

They were driven to the railroad station. She dreaded this moment. How odd that she didn't want to leave. But Fate was ripping her away from everything she had built and treasured, except for one thing: her dear Thaddeus sat beside her, too stiff to hold her hand, but there, always there.

The liveryman deposited them on the brick platform, and carried their bags to the green-lacquered express car. She watched the luggage vanish inside. Ahead of it a big locomotive chuffed idly, its engineer leaning out of the cab. Before her stood the shining green coach, its side gilded with the name of the Cashbox and Northern Railroad. The conductor helped her onto his iron stool, and then to the first step, and moments later she and Thaddeus worked their way down the aisle looking for seats near the rear of the car.

From the moment they had stepped inside the car, Cashbox ebbed from them. She settled in a window seat and peered out at the highlands and the mountains, but they seemed distant, and part of the past. She wanted to see her parents again.

The coach almost filled. They were people whose faces she knew, and some names, too. All of them were leaving Cashbox forever. She heard the conductor shouting, the clang of doors closing, and the shrill of the whistle. And then, with a thunderous huff and chuff, the train eased forward, its couplings tightening, and Cashbox slid from view.

CHAPTER 83

• • • • • • • • • • • • • • • •

Cornelius Daley could delay no longer. Urgent matters awaited him in Helena. He had to liquidate two western Montana mines that were done for; close an Idaho silver mine for as long as low prices made it unprofitable; sell a variety of shares in other mining enterprises for whatever he could get; and find ways of trimming expenses at two other mines.

He had also to retrench on everything, renegotiate loans made by two Helena banks, settle three minor lawsuits involving suppliers, and take care of odds and ends such as the repair of the house above Last Chance Gulch he had neglected for six years. His net worth had plummeted by seventy percent, and could continue to decline if he failed to act immediately.

He had lingered too long. The Giltedge was closed, the Webbs gone, the salvage work done. He had stayed for Sylvie. If only he could persuade her to come to Helena, where he had a splendid home awaiting her and a bustling city to entertain her. And a wedding ring engraved with their initials for her finger.

This was the last day of daily passenger service. The Cashbox and Northern had fallen into receivership in spite of the traffic. Starting Monday, the Northern Pacific, its principal creditor, would run one mixed passenger and freight train a week to Cashbox. The NP itself had fallen into bankruptcy, along with the Union Pacific and the Erie Railroad, but trains still ran.

He toted his heavy bags out of his suite and waited in

the clubroom for the hack to take him to the station. He had lived there alone for weeks.

He felt almost like a trespasser. The walls and damask drapes were still redolent with the cigar smoke of happier days, when scores of men got rich, swapped yarns, bought and sold stocks, made deals, sipped Sylvie's drinks, read papers from all over the United States, watched traffic on Cashbox Street, or listened to faint music or applause echoing up from the great hall below.

It filled him with a strange sadness to stand there in a place where men had won fortunes, fulfilled their dreams, lost all they had, and found the sort of company they preferred. It was all too quiet now, and the chill he felt in its air came from more than the autumnal weather outside.

Last evening had been haunting, and he relived it while he waited. She had served him steaks at her house, smiling awkwardly because the range had defeated her, as usual. He knew better than to press her again about leaving. She would come to it in her own good time, perhaps when she could no longer buy what she needed.

But he proposed one last time.

"I love you. I want you for my bride. Everything I have is yours. You've given me the happiest years of my life."

"I love you too, Con. I'll miss you."

"Come to Helena when you're ready. I'll wait for you."

She smiled.

They hadn't made love. They didn't very much any more. She built a small fire in the parlor stove and they simply sat on the sofa, his arm about her shoulder, through the silent evening. Out of some unspoken agreement, he knew she would not come to the station to see him off this morning.

He kissed her at her door and walked through a sharp night to the club. Maybe by Christmas Sylvie would have enough of Cashbox. Not many people would stay. Her real enemy would be loneliness. She might survive in Cashbox for a while, wrestling with boredom and melancholia, but it could not last. He could only pray that when she came to her crossroads, she would turn toward him.

The hack from the Overstreet OK Livery Barn took him and his two trunks and three bags to the station, where the last daily passenger train waited, its engine steaming lazily two cars ahead. He paid the liveryman, and watched his bags vanish into the express car.

When he walked to his coach, she was there on the platform. The sight of her astonished him. She wore her ermine-lined coat but was bareheaded. Her hair, as tangled as ever, looked barely under control. Her smile was as crooked as it was the day he had met her. Her beauty melted him, as it always did, but this time he felt both dread and joy. Would she join him after all?

"Sylvie, you came."

"Well how could I not come? I had to say good-bye."

Something in him sagged with those fateful words. "When I saw you, I hoped. . . ."

"Oh, Con, you know how I feel."

"Why, Sylvie? What's here?"

"I want to. Isn't that reason enough?"

It wasn't. He needed reasons and she offered none. "I'm glad you came. I'm touched."

"Oh, Con, I had to. I brought you a gift. Open it in the coach. It's something for you to remember me with." She handed him something thin, wrapped in tissue.

"Thank you, Sylvie."

"I think Cashbox is going to spring back. Isn't it a perfect place? I'm going to buy mines. Maybe I'll buy the Giltedge from you. There's ore in it. That mining engineer said so. I'd like to buy twenty mines. I want to buy the Delirium Tremens. That name always caught my fancy. Imagine having a mine like that. I'll hand people a business card that says I'm the owner of the Delirium Tremens Mine. They'll laugh and not believe me. There's lots of people here. Claude Baker thinks there's four hundred, and more up around the mines. That's a start. When the club reopens you'll be my first member."

"Sylvie—"

"Board," bawled the conductor.

"Sylvie—" But he couldn't find anything to say.

She threw her arms about him and hugged fiercely, her eyes bright. He crushed her to him one last time.

"Board, Mister Daley."

He let go and climbed up the steps and into the pungent coach. He found a window seat where he could see her, and she waved. He waved back while the car moved imperceptibly, and then faster and faster until she had vanished.

He sat quietly for a minute, feeling the rhythm of the pistons and hearing the clack of wheels over the joints in the rails, mixing with the wail of the whistle.

Then he gently untied the ribbon. He beheld a portrait of Sylvie in sepia, matted in an oval frame, taken by Octave Few, the portraitist. He had caught her very essence, somehow. She stood erect, her hair askew as well as her lips, her left hand on the back of a chair. She wore a high-necked blouse with a ruff that reached her chin, beneath a velvet suitcoat. She looked faintly amused, a little coquettish and maybe impulsive. But the tilt of her chin was willful. Her gaze revealed a woman who could love dearly, but a woman who would always reserve the larger part of herself from the world.

Octave Few had caught her, he thought. He studied the portrait, all he would ever have of her now, and was gladdened. For the rest of his days on earth, it would be wherever he would be. He wrapped it in the tissue again, and stored it in his briefcase beside the documents he had planned to read.

He didn't feel like reading. He watched the foothills roll by. He felt the engine loafing down three-percent grades and heard his coach rumble across a bridge over Allebaugh Creek not far from the old stagecoach road, taking him away.

It had been six good years. The best of his life. The Giltedge had been the best and most seductive mine he'd ever owned. After the railroad arrived, it had enriched him by a hundred thousand dollars in spite of dropping silver prices. Cashbox had delighted him as it transformed itself from a raw camp into a grand city with an opera hall, the private club, a great chophouse. And always there was Sylvie, who graced it and grew up with it. He had no regrets and, when his anguish passed, he would remember her with pure joy.

Chapter 84

· · · · · · · · · · · · · · · ·

Sylvie moved back to her apartment in the Exchange Building because she loved being there. Almost everything good in her life had happened at the club. She had enjoyed the sunny house on the hill for as long as Con stayed in town, but the day he left she knew she must go home.

She loved to take care of the club. She swept the rooms each day, or beat the rugs, or attacked the bottles on the backbar with a feather duster. She washed windows and mirrors and bar glasses so that no member would ever complain about dirt.

For weeks, giant Murphy wagons had been hauling mining machinery down the gulch to the railroad. Not only the Giltedge, but a score of mines were being stripped of their boilers, hoists, pumps, ore cars and rails. All that traffic made Cashbox seem lively again. Crews of men she had never seen before lived in the Silver Dollar Hotel and ate at its café, the only restaurant still open.

Everything seemed fine. She traded a pearl necklace to old Baker for a lot of credit. He said he would have it sold in Helena, and post the money to her account. With that in hand, he never hesitated to pull what she needed off the shelves behind the counter and fill her wicker basket.

But the town continued to shrink. Some left on the

weekly one-car passenger service, but the railroad didn't
mind when a man rode down to Livingston in the caboose
of the daily freight that was carrying the bones of Cashbox
south.

It surprised her that Willard Croker stayed on and published *The Plain Truth* faithfully week after week. He
didn't have a subscriber and not much advertising, either.
But he printed an armload of copies and then delivered
them to everyone for free. She couldn't imagine why. The
little paper had changed somehow. It didn't seem like
snake oil any more. Its tone was quiet. It had run half a
dozen letters from Senator Pride, each detailing the way
the special session of Congress was going. The House, he
wrote, had voted to repeal the Sherman Silver Act, 239
yeas to 109 nays, and had beaten back amendments offered by the Free Silver bloc. Now it was up to the Senate,
where things would be much closer.

One bright, sharp October day she stopped Croker when
he dropped by the club to deliver his paper.

"Come in, Mr. Croker. I'll make some tea. Or would
you rather have spirits?"

He seemed startled, but he did step in, looking around
the majestic club with a keen eye.

"Spirits, oh, that'd be good. A little Old Crow with a
dash of water if you have it. I haven't had a drop for so
long it'll be a treat. Why, it's as good as ever, Mrs.
Duvalier. It's a tiptop place."

"Thank you, Mr. Croker." She poured a drink for him,
a glass of her amontillado for herself, and joined him in
the club room. "I tell you what. You come and have a
drink now and then. That's how I'll pay for the papers you
bring me."

"You jokin'?"

"No, I'd be glad to have you come by. Besides, I want
to talk with you. I want to know everything about Cashbox."

He shrugged. "Not much to tell. We're down to about a
hundred and ten by my reckoning, but Baker says there's

a few more out at the mines. He says things are getting better, and he's ordered in some goods. Money's eased a bit. Worst is over."

"I should hope so. I've wanted to tell you for weeks that I've been enjoying your paper. Something's different."

"You really like it?" he asked.

"I do. I suppose these bad times have something to do with it. I like your editorials. Calling for people to help each other. I like your stories, too. You haven't missed a trick. I read every word. I'm glad you're not booming the town any more. It'd be strange to see that now."

"I suppose so. I'm doing things a bit different. You and Baker, you're the only two that said anything about it. I'm running out of newsprint, though. I'll go a few more issues and that'll be it."

"The end? Don't leave, Mr. Croker. We'll need a paper when Cashbox starts up again."

He grinned. "What'll I print it on? Shingles? No, I'll be walking out of here one of these times. I can't even afford to ship the press. Not that it's worth much. But the fonts are worth something. I guess I'll end up a gypsy printer."

"What's that?"

"They drift into a burg, work a while at the local rag, booze a lot, and drift to the next town. They can almost always get a job. Most are real fast, and the owners, they like having some old journeyman around for a spell."

"But that's not a good life."

"You want to name me a better one?"

"Oh, no. I'm a roots-down person myself."

"Well, you'll be leaving soon enough."

She shook her head.

He downed his drink and went back to delivering *The Plain Truth*. She thought that this Willard Croker was a better person than the one she'd known when Cashbox boomed. It was odd, what calamity did to people. Some got worse. He got better.

Early in November he stepped in to the club and handed her a two-page sheet.

"This's it," he muttered. "Came in just now."

The headline said, "Silver Repeal Signed by President." The text reported that the Senate had passed the repeal bill on October thirtieth, the vote being 20 Democrats and 23 Republicans in favor, and 19 Democrats, 9 Republicans, and 4 Populists against. On November first the House passed the amended bill, and it had gone to Cleveland for signing.

"It's over, Mrs. Duvalier," he said.

"Oh, it's never over. Have faith."

He looked pained. "Look, the railroad's cutting off service. They're running one last train outta here on Monday and that's it. Extra coach, a couple of boxcars. Read the rest. The post office is quitting. No mail. Baker's leaving. No food. Water company's not maintaining the works. One of these days, no water. The Silver Star's closing up. Anyone that can buy a coach seat can go that way; the rest can go in a boxcar if they have to. You'll have to pack up, go somewhere."

"There's no need. I don't want to."

He seemed exasperated with her. "There's gonna be no store, no potatoes, no one around here to cut firewood for you. There won't be a soul to talk to. No one you can go to for help. No way to send a letter. The telegraph's done, as of Monday. They'll be rolling up the wire. No one to help if you're drifted in. You'll be using creek water. No one up the gulch mining—this shut 'em all down, even the diehards. This did it. They all quit. Silver's at sixty cents and there's no one to take their ore to a smelter. Cashbox is a goner."

"What about the constable?"

"They're leaving. He stayed on because Daley paid him. But the work's all done at the Giltedge—everything's been pulled outta there, so he's free. He says they'll be on the coach. You won't want to stay here without a constable, Mrs. Duvalier. Bums'll come in here. They don't have scruples."

"I'll be all right."

"Not alone, not without protection."

"They'll be back, Mister Croker. I think I'll wait a while. Maybe I can buy Mister Baker's groceries—I've got credit. There's abandoned cordwood all over town."

He stared at her, looking puzzled. "Why? Tell me why?"

"Everyone asks me that."

He waited for an answer, but she gave him none.

"I've got to deliver these. I'll see you on the last train," he said. He paused at the door. "You're an adult. You can do what you want. No one can force you. If you stay, that's your choice. But my God, Sylvie—" He closed the door behind him.

She watched him from the window. He squinted up at her and hurried toward Main Street.

The club seemed very still after his booming voice had unsettled its peace. She remembered how it had been when it was filled with gentlemen, some at the walnut bar, some lounging in the overstuffed chairs, a few in the study or the billiards room. How she had been so busy until she got help, and then she'd become simply their friend, often sitting with them while they discussed stocks and wars and ores. She loved being among them.

They had all been grand. Never had any of them made an improper advance, and it wasn't just because she had enjoyed Con Daley's protection, either. They were gentlemen, and she had run a gentlemen's club. They had kept their bar tabs and none had ever cheated her.

They might return. Her Exchange Club might be filled with them again. This is where she had found the end of the rainbow. Everything within these walls whispered of happiness. Here she had made amazing amounts of money. Here she had found just the sort of company she wanted. Here she had been loved, and loved someone.

Oh, she was being absolutely crazy, but so what? It ran in the family. If her grandfather could eat gunpowder soup, then she could wait in Cashbox. And besides, everything would come out all right. Yes, she'd be as mad as she wanted to be. They all thought she was, and she did too.

When the sun was just right at midday, she could just see Old Jut-Jaw conning her into buying the Aurora Borealis. It didn't make her mad any more. She loved him now. And when she slipped into the empty suite and stared at Con's bed, where they had clung to each other so many wondrous times, it didn't sadden her either. She remembered only the joy.

CHAPTER 85

• • • • • • • • • • • • • • • •

May felt a terrible helplessness. She was being torn from the only home she had ever loved. It stood empty now. Everything had been taken to the boxcars. But Slug's rosemaling still twined up the cupboards, and his exquisite woodwork still glowed in the morning light.

"You all set?" he asked.

"It's so hard, Slug."

He didn't reply. Instead, he slid a burly arm around her shoulder, drawing her and Timmy to him.

"How can you give this up so easily?" she asked. "Your rosemaling—you're just leaving it."

"Can't take it with us. And besides, I'm going to do better with the next one. That was my first crack at it. I never got the petals right."

"You're such an optimist. I wish I could just let go the way you do. But I love this place so. . . ."

"May, there's always a better time down the road. All we have to do is go down the road, and not just sit."

"I should know that by now," she whispered.

She drew the blanket over Timmy's face against the sharp November chill and followed Slug through the door. He didn't lock it behind him.

"Want me to carry him?" Slug asked.

"No, just the bag."

He toted a Harvest Queen flour sack full of diapers in one hand and his shotgun in the other. It made her smile.

She felt the baby squirm in his cocoon, but he didn't fuss. He would be warm enough.

They walked along Main Street, which stood silent and lonely, each building the tomb of someone's hopes. The whole city seemed asleep. She had seen it like this on many a Sunday dawn, when no one stirred and a great silence hung over the town. On Sundays the mill up the gulch didn't roar and whistles didn't echo down to the business district. But this wasn't a Sunday dawn, and each building they passed had been orphaned. They all stood in a solemn row, fronted by a boardwalk and a cobbled street, waiting to die.

"It's so strange," she murmured.

They came to Cashbox Street, and curiosity overwhelmed her. "I want to see if he took that old press," she said, steering Slug to the right, and then to the old log building that slouched behind the mercantiles of Main Street. She peered into its gloom. Nothing remained. Croker had his typecases and press with him after all. The last issues of *The Plain Truth* lay under a brick in a box. She took one for a souvenir.

They returned to Main, and headed for the station.

"Not a live body in sight," Slug muttered. "I'm glad to get out."

A crowd milled at the station. The last train of the Cashbox and Northern consisted of two green coaches and four yellow boxcars, their doors open. Men were stuffing things into them.

She knew almost everyone standing on the brick platform next to the coaches. There was Willard, half a foot taller than anyone else, looking dapper. And One-Eyed Jack Wool, wearing a black silk stovepipe, a black woolen cape, a black suit, a black eyepatch, a black cravat, and shiny black boots. In all her years in Cashbox she had seen him only a few times. He had been a night creature, almost invisible to those who lived by day.

There were so many other familiar faces. Mr. and Mrs. Baker. The man who ran the Silver Dollar Hotel. Some miners and their wives. That night foreman at the Giltedge, Big Bull Focher. That Kermit Reilly who'd been so badly injured. Miss Prescott, the teacher, in a trim gray cape; rough men from the outlying mining districts, three saloon men in derbies. Fifty, she thought, and then raised her guess to seventy-five. Two veiled women in shapeless wool coats stood apart. She stared at them, remembering her temptation, glad in her whole being that she had resisted even when she was starved to dizziness. Oh, God, she thought. How close she had come.

They all looked so happy. As if they were going on a special excursion to some waterfall. They laughed and hooted. They clustered in groups, joking and yarning. Didn't they care that their town was dying? That hundreds of thousands of dollars' worth of property lay behind their backs, abandoned? That dreams had snapped, plans had fallen apart, and life itself had been sundered?

It bewildered her. How could they forget Cashbox so fast?

"Who wants to buy Cashbox?" said the gambler, in a voice as thick as molasses. "I have Cashbox for sale." He waved a sheaf of papers. Why, they were deeds! "I have in my slippery hand three hundred twelve lots, buildings and all, for sale," he said, enjoying the moment. "That's about two-thirds of the whole burg, gents. You get to be mayor, fireman, undertaker, and baker. You get to own The Oriental, that famous dive across the creek. Who'll bid a hundred clams?"

Men chuckled, but no one bid.

"You mean to tell me that no one wants a whole city for a hundred bucks?"

"You gonna pay the filing fees, Wool?" yelled someone.

"No, the sucker that buys will have to do that," he said.

"Well, how about seventy-five—on credit. Seventy-five clams for Cashbox."

Men laughed. May wished she could pull the money from her coin purse and buy it. She'd love to own Cashbox.

"Sell it to Sylvie. She'll buy," Baker said.

May looked around for Mrs. Duvalier, and didn't see her.

"Slug? Is she really staying?"

"Yup. I talked to her. Just about everyone's talked to her. But she's staying. I guess that's her right."

"Well, she won't stay long," May said. "Just wait until winter rolls in. Just wait until she's been all alone a month."

"We can't make those choices for her, May. Baker says she's got food. There's cordwood all over. And that coal chute's got enough railroad coal to keep her snug. She's just a loner."

"One person left in Cashbox," May whispered. "I wonder why."

"Fifty clams?"

Men laughed.

"Well if I can't sell a whole bustling, blooming, bright metropolis for fifty, I guess I'll burn the deeds," Wool said.

And he did. He built a tiny bonfire right there on the cinder platform, crumpling one deed after another and watching it turn to ash, laughing all the while like someone demented.

It chilled her.

"Where're you going, Wool?" Slug asked.

"Cripple Creek. Come on down and lose your last cent. I got my layouts in the boxcar."

"You all loaded up, gents?" asked the conductor.

Men standing in the boxcar doors waved at him. They had just run some horses and two wagons into the last car and slid the door shut.

"All right. Who's going by coach?"

A crowd gathered around the coach door. The conductor tipped his hat back and grinned. "I tell you what. I'm going to flip a nickel. If she comes up heads, you go free. If not, you owe this bankrupt outfit two bucks."

He tossed the nickel high, snatched it, and slapped it down on his wrist. "Heads it is, get yourself a seat."

He tossed for the next person, Mrs. Baker, and heads came up again. After that Claude Baker won, and then the next person, a miner, and after that, Willard Croker.

Men started laughing. The conductor winked. A dozen more clambered up the metal stairs and into the coach.

"Phony two-headed nickel," Slug said. "Everyone wins. Come on, May."

The conductor stepped aside and guided the whole crowd into the coaches. The pungence of varnish, ancient tobacco, wood ash, and sweat smacked her as she worked down the aisle. She chose a window seat and settled Tim in her lap. Slug threw his things in the luggage rack and sank down beside her. She felt so safe with him there.

She heard a wail from the engine. The empty platform outside of her window began to slide by. She craned her neck so she could see what she could of Cashbox, but she couldn't see much. They were leaving at last. It wouldn't be so bad, she thought. Slug would be the new night constable in Bozeman City, and that wasn't far away. He had wired and written several towns, and the chief at Bozeman had told him he wanted an experienced, level-headed man who could deal with drummers and hoboes, and to come along as soon as he could. The pay would be sixty dollars.

She felt the coach rock gently as they gathered speed in the long downhill run to the junction. She found Slug's hand and squeezed it. He kept her hand and wouldn't let go, smiling at her.

She peered out the window at the racing hills, remembering her desperate stagecoach passage to Cashbox, looking for a place to bury herself alive. She smiled. Cashbox had rescued her. Slug had found her. Slug had helped her forget the past. She had been given a new chance at life, and she vowed she would never falter and never fail, and she would love Slug and Timmy forever.

The baby opened his eyes and stared at her, and she marveled at her new boy. He would be a fine son, strong and good, with Slug's blood running in him.

"I can hardly wait," she said to Slug.

CHAPTER 86

• • • • • • • • • • • • • • • •

On a glorious April day in 1894, a white-flag special left the ornate station at Livingston and turned north on the spur to White Sulphur Springs. At a junction about forty miles north of the Northern Pacific mainline, the conductor and brakeman climbed down from a luxurious observation car and threw a switch that would turn the train east upon abandoned trackage.

After that, the engineer proceeded cautiously over rusty rails that led to the abandoned mining town of Cashbox. The conductor paused a moment beside the plush swivel seat that supported Senator J. Ernest Potter-Pride, to tell him that everything would be fine.

"We ran a handcar up there a few days ago. They pulled a limb off the track, checked bridges and trestles, and pounded down a few spikes. It's amazing how fast road-bed goes to pieces. We're holding it to twenty-five miles an hour."

The Senator nodded. "We're in no hurry," he said. "Mrs. Pride and I have taken the whole day. We'll enjoy the scenery."

Even at the reduced speed, they steamed into Cashbox before eleven. Something stirred the Senator's soul. Cashbox was, actually, his Montana address. He and Regina were coming home, but to a town that had died on the floors of the House and Senate in spite of everything Senator Pride and Representative William Jennings Bryan could do.

He sighed, wondering how his usually ebullient spirits would weather this sentimental journey. The engine chuffed and squealed to a stop, and then sat panting like a tired dog.

"Well, my dear, let's have a gander," the Senator said, clambering to his feet. He helped Regina, who wore a pink tent this bright day, to her feet and then into a duster.

He pulled a homburg over his locks and decided to brave the April zephyrs in his suit. He could always fetch his coat if he needed it.

The conductor helped them down to the platform. "We'll turn her around and wait," he said, even as the brakeman was uncoupling the engine and tender.

"Oh, look at it, J. Ernest. It's just like it always was," Regina said, gazing at the solid row of buildings along Main Street, and the clusters of them that climbed the slopes on both sides.

It felt grand to be back. Pride wished he could make a speech. In his mind's eye he saw himself addressing the multitudes here about silver and bimetallism and the pillaging of the West. But they were alone, walking up Main on a perfect spring day, with puffball clouds skidding across the sky and a delicious warmth pounding away the last of the drifts that lay on the north sides of buildings.

"A casualty of the federal government," he said to her. "Oh, how I wish those blind men could see this."

"Well, the Giltedge ore ran out, too," she replied.

"Why, there's ore, tons and tons of ore, under our feet. It really was Cleveland and the greedy bankers. They bled the last penny out of the West and then threw us to the dogs."

"Save it for a crowd, J. Ernest. What a day!"

He stopped suddenly, staring at an impossibility. His house had vanished. Nothing but a mortared rock foundation remained where his home and offices had stood. "Regina! My house! It's gone!"

It startled her, too. "Was it a fire? We would've heard. . . ."

He pushed through tender grass to the foundation. "No ash, no fire. Why, it's the farmers, Regina. The ranchers and farmers'll have all of Cashbox soon."

"Maybe your house is a pigsty, J. Ernest."

He laughed. Regina was irreplaceable. He was going to tell that one to the senators. Still, it shook him. *Sic transit gloria mundi,* he thought.

But as he stood there, grief pierced him. He had fought so hard for these people who wanted only to prosper in their daily business. He had come early to Cashbox, seen it blossom into a beautiful little city. . . .

"I know what you're thinking," she said. "It's almost unbearable to me, too." She plucked his hand and squeezed it.

They held hands as they strolled up Main, peering into empty rooms, some as clean as ever but others with windows broken or doors creaking in the breeze. These were laden with debris. He poked around the town lot building, studied the silent tonsorial parlor next door where Ike Cobb had sculpted his wavy locks just so. He peered into the dusky hotels, stood before the Cashbox bank, feeling its collapse, and the wound it left upon Cashbox, in his bones.

They headed for Regina's rooming house and poked through its icy halls silently. She insisted upon peeking into each room, and he knew she was remembering boarders. He could see her smiling, blinking back something tender in her eyes, her lips moving as if to communicate with ghosts. She retreated to the dining room, and then the kitchen where the great Majestic range still stood, noble and black.

"I wonder how many suppers I cooked there," she said.

Those were her only words.

They escaped into the joyous sunshine, needing its eternity and benediction. Walking through Cashbox seemed all too much like walking though a graveyard. He blinked in the sun. A pair of magpies, iridescent black and white, clamored up to a cottonwood limb.

They turned on Cashbox Street, and stared at the old Palace Hotel, rotting silently. Some of its windows had been broken. He remembered a moment when he had feared for his life right there where he stood, and it shook him. He climbed the steps to its portico and peered into its lobby. There were no potted palms any more. The chophouse contained nothing at all. Whitmore and Lake had stripped the place bare. He remembered when it seemed to radiate excitement.

"Are you glad we came?" she asked.

"I am. It reminds me what I stand for and what I must do. Yes, I'm glad. I'm also so shaken I can barely think."

"I am too. I just wasn't prepared for this. Where did they all go? They were all here, and now they've scattered."

They stood in front of the Exchange Building. Its dressed limestone walls looked as solid as the day it was built.

"Want to go up?" he asked.

"I do. More than anything else."

He tried the main doors to the hall and found them locked. The White Sulphur deputy had done that, he supposed. But the club door at the side gave when he pushed it hard. They stepped gingerly up the long stairway, through icy cold, and let themselves into Sylvie's clubrooms.

Everything looked exactly the same. It surprised him. Light still dazzled through the tall arched windows. The great damask drapes still hung beside them. The overstuffed leather and mohair chairs still stood where they always had. The billiard table remained in its room, and books still lined the study. The gorgeous whorled walnut bar still dominated the saloon next to the clubroom, but no bottles stood upon it. He supposed they had been stolen, or maybe the deputy had taken them.

He stared at the great sofa in the central room, almost

seeing her indentation in it. "This is where they found her," he said.

Late in February, a group of ranchers looking for salvage had found Sylvie's frozen body wrapped in a blanket on that couch. There had been no lack of tinned foods or firewood. She had taken sick and died, far from help.

"I can't bear the thought of it," Regina said. "Poor dear woman."

"I know, I know. But there's a consolation. Just as Cornelius said, she found what she wanted here."

His words didn't mollify Regina. "She should have been hogtied and hauled out kicking when she wouldn't go," she said. "Some people are like that. She was a little crackbrained."

But he scarcely heard her. He was seeing Sylvie's club in its palmy days, seeing Con reading the papers, seeing the perpetual poker game in the far corner, seeing Sylvie, who kept losing ivory barrettes all over the building, dispensing coffee or spirits or cigars, always enjoying herself, pausing to sit with each of her members, laughing at their silly jokes, loving her very own gentlemen in her gentle club. He saw those faces he had forgotten, remembered men who'd come and gone; and always Sylvie, carrying her sundazzle to her members, day after day.

He stood, dumfounded by grief, wrestling back something that welled up in him and would not be denied. Then he surrendered to it. "Regina, dear, you're going to have to forgive me," he muttered.

He led her downstairs and into the old hall, which lay deep in shadow. "You go sit out there," he said, pointing to some seats in the middle. "And just be patient with an old fool."

She saw the tears in his eyes. He didn't bother to hide them. He found the lectern and dragged it to the middle of the dais. He straightened himself, smoothed his hair, gathered his energies.

Before him the packed hall waited. Oh, there they all were. There was Croker with a notepad, and Thaddeus and

Portia looking handsome, and Cornelius radiating power and something else that seemed almost poetical. There were John and Henry Hammon in dark suits and cravats, and Hugh Trego hulking in a corner, and Whitmore and Lake, and Constable Svensrud and his gentle bride, and young Kermit Reilly, and the Widow Flower, and old Baghote looking like a Welch corgi, and Coke Timmons, and One-Eyed Jack, and scores of miners and their families: Cornishmen, Irish, German, Norwegian, Scotsmen. And the Chinese, too, standing against the far wall.

There they all were, the soul and blood of Cashbox, drawn together one last time before scattering to the farthest corners of the earth. Oh, there they all were, their eyes upon him.

"My dear friends and neighbors," he cried. "All of you who came to Cashbox looking for something. I pray God you found it."

Tears were spilling from Regina's eyes.

"I'm not here to talk about the past, but the future. I'm going to talk about the next Cashbox, our tomorrows, our dreams, our West!"

And he did. For a long time. Until he could talk no more and everything had rivered out of him. He talked about the settling of the West. How it had been a place that welcomed all the world's broken and oppressed. How we all need a West in our hearts. How the West offered second chances to those who hurt, or who'd failed, or who had done something wrong—like himself. He told them there always must be a West in America, or America would die. Then he told them all how much Cashbox had given him; why, it had given him that most precious of all gifts, his lovely Regina. . . .

She stood. "That was the most beautiful speech you ever made, J. Ernest," she said. She rubbed tears away.

They traded the Exchange Hall for some bright sunshine, walked across the bridge over Cashbox Creek, and down Granite Street on the disreputable side of town, until at last they reached the cemetery.

They found her grave at once, just as Cornelius said they would. They had buried her in the corner closest to her city beside someone unknown. A rectangle of black iron fence protected her grave, and at its head stood a gray marble stone, polished so brightly that J. Ernest could see his face in it. A weathered wreath lay before it, on top of the mounded clay. Someday grass would grow there but now it looked raw.

At Cornelius's direction, the stonemason had incised her name at the top. *Sylvie Duvalier*. It occurred to Senator Pride that he had never heard her called Sylvia, if that was her actual name. Always Sylvie. Beneath it was a legend: *She found the end of the rainbow.* That was all.

They reverenced the grave for a few moments, remembering Sylvie.

"I almost skinned her out of her rainbow," he confided to Regina. "Pretty near got it."

"J. Ernest, I've shed too many tears," she replied. "Let's go catch that train."

AUTHOR'S NOTE
....

Cashbox is loosely based on the real Montana mining town of Castle. In its brief life, Castle became an important silver and lead producer, but it received a mortal blow in 1893 when its most important mine, the Cumberland, was shut down. Later in that year the Sherman Silver Purchase Act was repealed, and hope vanished. The town lingered on into this century but never recovered its population or vigor. Castle got its railroad, known in Montana history as the Jawbone, but it arrived too late.

Only a few buildings remain today, most of them slowly surrendering to the elements. Some of them are elaborate Victorian homes. The foundations of some of the businesses along Main Street can still be seen. The cemetery is unguarded and cattle wander through it. Nothing remains of the Cumberland Mine, which became the Giltedge of my story.

It is alleged that Castle was, for a while, the home of Calamity Jane, and that Calamity's daughter attended school there. I find the story questionable. Castle did, however, give the world one of the great actresses and courtesans of the nineteenth century, Anna Robinson. At nineteen, she was regarded as "the most beautiful girl in Montana." In 1890 she appeared on Broadway as Jennie Buckthorne in *Shenandoah*. By 1900 she was the mistress of King Leopold of Belgium, and became one of the most celebrated women of La Belle Epoque.

Late in the writing of my story I was still wrestling with the elusive persona of Sylvie. Then, on Christmas Day, I received one of those epiphanies that seem awesome to any author. Only two words popped into my mind: *Baby Doe*.

I knew at once who Sylvie was and what her fate would

be. I won't rehearse Baby Doe's story here. There is an abundant literature about Leadville's silver king, Horace Tabor, and his young second wife, Baby Doe; their fabulous Matchless Mine; and Baby Doe's heartrending fate. Their story is so poignant that it inspired an American opera, *The Ballad of Baby Doe.*

I am indebted to Robert M. Clark, librarian at the Montana Historical Society, and his gifted staff. They swiftly unearthed a mountain of material about Castle. One important item was an 1894 United States Geological Survey report on the Castle Mining District. It supplied me with most of the geology that underpins this novel. The librarians also produced an 1892 plat map of the city, which I have followed faithfully, except that I converted Castle Street into Cashbox Street. The librarians also produced several issues of one of Castle's three newspapers, *The Whole Truth.*

I am deeply indebted to Stanley Gordon West, a gifted novelist who read these pages in manuscript, and offered numerous valuable suggestions. His thoughtful and sensitive criticism greatly improved this story. Mr. West's splendid novel, *Amos*, became an Emmy-nominated TV drama.

RICHARD S. WHEELER
January 31, 1993

ABOUT THE AUTHOR

• •

Richard S. Wheeler has written over thirty novels about the early American West. His carefully researched novels evoke the real West rather than the mythical one. They are largely historical and capture Western life from the fur-trade period to the end of the 19th century. They are noted for their warmth, optimism, literary quality, and the richness of his characters.

His *Fool's Coach*, published by Tor Books, is the winner of the Spur Award for best Western Novel of 1989. Three other novels have been finalists for the Spur, including *Winter Grass* in 1983, *Where the River Runs*, published by Tor in 1990, and *The Far Tribes*, one of the Skye's West series, published by Tor in 1990.

Mr. Wheeler is a former newspaper and book editor, and lives happily in Big Timber, Montana, in the heart of the country he writes about.